"You're digi-what? Can you say that in English?"

"A djinn, you blithering idiot. What you Americans so stupidly call *genies*." Ian managed to infuse the word with more contempt than he'd shown for me, a feat that couldn't have been easy.

I laughed. "Seriously. What are you?"

Ian extended an arm, and waved long and slender fingers at my dilapidated coupe. A spot of gleaming chrome burst on the front bumper and spread to become glossy turquoise along the body. Within seconds, a sleek two-door sports car—no brand I'd ever seen and no logo or name to identify it—stood in place of my former heap.

"I am djinn," Ian repeated.

I shut the flytrap that had replaced my mouth, surprised I wasn't drooling. "Right. Digie-inn. Got it."

"Imbecile! Just call me Ian. Surely you can pronounce that, at least."

"Sure," I said, not really listening to him anymore. I wandered to the car and ran a hand along the smooth roof. Cool, solid metal. My hand didn't go through it, and the paint didn't rub off. Okay, so maybe this Ian guy really had turned my rustbucket into a . . . whatever this was. ____ ever had it so good. All she got was a lousy ____ shoes. Maybe my luck actually wa ____ d be luckier than having a d ____

This ti ____

SONYA BATEMAN

MASTER OF NONE

Pocket Books

New York   London   Toronto   Sydney

Pocket Books
A Division of Simon & Schuster, Inc.
1230 Avenue of the Americas
New York, NY 10020

This book is a work of fiction. Names, characters, places, and incidents either are products of the author's imagination or are used fictitiously. Any resemblance to actual events or locales or persons, living or dead, is entirely coincidental.

First Pocket Books paperback edition April 2010

POCKET and colophon are registered trademarks of Simon & Schuster, Inc.

For information about special discounts for bulk purchases, please contact Simon & Schuster Special Sales at 1-866-506-1949 or business@simonandschuster.com.

The Simon & Schuster Speakers Bureau can bring authors to your live event. For more information or to book an event contact the Simon & Schuster Speakers Bureau at 1-866-248-3049 or visit our website at www.simonspeakers.com.

Designed by Jacquelynne Hudson.
Illustration by Gordon Crabb.
Cover design by Lisa Litwack.

Manufactured in the United States of America

10 9 8 7 6 5 4 3 2 1

ISBN 978-1-4391-6084-8
ISBN 978-1-4391-7142-4 (ebook)

For Andrew and Josh,
who give and—I hope—receive the most.

ACKNOWLEDGMENTS

SINCE THIS IS MY DEBUT NOVEL, AND ALL FIRST-TIME-OUT WRITERS are desperate to thank everyone who ever spoke a word to them in their paranoia that they'll leave someone out, this might take a while. Go ahead and grab a drink or something.

Everlasting thanks to my husband and son, who have put up with enough insanity to open their own mental institution. And to everyone else on the list, it's not ordered by importance, so please file your grudges away for something else I've done. Thank you so much: Mom, Dad, Rick, Tara, Jamie, James, Chris, Tim, Rissy, Alice, Deyon, Laurelei, Tru, Jill, Margaret, Linda, Kathy, Betty, Dave, Mamie, Wayne, Phil, Becky, and they'd run out of ink if I went on to list the rest of my relatives.

Thank you, thank you: The MB4 gang: Aaron (crit partner extraordinaire), Marta and Kim; Mark Henry, J. F. Lewis, and Jaye Wells for the awesome words; the Bradley crew: Gail, Ginny, Martha, Joe, Carol, Rose, Chris, Claire, Lisa, Jan, Nick, Carl, Bill, and Steve; and everyone at Once Upon a Nation.

Huge thanks to Cameron McClure, world's greatest agent, and Jen Heddle, world's greatest editor, for helping me hammer and polish this story into something much more than I started with. Thank you to the Design Department of Pocket Books for the best cover ever, and to Copyediting, Marketing, and Publicity, just because you rock.

And thank you, reader, for taking a chance on this book.

CHAPTER 1

Just once, I would have liked to get my shit together. Even accidentally. But I could already see that wasn't going to happen tonight. After all, I am the world's unluckiest thief. Ask anybody.

Especially my ex-partners.

The long-abandoned warehouse I'd stumbled across had seemed like a blessing, and the worn canvas bag wedged under my spare tire had been downright serendipitous. That was until I started stuffing my worldly possessions into it and the damned thing split down the seams. Out came everything, all over the concrete floor that was covered with dust and oil and Christ knew what else. The gunk would wreak havoc with my instruments.

As if that weren't enough, one of the banded stacks of bills popped loose. The draft in the place snatched a handful of hundreds and whisked them off into the gloom in a flurry of papery whispers. Like the building was laughing at me.

"Crud!" My voice echoed in the empty space. I froze, dropped to a crouch behind my car, and listened. Nothing yet. I'd ditched the tail half an hour ago, but they'd find me again soon. I figured Trevor must have had my ride bugged while he briefed me—which meant they'd been tracking me for a week. They knew I'd hit the place four days ago and hadn't shown up with the score yet. I might have found the bug if I hadn't misplaced my scanner on my last run.

Since I hadn't, my only chance now was to keep going on foot. I couldn't talk my way out of this one.

I kept my mouth shut and started stowing fistfuls of bills in pockets. The lost cash would have to stay lost. Next came the essentials: cell phone, Mag-Lite, lock jock, cutter, scrambler, electric pick, Bowie, SAK, wire, Magnum—unloaded, of course. I was a thief, not a murderer. Couldn't say the same for Trevor. He was a vicious bastard, for a fence. Hell, I'd met dealers who were calmer than Trevor. I did jobs for him because he paid well, but I suspected I'd be looking for a new contact to sell my scores to soon. One with a little less psycho in his veins.

I'd have to scratch the clothes, too. Not that they were much to look at. Bland, serviceable, meant for blending in. I'd buy more. Though I didn't need it for warmth, I shrugged into my windbreaker for the extra pockets and headed for the only point of entry and exit I'd seen in the rundown structure. It bothered me, being in a place with just one escape route. Made it hard to formulate a backup plan other than *get busted* or *die* . . . two alternatives I'd managed to avoid so far. I hoped this time wouldn't break my record, but I had my doubts.

Outside, a starless night in Middle of Nowhere, New York, waited for me. I tried to remember how far I'd driven from the last insignificant excuse for a town to get here. In my professional estimation, it was pretty damned far. The idea of calling someone for a pickup crossed my mind. I laughed at it and sent it on its way.

I didn't just burn bridges. I incinerated them. Everyone I knew had a legitimate reason to hate me—and none of them was my fault. Okay, maybe that thing back in Albany a few years ago was my fault, but everything else came down to sheer bad luck.

In the distance, a long and low howl rode the breeze, frustrated and almost human. I'd heard enough dogs to know the sound didn't come from a domesticated breed. A coyote, maybe even a wolf. Terrific. For the thousandth time, I reminded myself that I never should have taken this gig. At least, not alone. But with my reputation, only the greenest punks would agree to partner with me, which guaranteed I'd spend more time babysitting than working. I'd been in this game too long to bother breaking in newbies.

There was another reason I should've told Trevor to shove this job. It wasn't his style. I'd gotten a weird vibe when he laid it out. The flashy son of a bitch always wanted high-end vehicles or fine art or precious metals and jewels. But this score was ordinary. Small-time. Wouldn't fetch fifty bucks on eBay. He'd said it was for his private collection, but even then, the little voice I never listened to insisted there was something fucked-up about the whole thing.

I considered telling Trevor the truth, but hell, I didn't even believe it. Who'd believe a professional thief *lost* the item he'd been hired to steal? No way that unforgiving bastard would buy it. I'd seen Trevor shoot his own thugs for picking up the wrong kind of wine. Granted, it had been five hundred cases of wrong, but that was beside the point.

There was still a good ten feet between me and freedom when the drone and swell of an approaching engine sounded outside. Headlights swept the curve leading to the building and swung around to frame the doorway, pinning me in the glare. Hello, sitting duck.

The engine gunned. Tires screamed as the car shot forward. I darted back into the darkness of the warehouse and took a hard left. The car screeched to a halt somewhere behind me. I turned toward the front wall, held out a hand, and walked briskly until I encountered something solid. I flattened my back against the surface, and waited.

I had a knack for concealment, a trait that served me well on the job. A few ex-partners had sworn I could make myself invisible, especially when they'd gotten caught and I hadn't.

Car doors opened and closed. I counted four slams. Trevor had sent a lot more muscle than necessary. I almost felt honored, before I realized the son of a bitch probably wanted me taken alive. Should have seen that one coming.

Flashlight beams swept the main aisle. A rumbling bear of a voice delivered an order. "There. Search his car." I recognized it instantly. Skids Davis, Trevor's left-hand man. Left, not right, because Trevor only called on Skids when he needed something dirty cleaned up.

So I was dirty now. Fine. I'd been worse.

I held my breath and inched along the wall. The entrance stood five or six feet to my right, within my grasp. With a bit of luck, I could slip out before the creeping thugs reached my car.

A low shape broke away from one of the goons and headed straight for me with disconcerting clicks. Great. They'd brought one of the dogs. Though I couldn't make out features in the gloom, its build suggested Rottweiler, and its strut suggested that human flesh was its favorite meal.

I'd never been bitten by a dog during a gig, but they always managed to find me fast. This one was no exception. He padded to within two feet of me and sat down as if I'd promised him a snack. His mouth drew back in what looked like a smile. *My, vicious animal, what big teeth you have. Please don't bark.*

The dog licked his its a few times. And barked.

It was more of a sneeze, actually, but it sounded louder than a marching band in a tin can. Had the thugs heard that? Not daring to move, I scanned the building, convinced they could hear my eyeballs rotating in my skull. The idling sedan's headlights revealed just enough detail to count heads. *One, two, three...*

Something hard and cold pressed against my temple. I sighed. *Four.*

Thanks a lot, dog.

"Hey, Skids. How's it hangin'?"

A hand made of gristle and steel clamped on my upper arm. I caught a whiff of sour perspiration and cigarette breath when he said, "Going somewhere, Donatti?"

"Yeah. With you."

"You're a smart monkey." Skids jerked me toward the entrance and thrust me into the glare of the headlights. The semiautomatic trained on my head looked like a cap gun in Skids's meaty paw. "Unload."

"Come on, man. I need this shit. Gotta earn a living—"

The gun drifted lower. "Unload, or I ventilate your thigh."

"Fine." I emptied my pockets, dropping items one by one onto the ground with deliberate slowness. As if buying time would improve the situation. Even with an hour to spare, I couldn't come up with a way out of this. The other three wandered back toward the car and collected the dog, grinning the universal gotcha smiles of thugs everywhere. "I'm gonna get my junk back, right?"

"Doubt it. You won't be needing any of this. Unless you've got Trevor's item jammed up your ass." If Skids was amused, his cold features didn't betray the emotion. "Care to explain what in the hell you were thinking, Donatti? We know you had it. Who'd you fence it to?"

I added the last of the cash to the pile at my feet and glowered at Skids. "I'm not explaining jack to you. Trevor wants to know, I'll tell him."

"You'll have an easier time if you tell me. Trevor wants to hurt you. Extensively. I'll just shoot you now and get it over with."

"I'll take my chances, thanks."

"Suit yourself." Skids gestured with the semi. His free hand produced a key fob with a fat plastic tag. He aimed at the car, pushed a button, and the trunk popped open. "First class is full. You get to ride coach."

"Lucky me." I moved as slowly as I dared, figuring I had two options: climb into the trunk or run. If I picked the trunk, I'd have to tell Trevor I lost the score. Not that I knew why the bastard wanted the thing in the first place. Taking the trunk meant being taken to Trevor, where I'd be tortured to death.

And if I ran, I'd be shot. Great options.

I concentrated on the exit. To the right of the crumbling drive leading into the place, a few lone trees provided scant cover opportunities. I could run hard to the left, hope the hint of forest in that direction thickened fast. I'd probably take a bullet before I got out of range—*if* I got out of range—but Skids wouldn't shoot to kill. At least, not the first time.

Left it was, then. I tensed, slowed to a crawl. And stopped when a long, low shape streaked across the entrance from right to left, impossibly fast, and disappeared. Was it the wolf I'd heard out here earlier? I blinked and glanced at Skids, wondering if he'd seen it—or if I was just losing the few remaining ounces of sanity I possessed.

Skids displayed no reaction. His expression remained immutable. "Get in there."

I shook my head. Must have been a panic-induced hallucination. I stood in front of the open trunk, poised to climb inside. Drew a breath. And ran.

Gunfire snapped immediately. I lurched aside, hoping for a graze instead of penetration. I heard a faint, wet *pop* as a bullet met flesh, but I felt no pain, no weakness. I kept moving. Where had he hit me?

An unfamiliar voice rang out. "That *hurt*."

I misplaced a foot, stumbled, and went down with a grunt. Rolling onto my back, I located the source of the voice and froze. A tall stranger in a long, weather-beaten duster stood between me and Skids. The bullet had torn through the stranger's calf. Blood pooled on the cracked asphalt beneath him, thick and black in the red wash of the car's taillights, but the stranger showed no signed of distress. He seemed . . . insulted.

Skids didn't waste words. He shot the stranger in the chest.

The stranger glanced down at the massive wound. Blood practically poured from a two-inch hole in his ribs, and the torn flesh revealed a glimpse of bone. He glared at Skids. "I said that hurt, blast you. Do not do it again."

The fear skittering like June bugs through my stomach reflected in Skids's eyes. The gun shook in the thug's hand. He fired again. And again. The second time, the gun exploded— and took Skids's hand with it.

Skids howled. He didn't sound at all like a wolf.

The stranger pointed at me. "I need him." The disgust edging his tone indicated that whatever this guy wanted, it wouldn't be in my best interests. "Tell your master that Gavyn Donatti is mine. He is not to harm him."

Outright terror struck when my name left the stranger's lips. "How the fuck—"

"Be silent, thief." The stranger whirled to face me, eyes flashing pure hatred. "Unbelievably stupid . . . if I had no need of you, I would kill you myself."

Car doors slammed in rapid sequence. I stared past my bulletproof savior and saw the last thug dive into the backseat. The engine revved. The vehicle lurched back, executed a rapid single-point turn, and peeled away. I watched them go, too shocked to react.

I should have taken the trunk.

CHAPTER 2

"Okay. Who the hell are you, and why aren't you dead?"

The stranger ignored my demand. Not surprising. I would've ignored me, if I could take a few .45 slugs to the chest and stand there telling the guy who shot me to knock it off.

"On your feet," he said. "Take me wherever you live, so we can finish this quickly."

"Fine." I bit back a kiss-my-ass comeback. Whatever this psycho wanted to get over with, I wanted it done, too. Maybe he'd go away.

And maybe Trevor would call me up right now, apologize for the inconvenience, and send me a dozen roses and a bottle of bubbly.

I stood and caught a breath. At six-two, I'm no slouch, but I had to look up to the stranger towering over me. Hate-filled eyes glared at me. An unnatural shade of green-flecked gold, they were rounder than they should have been and ringed with black that looked like eyeliner on both upper and lower lids. The stranger's shaggy brown hair boasted occasional streaks of white, black, or gray. Made him look like a refugee from an eighties glam-rock band. He wore no shirt beneath the coat. Only an open vest and two ragged, oozing bullet wounds.

"What are you staring at?" the stranger snapped.

"Maybe I asked the wrong questions. *What* the hell are you?"

"I am furious. Now take me to your home."

"Sure. Follow me." I headed back into the garage. Time for a reality check. If this guy expected to rip off what I'd lifted for Trevor, he was in for a disappointing haul. Robbing me for his trouble wouldn't line his pockets much, either. He'd get more out of a McDonald's cash register. But if he really wanted my ancient Ford junker, it was all his.

The stranger hesitated and followed me inside. "What are you doing? You cannot live in this building."

"No, I don't." I stopped behind my thug-tossed car. "Right there. Home sweet home. Only I think I've just been evicted."

"You live in your car."

"Not anymore. Trevor bugged it, and I . . . misplaced my scanner, so I can't find the chip."

"Why, you idiotic, incompetent—" The stranger pressed his lips over whatever he'd been ready to say. "This is ridiculous. Why did it have to be you? How could you possibly . . . you are a thief. Not even a *good* thief."

"Hey. I'm an excellent thief." I had the distinct feeling the stranger was talking to himself, but I had to defend my honor—such as it was. "Just not very lucky."

The stranger's eyes narrowed. "Do you plan to continue your larcenous career, or are you actually going to do something with your life at some point?"

What was with the insults? The guy had told Skids he needed me. Maybe he really thought he did. I decided to try a different approach and propped myself casually against the car, as if I wasn't afraid for my life. "I'm not answering any more of your questions until you start answering mine."

"I am not interested in humoring you, thief."

"Okay. I guess we're through, then." I straightened and approached the scattered pile of stuff Trevor's thugs had left behind. Some of it looked salvageable. They'd even missed a few stacks of cash. Idiots. They'd smashed my cell phone. That didn't bother me as much as the mangled remains of my scrambler and the twisted-beyond-salvation lock jock. I couldn't see calling anyone in the near future, but I suspected I'd have to boost a ride. I pocketed everything that appeared intact and deliberately avoided looking in the stranger's direction.

"We are not through." The stranger spoke just behind me. I didn't turn. "I have business with you, and I'll see it carried out."

"Good luck with that."

"You will cooperate. Did you forget what happened to your quick-tempered friend?"

The cool front seemed to be working. I picked up the last remaining item—the wire spool, slightly bent—and slipped it into a pocket of the windbreaker. Straightening slowly for effect, I flashed a wry smile. "First, Skids is no friend of mine. I suspect you know that. And second, I didn't forget. But if *you* did that to Skids, it won't happen to me."

"I would not be so certain of that," the stranger growled.

"I would." My smile stayed put. "You need me. Remember?"

A flush suffused the stranger's face. He didn't correct me.

"That's what I thought. The way I figure it, you're the one who has to cooperate with me. So start cooperating, or I'm dust."

"You would be, if I had my way." The stranger's tone took on a silken edge that held more threat than his barbs. "Very well, Gavyn Donatti. What do you want?"

"Answers. Who are you?"

"You may call me Ian."

"Is that your name?"

"No."

"Fair enough." The people in my world didn't always use their real names. Skids's mom sure as hell hadn't named him after underwear stains. Probably wasn't what Skids had in mind when he took the handle, either, but I thought it suited him.

I let the name thing pass and stared at Ian's chest. The wounds still glistened red, their edges puckered and drawn. He shouldn't be standing—*couldn't* be—but I'd learned to believe what my eyes told me, no matter how impossible it seemed. "How do you know my name?"

"From the telephone book."

"Nice try. I'm not listed."

"I know because it is my business to know. I cannot explain further."

"Fine. I have a more important question, anyway." I wasn't sure I wanted the answer, but I had a feeling it was a need-to-know kind of thing. "What are you?"

Ian hesitated. He stared at me, as if he was trying to gauge my capacity to handle the news. A few insane ideas flashed through my head: werewolf, vampire, figment of my imagination. I would've preferred the latter. At last, he said, "I am djinn."

"You're digi-what? Can you say that in English?"

"A djinn, you blithering idiot. What you Americans call *genies*." Ian managed to infuse the word with more contempt than he'd shown for me, a feat that couldn't have been easy.

I laughed. "Seriously. What are you?"

Ian extended an arm and waved long and slender fingers at my dilapidated coupe. A spot of gleaming chrome burst on the front bumper and spread to become glossy turquoise along the body. Within seconds, a sleek two-door sports car—no brand I'd ever seen and no logo or name to identify it—stood in place of my former heap.

"I am djinn," Ian repeated.

I shut the flytrap that had replaced my mouth, surprised I wasn't drooling. "Right. Digie-inn. Got it."

"Imbecile! Just call me Ian. Surely you can pronounce that, at least."

"Sure," I said, not really listening to him anymore. I wandered to the car and ran a hand along the smooth roof. Cool, solid metal. My hand didn't go through it, and the paint didn't rub off. Okay, so maybe this Ian guy really had turned my rustbucket into a . . . whatever this was. Cinderella never had it so good. All she got was a lousy coach and breakable shoes. Maybe my luck actually was starting to turn. What could be luckier than having a digie . . . a genie . . . an Ian on my side? Or at least saving my ass from Trevor's thugs and giving me sweet wheels. "So, Ian," I said, without taking my attention from the car in case it disappeared. "Why do you need me?"

Ian didn't answer.

I turned. The self-professed djinn's fierce glare had become almost feral. I had to admit, I was impressed with Ian's restraint. Not even Trevor hated me this much. "If you're not going to answer me, I'll just leave. And you can find somebody else to get whatever it is you want."

"I cannot do that. It must be you."

"Why?" I leaned back and propped my elbows on the car's low roof. Still there. Hot damn. "What's so special about me?"

"You—" Ian snapped his mouth closed. The intensity of the hatred in his eyes flared to inferno proportions for an instant. At last, he said through gritted teeth, "You are my master, Gavyn Donatti. And I must serve you until your life's purpose has been realized. But—and heed me well, thief—I will not enjoy it in the least. And if you attempt to humiliate me, or do anything stupid while I am around, you will regret that I ever found you. I despise you, and I am not your friend. Understand?"

I managed a small nod. Maybe having a djinn wasn't so lucky, after all.

IF I THOUGHT TOO HARD ABOUT THIS, I WAS PRETTY SURE I'D LOSE my mind. I couldn't dismiss the fact that the man—the *creature* next to me—was real. Not when I was driving the evidence.

At least I'd found the bug stuck to the frame under the passenger side, so I wouldn't have to worry about Trevor's thugs for a while. If they were even still trying to find me after Ian's little Superman act back there. Which I doubted. The look on Skids's face had said Trevor wasn't paying him enough for this shit.

I pulled onto something resembling a main road and headed south. No idea where I'd end up, but the farther from Trevor, the better. Ian sat silently fuming in the passenger seat. When I couldn't stand the quiet anymore, I said, "We'd better talk."

"I would rather not."

"Tough. There's a few things we have to sort out if we're going to be stuck together."

Ian sank further into the seat. "Must you remind me of that?"

"First, you've got to stop calling me by my full name." I ignored the sulking and concentrated on bland details that wouldn't strain my brain. "It sounds weird, and people will get curious."

Ian's lip curled. "What would you have me call you, then . . . *master*?"

"Not that." I shuddered. If words could kill, I'd be laid out right now. "Just Gavyn, or Donatti. Take your pick."

"Fine. Anything else?"

"Yes. Wear a shirt. And how long are you going to bleed? You can't go around all bloody and exposed. People wear shirts under vests, you know."

"I am djinn, not *people*. And I hate shirts."

"Christ, you're a surly bastard." My jaw clenched hard enough to sink my teeth into my gums. I stared through the windshield and entertained the notion of ramming his side of the car into a tree. "Is there anything you don't hate?"

"Not at the moment."

"Well, you're going to have to dress like a person. Sorry." A sign ahead proclaimed GENOA—25 MILES. FOOD—LODGING—BEER. That sounded good. Especially the beer part. "Maybe we should head there. Listen, do you need a doctor or something?"

"Gods, no. Your doctors would panic if they examined me."

"You're still bleeding."

Ian glanced down at his chest. "Yes."

"Okay, then." I concentrated on the road. "Look, I'm going to pull off in this Genoa place. We can grab a room for the night, and in the morning—what exactly are we doing, again?"

"Must we stop? I want to be rid of you."

"That makes two of us. But I'm people, remember? I need food, sleep, shit like that. If you don't want to tell me what you're planning, fine. Surprise me. But we're stopping for the night."

Ian frowned. "What I am planning is not that simple. I cannot just lay it out step by step. I have to serve you until your life's purpose has been realized, and then I can go home." The word *home* emerged on a longing sigh.

I almost sympathized with him for a minute. If I had a home, I'd want to go there, too.

"Uh-huh," I said. "So, what's my life's purpose?"

"I do not know."

"That's great. Neither do I." The road entered a sharp and unexpected curve. I gripped the wheel tighter and eased off the gas. Damn, it was dark in the country. No streetlights, no city glow, and I hadn't seen another car for miles. "How does this work? You serving me, I mean."

"Excuse me?"

The warning note in Ian's voice gave me pause. I chose my words with care. "Well, I have to admit, I don't know much about djinn. Okay, I don't know anything. Do I get three wishes?"

Ian muttered something that included *television* and *idiotic*. "No wishes," he said. "If you need or desire something, I will attempt to fulfill that need or desire . . . in a way I see fit."

"Oh, good." Wasn't there a story about magic backfiring? Something about an animal . . . a monkey. The Monkey's Paw. An old couple wished for money, and their son was killed in a horrible accident, for which they were compensated. I wouldn't put it past this djinn to try something like that. *Be careful what you wish for . . . you just might get it.* "So, should I just ask for what I want?"

"You can try."

"You're not making this easy."

"I do not intend to make things easy."

"Yeah, I can see that. Look, you want to go home, right?"

"Yes," Ian snarled.

"Don't you think this situation would be easier and done faster if you cooperated? If you didn't have to put up with my stupid questions, we'd avoid all this dancing around each other. Just be straight with me."

"Fine." Ian seemed to relax. A little.

I grinned. Time to push some buttons. "I'm thirsty."

"How fortunate, then, that our destination has beer." Ian pointed to a sign indicating ten miles to Genoa.

"Aren't you going to fulfill my desire?"

"Idiot. If we were close to a lake, I would throw you in." Ian straightened in his seat and glared. "We do not use magic for trifles. My power is a disruptive force, not a . . . a parlor trick."

"Okay. No disruptions. Got it." I tapped the steering wheel and made a mental note to strike the frivolity button. "Speaking of disruptions, you're a big walking one. And I don't think that bleeding is going to stop. Have you ever been shot before?"

"No." Ian made a face. "If I had, I would have known how painful it is."

"We're going to have to do something about that. There has to be someone . . . let me think a minute." I knew all about avoiding hospitals. In my profession, I couldn't exactly show up at the ER with most of the injuries I received in the line of duty. They always wanted explanations. Had to be someone in the area I could contact, preferably someone not associated with Trevor.

Oh, damn. She wasn't going to be happy to hear from me.

"Here's the plan." I tried to sound more convinced than I felt. "We'll check in, and I'll get in touch with Jazz. She'll patch you up. Might even bring you some real clothes."

If she doesn't kill me first.

CHAPTER 3

Lodging in Genoa consisted of a squat, sagging one-story motel painted what used to be pink, with a row of nine doors that I assumed led to eight rooms and an office. The Wandering Inn. How bloody charming. I pulled into the deserted lot and parked as far as possible from the only door not bearing a hand-carved wooden number, hoping the owner was a vampire. Otherwise, whoever ran this backwoods place would have no reason to be around to rent a room at this time of night.

I cut the engine and unfastened my seatbelt. "You stay here. If they see you, there'll be trouble. I'll be back in a few minutes, all right?"

Ian nodded. His skin had paled considerably, and his hands lay fisted in his lap.

"You look like hell. Are you gonna make it?"

"I will be fine. Go."

I slid out and started across the lot, less than assured about the djinn's condition. What would I do if Ian died on me? Scratch that—not happening. The guy was a magical creature or something. Had to take more than a few bullets to kill him. I hoped.

A light above the office door snapped on when I got close. Something at the window shifted. I caught the impression of a face peering out. At least someone was awake, but whoever it was probably didn't have a happy reason for monitoring the parking lot at midnight. I reached the door, and before I could knock, it opened.

A double-barreled shotgun greeted me. I damn near laughed. How many people were going to try to shoot me tonight?

"Didn't think I was serious, didja?" A gravelly voice rolled from the shadows inside the door. "I toldja you punks ain't gettin' me out. Toldja I'd blast you if you came back. I already talked to the sheriff, and he said if I hadda shoot, go for it."

"Uh . . ." I cleared my throat. "I just wanted a room."

A pause. "You ain't with that Trevor fella?"

Trevor? Shit. Just my luck that the only motel for a hundred miles was a target for Trevor's "real estate" endeavors. I should have done what Ian wanted and kept driving. Too late now—neither of us was in any shape to head back out. "No. Never heard of the guy." I managed to sound normal.

The shotgun stayed in place for a moment and finally lowered. A light flickered on inside, revealing the gun's owner. Sixties, salt-and-pepper hair, sun-weathered skin, and a solid build just beginning to soften around the edges. The aging Marine look.

I felt sorry for him. No one stood up to Trevor's thugs for long. If the bastard wanted something, he got it—one way or another. And it looked as if he'd get this place over the owner's dead body.

"Hmph. Thought that was his car." The old man pushed past me and stepped out into the lot, his finger still resting on the trigger. He peered at the sleek blue car. I wondered if he'd notice the fine craftsmanship that made the thing stand out like a clown at a funeral. Finally, he said, "Got another guy with you. You a faggot?"

So that was it. He didn't want any degenerates fouling his upstanding establishment. "Uh, no. He's my . . . brother." *Damn it, Donatti, don't hesitate.* "We had a convention up in Auburn. We were gonna drive through the night, get home tomorrow. But the bastard got sloshed on me at the after party, and I'm too beat to keep going."

The old man grunted. "Yeah, my brother's a lazy asshole, too. Room's two hundred a night for double occupancy. You can take number eight, since you're already parked there. You want it?"

"We'll take it." As if there was another choice. Two hundred seemed a bit steep for a middle-of-nowhere dive, but the old man probably figured me for loaded, considering the car. Good thing I'd kept the cash handy. I dug in a pocket and produced two hundreds. "Since this is a cash transaction, I don't have to sign anything, right?"

Damn. I hadn't meant to say that out loud.

The old man's eyes narrowed. "You ain't doin' anything illegal, are ya?"

"Nope." Technically, it was the truth. I wasn't stealing anything at the moment, sure as hell not from here, and saving my own ass wasn't against the law. "Just keeping out of the spotlight."

Nodding, the old man took the bills and pocketed them. "Hang on. I'll get your key." He tromped back inside and returned a moment later without the shotgun. Instead, he carried a key fastened on the end of a sanded wooden oval and a six-pack of Busch Light dripping with condensation. "Ain't got an ice machine, but there's a mini-fridge in the room. Beds're made. Cable's out, but you can probably get a couple local channels, weather and crap."

I accepted the key and the beer with a heaping side of confusion. I had to know. "Do you always hand out booze with room rentals?"

"You jus' looked thirsty." The old man shrugged and headed back inside. "Checkout's at eleven," he called over his shoulder. "If you're late, you gotta pay another night."

"Wait. Can you turn the phone on? I have to make a few calls."

"No phones in the rooms. Pay phone around the corner of the building."

Jesus. No wonder the place was so dead. All the cost of an upscale room in the city and none of the amenities. Why didn't he just take the beds out and charge three hundred a night to let people sleep on the floor? "Fine. Can I get some change, then? I've only got bills."

"Don't keep change around nights. Have to wait for the bank to open in the morning." With that, the old man entered a room I guessed was his office and closed the door.

I stared after him, more than a little ticked. I'm normally an easygoing guy, prepared to grab the short straw every time, but this was pushing it, even for me. Now I'd have to call Jazz collect. Thank you, phone-smashing thugs and tight-wad motel owners. If she showed up, it would only be to disembowel me.

I headed back to the car and opened the passenger door. Ian slumped in the seat, motionless, eyes closed. I had to fight the urge to shake him—not so much to wake his sorry ass but because it would've made me feel better. "Hey. Are you all right?"

Ian opened his eyes and fixed me with a glare. "There is no need to yell. I am right here."

"Yeah, well, that's great. You looked dead. How am I supposed to know . . . shit, never mind. I got us a room. Come on."

The djinn unfolded himself from the car. "I see you have your beer," he said.

"Uh-huh. How about that." I looked up at him and thought about asking him to shrink a few inches. This towering bit unnerved me. "See, the owner, he just gave it to me with the room key. I didn't even ask for it."

Ian arched an eyebrow. "You did say you were thirsty."

"So you did have something to do with it."

"I simply made it possible for your desires to be satisfied. Can we go to this room, please? I tire of your company. Perhaps you will be more tolerable in your sleep."

I grunted. "I don't know that I want to fall asleep around you. You might slit my throat or something." I headed for number eight, key at the ready.

Ian followed at a languid pace. "Djinn do not kill humans. We do not even hurt them."

"Really? Then why'd you blow Skids's hand off?"

"He shot me. Besides, technically, I did not hurt him. The gun did."

"Oh, I see. So *technically*, causing a heavy blunt object like a television set to fall on my head wouldn't be you killing me or even hurting me. Right?"

"I told you, I cannot hurt you. You are my—"

"Don't say it. I know." I unlocked the door and felt inside for a light switch, suddenly as eager to get rid of Ian as the djinn was to ditch me. Being this surly bastard's *master* was about as useful as ordering the weather around. And if achieving my life's purpose depended on coaxing a flesh-bound hurricane to cooperate with me, I'd take eternal bad luck. Why couldn't I get the djinn of lollipops and happiness? I'd take a stereotypical genie in a bottle—a female, easy on the eyes—any day over this lanky, overgrown jerk.

I found the light at last. As the owner had promised, the beds were made, one with an olive-green paisley spread, the other with a ruffled pink blanket.

"The pink one's yours." I walked into the room and thumped down on the ugly green cover. While waiting for Ian to make his way inside, I gave the place a quick once-over. One nonopening window, three doors—bathroom, closet, entrance. Crud. I'd have been more comfortable sleeping in the car. At least it had two outs. Three, if I counted driving away before any threats-to-come managed to get inside.

I spotted a mini refrigerator beneath a desk on the left-hand wall and crossed the room to stow the six-pack. Twisting two cans from the rings, I closed the vaguely mold-scented appliance and offered one to the djinn, who'd settled uncertainly on the edge of the pink bed.

Ian stared at it and seemed about to refuse. After a moment, he accepted it silently.

I cracked mine and took a seat facing him. "So. Here we are."

"Indeed." Ian made no move to open his beer.

"What's wrong? Don't genies drink?"

"I despise that word. I am djinn."

"Whatever." I took a slug and damn near moaned in pleasure. Nothing like a cold beer after a hard day of running for your life. "By the way, any chance you could tell me how you found me out there?"

He took his time responding. "I have known your whereabouts for quite some time now."

"And you just happened to catch up when I was about to die."

"It was no coincidence. I have always been close."

"Really." I gulped more beer. The taste soured in my mouth—or maybe it was the feeling that I didn't like what I thought I was hearing. "So you've been following me."

"More or less."

"For how long?"

Ian shot me a nasty look. "Long enough to know why those men were attempting to bring you to their master."

I laughed at the idea of Skids calling Trevor "master." The cold bastard would probably shoot him for being a wise-ass.

"I fail to see why this amuses you." Ian flicked at the pop ring on the can he held but still didn't open it. "I, for one, do not enjoy being forced to . . . serve a petty thief."

"Hey. I told you, I'm not petty. I'm good at what I do."

"You steal. And for baser slime than yourself."

This time, I gave the dirty look. "The door's right there," I said, gesturing with my beer. "I didn't ask for your services. This slime can take care of himself, thanks."

"Oh, yes." He sneered at me. "You were doing so well before I arrived. Just about to escape, were you?"

"As a matter of fact, I was. I could've made it." Probably. Maybe. Okay, there'd been a slim chance—but it was still a chance.

Hell, I'd have been a dead man without him.

I sighed and stared at the worn carpet. "Fine. Thank you, okay? Just don't call me slime. I'm nothing like Trevor or his goons."

"Perhaps not." Ian didn't sound convinced. He tapped a finger on the top of his can. "How does this container operate? The opening is sealed."

I blinked. "You don't know how to open a can? Man, what rock have you been living under?"

His momentary surprise rolled over into disgust. "I have been away for some time. And I have never had occasion to open such a can."

I stood and showed him how to work the pop-top, wondering where the hell he'd been away. He'd never seen a beer can, didn't seem to understand that guns shot people . . . maybe he'd been helping Santa and the elves out at the North Pole, or herding unicorns, or whatever magical creatures did in their spare time. I handed it back to him with a frown. Enough stalling—time to give Jazz another reason to hate me.

"I have to make a call," I said, finishing off my beer and grabbing a fresh one. "Apparently, the only available phone is the one outside. I won't be long, so just stay here."

"Where else would I go?"

A smart-ass remark froze on the tip of my tongue. The question lacked the djinn's usual acerbic timbre. Ian hadn't looked at me. His gaze rested on the beer in his hand, and he seemed almost sad.

"I'll be right back," I said, modulating down to nicer than normal. I left the room, closed the door. Outside, I popped the new can and drank half the contents in one long swallow.

Two beers weren't enough to prepare me for the groveling I'd have to manufacture for the less-than-decent chance of getting Jazz out here. I gave the can a rueful stare. Liquid courage, my ass.

Too bad it wasn't tequila. At this point, I'd down the bottle and eat the worm.

I FOUND THE PHONE WITHOUT DIFFICULTY. DIALING PROVED harder. I punched in a zero and half of Jazz's cell number. Hung up. Drained the rest of the beer. Tried again and managed all but the last two numbers before disconnecting.

With the receiver in a clammy hand and a finger on the cutoff, I stood there trying to convince myself that the worst she could do was refuse the call. It wasn't—she could track me down and beat the crud out of me or take the hands-off approach and send the cops, if she wanted to.

Since she hadn't done either in the three years since I ditched her, maybe I had a shot.

It was enough to get me dialing. I waited for the recording to request my name and said in a rush, "I'll pay you triple please don't hang up."

The canned voice finished its spiel. A click sounded, a beat of dead air. The call went through. I clenched a fist, my jaw, anything that would tighten. *Please please please be there.* One foot involuntarily tapped out a jackrabbit thump on the pavement.

Jazz answered on the fourth ring. "Yeah, what?"

God, she sounded just the way I remembered her. Pure pissed-off female, with the walk to back up the talk.

The drone dividing her end from mine switched on. *"You have a collect call from* I'll-pay-you-triple-please-don't-hang-up. *Press one to accept the charges, two to decline."*

"Son of a . . ." she whispered. I didn't hear any buttons being pressed.

"You have a collect call from—" Beep.

"Please let that have been a one," I muttered.

Another hollow click. More dead air.

"You should've stayed in whatever hole you crawled out of, Houdini."

"Jazz." I closed my eyes, only partially from relief. "I know I'm the last guy you want to hear from—"

"Damn straight you are. Last time I mixed with you, you just about got my ass busted."

"It wasn't my fault."

"Really. So somebody else ditched me and skipped town right before that gig for Jonnessey? I had to make the run myself. There were cops all over the place."

"Hey, at least you didn't have to split the payout with me."

Jazz heaved a sigh. "What do you want? Make it fast, you're on my dime. You're paying for this call, you know."

"Yeah, I know." Momentary panic stilled my tongue. I hadn't come up with a story. I'd have to keep it simple for now. "I'm in the area, and my partner is injured."

"Oh, good. Another partner. How injured?"

"Gunshot." I paused. Couldn't fudge on that—if she came, she'd notice. "Okay, multiple gunshots. They're just flesh wounds, though." *I think.*

"Where are you?"

"The only motel in Genoa. Room eight."

"That's an hour away." Jazz made a sound that could only be described as a growl. "Anything else I should know?"

Crud. I'd hoped to avoid this little fact. "Er . . . Trevor's gunning for me."

"Christ, Donatti. How do you get yourself into these messes?"

"Just lucky, I guess."

"Yeah. You're a regular friggin' leprechaun. Well, for once you can count yourself lucky that I hate Trevor more than you."

"You mean you'll come?"

"Pay my regular rate, cover my gas, supplies, and this damned call, and yeah. I'll come. Give me two hours, tops."

Relief made a temporary comeback. "Thank you, Jazz. I—"

"Don't say you owe me. You'll never be able to make it up."

"Right." I started to sign off and remembered Ian's lack of fashion sense. The bullet-riddled-fugitive look just wasn't in. "Can I ask for one more favor?"

"You can ask."

"I . . . that is, my partner needs clothes. Shirt and pants. His are wrecked."

"You know, you ought to give your partners some warning before they sign on with your sorry ass. 'Caution, I screw people over, but don't worry, it'll be an accident.' I suppose you're completely unscathed as usual?"

"Yeah, but . . ."

"Never mind. What size?"

"Uh . . . tall?"

"A little more specific, please."

I tried to picture the djinn. "About my build, maybe a tad slimmer, and half a foot taller. Long legs, long arms."

"Oh, that helps. C'mon, Donatti, I never looked at your underwear tags. What size are you?"

"Thirty-eight." Damn it. Why did she have to bring up underwear? I'd noticed hers. They'd looked great wadded on the floor of her van. Almost as great as she looked naked . . .

I had to think cold thoughts to stop my size thirty-eights from stretching. Snow. Ice. Antarctica. Trevor.

That did the trick.

"Fine. I'll do what I can." She hesitated, and for an instant I thought she'd hung up. At last she said, "Look, Houdini, you'd better not pull another disappearing act on me. I still don't know whether to kiss you or kick your ass."

Before I could formulate a response, she hung up.

CHAPTER 4

When I returned to the room, I found Ian's coat tossed on the bed—without Ian. The pink blanket bore a few smears of blood. A trail of fine crimson droplets on the tan carpet led from the bed to the closed bathroom door. How much blood could this guy lose? This couldn't be healthy, even for a djinn.

I headed for the bathroom, raised a hand to knock, and hesitated. Did genies take dumps? I had no idea whether their bodies worked like people—though they certainly bled like one when they got shot. They might not need to eat or drink. Maybe he'd just decided to clean himself up, but I didn't hear any running water.

A low, muffled voice drifted through the door. Ian, but he wasn't speaking English. I cupped my hands on the door and rested an ear between my thumbs. The language wasn't one I recognized, though it sounded vaguely Middle Eastern. Ian fell silent after a modulated upswing that sounded like a question.

Another voice responded. A female voice.

I jerked back, reached for the handle, and twisted hard. Locked. Where in hell did he find a woman this time of night . . . and why wasn't she freaking out over all the blood? Whoever she was, she had to go. I pounded on the door. "What the hell's going on in there?"

A sharp crack sounded from inside. Ian gasped. "Blast it, thief!" he shouted. "Do you not have any manners?"

"Who's in there with you?"

"No one."

"Bullshit. I heard someone else. And she wasn't you, unless you were squeezing your balls and practicing your *I Dream of Jeannie* imitation."

A long pause. The door opened slowly, just enough to reveal Ian's haggard face. "There is no one here but me. You must be imagining things."

"Prove it."

Ian's eyes narrowed. He stepped back and to the side and let the door swing open on a scene straight from a cheap horror flick. Blood drizzled the edge of the sink and pooled on the floor. Drops of the stuff decorated the faucets, the wall, even the toilet. A crack scarred the mirror above the sink, segmenting the lower right corner. On the unscathed upper left of the glass, there appeared to be a symbol drawn in blood—a wavy vertical line and a dot enclosed in a crescent. For some reason, the symbol seemed familiar to me, though I was sure I didn't know how to read djinn.

"Jesus Christ. What'd you do, sacrifice a few chickens?" At least there was no mystery woman in sight. Only Ian and a gallon or two of blood. Still, I knew I'd heard the voice. Had he shoved her in the shower? Flushed her down the toilet?

"Idiot. I was trying to get the bullets out." Ian looked down at his chest, now bathed in deep red. "For some reason, I do not heal as quickly as I used to."

"I thought you said you've never been shot before."

"I have not. But I have been injured. Guns are not common in—"

"Gahiji-an?"

I flinched. The distinctly female voice sounded hollow and distant, like a cell phone with a bad connection. I scanned the room and finally noticed the ghostly image in the mirror. A woman's face, eyes ringed with black like Ian's, almond-shaped instead of round and more than a little unsettling. Took me a minute to realize it was because she had no whites, just a thin black border around pale gray irises that extended to the edges. Dark hair, dusky skin, a beguiling smile—only half visible, since the image didn't extend beyond the crack in the glass.

My mouth fell open. No words came out. The image copied my expression and then offered a musical laugh. "You are Gavyn Donatti," she said.

"Last I checked." I swallowed and glanced at Ian. The djinn's features had darkened, and he stood rigid and mute, as though he didn't trust himself to speak. My earlier reservations about falling asleep around him returned in full force. I'd pissed him off without half trying. Go, me.

I turned back to the woman in the mirror. "Who are you?"

"I am Akila."

Ian shook himself. He strode toward me and shoved me away from the mirror. "This is not your concern, thief. Get out."

"Gahiji-an. Do not be so hard on the boy. He seems quite strong."

"Akila, please. Do not encourage him. He is already full of himself." The look he sent her contained equal parts fury and pleading.

"Boy?" I asked. She had my attention. I decided to ignore Ian's latest slur and indulge my curiosity. "Uh . . . how old are you? Sorry, I know it's not polite to ask a lady her age and all, but I'm not exactly fresh out of high school."

Ian whirled on me and spoke through clenched teeth. "This connection is weak. I have little time left, so if you do not mind, my wife and I would like some privacy."

"Your . . ." Did he say *wife*? I couldn't imagine anyone putting up with this world-class asshole long enough to hold a decent conversation, much less promise to love and cherish him for life. Maybe the djinn had a different arrangement for marriage, something that didn't involve the couple being around each other for longer than it took to procreate.

Ian in the sack. Another idea I didn't want to wrap my head around.

"Donatti. Get out." Ian closed his eyes and added, "Please."

Whoa. He'd used my name and asked nicely. "Uh, okay. Sure."

"Good-bye, Gavyn Donatti," Akila said. "Luck be with you."

I had to laugh. "Luck. Yeah, right." I stepped out, and Ian slammed the door in my face.

By the time Ian emerged from the bathroom, I'd drained two more beers. I watched him move slowly to the bed and all but collapse. Either whatever he'd done to contact his wife had drained him, or he'd been putting on one hell of a front from the start. He was in rough shape.

For the first time, I noticed the tattoos encircling his upper arms: identical bands of curving, fluid points overlapping straight lines. Like stylized barbed wire or thorns. The ink, or whatever djinn used for tattoos, was shades of brown and black. The markings appeared to have a raised texture, but I wasn't about to touch him and find out.

"I take it they don't have phones back in genie world," I said. "You all should invest in some technology. Your disruptive force seems a little defective in the communication department."

Ian glowered. "It would have been fine, if you had not interrupted."

"How was I supposed to know you were talking to a magic mirror? I thought that was a witch thing. Besides, I . . . never mind." I stomped to the fridge and grabbed the last beer. If I drank enough, maybe all this insanity would go away.

"Besides what?"

"I was worried, all right?" I popped the can and studied my feet. "You're bleeding all over the place. I don't want you dying on me."

Ian made a strangled sound. "Not before you get your riches and fame from me."

"Wrong. I just don't know how I would dump your sorry carcass, you impossible son of a bitch." I took a long swallow, exhaled sharply. Wasn't enough beer in the world to make him disappear. "What makes you think I want riches and fame, anyway?"

"You are human."

"And?"

"I've seen your world. All humans are greedy, selfish, and shallow."

"Damn it, you don't know me!" I resisted throwing the beer can across the room and drank more instead. I couldn't believe he was getting to me. I might have been a thief, but as humans went, I considered myself halfway decent. I held doors open and helped old ladies cross the street, and I always tipped at restaurants. Besides, stealing was just a job—and the only thing I'd ever been good at. I didn't want to be rich. I just wanted to survive. "Are all djinn miserable, secretive bastards?" I muttered. "If I hadn't seen your wife, I'd be inclined to believe that."

"My wife is none of your business."

"*Nothing* is my business. How the hell are we supposed to work together and get you home if I don't know what's going on?"

Ian's brow lifted. "You want to get me home?"

"I don't want you hanging around pissing and moaning about how much you hate me." I moved to the bed and sat down. Hard. "Honestly, I couldn't care less about my life's purpose, or whatever it is you're supposed to be here for. It wouldn't matter to me if you left right now. Christ, I need a cigarette."

"Look in your jacket pocket." Ian waved vaguely at the windbreaker I'd tossed onto the nightstand between the beds.

I shook my head. "One of Trevor's goons snagged 'em."

"Just look."

"Whatever." I grabbed the jacket and inspected the pockets one by one. The upper right yielded a sealed pack of filtered Camels. I grinned and tapped the top of the box against my leg a few times. He'd even gotten the brand right. "Thanks for determining I needed this. Got a light?"

Wordlessly, Ian reached for his own jacket and produced a plain gold Zippo.

I lit up and offered the pack. "Want one?"

"No." Ian dropped his gaze and added as an afterthought, "Thank you."

Shrugging it off, I tossed the pack and lighter onto the table. "So I take it you're not going to die anytime soon?"

"I am afraid not. In fact, I should be fine if I can get these blasted bullets out."

"Jazz'll take care of that. She'll be here soon." I finished off all but a few sips of beer and flicked ash into the open can. A quick hiss echoed inside the hollow space. Pleasantly buzzed, I ignored the logical part of my mind that insisted none of this could be real—the car that shouldn't exist, the beer I shouldn't have been offered, the cigarette I smoked that couldn't have been in my jacket, the speaking phantom in the mirror . . .

The blood in the bathroom. Jazz might not freak, but the motel owner sure as hell would.

"God damn it." I stood and dropped the cigarette into the can. "We've got to do something about that mess. Well, I've got to do something. You'll just make it worse. You stay there and bleed. I'll figure it out."

Ian sighed. He made a dismissive gesture toward the closed door. "It is done."

"Crud." I sat back down. "This is really happening, isn't it?" Propping elbows on knees, I pressed the heels of my hands against my eyes, as if I could push every crazy thing that had happened tonight out of existence. When I looked again, I was still in a shitbag of a motel room in the middle of nowhere, with a grumpy magical dude sitting across from me. "Why are you being so nice now? I don't trust you."

"I am simply doing my job. *Master.*"

"I thought we agreed you wouldn't call me that."

He had the decency to appear mildly apologetic.

I sighed. "Can we call a truce? You try not to hate me for

existing, and I'll try not to hate you for making my already shitty life worse. Deal?"

Ian's gaze flicked down and back up. "I will try."

"Gee, thanks." He sounded about as enthusiastic as a fast-food employee asking if I wanted fries with that. "You know, I really don't get you. Are you allergic to humans or something? Because I don't remember doing anything to make you despise me this much."

Before Ian could reply, the rumble of an approaching engine swelled outside, revved for an instant, and cut out. "Hold that thought," I told him. "Jazz is here. Cover yourself up, wouldya? She's tough, but it's better to ease into stuff like life-threatening wounds that don't make you dead."

Ian grunted and moved for his coat. I pushed myself off the bed, crossed the room, and opened the door—only to find myself at the wrong end of a gun for the third time in a night. A new record.

CHAPTER 5

H ey, Jazz. You know, if you shoot me, there's a good chance you won't get paid."

Jazz offered a crooked smile. "There's more to life than money."

"True. But I hear it's hard to get much out of life behind bars."

"If I took you out, I'd probably get a medal. Don't worry too much. I'm just taking precautions." She leaned aside and looked into the room. "That your partner?"

"Yeah, that's him."

"He's prettier than you. Looks pissed. What's his problem?"

I shrugged. "He hates me."

"I like him already." Jazz lowered the Glock and gestured toward the parking lot. "Go get my bags, Houdini. I'll see to your friend, and then we need to talk."

I didn't move.

"What are you staring at?"

"Nothing." *You.* Jazz had captivated me from the first time I'd seen her lay out a man twice her size without breaking a sweat—which described just about every man she'd ever laid out, since she stood all of five feet in boots. Her mixed heritage had given her the best of both worlds: glossy black hair, elegant features, golden brown skin. At night, she couldn't wear the sunglasses she favored to hide her unusual eyes. One deep brown, almost black, the other a pale and penetrating green.

"It's good to see you," I said. Understatement of the century, but I couldn't come up with anything more profound at the moment.

She rolled her eyes. "I can't say the same yet, but I might change my mind. Would you get moving? It's two in the goddamn morning."

"Right. Sorry." I edged past her, and she held the room door open while I snagged two worn leather bags from the back of her white panel van. Couldn't believe she still had this thing. We'd used it for a job up by the St. Lawrence, and she'd put it through some serious shit. But I guessed getaway drivers never dumped a vehicle if they could help it. She must've fixed it up and stashed it for a while until the heat died down.

I hauled the bags back to the room, pushing away memories of what we'd done in the back of that van. Jazz closed the door behind me.

"Just put them down." She waved a hand at the floor and turned her attention to Ian, who stood as she approached him. "Guess you can't be that bad off, if you can still get up. You're a bit tall for a thief," she said. "Are you the driver or the distraction?"

Ian bristled. I dropped the bags, hustled toward them, and cleared my throat. "Ian, this is Jazz. And Jazz, Ian. My partner." I leveled a keep-your-mouth-shut look at the djinn, sure he'd take offense at the partner bit. "He's a little on the green side, but he specializes."

"Hello, Jazz." Ian gave a slight bow. "It's an honor to meet such a lovely and no doubt talented lady."

Jazz laughed. "Oh, I definitely like you. Even if you are a little weird. So what's your specialty, cowboy?"

"Let's not talk shop right now," I cut in. The bastard could be civil when he wanted to—and if I'd said the same thing to Jazz, she'd have slugged me. "All right, Jazz, this is your show. Just tell us what you need us to do."

Jazz pursed her lips. "I'm guessing I'll have to take a few bullets out, so it's going to get messy. We can do it on the bed, if you don't mind lifting the blankets when you check out."

"No problem." That wouldn't be necessary, but I didn't have to tell her that Ian could just magic the bloodstains away after she left.

"Didn't think it would be." Jazz eyed Ian again. "You took one in the leg. Where else?"

"Uh, Jazz?" Tough as she was, the sight of his mangled chest would be hard to take. "Before you check him out, I need to explain something. Ian is . . . resilient."

"Fascinating. And I need to know this because?"

"Well. He's tough. Tougher than Teflon. It's almost hard to believe—"

"I've dedicated years to the art of separating mind and body, in order to manage pain," Ian interrupted smoothly. "I have studied many different techniques, including those of the sumo, Yogi masters, and ancient Egyptians. I believe Donatti is attempting to warn you that the extent of my injuries may prove shocking."

"Yeah. What he said," I muttered. Son of a bitch was a better liar than me, too.

Jazz grinned. "If you can shock me, I'll be impressed."

With a small smile, Ian removed his coat.

"Okay," Jazz whispered. "I'm impressed."

"I thought you might be. Should I lie down?"

"Yes. No . . . strip first. I'll have to get at that leg, eventually." Jazz stepped back and finally tore her gaze from the sight of his ruined flesh. "Donatti. Get the basin out of the big bag—wait, hand me the small one first."

I did as she asked and put a hand on her shoulder. She flinched. "I'm sorry," I said. "Shouldn't have sprung this on you."

"I'm all right." Jazz released a shallow breath and visibly pulled herself together. "Well, Houdini, at least I can say you're never boring. Got any more . . . whoa."

I followed her stunned gaze. "Christ, Ian."

"What?" he countered.

"Don't you believe in underwear?"

Ian scowled. "As a matter of fact, I do not. And why should it bother you? Do you not have the same equipment?"

"Yeah, but I don't go showing it off to everyone. And you said *I* didn't have any manners. Get a towel or something."

"What the hell's goin' on in here?"

Shit. The motel owner, shotgun in tow, stood in the open doorway with a grim expression, holding what I assumed was a master key. "Not much," I said, resigned to a lack of explanation. Anything I came up with now would sound ridiculous. Yes, sir, we're just rehearsing for an off-Broadway show, and Ian's really bad at death scenes. Don't mind the blood. Or maybe: My friend here is a masochist, and we hired this dominatrix to shoot him a few times. He asked for it. Me, I'm just holding the bucket. I'm a voyeur.

Oh, yeah. He'd buy that. At least the gun wasn't pointed at me this time.

"You freaks get outta my place. Right now."

I glanced at Ian and shook my head, hoping he would take the hint and leave things alone. I hated this dump anyway. "Don't I get a refund?"

"Out!"

Sighing, I hoisted Jazz's bags and caught her eye. Her hand hovered near the pocket in which she'd stowed her Glock. *Don't,* I mouthed, noting with relief that Ian was getting dressed. *No trouble.* Her lips firmed in disapproval, but she dropped her hand.

We filed out under the owner's paranoid watch. In the parking lot, I replaced the bags where I'd found them and turned an apologetic grimace on Jazz. "Know any decent motels nearby?"

Jazz shook her head. "I can't believe I'm saying this, but . . . you two had better come with me."

WE LEFT IN RECORD TIME, UNDER A BARRAGE OF THREATS FROM the owner to alternately call his buddy the sheriff and just shoot us all. After stashing the odd little car in a wooded area just off the road outside town, I climbed into the passenger seat of the van when Jazz curtly declined my offer to drive. I couldn't argue. She was the expert. Ian stretched across the van's far backseat, apparently asleep. Jazz hadn't looked in my direction since I'd gotten in, and I hadn't been inclined to initiate conversation.

Since I'd nixed letting her put the motel owner in his place, I worried she might turn the Glock on me as a substitute. Jazz never allowed herself to get pushed around.

She swung onto 34 North, switched the radio on at low

volume, and glanced into the rearview mirror. "He's not from around here, is he?" she said softly.

"Not exactly." I pushed back the temptation to confess. Barely believed it myself, so how could I convince her? The best idea for now would be to elaborate as little as possible. Keep it simple. And lie my ass off. She'd taken it well, but we'd both seen some insane things on the job. Most of the time, it was better to adopt a "don't ask, don't tell" policy. So far, she'd stuck to the thieves' rulebook. I hoped she didn't plan any detours.

"Somehow I get the feeling there's something you're not telling me. No," she said, holding up a hand. "Right now, I don't want to know. But we need to talk, and we might as well do it now."

"All right." I suspected I wouldn't like what was coming. "Let's talk."

Jazz hesitated. When she finally started speaking, she kept her gaze straight ahead. "First off, Trevor has an open contract out on you. Big money. He wants you alive."

"Son of a bitch works fast, doesn't he?" I gripped the armrest hard. "I hate to ask, but you know I have to. Are you planning to cash me in?"

"No." She gave a short laugh. "The thought crossed my mind. Like I said, though, I hate him more. Don't worry—I put out word that you were on my shit list a long time ago. No one will come looking for you with me."

"Great. That's reassuring."

"If I wanted to reassure you, I would've lied. What'd you do to Trevor, anyway?"

"Stepped on his foot and scuffed his loafers."

"Come on, Donatti."

I had to fess up. How embarrassing. "He hired me to lift something, and I . . . lost it."

"You're kidding." Her laughter was genuine this time. "You *lost* a score? Shit, you really do have the worst luck."

"Tell me about it. Of course, Trevor thinks I double-crossed him, fenced it to somebody else. He wants me alive so he can torture me to find out what I did with it. And I'm sure he won't take 'I lost it' for an answer."

"That's rough." Jazz tapped the brake a few times as we passed a posted speed limit of forty-five heading into a small town. "What'd he have you lift, the Hope diamond?"

"Actually, it was some crappy old knife. Piece of junk, far as I could tell. But you know collectors. They have the most screwed-up reasons for wanting things."

Jazz nodded and fell silent.

I watched her concentrate on the road for a few minutes. She picked up speed again when we hit the edge of East Bump-in-the-Road, or whatever that little huddle of buildings called itself. "Was that all we had to talk about?" I asked.

"I wish." Jazz drummed her fingers on the steering wheel. "Aren't you wondering why I agreed to help you after all this time?"

"I figured it was because of my charming personality. Or, barring that, the money."

"Charming. Not the word I'd use."

"How about eccentric?"

"Would you lay off the wisecracks for a minute? This isn't easy for me to say." Her expression hardened, and her hands clamped the wheel. "I have a son."

"*What?* Where?" I glanced back, half expecting a kid to materialize behind my seat.

"You moron. Do you really think I'd bring him out in the middle of the night to hang out with a bunch of thieves? He stays with my sister when I'm working."

I smiled. "How is Molly? Haven't seen her in a while."

"She's fine." Jazz gave me an odd look. "My son just turned two last week."

"Okay." My mind raced. Obviously, she wanted me to understand something, but my exhausted brain refused coherent thought. Was she trying to say she was getting out of the business? I'd certainly buy that—thieves weren't good role models for kids. "I'm . . . uh, sorry?"

"Damn you, Donatti. Don't you get it?"

I started to shake my head and froze. I hadn't seen Jazz in almost three years . . . and there'd been no shortage of baby-making activity between us back then. Jesus. She couldn't be telling me what I suspected. What would rip the rest of my soul out and crush it—because, for fuck's sake, being a thief wasn't enough to ensure my spot in hell. No way Jazz could be saying I'd accidentally become a father.

But she was.

When my tongue failed to move, Jazz spoke for me. "I have a son. And so do you."

CHAPTER 6

If I had been driving, I would've wrecked us right then.

Since I wasn't, my body's sudden, stiff reaction to the news jerked the seat belt tight across my chest and squeezed the breath from me. I stilled, closed my eyes, and felt shock leach through a constricted windpipe to clot in my gut. "Why?" My voice scratched across the sandpaper on my tongue and slithered over dry lips, as if I was expelling snakes instead of words. "Why didn't you tell me?"

"Don't you think I tried, you jackass? You're never easy to find, not even when you want to be accessible. And obviously, you didn't." Jazz kept her furious gaze averted. "I spent a year looking for you. From when I found out I was pregnant until Cyrus was three or four months old."

My throat tightened further. If it shrank any more, I'd asphyxiate. "You named him Cyrus?" More snakes, wiggling in the air between us. I'd been utterly trashed back when I confessed to Jazz the bizarre middle name my unknown parents chose to inflict on me. Not that the rest of my name was much better. But since they were dead, I'd never been able to unravel that particular mystery. There had only been a birth certificate, and it wasn't talking.

"We call him Cy." Her expression softened for an instant and then returned to rage. "I couldn't take worrying about where the hell you were, what you were doing, whether you were even alive. A few times, I thought you must have figured it out and took off so you wouldn't have to deal with me. With us. Finally, I decided you'd have to be all or nothing. And since you weren't around, you became nothing."

"Terrific. So what does this kid—Cyrus, I mean—think about not having a father?"

"He isn't old enough to understand. And don't you dare get pissy with me because you pulled a disappearing act."

"I didn't disappear." I drew a deep breath and tried to calm my stuttering heart. It didn't help. "I mean, I wouldn't have, if I'd known. I'm sorry, Jazz. It's just . . . this is a lot to take."

"I know." Her scowl softened. "I'm sorry for that, but there wasn't a way to ease into it gradually."

"Yeah. I guess not." I stared through the window, watched the silhouettes of rolling hills and staggered trees rise and fall over the darkened landscape. Such a bleak picture—nothing out there for miles. I'd never considered having kids. As far as a serious relationship, Jazz was the closest I'd come, and only because the word *marriage* had actually crossed my mind a few times before I took off. Hell, once I even came close to stealing an engagement ring for her.

But I hadn't acted on the thought. In fact, I'd barely considered the future at all. The farthest ahead I ever looked was the next score. Even that didn't matter. I only kept stealing because I didn't know how to do anything else.

"I took an out-of-town gig when I bailed on you," I finally

said. "Thought it'd be best to lay low for a while. Figured you could take care of yourself."

Jazz made a thick sound, not quite clearing her throat. "Where'd you go, Mars?"

"No, Canada." At the time, it was the most desolate place I could think of that was still habitable, and I'd wanted to get as far from humanity as possible, before I screwed anyone else over.

"Is that where you found him?" Jazz indicated the still-slumbering djinn with a jerk of her head.

I laughed. "No. He found me. I've tried to steer clear of partners, ever since . . . the thing with Lark."

"The hookup out in Fremont? What'd you do to him?"

"You mean he didn't spread the word? Thought he'd have a contract out on me by now." I returned my attention to the window. This was one conversation I didn't want to have.

Jazz had other ideas. "What happened, Donatti?"

"Nothing." I clenched a fist. "Just me being me. I fucked up."

"Fine. Don't tell me."

I groaned. One of the few things I'd learned about women was when they said something was fine, they actually wanted to rip your entrails out and strangle you with them. "We hit a place up in Albany," I said. "Some Egyptian artifact—you know that stuff he collects. He was hot for this one. Practically drooling over it."

"I didn't know Lark went out on active gigs. Isn't he a techie?"

"Yeah. But he wanted to be there, and I thought I could handle it." I let out a shaking breath. "The place was wired to hell and back. Lark broke through everything in less than three, and we had a fifteen-minute window. I figured we'd make it in five, with two of us. So I brought him in."

"Jesus Christ."

I gave a weak laugh. "Seemed like a good idea at the time," I said. "It should've been a simple in-and-out. I'd canvassed the place myself, but I missed something in the sweep. One lousy sensor, hooked to a separate rinky-dink tertiary system. God-damned alarm sounded like a cheap doorbell. But it still triggered a downline. Everything sealed off before I could even remember where the entrance was."

Jazz shook her head. "You didn't have a backup?"

"Lark was the backup. At least, he would've been, if I'd left him outside." My stomach clenched at the memory of what had happened next, but my mouth went ahead and spilled. "I brought us out on the roof. Didn't know there was a little construction going on up there. And. . . well, Lark isn't exactly sure-footed. I was helping him cross some open beams, and I kind of dropped him. Two stories."

"My God," Jazz whispered. "You didn't . . ."

"No. He survived. I scaled down the back while the cops swarmed the front and dragged him into the van we were using. Drove him to the hospital. Told them we'd been out drinking, and he took a header down some stairs on his way to piss." I couldn't look at her anymore. "They told me his spine was damaged. That he might never walk again. I stuck around until he regained consciousness, and he gave me one chance to live. He said if he ever saw me again, he'd kill me. So I left."

No, I countered silently. *I didn't just leave. I ran.* From Lark, from the life and the guilt. From her and from myself. But I still hadn't managed to get rid of me.

"When did this happen?" Jazz asked after a moment's silence.

"Two days before I planned to hook up with you."

She didn't react to the admission, but I suspected she'd formed her own opinion of my actions. Coward, she probably thought, or worse. The truth was that I hadn't wanted anything to happen to her because of me. I didn't want to ruin her life—or anyone else's—the way I had ruined Lark's.

Apparently, I'd done it anyway. I left her alone to raise a child I'd fathered.

While my brain tried to work out a coherent explanation, bright flickering light at the corner of my eye commanded attention. A glance in the side-view mirror confirmed what I feared. Cops.

"Oh, shit."

"What . . ." Jazz began. A siren interrupted. "Damn it." She eased down on the brakes and guided the van toward the roomy, deserted roadside. "Think that guy at the motel called them?"

"Maybe. If he could manage to find a phone." I leaned over and twisted to face the back. "Ian, wake up. We have a problem. Maybe two or three problems."

No response.

"Ian!" I shouted this time. "We could really use your help, like *now*."

Silence.

Jazz gave me a curious look. "How could he help? If anything, he'll only make them more suspicious. Especially if they see he's been shot."

"He . . . uh, you're right. He can't help." *Or won't*. Didn't this qualify as a need? If nothing else, I *desired* to stay out of jail. This master gig was highly overrated. I felt less like Cinderella and more like used drywall. Perpetually screwed.

Cops could smell panic. I forced myself to relax. Probably

just a routine stop, some small-town fuzz trying to fill a quota. I'd offer to pay the ticket later.

Jazz glanced at me. "This is going on your bill."

"Right." I shook my head and fought a smile.

Blue-white light flooded the driver's-side window. A cop's flashlight. Jazz turned her head, and I squinted against the glare. The beam remained steady for long seconds. The cop moved off. Footsteps circled the back of the van. The figure reappeared at my window and repeated the holding pattern with the light. At last, the cop switched it off and tapped on the glass—my first clue something about this situation didn't wash. I wasn't the one with the license and registration.

Grimacing, Jazz lowered my window with the controls on her side.

The backwash from the headlights revealed the cop's movements clearly. He stepped back, still gripping the heavy flashlight in one hand, and with the other drew his piece.

"Step out of the vehicle. Both of you. On this side."

I stared at the gun and reached for my seatbelt. This made four. Not that I was counting.

THE COP DIRECTED US TO STAND AGAINST THE VAN, FACING HIM. "If either of you have any weapons, toss 'em now." He gestured with the flashlight to the weed-choked ditch beyond, keeping the gun trained on us. Mostly on me.

My stomach clenched. This wasn't routine. "What the hell's going on?"

"Conner, you dirty son of a bitch." Jazz pulled her Glock and threw it hard, narrowly missing the man in uniform. "This wasn't part of the deal."

"Deal?" I barely managed to get the word out. The world

tilted viciously, like a carnival amusement ride at double speed, and my legs threatened to fail at holding up the rest of me. Once again, reality refused to make sense. "You made a deal with the cops?"

"Not the sharpest pencil, are you, Donatti?" Conner sneered. "Your little friend is dealing with Trevor. I'm just here to make sure she follows through."

The carnival ride screeched to a stop. Anger and pain focused my thoughts. I should have seen this coming—though it still hurt, more than the ass-kicking I'd expected from her in the first place would have. Jazz was a thief, just like me. Wouldn't I have done the same?

No, I decided. I wouldn't have. Not to her. Even before I knew about the kid.

"Gavyn . . ."

She gutted me with a word. She'd never called me Gavyn before. Too late to start now. Ignoring her, I eased away and assessed the situation. Jazz obviously wasn't going to be any help. If I could throw this Conner guy's guard off, I might be able to take him down. But what about Ian? The djinn must have truly passed out . . . if he was still alive. Even he wouldn't be callous enough to ignore this disaster.

The distance between Jazz and me grew by subtle degrees. I'd gained almost two feet when Conner swung the flashlight and belted me across the face, knocking me to the ground. I snarled and cupped a hand against the blood streaming from the corner of my mouth. Fuck, that hurt. Tasted awful, too. Like sucking salt from a hot nail.

"Don't even think it, Donatti. Next time, it'll be a bullet. Get up and empty your pockets."

Coughing out a mouthful of wet warmth, I struggled to my

feet and sent a glare at Jazz. She looked away fast. I faced the cop—or whatever he was—and spoke slowly in deference to my throbbing jaw. "I'm not armed. Trevor's brute squad took care of that earlier tonight."

Conner's gun stayed steady on me. "Jazz. Take his jacket off and hand it to me."

"Don't touch me." I spat blood on the ground at her feet. The gesture lost some of its effect in the dark, but she'd get the point. I shrugged free of the jacket, yanked my arms out, and tossed it in Conner's general direction. "Happy now?"

The cop kicked the jacket into the weeds. "Turn out your pockets."

I complied in silence. Nothing in the right. The left held a small folded wad of hundreds. With a one-sided smirk, I held it toward Conner and said, "Here you go. Buy yourself some balls with it."

Conner grinned a nasty promise. He spun the flashlight, stepped forward, and rammed the butt end into my crotch.

Every muscle in my body liquefied. The cash fell from limp fingers and hit the ground some time after me, as far as I could tell through the dazzle curtain bursting over my vision. Somewhere outside the high-pitched whine filling my ears, Jazz shouted. I didn't care. Wished her dead. Wished myself dead, if it would stop the agony flooding my groin. Gradually, the pain eased enough to let the world emerge through the fog.

"Thanks. But why bother buying some, when I can just take yours away?" A shoe prodded my shoulder. "On your feet. We're going for a ride."

It took longer to get up this time. I leaned back against the van, panting, and watched Conner slam the flashlight into a belt holster, then detach a set of standard-issue handcuffs and hand them to Jazz.

She snatched them. "Bastard. You didn't have to do that."

"No, I didn't. But it was fun." Conner fished in a pocket and produced a single key. "Put them on. Your right, his left."

Jazz fumbled with the cuffs and after a minute managed to bind us together. I didn't resist. I'd have to try to escape from Trevor before the bastard killed me—which put my odds of survival somewhere around the chances that a bolt of lightning from the now cloudless, star-strewn sky above would strike Conner dead in the next five minutes.

Conner extended the hand without the gun. Jazz thrust the key into it. The cop pulled another set of cuffs from a pocket, this one with a longer chain. "Turn around and face the van."

With a sorrowful glance, Jazz started around me to achieve the directed position. I failed to return her pity. "You wanna stick another knife in while you're back there?" I said.

She kept going without a word. The minute my back was turned, Conner's gun dug into my spine. "Your left."

I extended my free hand. The bracelet snapped around my wrist. Conner tightened it one-handed, pulled my arm toward Jazz, and fastened the other cuff to her right wrist.

The cop ordered us to face him. He moved toward the van's side door. "Let's see what you've got in here." Popping the handle, he slid the door open, retrieved the flashlight, and shone the beam inside. "Well, look at that. Tall guy in a trench coat. Heard a little something about him." Conner turned a sickly grin in my direction. "Doesn't look dangerous to me. Looks dead. Let's just make sure of that, shall we?"

My eyes closed against helpless fury. Two shots sounded

in solemn progression. I managed to keep my legs under me. If Ian wasn't dead before, he sure as hell was now.

"That should do it." Conner replaced his gun. "But just in case, why don't you get in there and find out?" He prodded my shoulder with the flashlight.

"Are you as stupid as you look? How am I supposed to do that?" I rattled one of the chains for emphasis.

"Figure it out."

You asshole. Whatever Trevor had told him, it was apparently enough to make him worry. I sat on the edge of the van floor, swung my legs inside, and glanced at Jazz. She hadn't moved. "A little cooperation would be nice here," I said through my teeth.

She sat next to me without a word.

I inched between the seats, dragging Jazz with me, far enough to catch sight of Ian's still form. Under the van's dome light, his skin looked gray. One of Conner's bullets had gone through his foot. The other was a straight hit to the heart—at least, the place a human's heart would be.

His chest didn't move at all. I leaned over his face, checking for a faint breath. For an instant, I thought air moved across my cheek . . . but it was cold. Lifeless. Probably a draft from outside.

"Is he . . ." Jazz whispered.

I glared at her and decided not to dignify that with a reply. "Move out."

She scuttled sideways and must have caught a foot on a seat leg. She jerked suddenly. The movement pushed me against Ian.

Light infused his body the instant I made contact with him, a faint and ghostly aura. It faded quickly. I blinked and would've rubbed my eyes if I could use my hands, positive I'd hallucinated that. I hadn't seen him glow before.

We made it back outside. "He's dead, you fuck. Satisfied?"

"Supremely. Don't worry too much, Donatti. I'm betting you're about to join him." Conner slammed the van door and grabbed Jazz by the arm to steer us toward his idling cruiser.

Even if I was in a gambling mood, I wouldn't have taken that bet. I suspected Conner was right.

CHAPTER 7

Silence smothered the back of the squad car. Conner, separated from us by a thick layer of reinforced glass with a small sound grate low and center, pulled off 34 and headed east, toward Owasco Lake. Toward Trevor.

The aching sorrow residing in the vicinity of my chest surprised me. I'd hated Ian—or at least thought I did. Still, to borrow a phrase from Benedict Arnold there, at the moment I hated Jazz more. He hadn't deserved to die for her treachery. Would his wife ever know what happened to him? I couldn't tell her. Didn't know where to find a magic mirror. Maybe there were other djinn somewhere in this world—but would they be able to find Ian? I had no idea how they operated. It wouldn't surprise me if they all hated each other.

I turned my attention to what I could recall of Trevor's place, hoping to remember something that might help me escape once I was inside. There was the fortress of a gate surrounding the house and the grounds on three sides and the lake on the fourth. Guards manned checkpoints at the gate 24-7. Dogs—well—dogged the stretches between the checkpoints.

The house itself, a three-story Victorian, featured barred windows, electronic locks, and a remote-monitored alarm system that kept items in and people out. Of course, it also kept people in, if Trevor didn't want them to leave.

I grimaced and considered trying to swim the lake. If I didn't drown, Trevor's thugs would have plenty of time to boat across and either pick me up on the way or secure the opposite shore before I got there.

Option three: offer to become Trevor's servant for life. And die anyway.

"Donatti."

Jazz's whisper pierced my thoughts. I refused to look at her. "I don't feel like talking anymore," I said through clenched teeth.

"There's something you should know." She continued to whisper, as if Conner couldn't hear her. The wire leading from the sound vent probably connected to a microphone somewhere up front.

"Whatever it is, I don't care."

"Tough shit. I'm telling you anyway."

I faced her slowly. Her expression, grim but determined, bore no trace of the sadness she'd exhibited earlier. "If you're having an attack of conscience, it's too late," I told her.

"Fuck you."

"No, thanks. Tried that already, and look where it got me."

"You . . ." Jazz closed her eyes, opened them. "Look, it's real simple. I love my son, and I would do anything to keep him safe. *Anything*. Understand?"

I flinched. "You mean, Trevor has . . ."

"Yes. He does."

I forced my mouth shut against a flood of profanity. Could the sick bastard sink any lower? "He was at your place when I called. Wasn't he?"

She shook her head. "I was at his."

Conner banged a fist on the partition. "All right, that's enough. It's lovely that you two kissed and made up, but now it's time to shut your fucking mouths. Or I'll shoot her. Trevor only wants you alive, Donatti. Think about that."

I pressed my lips together and winced when fresh pain shot through the split corner. *That was stupid.* Resolved to keep better track of my injuries—without doubt, there would be more to come—I looked at Jazz. Her sorrow had returned. Her eyes shone with it, threatening to spill over.

I'd never seen her cry. Didn't want to now. If she broke down, I might follow her lead.

Momentarily forgetting the handcuffs, I moved to touch her face and succeeded only in scoring my wrist when the chain jerked taut. I swallowed a curse, lowered my hand. She released a slow, controlled breath and faced forward.

I eased over and slipped my fingers between hers, trying to convey with gestures what couldn't be said. Not that I enjoyed being turned over to Trevor, but I understood why she had to. She faced me, her mouth forming an O before settling into a small smile.

I held her gaze for a moment and looked away to refocus my rage. Trevor had her son. *Our* son. I'd make sure the bastard didn't hurt him, even if I had to die for it.

Unfortunately, I had a feeling that was exactly what I'd end up doing.

———

FIVE, SIX, SEVEN, EIGHT. DEFINITELY A NEW RECORD. AND THE night was still young.

Not all the thugs on Trevor's porch had guns. One carried an aluminum baseball bat. Another held a Taser. The seventh and last had enough mass and muscle to qualify for his own zip code. No external equipment required.

Conner removed the cuffs, then drew out his pistol and offered it handle-first to the nearest goon. Criminal protocol demanded that we all be subjected to a pat-down. The guy with the bat collected Conner, and Taser Boy claimed Jazz with a grin that said she wouldn't escape this with her dignity intact. Since the firepower had to stay in place, that left me to the land mass.

Lucky me.

Several minutes later, shoeless and with a few extra bruises to catalogue, I joined Jazz to be marched inside and led to a spacious and richly furnished den complete with indoor columns and a full-sized dry bar—Trevor's sitting room. There, we found Trevor, sitting.

With a prison-style buzz cut, hard features, and dark eyes that held the promise of fucking you over, he should've resembled a gorilla stuffed in a suit. But Trevor wore his Italian silks and English wools like a birthright. He'd blend right in at a country club or a yacht party, until he started shooting the other suits for looking at him funny.

And the bastard wasn't alone. A small boy with a riot of silky black curls perched on his lap, half-dozing, a tiny thumb thrust into his mouth.

"Cy!" Jazz lunged forward, only to be stopped by an arm as thick as a roof beam and just as solid. "God damn you, Trevor. You were supposed to bring him home."

The boy perked up. His eyes widened, and his thumb left

his mouth with an audible *pop*. "Mommy?" Cy wiggled and slid down to the floor. Trevor made no move to stop him. "Mommy, I wet." He toddled toward the forest of thugs, eyelids drooping as he walked.

Trevor gestured. The land mass moved aside, and I saw the silencer-fitted Ruger .45 the seated man had been holding on the boy.

"Was he that dangerous, Trevor?" Somehow, I managed to speak evenly.

"Insurance, Mr. Donatti. You understand, of course."

"Oh, God. Cy . . ." Jazz fell to her knees as the boy neared and swept him against her. She buried her face in his curls, rubbed his back. After a moment, she directed a look of absolute rage at Trevor. "He'd better not have so much as a hangnail, you sick asshole."

"Not to worry, dear lady. The boy's been an angel." Trevor rose and passed a hand over his shaved head, then brushed at a damp spot on his tailored slacks. "He is, however, wet."

Jazz scooped Cyrus into her arms and stood. The boy snuggled against her with a contented sigh, and his thumb migrated back to his mouth. "Is there some reason you sent your puppet after me? I told you I'd bring him in."

Trevor moved two paces forward, the gun held casually at his side. "I don't believe in trust. I believe in control." Frigid green eyes settled on me for a moment and then languidly scanned the rest of the group. "Conner. Come here, please."

The cop approached Trevor, his expression neutral. "What's up?"

"Where is our friend in the trench coat?"

"Still in her van. He's dead."

Trevor stared at him. "You must be mistaken."

"Uh . . ." A flicker of unease penetrated Conner's features. "No, he's gone. I shot him a few times, just to make sure."

"Did I tell you to shoot him?"

Those flat words were Conner's death sentence. I knew it. Conner did, too.

"Wait." Conner stumbled back. "Trevor, I—"

Trevor's arm jackknifed up to press the gun against Conner's forehead. He fired without hesitation. The silencer allowed a whining snap, no louder than a breaking branch. Trevor didn't even blink when the cop's blood spattered his face and his pristine linen shirt. The body dropped to the floor. Trevor released a short sigh and shook his head.

"Leonard. Dispose of that, and tell Mari to bring me a new shirt and clean the carpet." Trevor lowered his arm, stowed the gun in a back pocket, and started on the buttons. "His car has to go. John, bring it to the docks . . . wait, take this and burn it somewhere first." The last button released, he stripped the shirt off and held it out. Bat Man ambled forward to take it.

I blinked more than a few times at the intricate mass of snakes tattooed on Trevor's chest, stomach, and upper arms. The work was unusual—done in shades of black and brown, it didn't look so much inked as burned into his skin. In addition, a pendant on a thick silver chain hung around his neck. The medallion was etched with symbols that once again seemed strangely familiar. The thing looked a few thousand years old, like a coin from a forgotten Chinese dynasty. But it gleamed as if it had just been minted yesterday.

With the shock of the emotionless execution wearing off, I tore my gaze from the strange markings and looked at Jazz. Her eyes hadn't left Trevor. Cold fury radiated from her and promised retaliation, while her arms formed a shield around

Cyrus. The muffled shot hadn't freaked the kid out too bad, but he whimpered and squirmed against Jazz.

The land mass, otherwise known as Leonard, crossed to the body and produced a folded plastic trash bag. The fact that he apparently carried them around just in case chilled me to the core. If I didn't pull a miracle out of my ass soon, I'd end up right where this sorry sack was headed—in a thirty-gallon plastic coffin at the bottom of the lake. Leonard opened the bag and drew it over the corpse's head. He tied the bag closed at the waist, lifted the body as if it weighed no more than a bag of leaves, and tossed the eternally surprised Conner over a shoulder.

Trevor watched the giant leave the room. He'd made no attempt to remove Conner's blood from his skin. The spray had darkened to a tacky maroon, creating an almost tribal pattern across one side of his face, up his skull, and down his neck. Even his ear bore the gruesome freckling. He bestowed a benevolent smile on Jazz. "Don't be troubled, now. You've met my expectations, and you're free to go." He addressed two of the gun-toting thugs. "Pope, Harmon, bring the lady and her child back to her vehicle. If there is a body, collect it. If not, call for reinforcements."

My skin crawled. Why would Trevor think there wouldn't be a body? An instant later, I realized Skids must have reported exactly what happened at the garage, and if Trevor even half believed it, the vigilant son of a bitch was just covering his ass.

With a defiant glance at Trevor, Jazz approached and stopped in front of me. The boy in her arms stirred, blinked sleepily . . . and a lump lodged in my throat when my own blue eyes looked back at me from the small face that bore a striking resemblance to Jazz's.

In that instant, I would have died a hundred times for both of them.

Jazz attempted to smile. It didn't work. "Try to stay alive, Houdini."

"Ga," the boy pronounced.

"I think he likes me." I summoned a grin, though I imagined it looked as if I'd just dropped something heavy on my toe. "Maybe I'll see you around."

"Let's not give the lady false hope," Trevor cut in. "As I believed my former associate mentioned to you earlier this evening, Mr. Donatti, that isn't likely to happen. Pope, if you would."

One of the goons grabbed Jazz by the shoulder and steered her away. I watched them escort her out in silence, too furious to release the useless barrage of insults and threats building inside. At last, I faced Trevor with fists and jaw clenched and waited.

Trevor smiled, this time without benevolence. "Take Mr. Donatti downstairs, and let him hang around for a while. I have a few matters to attend to before we begin. Mr. Donatti, I suggest that you consider very carefully what you're going to tell me, and make sure I like your answers to my questions. I have many of them."

Two of the remaining thugs flanked me. The one with the Taser moved in front. While the others held me, the third thumbed a trigger on the pronged device and produced an ominous buzzing crackle. The insouciant grin he'd flashed Jazz outside resurfaced. He thrust the posts under my ribcage and held.

Tasering didn't feel like sticking a finger in a light socket. It felt like swallowing a box of sewing needles, then being thrown into a giant blender to get them moving around.

Five long seconds into the shock treatment, I sagged in the thugs' grip. Taser Boy gave me another quick jolt for good measure and finally left me to droop. They dragged me across the room opposite the direction everyone else had left, toward a tall black door.

I could hardly wait to see what was on the other side.

CHAPTER 8

Split lip, bruised balls, fried ribs, and now, shredded wrists. My running tally of injuries insisted on playing itself out in my head like a demented game show. *And what do we have next for our fine contestant? Why, it's a drawn-out and brutal death, accompanied by a fabulous voyage to the bottom of the lake!*

"And the crowd goes wild," I muttered. Hysterical laughter bubbled just beneath the surface. I couldn't let it out, or I'd never stop.

Downstairs was a basement, where the thugs had strung me from the rafters like so much meat. Dim lighting revealed enough to confirm that this room had only one purpose: to inflict pain. I scoped the scenery, automatically looking for possible escape routes. My initial analysis proved less than encouraging.

I had to give it to Trevor. The place had atmosphere. I'd done a brief stint in a Cuban jail, and though those quarters had been less than modern, they'd been a four-star motel compared to this. The stone walls glistened with just enough moisture to dampen the already stifling air, and the slab floor that chilled my feet through my socks showed layers of blotched stains, the ghosts of fluids that couldn't have been water.

I knew he was into torture, but I never imagined he'd elevated it to an art form.

The light came from a dense cluster of flickering candles at various stages of melted, arranged on a small curtained table. Wax buildup, the thick and blackened kind that could only have come from years of burning candles in the same spot, clumped along the edges and descended in stippled waves down the fabric draping the sides. It reminded me of the bless-me-Father-for-I-am-fucked displays common to low-income ethnic neighborhood churches. I'd seen plenty of them growing up. Nobody's Aunt Maria ever recovered from cancer because of them. Nobody won the lottery. And nobody's parents miraculously returned from the grave, either. I knew—I'd spent every Sunday afternoon for two years confessing sins, regurgitating Hail Marys, and lighting those damned candles. They were false advertising.

Back to the inventory. What basement torture chamber would be complete without the requisite instruments? Despite the high-tech gadgetry controlling the fortress upstairs, Trevor remained downright medieval in his choices of pain-causing devices. A pegboard displayed a collection of pliers, good for the wholesale yanking of nails and teeth. Ball-peen hammers ranging in size from miniature to skull-crushing marched down the right side of the board.

Restraints seemed a common theme, too. There were chains, cuffs, collars, and lengths of rope, like the one keeping me suspended in place and rubbing my wrists raw. A bundle of smooth rods stood in a far corner. From here I couldn't tell what material they were made with, but it looked as if they'd hurt. An enormous gilt-framed mirror hung on the wall to the right of the stairs. He probably liked to have his victims watch themselves being tortured.

Best of all was the long table encompassed by a sectioned wooden frame, complete with an oversized gear and a crank handle. A good old-fashioned rack.

I couldn't wait for Trevor to come down. What fun we'd have.

A whispered rustle of sound crept from a shadowed alcove to my right, at the opposite end of the room from the stairs leading up. I squinted in that direction, but the candlelight refused to penetrate the blackness there. The sound didn't repeat. Maybe I'd been hearing things. Might have been a rat or some other basement-dwelling creature.

Another sound commanded my attention. Measured footfalls on the stairs. Oh, good. Time for pain.

I tried to hold the guttering hope that the alcove, with its mysterious noises, contained a way out. A crumbling wall, a secret passage, a sewer grate. I wasn't picky. Since I didn't intend to tell Trevor anything just yet, he wouldn't kill me right away. Maybe the rope would loosen or weaken while he beat on me. It could happen.

So could Armageddon. At least that would take Trevor, too.

Trevor entered the room alone. A point in my favor—no thugs to witness my forthcoming screams. He'd cleaned himself up but hadn't bothered to button his fresh shirt. He still wore the pendant. The snake tattoos seemed alive in the flickering candlelight, writhing hungrily over his torso, devouring him. His eyes shone with carefully contained insanity. And he'd brought the Taser.

I was so dead.

He stopped in front of me. "Mr. Donatti."

"Present."

Trevor jammed the Taser against my thigh and pulled the trigger.

I went limp. Fortunately, the rope held me up. He kept the jolt short, and when he pulled back, I gasped. "Jesus Christ. Aren't you supposed to ask me a question first?"

Trevor shook his head as if he was disappointed. This time, the damned thing juiced the side of my neck.

The charge exploded in my head, blinding me. My mouth opened. No sound emerged. I figured smoke would start billowing out, but saliva foamed over my lip and dribbled down my chin instead.

This was Trevor's subtle way of telling me to shut up. It worked. Couldn't speak if I wanted to.

"If you had my item, Mr. Donatti, you would have given it to me by now." His voice wavered and splintered against my pounding eardrums. "Eventually, you will explain what happened. I'm not ready to question you yet. At this point, your job is to listen."

"Listenin'," I slurred, slopping more drool onto the floor.

Trevor zapped me again. I screamed.

"You believe if you don't cooperate, I'll kill you. I won't. You believe if I leave you alone long enough, you'll find a way out. You can't. You believe torture is the worst that can happen to you, and death is preferable." He moved in and brought his face inches from mine. "It isn't."

I believed that.

Had to pull myself together. I drew several deep breaths and tried to calm my jittering muscles, aware that short Taser bursts didn't cause death. Only temporary paralysis and incredible pain. My legs responded slowly, and I managed to hold a little weight with them. I lifted my head. "You're not . . . giving me a lot of . . . incentive."

Trevor grinned. There were icebergs in his smile. "I don't have to, Mr. Donatti. You see, I don't need your cooperation."

"What?" My voice cracked. If he didn't need me, why hadn't he just shot me?

He acted as if he hadn't heard me. "Regarding other things I don't need, your lovely friend Jasmine is a liability. The boy, too."

"Don't you touch him," I snarled—seconds before my brain worked out that I'd chosen the wrong pronoun. *Oh, Jesus, no . . .*

"Him?" Trevor stared at me. The icebergs flashed. "Why, Mr. Donatti. What blue eyes you have."

HE LET ME HEAR HIS PHONE CONVERSATION WITH THE THUGS.

"Have you gotten to her van yet? All right. When you do, let her and the boy go, and follow her. Don't alarm the lady. Remember, I want that body. If it's not there, I'll send others to look for it. I have a different job for you." Trevor paused and sent a smile in my direction. "Wherever she ends up, I want a silent hit. Kill her, finish anyone else you find, and bring the boy back to me."

I couldn't breathe.

Trevor disconnected and pocketed his phone. "Well, Mr. Donatti, it seems we're going to have company."

"Why?" I finally managed. "You have me. Why hurt them?"

He grinned. It was an awful expression, full of bitterness. "Because I need that item you lost. You have no idea how much. But mostly, because I can. And I did warn you that being tortured wasn't the worst thing that could happen."

"I'll kill you, Trevor. Believe that."

He looked at me as if he was actually considering the possibility. "I believe you're convinced that you will. You can't, of course. But you do possess more fortitude than I gave you credit for, and that is saying something." He crossed to the pegboard, scanned it. After a moment, he reached out and selected the smallest pair of needle-nose pliers, just three or four inches from tip to end. "If you'll excuse me, I must prepare for our guest. Don't worry, Mr. Donatti . . . I'll let you see him first. I'll let you see everything."

My mind emptied. I couldn't threaten him, couldn't insult him. Couldn't even move, despite my body's desperate desire to lunge, snap the rope, gouge the sick bastard's eyes out.

"You're speechless?" Trevor approached me, Taser back in hand. "And I thought you'd never shut up." He stopped and thumbed the trigger a few times. Sparks snapped from the prongs in the semidark, bright as fireflies. "Where would you like it this time?"

He couldn't bring me any lower, so I spat in his face. "Up your ass."

"Oh, that's far too much trouble."

I had time to think that at least I'd wiped the smug smile from his face before he jammed the Taser into my stomach and held.

For a long, long time.

Seconds, maybe minutes. I couldn't tell. Everything shut down—sight, sound, smell—everything but sensation. I could still feel. And what I felt was pure pain in every cell of my body. Was I breathing? I'd forgotten how to bring air into my lungs.

Forgotten how to think. Mr. Donatti isn't in right now. Please try your call again later.

At last, I realized there was no new pain being generated. The source had been removed. It took my scrambled brain a few tries to recall the source. Trevor. In the basement. With a Taser.

Trevor. Ordered a hit on Jazz. Going to torture and murder my son in front of me.

I'll kill you. I will. Kill you. Believe my ass.

Something burned in my chest. My lungs. I needed oxygen. Lots, fast. Still blind and deaf, I heaved in air and gasped it out. Did it again. And again. Finally, my body took over the task, and I concentrated on regaining the rest of me.

The vacuum of sight and sound became a humming white blur. The blur faded gradually and returned me to a muffled version of reality that didn't include Trevor. Only me and the basement. I still hung in place, head down, legs bowed and limp beneath me. A few spots of fresh dark liquid adorned the floor. Blood? Tasers didn't cut.

Another drop burst into existence below. The consuming anguish eased, allowing me to feel more specific pain. My lip had resplit during the prolonged shock. Hence the blood. My shoulders screamed, and my wrists were on fire. Though I couldn't lift my head, I knew blood streaked my arms, too. And despite the damage, I would live.

Not something I looked forward to.

A soft sound penetrated my muted hearing. For an instant, I thought it came from the alcove. It sounded again, a muffled scrape reminiscent of sandpaper on wood. The stairs. Another scrape, a light clicking, like the claws of an animal. Rats came to mind again. Weren't they drawn by the scent of blood?

Raising my head took tremendous effort. I tried to focus on the stairs. Didn't see anything. Squeezed my eyes shut, opened them. Some of the blurriness dissipated. At last I caught a glimpse of rippling fur. The shape poured from the landing, refusing to pull itself together. I strained until my eyes watered and realized it was bigger than a rat. Much bigger. Maybe Trevor had sent one of his dogs down to guard me.

The creature stood absolutely still, facing me. A long, low growl rumbled in its throat. It slunk toward me, hackles rising. When it reached the strongest pool of candlelight, I made out features that shocked me harder than the Taser.

Not a dog. A wolf. A really big fucking wolf.

No wolf had ever been that big. The thing was the size of a small pony. It stopped and stared at me. Round amber eyes ringed with black. Filled with an almost human awareness . . . and recognition.

"Ian?"

CHAPTER 9

The wolf nodded.

I stared at it. Wolves didn't nod. This was a little harder to swallow than the car thing. I didn't doubt that it was a wolf. I'd seen its teeth. All hundred or so of them. Only my sanity was in question here.

The suspicion that I'd lost my mind shifted into certainty when the wolf started to glow.

Within seconds, the animal became pure light in the shape of a wolf. The limbs thickened, the body stretched, the snout shortened. The light formed a man on hands and knees and faded to reveal Ian.

The djinn stood quickly and held a finger to his lips.

I laughed. "It doesn't matter," I told him, though a rasping whisper was the best I could manage. "He's gotta have cameras down here somewhere."

"Be silent, thief. It is not Trevor I am concerned about."

"Well, I am," I muttered, wondering briefly how he knew Trevor's name. He must have heard me say it at some point. I turned my confusion to how in the hell he'd gotten here, uninjured, because there wasn't a mark on him. Even his bullet-torn pants were whole again. The fact that he'd somehow retained his clothing baffled me. Shouldn't he be naked?

"Trevor is busy. And if you speak again before we get out of here, I will gag you. You will get us both killed."

He sounded serious. I decided to take his advice and shut up.

Ian approached me and laid his hands over my wrists. I felt the ropes loosen, the knots seem to untie themselves. *Bad idea,* I thought frantically. *I'm gonna . . .*

The ropes released. I dropped to the floor.

Fall.

Concrete wasn't the softest landing pad. I groaned and curled inward, convinced that I'd broken something.

"What is wrong with you?" Ian whispered. "Get up. You do not look that badly injured."

"Tasers don't leave marks." I panted. "Why can *you* talk?"

"Not another word. If you—" He froze. A scuffling noise whispered from the dark alcove, stronger than the first one I'd heard. Something scraped, metal on stone. Someone coughed—not him and not me.

"Gahiji-an?"

The voice sounded like rocks in a tumbler, filtered through cotton. Horror painted Ian's features. He produced his Zippo, fired it up, and stretched the lighter toward the recess. The flame shook at the end of his arm. He approached slowly, stopping when the light revealed enough of the figure in the darkness to make everything inside me twist the wrong way.

A man. No, a breathing corpse. Suspended, practically crucified on a wooden frame. Chains around his ankles, his neck, his arms just above the elbows and at the wrists. Hairless, toothless, naked save for a filthy and bloodstained cloth tied around his waist. Scars and fresh cuts, scores of them, covered his body—all two to four inches long, in apparently random directions. And empty, blackened sockets where his eyes should have been.

Trevor was more than insane. He was a monster passing himself off as human.

"Shamil . . ." Ian's voice broke. He stepped forward.

"No," Shamil whispered. "It is sealed."

Ian stopped and glanced back at me. I forced myself to move, get on my feet. With a better view of the horror show in the alcove, realization struck me dumb. The battered figure was tall and long-limbed, like Ian. Dark brown armband tattoos, similar to Ian's, were still visible between the wounds. His eyes had probably been ringed with black before they'd been burned out.

Another djinn. In Trevor's basement.

Shamil lifted a face streaked with grime and dried blood. The skin around his eye sockets twitched, as if he was trying desperately to see. "Free me. Please."

Ian flinched as though he'd been shot. "Your tether?" he said in thick tones.

"The pendant."

Nodding once, Ian closed his eyes, opened them. "It will be done, brother."

"Thank you." Shamil released a shuddering sigh and let his head fall.

Ian turned away and snapped the lighter closed. A thousand questions begged for release from my tongue. I denied them a voice out of respect for the stricken djinn, and hoped Ian hadn't used the term *brother* literally.

"Head for the stairs," Ian said. I started toward them and

stopped when a distant click drifted across the room that sounded far too much like a door opening.

Descending footsteps. Trevor.

"I will need the wolf," Ian whispered. "Climb onto my back. Hold tight, do not move, and do not make a sound. He will not see you."

Protests screamed through my mind. A glimmer of light behind me. A furry head butted the small of my back. My body moved despite my brain's insistence that riding a wolf as if the damned thing was a horse with fangs constituted a Very Bad Idea—almost as bad as convincing myself that Trevor would somehow fail to notice that the guy he'd left strung up from the ceiling had escaped to mount a giant fucking wolf and amble off into the sunset. Well, sunrise by now, or close to it. I straddled the squat, muscular body and felt compelled to flatten myself along his back and clutch the scruff of his neck with both hands.

Snug as a bug in a Venus flytrap.

The moment my grip was secure, the Ian-wolf moved along the perimeter of the room, approaching the stairs. Trevor reached the basement when we still had several feet to go. The wolf froze and tensed beneath me. Panic dried my mouth and pushed needles through my chest. How in the hell could he not see us?

Trevor moved across the room, away from us, toward the empty rope lying on the floor. He nudged it with a foot. His lack of a violent reaction to my absence sent spikes of fear to join my panic. Gavyn Donatti, the amazing human pincushion. Trevor turned in a slow circle, scanning the room. His gaze skated past us without pause. "You are still here, aren't you?" he said softly. His voice seemed suddenly un-Trevor-like. "I feel you . . . Gahiji-an."

Tremors rippled the wolf's body. It was all I could do to keep my teeth from chattering. Slowly, he crept toward the stairs. We progressed an inch, six inches, two feet. My lungs burned with the breath I held.

"I suppose you haven't told him." Trevor performed another languid rotation. "No matter. You and your bastard offspring won't survive much longer." He pulled a knife and moved toward the alcove, a frozen grin splitting his face. "Would you like to hear your friend scream, Gahiji-an? I don't know about you, but I find the sound pleasing."

The tremors became shudders, but the wolf still gained ground. I bit my tongue and tried not to dwell on what Trevor had said . . . especially the part about bastard offspring. Didn't like the sound of that. Not at all.

We reached the stairs and began the ascent before Trevor got to the chained djinn. Though we were spared witness, sounds followed us. Trevor muttering. Shamil flinging a curse, chasing it with hollow, crazed laughter that burrowed beneath my skin like undead ticks. The screams came just before we made the door.

And the wolf ran.

I MIGHT HAVE SCREAMED A LITTLE. MAYBE JUST A GRUNT. Couldn't help it. Ian walking had been difficult enough. Ian running felt like holding the wing of a plane in flight under heavy turbulence. I knew I'd fall off, and that would be the end of whatever mojo kept Trevor from seeing me.

The wolf growled low in his throat but didn't slow the relentless pace. We streaked through Trevor's house, bounding around corners and skirting loose carpets on smooth floors. The front door stood open. We shot through and cleared the porch steps in a single bone-jarring leap that forced me to tighten my grip. The wolf yelped once and tore around the corner of the house toward the lake.

Outside, I smelled smoke.

A glance behind us revealed the source. Just inside the gate stood a smoldering heap, shaped vaguely like a car. A few thugs with spent fire extinguishers milled around the wreckage. One had dragged a hose over and stood spraying down what was left. This must have been what Trevor was busy with. Fantastic. Now the bastard would blame me for blowing up his car, too.

After all, Ian was my djinn—sort of—and somehow, Trevor had known.

Wouldn't think about that now. Wanted to be breathing when we got out of here, and if any of his thugs saw me, they'd provide me with some rather inconvenient ventilation holes. I had to concentrate on maintaining my grip.

We'd covered half the distance between the house and the lake when I caught a dark shape streaking toward us from the direction of the gate. My heart rate ramped up from beat to vibrate. One of Trevor's dogs had caught our scent. Oh, good. Dogs trusted their senses and would believe what their olfactories told them even without visual confirmation.

If Trevor knew anything about the djinn, he probably counted on that.

The wolf slowed and changed direction, heading for a small shed to the right. The dog followed, already barking a strident alert. We rounded the shed, skidded to a halt out of sight of the main house, and the wolf bucked me off.

I hit the ground, rolled once. By the time I gained my feet, Ian stood in the wolf's place. Still clothed. I'd have to ask him how he did that, if we lived long enough.

He grabbed my wrist before I could spit anything out. "Silence." He snarled the word, as if he hadn't completely shaken the transformation yet.

I didn't argue. The fewer teeth marks I ended up with, the better.

Like its master, the dog didn't know the meaning of hesitation. A furry projectile launched at Ian and sank fangs into his shin. Ian reached down and stroked its head, crooning to the growling beast in the language he'd spoken with his wife, as though it was an overgrown puppy. The dog wrenched its massive jaws open, sat on its haunches, and looked up at the djinn with doggy joy. Its tongue lolled between teeth marbled with Ian's blood.

"Sleep," Ian whispered. Obediently, the dog lowered itself to the ground, laid its head on folded paws, and closed its eyes.

I was sufficiently impressed.

Ian still held my wrist, and something about him seemed strange. I squinted at him. The edges of his body shimmered, like a car on the road under a blazing sun. A glance at my hand revealed the same flickering outline. I guessed this was what invisible looked like from the inside. Would've thought it was pretty cool, if I wasn't worried about dying in the next five minutes.

"Okay," I whispered. "Now what?"

Shouts and running feet sounded in the distance as the thugs headed our way to investigate the dog's warning. Ian faced me, wearing the most disgusted expression he'd manufactured yet. "You will have to climb onto my back. Hold on. And for the love of the gods, do not strangle me, or I will drop you."

I goggled at him. "You planning to turn into a shark and

swim the lake? Because I don't think you can run faster than a bullet, especially carrying me around."

Ian turned away. He didn't have to say *Just do it*. I did.

For an instant, I felt like the world's oldest annoying little brother. Giddyap, horsie. Heat crept up my neck and singed my ears as I clung to his back, hands gripping his shoulders, legs locked around his waist. "Whatever you're gonna do, do it fucking fast," I mumbled near his ear.

Ian spat something in his language. Probably a curse. He tensed, bent his knees, and jumped.

And kept going up.

In seconds, the ground lay a good hundred feet beneath us and still dwindling. I wanted to go back down and retrieve my stomach—and stay there. I'd almost prefer torture to being airborne, and an open-air djinn was far more terrifying than an enclosed plane. My eyes squeezed shut, and my teeth chattered like ice in a blender. "You're f-flying," I stuttered.

"Yes. I cannot do it for long."

"Jazz!" I shouted. The wind snatched my words from me and whipped them away. I leaned in the direction of Ian's ear, without opening my eyes. "Have to get to Jazz. Trevor ordered a hit on her."

"Your lady friend seems capable of handling herself. We have bigger problems."

"We're going. Wyckoff Road, just outside Elmwood. Go!" The shouts tore from my throat, forcing me to gasp frigid air.

"Idiot. Do you really think I know where this Elmwood is? I am not a human. And we are not—"

"*We're going.* I won't let them kill her—and Trevor wants Cyrus!"

"Who in the name of the gods is Cyrus?"

"Her son. *My* son!"

Ian lurched in midair. And dropped.

I screamed.

When we failed to hit the ground and splatter across the landscape, I wrenched one eye open. Ian hovered fifty feet above a stand of trees, stiff as cement. "Your son?" He choked the words out, half disbelief, half something else. Hope?

"Yes. He's my son. Jesus Jefferson Christ." I gasped. "Don't ever fucking do that again."

"Which way?"

I looked down. Panic flooded my circuits. The ground swam, doubled, contracted. "Shit. Where the hell are we?"

"Never mind. I can find him. Hold on."

How? I wanted to shout, but I couldn't. We were moving again—fast. I'd have to trust him. I closed my eyes and prayed to the god of losing lottery tickets and dying Aunt Marias that we weren't too late.

And if it wasn't too much trouble, maybe he could throw in a barf bag.

CHAPTER 10

Dirt never made a man happier than I was when I slid off Ian's back and landed in it facedown. If I'd found a worm, I'd have kissed it.

"Let's not do that any more, 'kay?" Groaning, I pushed up with trembling arms and stood on equally shaky legs. The dirt beneath me was a clearing in the woods, sullen and gray in the predawn light. A rhythmic, gentle rushing rose and fell in the distance. Lake water. Nature's symphony hummed through the air. There wasn't a road or a house in sight. "This isn't Wyckoff. You said you could find them." Fear banished the last of my weakness. We could be miles from them, and getting anywhere from here would take too long.

"They are close. Come on." Ian pivoted and plunged into the thick of the woods.

I stumbled after him, painfully aware of my inadequate foot-wear. My shoes were long gone by now—Leonard the Land Mass had probably eaten them. "How?" I shouted, kicking at a tangle of vegetation that tried to claim my sock. "How could you possibly know where they are? I'm starting to think you're not really a djinn. You're just out of your goddamned mind."

Ian stopped. "You are the most pathetic thief I have ever met. Could you make any more noise?"

"Answer the question." I fought through more brush, wincing when a sharp branch stabbed my instep. "Tell me how you think you're going to find them."

"The same way I found you."

"And how did you find me?"

Ian bared his teeth. "I sensed you. And since the boy is your son, I can sense him. Now, be quiet, idiotic thief. There is a good chance Trevor's men are out here looking for them, too."

I hadn't thought of that. Why hadn't I thought of that? Taser'd definitely fried my brains. Maybe I could convince myself I'd hallucinated everything from the wolf on. It wasn't a bad alternative. I could still be tied in Trevor's basement, imagining this insanity.

But that would mean not saving Jazz and Cyrus. Besides, all these cruddy trees and branches felt real enough, especially when they whacked my shins or skewered my feet.

Ian moved on. I tried to keep quiet, but it wasn't easy. This wasn't my element. Give me a warehouse, a mansion, an office building, hell, even a cluttered basement, and I'd be as silent as a sleeping monk. Here, there was entirely too much nature. Nature had no structure, no detailed blueprints to study. Randomness threw me off.

As though the woods wanted to reinforce my unease, my foot—the one with the torn sock, of course—squelched through a pile of random nature. I gagged and damn near collapsed.

"What is wrong with you?" Ian whispered. "Evolution moves faster than this."

"Sorry," I shot back. "This turf isn't made for walking without shoes."

Ian muttered something and gestured. My feet tingled. Solid footwear materialized. "Now, move."

The shoes felt strange. "What happened to my socks?"

"Live without them."

"Fine." I wiggled my toes. "You didn't do anything to my feet, did you? I mean, you keep ending up with clothes on when you come back from being a wolf. Doesn't seem like it should work that way."

Ian made a sharp sound. "Fur covers the wolf. This covers me." He swiped at his coat. "Enough foolish questions! We've no time for this."

I decided he was probably right.

With less hesitation on my part, we made good time. Somehow, Ian managed to cover the ground in silence, while my progress made Godzilla seem light-footed. I must have snapped every twig in upstate New York. And after five minutes of blundering through endless trees, I couldn't have found my way back to civilization with a GPS and a forest ranger to guide me.

I hoped Ian could sense blacktop and gas stations.

The djinn stopped and motioned me into silence. Some distance ahead, leaves rustled, and branches crackled under human intrusion. Jazz or the thugs? Ian pointed to a thick spray of downed pine branches five feet to his right. The boughs arched out from two or three close-set trunks and appeared to create a natural cave. *Jazz?* I mouthed.

He nodded.

Damn. All that crashing up ahead had to be the thugs, and they weren't far. I could render a person unconscious if I caught him by surprise, but I knew there were at least two of them. If I brought one down, the other would shoot me before I could say

Just turn around and pretend I'm sneaking up on you. And hadn't Ian said he wasn't allowed to kill humans? Not that it stopped him from relieving them of a hand or two. He'd have to pitch in.

I moved toward the spray, trying for silence so I wouldn't startle her . . . if she was even in there. I still had my doubts. "Jazz," I whispered. "Are you—"

Pain splintered my left shin seconds before my ears registered the gunshot.

"Fuck." I pronounced the word solemnly and plopped on my ass in a carpet of browned pine needles. Eight people gunning for me tonight, and the good guy—well, girl—scores. At least, I hoped it had been Jazz firing. "Whatever I did now, I'm sorry."

Something rustled behind the boughs. "Donatti?" A breathless whisper.

"Yeah, that's me." My ability to speak was a surprise and a concern. The pain had all but vanished, and my lower leg was a block of concrete glued to my knee. I knew it would hurt again soon. A lot.

"Are they gone?" She didn't come out. She meant the thugs.

"Not exactly. But they're not right here."

At once, Ian stood over me, glowering. "Be silent."

"Jazz, don't shoot again. It's Ian," I whispered harshly. Looking up at the angry djinn, I threw his expression right back. "Yeah, I'm fine. Thanks for asking."

"You will live. Your woman has just announced exactly where we are. Get in there with her, and do not move." Light suffused his body, and the wolf returned. He darted off into the trees.

"What the hell just happened out there?" Jazz demanded in rough undertones.

"Hold on," I whispered back. "I'm coming in." Walking was

out of the question. I shifted until my back faced the branches and scooted through the wooden curtain, pushing with my arms and good leg.

Inside, Jazz knelt on the ground, a gun still trained toward the cover. "Holy hell," she whispered. "You really are Houdini. How did you get out of there?"

No nonsense, no apologies. That was Jazz. I had to smile, despite the first twinges of real pain announcing themselves in bursts of heat from my leg. "Long story. Where's Cyrus?"

She hesitated and then pointed. The boy sat at the base of the center tree, a thumb settled securely in his mouth, wide-eyed and pressed back against the trunk. "He's a trooper," she said. "What was that light?"

"Uh, it was Ian. See . . ."

At once, she swung the gun in my direction. "Don't think for a second I won't choose him over you. Get out, if you want your brains to stay inside your skull."

"Whoa." I held my hands out in surrender, completely baffled. "Choose who over me? Does there have to be a choice? I mean, I'm on your side . . ."

"I'm not stupid, Donatti." The gun didn't waver. "Ian is dead. And the only way you could have gotten out of Trevor's place is if he let you go. That bastard's not getting my son. You can tell him that."

Crud. If things were logical, she'd be right. Unfortunately, I'd entered the Twilight Zone the minute Ian had invaded my life, while she was still planted firmly in reality—and her reality included protecting Cyrus from a madman with serious firepower. "Jazz, please. I'm not telling Trevor anything. I don't work for him. You have to trust me."

"I don't."

"I knew you'd say that." Sighing, I lowered my arms a few degrees and tried to come up with something that would convince her of my loyalties. "Look. If Trevor had sent me, I'd be armed, right? You can search me."

"If you're not out of here in five seconds, you're a dead man."

"Jazz . . ."

"Four."

Damn. I was going to regret this.

Moving as though I meant to comply with her demands, I shifted forward slightly and watched her face. The next time she blinked, I wrestled the gun away, then turned it on her.

"You asshole," she said through clenched teeth. "He's your son, too."

"I know. That's why I'd never work for Trevor. But since you don't believe me, I couldn't think of another way to survive long enough to prove it. Come on, Jazz, don't you think—*ow!*" My righteous little speech ended in a howl when something pinched my arm hard. I glanced down to see Cyrus clinging to me, his tiny teeth sunk into my flesh like an oversized piranha.

Jazz flashed me a look. "Please don't hurt him."

"I told you I'm not going to hurt him," I said, with gritted teeth of my own. "Can you please ask him to stop biting me, if I promise not to blow anyone's brains out?"

She scuttled closer. "Cy, baby, it's all right," she coaxed. "Come over here."

Cyrus released me. For an instant, he glowered, his hands clenched in small fists, and then he toddled over to Jazz's waiting arms. Jesus, the kid was just like his mother. A pint-sized bundle of guts.

"Thanks." I rubbed at my chewed arm and winced. My leg

had stopped humming and started to sing—a full-blown choir of pain. I had to stop the bleeding, at least. "Okay. If I put this down for a second, will you promise not to attack me? Either of you? I have to wrap my leg."

"What's wrong with it?"

I stared at her. "Uh . . . you shot me."

"I did?" She frowned. "That was a wild shot. Didn't think I hit anything. Here, let me see." She settled Cyrus on the ground. "Stay here, baby, okay? Just for a minute."

"'Kay." Cyrus gave a huge yawn and thrust his thumb back in. How did she get him to do that? All the little kids I'd encountered were tantrum factories. This boy was as calm as a desert mirage.

Jazz scooted toward me—and without thinking, I handed her the gun.

She smiled. "All right, Donatti. I believe you."

"Good." Relief kept me from blurting that I hadn't meant to do that and would still feel safer with the weapon in my possession. After all, she'd conned me before. But I'd cross those shark-infested waters when we weren't in fear for our lives, which probably wouldn't be until someone killed Trevor. Preferably me.

I'd never actually wanted to kill anyone before. The feeling terrified me.

Though sunrise had brought color to the woods, the thick shade beneath the branches made things difficult to see. Jazz prodded my leg, gently at first, and then with a firm grip. I hissed. "Sorry," she said. "It went through."

"Hey, it's a stroke of luck. We won't have to dig a bullet out with a stick." Grimacing, I peeled off my shirt, used my teeth to tear it open, and worked a strip free. Jazz took it and cinched it around my calf while I formed another makeshift bandage, mostly to keep my mouth shut against the pain. When half the shirt was gone, I dropped the rest and let out a hard breath. "I think I can learn to appreciate being shot," I said. "Doesn't hurt as much as Tasering."

"Oh, God. Did Trevor . . ."

I laid a finger on her lips. "I'm okay now. Let's work on getting the hell out of here, and then—"

Not far away, a medley of sounds exploded. Harsh growls, breaking branches, shouts, gunfire. A startled yelp. Silence. Cyrus shifted closer to Jazz, eyes wide, and she drew him in with an arm. "Bad guys," he murmured around his thumb.

"You got that right," I said. *God damn it, Ian, stop getting yourself killed.* I hoped he could pull out of this. He'd done it before—he would be all right. Wouldn't he?

Jazz gripped my arm. "Was that a dog?" she whispered. "Jesus, how did they get the dogs out here? We've got to move, now."

I shook my head. "It wasn't a dog. Just . . . trust me. Stay here and keep him safe." I had to see if Ian had taken one or both of them out—or if they'd gotten him first. "Can I borrow your gun?"

She handed it over. "Try to stay alive, Houdini."

"Funny. I think I've heard that before." I hitched a half-smile and glanced at Cyrus. The kid had stayed put. His big blues stared at me, and I could have sworn I knew what he was thinking: *Boy, you're pretty stupid going out there, Mister. It sounds scary.*

I had to agree. So far tonight, stupid had been my middle name. Good thing Jazz hadn't known that before, or she might have named the kid Stupid Donatti.

CHAPTER 11

After Jazz handed me a couple of spare cartridges and a peck on the cheek for luck—useless, but it felt nice—I hop-crawled out of the shelter and hunkered beside it to listen, gun at the ready. The weapon seemed on the flimsy side. I glanced at it in the stronger light and understood why my bones hadn't shattered with the shot. It was a .22 Browning. Practically a cap gun. What was she doing with this peashooter? Oh, right. Conner the Barbarian had forced her to toss the Glock. This must have been her spare.

I was no marksman. I'd probably fare better armed with a big stick.

It would have been silent, except for the birds babbling their feathered heads off. Didn't they know there were people with guns down here? I straightened slowly and shifted my weight to my good leg. Had to move away from Jazz before someone showed up looking for trouble with a capital Shoot to Kill. I limped in the direction Ian had disappeared earlier and realized that whoever had been left standing would have no problem finding me—with my foot dragging on the ground, I was about as stealthy as an elephant.

Ten feet, then twenty, and no sign of anyone. Ian or otherwise. Much farther in, and I'd have trouble finding Jazz again. Everything looked the same. There were probably fifty different varieties in here, but to me, a tall brown thing with green stuff was a goddamned tree. I would have stopped and waited for them to come to me, but Jazz and Cyrus were still too close. I picked up the pace, unmindful of the racket I made, and blundered another fifty feet.

On a tangle of dried weeds, I found my answer. The score was tied—one for us, one for the thugs. Harmon or Pope, minus his throat, sprawled face-up with clouded eyes fixed on the branches above. I guessed Harmon, because only a guy called Pope would take the time to thumb a cross on his dead buddy's forehead with his own congealing blood after shooting the wolf that brought him down.

The wolf lay on his side a few feet from the body. Crimson stained his white muzzle, and his fur glistened darkly in at least three spots I could see. At least his eyes were closed. *Jesus, Ian, I thought you couldn't kill humans.* Apparently, there were exceptions to this rule. Maybe they could only kill people while they were wolves. I stood and watched him, hoping to see a twitch, a shallow breath, anything that might herald another miraculous recovery.

When nothing happened, I made yet another colossally stupid decision.

"Hey, Pope!" I bellowed. A handful of startled birds burst into flight above me. "Trevor's gonna hand your ass to you in a basket when he finds out you two morons couldn't even bag a chick and a kid." I turned in a slow circle, alert for any sound. At least the birds had given it a rest.

Something crunched to my left. I swung the gun and fired blind.

An answering shot thundered. Splinters burst from a tree behind me. I dropped and rolled, crouched opposite the wounded side of the trunk. "You're a lousy shot, Pope. What's your regular job, doing Trevor's laundry?"

"That you, Donatti?" Pope's voice sounded holy, all right. Like he'd eaten a cactus. I hoped Ian had gotten a few chomps in before he went down. "We figured you'd turn up eventually. Too bad about your dog, huh?"

We? Did he mean Trevor we, or dead-guy we . . . or were there more of them out here? "Shame about your buddy, too," I shouted. "Hell of a way to go. You ready to join him?"

Pope's gun roared. The bullet skimmed the side of the tree, inches from my head. "Ladies first."

"Oh, you're clever. Did you pick up your insults at Thugs R Us?" Jesus, that was close. I tried to remember what I planned on doing after I'd gotten his attention. And then I remembered that I didn't have a plan. Shit on toast.

No response from Pope. The silence highlighted my heart pounding in my ears. Took him long enough to figure out what I was up to. Trevor didn't make a habit of employing idiots. Seeing a wolf tear his partner's throat out must have unhinged him a little, but he'd recovered now. Nothing I hated more than smart thugs.

I had to move soon. My leg screamed a protest under my weight. Sweat soaked my temples and dripped cold down my back. Holding my breath, I felt the ground beneath me and closed my fingers around a good-sized rock, then inched up the tree trunk slow and easy.

A whisper of sound behind me. Couldn't let him get the advantage—he had a bigger gun. I lurched around the tree, ready to brain Pope on the other side. He wasn't there. I knew I'd heard something. Before my mind could process this development, a sensation I'd experienced too often tonight presented itself: a gun jammed against me. Right between my shoulders.

"Drop it, Donatti."

He must have come around the opposite side. The .22 tumbled to the ground. Useless thing, anyway. I almost dropped the rock that he hadn't even noticed, but in a snap, I realized that if Pope intended to kill me, he'd have done it by now. Which meant Trevor's arrogant ass still wanted me alive.

Not gonna happen.

I stilled and transferred all of my weight to the leg without the hole in it. Had to act fast, before Pope decided what to do with me. If I missed, I'd take another bullet for my trouble. I leaned forward and spun around, arching the rock up and out, then sling-shotted in for his head.

The dull crack of stone-meet-Pope sounded like salvation.

He didn't go down right away. He blinked, stumbled back, and jerked. The gun went off, and the bullet sailed away through the trees without my body to block it. At last, the thug toppled to the ground with an expression that said, *Where'd you get that cement fist?*

I snagged his piece from limp fingers and foraged for the Browning. I hoped the blow had only knocked him out. I'd leave killing him to Trevor. Sometimes my morals really interfered with the job. Kind of pathetic, if I thought about it too hard. When it came to stealing, I'd break the law six ways to Sunday, but murder, now, that was a crime.

Going through his pockets was second nature. Toss the wallet, didn't need it. Crunch the cell. If he woke up, he could thumb his way to call for a pickup and execution. I would've kept it, but I knew Trevor would be able to track it. Don't even try to figure out why Pope carried a travel-sized lube tube and the barrel of a mechanical pencil.

I kept the spare cartridge and the butterfly blade with the cross etched in the handle. Felt good to be armed properly again. I'd leave him the string of mint-flavored condoms, though.

With no idea how long he'd be out, I had to immobilize him. I dragged him to the base of a slender tree, positioned his arms on either side of the trunk, and took off his shoes and socks. They stank like last week's dinner left on the counter. I knotted the socks together end to end and used them to bind his wrists on the far side of the tree. Not satisfied, I repeated the process with his shoelaces.

As I lashed the end of a lace to a thick root arching up from the ground, twigs snapped, and vegetation crunched in the distance with foot-stepping regularity. I pushed away the faint hope that the sound had come from Ian and ducked behind a fat pine.

If this was the "we" Pope had mentioned, I might have to injure my morals.

The footsteps stopped somewhere in the vicinity of Pope's trussed form. I waited for an indication of who owned the brush-cracking feet. When it came, I experienced a figurative desire to kill her for being dumber than me.

"Guess I won't need this after all."

I stumbled out and glared at Jazz, who'd armed herself with a big stick and Cyrus with a little one. "You were supposed to stay hidden. What if something happened to him?" *Or you?* I couldn't vocalize that part. She'd never welcomed protectiveness, and I wasn't ready to proclaim a feeling I didn't understand.

"Relax, Donatti. I knew you had it under control. Just had to make sure your compassionate streak didn't limit you to giving this asshole a stern lecture, instead of knocking him the hell out."

"Thanks for the vote of confidence. Put the damned stick down, will ya?" I handed her piece over and watched Cyrus poke at the ground, as if he was prospecting for treasure. "I take it there were only two."

"Yeah. But they didn't bring a wolf." Jazz looked at me, her expression perfectly calm—the closest I'd ever seen her to fear. "This piece of trash said something about your dog. If you don't mind my asking . . . what the hell is going on?"

I frowned. If Stupid was my middle name, Pragmatic was hers. She'd no sooner believe in magic than she would don a pink dress and take high tea with the queen. "You know, I have no idea what he meant," I said, going for casual and probably scoring a ten on the bullshit meter. "I don't have a dog."

"No. But apparently, you have a wolf. Or had one, at least."

"Uh, right. About that . . ." I trailed off, glanced around, and my stomach took a dive. "Where's Cyrus?"

Jazz whirled. "Cy? No, don't go over there!"

She ran off, and I spotted the kid at the edge of the clearing where Ian and Harmon lay. Cyrus moved with determination toward the wolf, head cocked, stick abandoned in favor of this new discovery. I dragged after them as fast as I could manage and reached the clearing to see Cyrus burble something that sounded like *doggie* and stroke the wolf's massive head.

At his touch, Ian glowed.

"Oh, my God." Jazz bent, snatched the startled boy around

the waist, and yanked him back. Cyrus turned a quizzical glance to his mother, who stared at the changing form on the ground as if she'd burst into flames if she looked away. "Donatti," she whispered. "What . . ."

I couldn't suppress a grin of relief. "Like I said before. It's Ian."

The light seemed to run off him like rainwater. Ian, unharmed once again, sat up slowly and blinked at his audience. "I assume you have taken care of the other one, then. Partner."

"I think we can drop the partner bit," I said.

Jazz backed away. Cyrus squirmed in her arms, but she tightened her grip. "How the fuck did you do that? Sorry, Cy. Don't say fuck. Was it a costume? Secret government technology? I never thought you were really a magician. . ."

Oh, boy. I glanced at Ian, who didn't look too pleased with me, and wondered what I'd done now. "Uh. Can we tell her?"

Ian nodded.

"You know what? I don't want to know. Just get me the hell out of Freaksville."

"You have to know." I moved toward her. She backed up another step, maintaining a lock around an increasingly struggling Cyrus. "Trevor does want him—so he can get to me. You've got to understand what we're facing so you can help me protect him." I was spitballing, but it sounded good. Unfortunately, it also sounded like the truth.

Jazz paled, appearing on the verge of a slump. "All right," she said flatly. "What do I have to understand?"

"Ian is . . . well, he's not exactly human. He's a djinn."

"A djinn." Her lips pursed, and her body relaxed. Cyrus, sensing freedom, slid to the ground and headed for Ian. Jazz didn't try to stop him. She'd apparently decided we weren't dangerous, just nuts. "That's fascinating. I'm actually a unicorn. Lemme guess, Donatti. You're a fairy prince, right?"

"Come on, Jazz. I'm serious." I turned to Ian. Cyrus had reached him and stood tugging on his coat. "Can't you magic something so she'll believe it?"

Ian reached down and almost absently scooped up the kid, who promptly snuggled into the crook of his arm and popped in a thumb. "I told you before—"

"Yeah, I know. No trifles. Christ, this is ridiculous." A sharp twinge in my leg reminded me that I had a rather untrifling need. "Think you could fix the bullet hole before I bleed to death?"

"That little scratch? It is hardly necessary."

"Ian . . ."

"Fine." Ian held his free hand out and murmured something. After a minute, blessed normalcy returned to my calf.

"Give it a rest." Jazz folded her arms and glowered. "If he could just fix you up like that, why did you call me to patch him after . . . wait a minute." Her eyes widened, and she seemed to notice the unbroken skin of his chest for the first time. Her mouth opened in silence.

"At the time, I did not have enough power to transform myself," Ian replied. "It is the only healing method available to djinn in this realm." A small smile played on his lips, and his gaze met mine.

"That's not funny, Ian. I'd better have a human leg under here." I went down on a knee and used the knife I'd relieved Pope of to cut the shirt strips free. A small, ragged hole still adorned my jeans. I tugged them up and found my own un-damaged leg attached to my knee.

Ian chuckled. "Relax, thief. I said it was available to djinn, not humans."

Jazz sat down hard on the ground. "You are serious." Her voice came out small and awed, like a kid finding Santa in the living room on Christmas Eve. She shook herself and grew solemn. "What does Trevor have to do with this?"

I crossed to her, offered a hand, and helped her up. "He knows about them. The djinn, I mean. He . . . has one in his basement."

A pained look crossed Ian's face. He said nothing.

"Wait a minute. Trevor has a djinn on his payroll?"

"I don't think Trevor's djinn volunteered for the position." I shuddered at the recollection of Shamil's tortured body and his plea for release. The questions I hadn't asked in the basement returned to demand attention—but first, I had one that had formed more recently. "Ian. Why didn't you get up until Cyrus touched you?"

"I would have recovered sooner, if you had bothered to concern yourself with my condition." The anger he displayed broke Richter-scale records. "It is far more difficult to transform from the wolf state, but I can amplify my power through proximity, and especially contact, with—" He broke off and looked at Cyrus, who'd just about fallen asleep against him. Poor kid had to be exhausted. "Blast it. Why did it have to be you?"

I knew he meant me. Though I was tempted to adopt Jazz's don't-wanna-know philosophy, my traitorous mouth had other ideas. "Contact with what?"

Ian's jaw clenched. He raised his head, and his eyes blistered me.

"With my descendants."

CHAPTER 12

I could have sworn Ian had said *descendants*. Of course, that was impossible. So I asked him to repeat himself—and he said it again.

"Around here, descendant means direct relative," I told him. "What does it mean on your planet?"

"The same," he said. "I like it no more than you, and I would appreciate it if you would stop playing the fool."

"But . . . Ian, this isn't funny. If you're gonna mess with me, at least try to come up with something remotely believable."

"Do you really think I would claim you as a descendant if it were not true?"

That made sense. Nothing else did, though. "So you're telling me that I'm a djinn? Why can't I transform into a wolf or fly or turn rustbuckets into slick cars?"

"Idiot. You are not djinn. You are descended from one of the bloodlines I created with humans."

"Right. You and humans." He couldn't even stand talking to us. I wasn't about to believe he'd slept with a human woman. "Just how many bloodlines did you create?"

"Dozens."

"Jesus." The ground looked awfully inviting. Sit down, take a load off, hop a train back to the real world, where I was just a thief with lousy luck and not some distant relative of a djinn. "Sorry, Ian, but I don't buy it. I think you got your wires crossed somewhere. I'm just a regular guy."

Ian cocked an eyebrow. "Have you ever hidden in plain sight and not been found?"

"Yeah. It's called concealment. Thieves have to be good at that."

"In your case, it is called invisibility. The one trait that is invariably passed through djinn blood. You are not merely hiding. You are invisible to others."

Jazz cleared her throat. "He might have a point there, Houdini. You can disappear when you want to."

"Oh, so you're on his side now?" I threw up my hands. "Fine. Let's say you're right, and I'm your descendant. When did you start planting this human garden of yours?"

"I do not know that I should explain much of this to you. Your human mind may not be able to process—"

"Try me."

A strange look shadowed Ian's features. "Four hundred years ago. Give or take a decade."

For an instant, I thought Ian had been right. Something in my head tried to shut down and refuse the offered information. I forced it open. "All right. If you created dozens of bloodlines back in the Stone Age, shouldn't you have a few hundred descendants running around by now? I mean, why me?"

"I have my reasons."

"Oh, come on. You hate me. Why can't you go bother some other descendant?"

A moan drifted from the direction in which I'd left Pope. Ian stared at me. "You did not kill him?"

"No. I'm not a murderer." *Not yet, anyway.* "Maybe we should get out of here before we continue this enlightening conversation."

Jazz frowned. "I'd say we could take my van, but those assholes shot the hell out of it. It'll kind of stand out on the road. Besides, once Trevor realizes they aren't coming back, he'll look for it."

"Ian," I said. "Can you . . ."

The djinn nodded and approached Jazz. "Take the child. Is your vehicle close?"

"More or less." Jazz arranged Cyrus against her like a forward-facing backpack. The boy stirred a bit but remained asleep. "What are you going to do to my van?"

I nudged her. "Remember that car I had at the motel?"

"Yeah."

"It used to be an '89 Ford Escort."

"Oh." Jazz offered Ian a weak, incredulous smile. "Can you do a Kia Sorento? I've always wanted one of those."

There was no hint of sarcasm in her tone. She'd accepted the bizarre truth. I would have been relieved at having one problem solved—if there hadn't been a thousand more to go.

THE NEW, IMPROVED VAN WAS NO SORENTO, BUT IT CAME CLOSE.

Jazz had somewhat graciously agreed to let me drive—if gracious meant threatening me with bodily harm if anything happened to her van. I was just glad she'd brought clothes for Ian that he didn't need, since my shirt had been sacrificed for a tourniquet. I didn't like driving around half-naked.

She'd given me her sister's address, just north of Auburn.

We had to get Cyrus somewhere safe, and I hoped the thugs hadn't keyed into Molly yet. Jazz had been home with Cyrus when they hauled her in to Trevor. If we made her sister's place soon, we might be able to grab a few hours of sleep before making any monumental decisions. Jazz lay on the backseat with Cyrus, getting an early start.

Ian sat in the passenger seat and entertained me with his jackass impersonation.

"Okay, look," I said when he refused to respond for the hundredth time. "Whatever this life-purpose thing is supposed to be, it has to include me staying alive, which obviously goes against Trevor's plans. That means Trevor has to factor in here somewhere. And you know something about him that I don't."

"How observant of you."

"So, if you tell me what you know, maybe we'd get closer to figuring out how to solve this problem and get rid of the bastard."

Ian shook his head. "What I know has nothing to do with you, thief. It is a concern of the djinn."

"What about Shamil? Is it his concern? Because I think he'd be glad to see Trevor gone."

"I will take care of Shamil." Ian practically vibrated with suppressed rage. "Do not speak to me of him. You know nothing."

"You're right. I don't know jack." I gripped the wheel and forced even breaths. "And if you can't see why that's a problem, you must've eaten a bowl of stupid for breakfast."

Ian closed his eyes. "No good has ever come of our cooperation with humans."

I wanted to feel offended, but the pain in his statement came through clear as crystal. He spoke from experience. And having seen what Trevor had done to his friend, it wasn't a stretch to understand why he'd get that impression. The bastard in me wanted to tell him tough shit, the world ain't fair, take your lumps and move on . . . a lesson I'd learned the direct way.

Unfortunately, the rest of me insisted on feeling sorry for him.

"All right, maybe that's true," I told him. "Maybe cooperating with me won't change a damned thing. But I can promise that I won't make things worse—at least, not intentionally. I trust you. God knows why, but I do. And you're going to have to trust me."

A long pause followed. At last, Ian said, "Trevor is working with a djinn."

"Uh, yeah. I saw that. You going to tell me something I don't know?"

"Not Shamil." Ian scrubbed a hand down his face. "The blood is the bond. Direct human descendants are most powerful, but any human containing djinn blood can be used to amplify power. Even if the containment is temporary." His features twisted in pure fury. "Trevor is keeping Shamil merely to supply him with djinn blood, in order to prime himself for another djinn to work through."

Bile scalded my throat. "You mean he drinks his blood?"

Ian nodded stiffly. "The one who uses him is of the Morai, the snake clan. The banished. They are not permitted to return to the djinn realm."

"Why not?"

He sent me a look that suggested I was as dumb as a bag of marbles. "They are banished. Do you not know this word? It means—"

"I know what banished means."

"Then why did you ask why they cannot return?"

I forced back a surge of annoyance. "I mean, what did they do?"

"They are evil. Bent on power and destruction."

"That's it? They're banished because they're evil?" If humans practiced that policy, we wouldn't have to worry about Trevor right now.

Ian's mouth twisted down. "It is enough."

His tone said he'd already told me more than he wanted to. I knew it wasn't even approaching enough, but I decided to leave it alone for now. "I take it Shamil isn't one of them. The Morai, I mean."

"Shamil is Bahari."

"Let me guess. The wolf clan."

"No. Hawk. The wolf clan—my clan—is Dehbei." His voice caught, and he turned away.

I drove in silence for a few minutes. Trying to make sense of this felt like absorbing a steel plate with my brain. It was incompatible, and it made my head hurt. Trevor had gone from garden-variety psychotic fence to blood-sucking overlord with an evil snake djinn at his disposal. Fantastic. Even as a regular guy, he was untouchable. To have a shot at the bastard, we'd have to take the snake out of the picture.

We'd passed Auburn proper. I slowed and turned onto Route 5, hoping to make the next six or seven miles fast. My body begged for rest. I didn't know how much longer I could fight the urge to close my eyes, just for a minute, despite the knowledge that the van would end up intimately acquainted with a tree if I succumbed. "Ian," I said slowly. "How do you kill a djinn?"

Ian shot me a dagger gaze. "Excuse me?"

"I just figured if we could snuff the snake dude, it'd leave Trevor open." I flashed a brief smile. "Christ, did you think I wanted to bump you off?"

"The idea crossed my mind," Ian muttered. "Besides, I thought you were not a murderer."

"I'll make a few exceptions for Trevor." A memory throbbed in my head: Trevor selecting tiny pliers, smiling and telling me I could watch while he tortured my son. The son of a bitch deserved worse than death, but death was all I could bring him, and I intended to follow through.

"So what's the deal?" I said. "Obviously, bullets don't work."

Ian hesitated. "To destroy a djinn in this realm, you destroy the tether that binds him to it. There is a ritual spell that must be performed."

"Tether?" I frowned. "The pendant Trevor wears. That's Shamil's tether, right?"

"It is."

"Great. How much you wanna bet he never takes it off?"

"I am sure he does not. But I must get it somehow."

"Far as I know, the only way to get something that belongs to Trevor is over his dead body." I cursed and slammed on the brakes. I'd almost missed the turn for Molly's. Easing the van back on track, I added, "So how do we find this other djinn's tether? What are we looking for, another pendant?"

"They are not all pendants. Do you not know the story of Aladdin's lamp?"

"You're shitting me. That was for real?"

"More or less. But I assure you, there were no wishes involved." Ian shifted and slumped down a few inches. "It will take some effort, and time, but I should be able to locate it.

Unfortunately, the Morai is likely to have it in his possession, wherever he is. The best we can hope for is the possibility that Trevor has it somewhere."

"Oh, yeah. That'd be a piece of cake, stealing something from Trevor."

"A simple matter compared with stealing from a djinn."

He had a point.

I made a token pause at a deserted all-way and continued on a road suddenly swaddled in forest on both sides. "So what's your tether?"

"Never mind."

"Come on. Even if I knew, I couldn't do anything with it. There's some kind of ritual, right? I'm curious. Indulge me."

"Gods take you! Leave it, thief." The edge in his voice could have slit a few throats.

I shook my head. "So much for trusting me, huh?" It was mostly a joke. I guessed if I had some item that dictated whether I lived or died, I wouldn't want to go around pointing it out, either. Still, it did sting to think Ian believed I'd use it against him.

Ian jolted straight. "Stop."

"What's . . ."

"Stop driving."

I hit the brakes. The van lurched and settled back. "Why?"

"Do you not smell that?"

I started to say no, but at once I caught the unmistakable pungent sting of smoke. "Shit. Is that coming from the engine?"

"No." Ian pointed to the passenger window. "Look."

Unease stirred in my gut. I leaned forward and sucked a breath. Ahead, the road curved to the right, and thin ropes of black smoke shuttled through shafts of sunlight in the air like ghostly snakes. "Jesus," I whispered. "Think there's a forest fire up there?"

Ian's lips compressed. "Keep going, but slowly. We may have to turn back."

Nodding, I eased down on the gas and nudged forward. We rounded the bend. Several yards down the road, thick gray-black clouds billowed skyward from a cleared area on the left. My unease plunged into sick fury when I realized the source of the smoke: the smoldering remains of a house. Right where Molly's place should have been.

CHAPTER 13

I glanced in the rearview mirror, relieved that Jazz hadn't woken yet. How could I tell her this? *Sorry, Jazz, but while you were sleeping, we found your sister's place, and we didn't stop. Why? Oh, we just weren't in the mood for barbecue.* "Ian, any chance you could tint the windows or something? Like, now?"

For once, he didn't question or protest. He gestured, and the glass around us darkened to blue-gray. "You think there might be someone there waiting for us," he said.

"Exactly. I'm just going to keep driving. They won't recognize the vehicle."

Ian almost smiled. "You are smarter than I credited you, thief."

"Thanks. I think." I slowed as we passed the smoldering wreck. Anyone would—I knew it wouldn't look suspicious. Only a few charred and crooked timbers remained upright, marking three of four walls. The rest had been reduced to piles of blackened slabs and ash. They must have doused the place first. Otherwise, it wouldn't have burned so thoroughly. Had they killed her before they torched it? I squinted, searching the rubble for signs of a body.

"Donatti? How close are we?"

Jazz's voice, thick with sleep, rolled from the backseat and slugged me with regret. Crud. I'd hoped we could somehow skip the part where she saw what was left of the place.

She hadn't sat up yet. Maybe she wouldn't look. Making my way back to normal speed, I glanced at Ian and cleared my throat. He nodded once, but I wasn't sure whether he was encouraging me or saying *You do it.* "Jazz," I said softly. "They've been to your sister's place."

"Oh, God. Molly. Is she all right? Why didn't you tell me when we got there?"

I couldn't look back anymore. "We didn't stop."

"Why?"

No response came to mind. I shook my head.

"Donatti." Her voice shook. "Why didn't you stop?"

"I . . . there was nothing left to stop for. Shit, Jazz . . . they torched the place."

"No." Jazz whirled and looked out the rear window, as if she expected her sister's house to be right there waiting. "Go back. Go back! What if she's still in there?"

Something inside me broke at the pleading in her tone. My stockpile of reasons to kill Trevor stood at about Empire State Building height. I had to drag the words from my mouth. "She can't be. It's burned flat. I'm so sorry . . ."

With excruciating slowness, she faced forward again. She said nothing.

The hum of tires on pavement filled the silence. Jazz's lack of reaction concerned me more than if she'd screamed or cried or threatened to kill someone. Trevor. Possibly me.

A sick certainty twisted my stomach. If I were her, I'd blame me. I was the reason Trevor had targeted her in the first place.

"Jazz?" I croaked. "Are you . . ." I checked the rearview.

The muzzle of her Browning greeted me. "Turn around and go back. Right fucking now."

She'd shoot me. I knew she would. But I still had to try to talk her out of it. "We can't. They might be hanging around waiting for us to show up."

"If they are, they're dead. Turn the hell around."

I sent Ian a do-something look. He didn't. Teeth clenched, I swerved right and made a sloppy three-point. "We're going to regret this," I muttered.

"You would've regretted it more if you'd kept going." Jazz checked the seatbelt she'd fastened around a still-napping Cyrus. She moved up to the seat behind us and thrust the Browning at Ian, handle first. "Can you give this thing some more kick?"

"Perhaps." Ian accepted the weapon. He passed a hand over it, and his eyes closed briefly. The gun's grip and body thickened. The barrel lengthened. His finished product didn't resemble any gun brand I'd ever seen, but it looked as if it could punch a hole through steel at a hundred yards. He handed it back to her. "Will this do?"

"Oh, hell yes. Thank you."

My hands tightened on the wheel. Wasn't that impossible bastard supposed to be helping me? I failed to see how arming Jazz, who'd shifted from protective mother to vengeful hellion, would be useful to anyone. He should've done his dog trick and put her back to sleep.

Smoke came into view first, followed too fast by the pile

of blackened debris. Jazz made a small, helpless sound. But she didn't scream.

She also didn't change her mind about searching the devastation for her sister.

"Pull over." She crouched, hand on the door, ready to fly. "Donatti, I need you to stay with Cy. Keep him safe."

"No."

She glared at me. "He's your son—"

"I know. Christ, just listen to me a sec." I edged off the road, threw the van into park, and took a hard breath. "If you want him safe, Ian should stay. He can protect him better than me. I'm going with you."

"I don't need your help. Cy's more important."

"Damn it, Jazz, *you're* important. To me. Cyrus, too. But that doesn't mean I'm going to sit here and watch you walk into a trap. He's staying. I'm going. If you want to stop me, you'll have to shoot me."

Her brow lifted. "You finished?"

"Yeah."

"Good. Let's go." She jerked the door open and stepped out.

I groaned. "Women. Do any of yours make sense?"

"No more than yours, I suspect." Ian smirked and glanced back at the sleeping boy. "You should go. I will protect him."

"Thank you." I jumped out and hustled after Jazz, hoping there wouldn't be anything to protect him from.

THE ROOF HAD COLLAPSED AND BURIED EVERYTHING UNDER chunks of charred rafters and melted insulation. Parts of the flooring poked through here and there like jagged wooden teeth. Small reminders that life had been here lay scattered among the broken structure—the corner of a mattress, a snarl of wire hangers, the bare springs of a recliner with shreds of burnt material still clinging to them.

Jazz picked her way through the wreckage with dogged determination. I wanted to grab her and drag her away before she found what I knew had to be there—her sister's body, probably in a condition Jazz should never have to see. She might thank me later, but right now, all I'd get for my trouble would be a swift kick to my manhood. Maybe a busted jaw, too.

I'd take a pass on that experience. Already had my balls bashed enough for this lifetime.

I followed her, close as I dared. Piles of blackened debris, weak and unstable, made moving a dangerous balancing act. And the smell didn't help. Sharp traces of whatever accelerant the thugs had used to start the blaze—probably kerosene— edged the heavy black stench of burnt everything. Each breath felt like sucking in a mouthful of tar. Heat rose in visible air shimmers from some of the deeper mounds of rubble, but overall the temperature was bearable.

They must have hit the place the minute Jazz left Trevor's. Maybe even before.

Jazz stopped moving, as if she'd just realized the same thing. But she remained frozen in place for so long that I knew she hadn't paused to consider the asshole-ness of Trevor. I made my way closer, dreading her discovery, knowing without having to see what had riveted her gaze and sketched rigid shock into every line of her body.

When I found it, I wanted to unsee it for her. Just take the image and absorb it from her memory, so she wouldn't have to spend the rest of her life with the vision of a bare brown leg and a naked foot jutting at an impossible angle from a snarl of broken things. The idea that the rest of Molly lay mangled beneath made this almost perfect, visible portion somehow more gruesome. More final. Deader than death.

"That's not her," Jazz whispered. "It's not. Not. M-molly."

Her denial kicked me in the gut. I tried to put myself between her and the body, to spare what I could of her witness. "It is her," I said, as gently as I could manage. "Jazz, you've got to accept it. You'll only feel worse if you don't."

"It's not." She almost screamed but seemed to rein herself in with formidable effort. Closing her eyes, she shuddered and swallowed back dry heaves. "She has tattoos. Circlets. Both ankles. That's not her."

I looked again and saw what Jazz couldn't—or wouldn't. The heat of the blaze had melted her skin. Rough, uneven texture and discoloration bore evidence that she'd been exposed to air long enough to cool. If I squinted and stared hard enough, I could make out faint traces of ink streaking the ridged shin.

"Jazz . . ." I turned back to her.

Devastation stamped her features. She'd noticed.

"Excuse me." She made a vague gesture, telling me to get out of her way.

Though instinct told me to force her away from this horror show before things got worse, I stepped aside. She wobbled across rubble to the forlorn leg, stopped. Knelt, bowed her head.

"Molly. I'm so sorry . . ."

She didn't blame me. She blamed herself.

Feeling like an unwanted extra, I gave her some distance and scanned the wreckage and the property beyond. A brightly colored child's swing set, smudged with soot and leaning forward as if the front legs had weakened in the heat, served as a sharp reminder that Cyrus had spent a lot of time here. A large shed sat untouched several yards back, and a good half-acre of trimmed lawn expanded behind the house to dense woods. The shed worried me. Someone could be hiding in there, waiting to see who showed up to investigate. With no neighbors for miles, it might be hours before any cops arrived. Maybe never. No doubt Trevor had influence on the cops around here, too.

Something unnatural in the distance caught my eye. A flash in the treeline beyond the cleared property. Sunlight on glass.

They were waiting for us.

CHAPTER 14

azz." I started for her, but my foot sank through charred debris. I cleared falling on my face by a few frantic arm flaps. "They're out there. Come on, we've gotta get back to the van."

She looked at me and then at the yard. "Where? I don't see—"

The distant, unmistakable sound of an engine starting stemmed her words. She stood—and headed the wrong way. Toward the thugs.

"What are you doing?" I yanked my leg free and clunked after her, but she scrambled lightly over the jumbled wreckage as if she was crossing a parking lot and pulled ahead of me. "The van's *that* way." I pointed back.

She failed to notice my helpful directions.

"Murdering bastards." She whipped out the Ian-modified gun, sailed over the last of the rubble onto clear ground, and took aim at a black Jeep trundling over grass toward us.

I didn't waste my breath telling her to stop. I ran, intending to knock her down and drag her back if I had to. Somehow, my usual elephantlike grace failed to slow me this time.

She still fired before I cleared the house.

"Are you nuts? You can't hit—"

Another blast cut me off. The Jeep lurched, swerved, and almost tipped over before rolling to a stop sidelong in the grass.

I gave a low whistle. "Nice shot."

Jazz didn't move. I made my way to her, hesitated, and put an arm around her shoulders. Her body vibrated like a power line.

"Come on," I said. "We'd better get out of here."

"Look," she whispered.

The Jeep bounced and rocked. Stopped. The driver's-side door opened, and a body tumbled out. An arm closed the door. The Jeep backed up, skirted the heap on the grass, and headed for us at a fast clip.

Behind the advancing vehicle, the body stirred and attempted to rise.

And Jazz leveled the gun again.

"No." I grabbed her arm. "Van. Now. Don't argue."

"Don't go caveman on me, Donatti. These bastards are meat."

Tugging on her was like trying to pull a telephone pole out of the ground. I glared. "Don't make me carry you back. Because I will." She'd beat my ass into hamburger for it, too. But I wouldn't let her get killed—or live to regret being a murderer.

She must have seen something in my face that convinced her I meant it. Or she'd decided to just plug me instead. Either way, she relented and ran with me. We skirted the wreckage and pounded over brittle brown grass. I couldn't shake the image of the wounded thug shoved from the Jeep like so much litter. That meant the one Jazz hadn't hit was a ruthless, cold-blooded bastard . . . or knew damned well that Trevor would kill him if he came back empty-handed. Probably both.

We hadn't reached the former front of the house when the sharp stutter of an automatic sprayed the air.

"*Move!*" I practically threw her ahead of me. If only one of us survived, I'd rather it was her. I didn't know how to change a diaper.

She sprinted and slammed into the van's side door seconds before I skidded hip-first against the front panel. I raced around the hood, scrambled into the driver's seat, and made a mental note to teach Ian the finer points of getaway driving. Provided we lived long enough.

With a quick glance to make sure we still numbered four, I wrenched the gearshift to drive and took off. Navigating the remains of the house must have slowed the remaining thug down, but the bastard still made pavement before we'd gotten out of sight.

"Everybody buckle in," I said. "It's gonna get rough."

A four-way stop loomed ahead. I kissed the brake just enough to manage my own seatbelt with one hand and peeled right, deeper into unpopulated area. If I risked heading for straighter roads, he'd have a clear shot. Of course, this meant I'd have to speed through unfamiliar territory.

Maybe I should've let Jazz drive.

I stomped the accelerator, moving as fast as I dared on the narrow, curving road. Behind us, the Jeep made the turn and picked up speed.

Ian twisted to look out the back window, then faced forward again with a blank expression. "When I tell you, drive faster."

"I'm already going—"

"Do it. You will only need to continue for a few seconds."

"Right." I'd already hit sixty and either felt or imagined the wheels lifting around the bends. Much faster, and we'd end up rolling the thing. "I hope you're gonna tell me soon."

"Be silent. Drive."

I risked a mirror glance. The Jeep couldn't quite match our speed, but at the rate it was falling behind, it'd take hours to lose him. For an instant, I wondered what in the hell Ian planned to do. Then I decided against asking. I didn't want to know.

The answer came when we rounded another curve. A massive tree alongside the road just ahead of us started to lean, and Ian said, "Move."

I floored the gas. The van responded with a smooth jump to seventy, then eighty. I tried not to envision the thick trunk landing square in the middle of the roof, crushing us into fugitive paste, or smacking the back bumper to send us flipping end-over-end through the air and eventually crashing down to grisly death.

We cleared the falling tree with a few feet to spare. I rounded on Ian. "You asshole. Warn me next time you're going to drop half a ton of wood at me." A thud shook the ground, punctuating my statement as though the tree agreed.

Ian smirked. "You are still alive. You can slow down now."

I tapped the brakes. Behind us, screaming tires announced the Jeep's attempt to avoid the impromptu roadblock, and the crunch of metal and glass proclaimed its failure.

Shaking, I slowed to a crawl and sought Jazz in the rearview mirror. She sat straight as a poker, slack-featured, her pallor practically green. "Nice driving, Donatti," she whispered.

"Yeah. Just call me Jeff Gordon." I swallowed hard. "Is Cyrus okay?"

"He's fine."

"Boom!"

The small voice piped up from beside Jazz and startled laughter from me. "I guess he is. Doesn't anything faze that kid?"

"Not really." Worry creased Jazz's brow. "All right, we're not being followed anymore. Now what?"

"Good question." I glanced forward to make sure I'd stayed on the road and watched her again. She still hadn't let it sink in, but she was getting there. I could practically see the adrenalin draining, the despondency taking its place. "I think we need to find a safe place, get a little rest. Any suggestions?"

Jazz blinked once and dug something from a pocket. Her cell phone. She must have set it on vibrate. After favoring the phone with a lackluster stare, she met my gaze in the mirror.

"It's Trevor."

I pulled off the road and crouched between the front seats. "Don't tell him we know. Can you put it on speaker?"

Jazz stared at me. Didn't move.

"Come on, Jazz. You've got to snap out of it, just for a minute. You can snow this bastard." I didn't dare touch her, not even for comfort. She might break. I knew shock when I saw it. "You fooled me. You can fool him."

Her mouth twitched. "Molly. He killed her . . ."

"Yes, but he didn't get Cyrus. Your son needs you."

That brought her back. She shook herself and reverted to her usual no-bullshit demeanor. Lifting the phone to the back of the seat, she hit the speaker button. "What do you want?"

"Jasmine. Have you been to your sister's house lately?"

Jazz closed her eyes. For an instant, I thought she'd lose it, but a sneer curled her lip, and she replied evenly, "No. Why, have you?"

"Not personally. But I've sent a few of my associates to pay her a visit. I understand she wasn't happy to see them."

She looked at me with *Now what?* in her eyes. I shrugged and pantomimed slitting my throat. *Hang up on him. Kill the call.*

Fury hardened her features. "You son of a bitch. If you've hurt her, I swear to God, you're a dead man."

My jaw dropped. Not exactly what I meant, but maybe this was better.

"If it comforts you, dear lady, I can assure you that your sister is not feeling any pain at the moment. Nor will she ever again."

"Trevor, you disgusting—" The phone shook in Jazz's hand. "She wasn't a threat to you. To anyone. How could you?"

"Bring Mr. Donatti and his resourceful friend to me. It's your only chance for survival."

"Kiss my ass."

In that instant, I knew I loved her.

It took Trevor a few seconds to recover. "Bring them to me, and I'll refrain from killing your son."

I shook my head fiercely, hoping she'd understand that I meant he wouldn't refrain.

She did.

"Trevor, you're a lying dog. And a coward. I won't refrain from blowing your ass off the map." The muted beep of the phone disconnecting sounded almost anticlimactic. Jazz dropped the device on the seat in front of her. Her eyes lost focus. "Oh, Molly. It's my fault . . ."

I shuffled around the first seat and wedged myself beside

her in an awkward crouch. "Jazz, don't. This is all on Trevor. Not you." Hoping she wouldn't haul off and deck me, I took her hand and squeezed. "He's going to pay for this. In blood."

Jazz leaned in close. Her lips feathered my ear, and I swallowed a groan. Christ, this was bad timing. I couldn't help wondering if she felt the same rush of heat, the urge to ignore the presence of children and genies.

"Donatti."

"Mm-hm."

"Shouldn't you be driving us out of here?"

The crunch in my head was the sound of my ego shattering.

"Uh, yeah. Driving. Sorry." I released her and fumbled my way back to the driver's seat. Ian regarded me with a knowing smirk. "Stuff it," I mumbled. "Okay. Anyone know where we're going?"

"Head north." Jazz fell back against the seat. "We all need to crash before we figure out . . . something else." A tremor shook her voice, but she gained resolve quickly. "Weedsport isn't far, and it's a big concert town. Plenty of hotels. Can you find 34 from here?"

"I guess. But we can't stay too long. Trevor has eyes everywhere." More than I ever suspected. Probably human and djinn. No wonder I'd never managed to ditch the bastard. "You and Cyrus have to leave the state. Maybe the country." I tried to smile. "How do you feel about Canada?"

Jazz shook her head. "I don't know. I just . . . I can't think straight. Just get me away from here. Please."

I swung onto the road and maintained a legal speed, watching for road signs or turnoffs or thugs in wait. The longer I thought, the more I realized even Canada wouldn't be safe. Trevor had already demonstrated an uncanny ability to find any of us when he wanted to. I suspected it had something to do with magic and that snake djinn he was working with. "Ian. Got any brilliant ideas?"

"No. But I may have a bad idea."

"Better than nothing. Let's hear it."

Ian glanced in the mirror. For the first time since I met him, he seemed concerned. "It may be possible to send them to Akila. They will be safe with her."

"I think you're right. That's a bad idea." I envisioned a mysterious and ancient ritual involving a blood sacrifice—and with my luck, it'd be my blood. Besides, what if something went wrong, and Jazz and Cyrus ended up horribly disfigured or lost forever in some dimensional limbo?

"Hey. Maybe it's not a bad idea," Jazz said. "Who's Akila?"

"Jazz, it's really not so great. He wants to—"

"Shut up, Donatti. Let Ian talk."

Ian smiled. I managed to keep from knocking his teeth out.

He turned sideways. "Akila is my wife," he said. "I can send you and your son to the djinn realm, and she will care for you until it's safe to return. I need only a reflective surface—a mirror will do nicely."

"Whoa." Jazz hesitated for a long moment. "Are you talking off the planet or something?"

"No. Our realm exists here but in a different space. I am not certain how to explain. There are pockets that lead to our world. Reflective surfaces, like mirrors or bodies of water, can serve as bridges."

"That's . . . amazing. And you can send us to your world through a mirror?"

Ian nodded. "Trevor will not be able to reach you there. You will be safe."

Another stretched silence. "All right. Let's do it."

"Wait a minute," I said. "What about those evil snake guys—the Morai? If you send them over there, won't it be easier for them to find Cyrus?"

Ian looked at me. "I told you, the Morai have been banished. All that live are here, in your realm. They cannot return."

"How can you be so sure? I mean, you've found ways to get around djinn rules. Doesn't seem like you follow any of them."

"They cannot return," he repeated in tones colder than a meat locker. "I have ensured it."

"Okay, fine." I recognized a sore subject when I prodded one. Still, I wasn't sold on the idea of shoving Jazz and Cyrus through a mirror into God-knew-what—and if the other djinn were anything like Ian, they wouldn't exactly throw a welcome party. "What about the rest of the clans? How many humans do you have kicking around over there now?"

"They will not be harmed."

"You didn't answer the question."

He paused. "Humans have crossed to the djinn realm in the past."

"And? What happened to them?"

"They . . . decided to stay."

I didn't like the hesitation. "Did they, or was the decision made for them? Come on, Ian. I know you're leaving something out here."

He uttered a sharp string of djinn words. Looked away. Finally, he said, "There are places between the realms that are thin. Natural bridges that can open by themselves. Occasionally, a human has stumbled through a thin place and into our realm."

"Really. Like what, the Bermuda Triangle?"

"That is one of them, yes."

Terrific. Amelia Earhart hadn't really disappeared. She'd just fallen into some djinn. "So what happens to them once they get there?"

"As I said, they generally decide to stay." Another long pause. "No djinn has ever sent a human to the realm intentionally."

"Great. You're really selling me on this plan of yours."

"They will be safe," Ian insisted. "Akila will protect them."

"See, that's why I'm worried. If they'll be safe, why will they need protection?"

"Donatti." Jazz reached up and brushed my shoulder. Her touch sent a jolt through me. "Ian says we'll be all right. I think we should trust him. Besides, what else can we do?"

My hands clenched the wheel. She was right—we'd run out of options. "You'd better know what you're doing, genie boy. I want them back in one piece. Well, two pieces. You know what I mean."

Jazz laughed. "I think I'll get to know a few more djinn guys while I'm there. You're cute when you're jealous, Houdini."

I grunted and forced back the grin trying to spread across my face. Cute. I could live with that.

CHAPTER 15

We rented a double-occupancy room at the Days Inn in Weedsport. Cyrus, who'd fallen asleep on the way, didn't wake when Jazz carried him in and laid him on one of two tightly made beds. At least the blankets matched, even if they did look like a bear had wandered in and vomited a forest on them.

I shut and locked the door. The room had a window that opened, but its two-foot proximity to the entrance negated its utility as an alternative escape route. If anyone came through that door, I'd have to move at somewhere around Mach 4 to make the window.

Ian drifted over to a wall-mounted mirror behind a low desk opposite the beds. He ran the fingers of one hand across the surface, then gripped both sides of the frame and pulled. The mirror just about popped off the wall. Frowning, he headed into the bathroom.

"This one will do," he called. "Give me a few moments." The door slammed, and the lock engaged.

Jazz stood beside the bed, looking down at Cyrus. "What do you think, Donatti? Will we make it through this?"

"Absolutely." It was the most confident word I could come up with. I hoped it made up for the lie it formed—certainty had deserted me somewhere between Skids's trunk and Trevor's basement. "Ian knows what he's doing."

"I meant all of us." She faced me with resignation. "Including you."

I didn't want to think about whether I'd make it. Too easy to come to a negative conclusion. At this point, the best I could offer was the truth. "I don't know."

"When we're gone . . . what are you going to do?"

"Kill Trevor." *Or die trying.* I'd prefer option one.

"Donatti, please. Be serious. I really want to know." She stepped toward me, stopped. "You've never killed anyone. You go out of your way to make sure you don't. You're the most compassionate thief in history. Hell, I bet you've never even squashed a spider."

"Have too." I caught myself looking for one just to prove it—and realized she might be right. "Okay, but I've definitely swatted flies. And I shot a guy once."

She frowned. "Accidentally. In the foot. With a beebee gun. I remember the story."

"It was dark. I thought it was a rat." This wasn't helping my case. I let out a long sigh. "All right. What do you want to hear? That I think Trevor makes Hitler look like a saint? That he could give Satan some competition in the twisted bastard department? All that's true, but this is personal. The shitbag told his thugs to kill you and bring Cyrus in so he could torture him to death in front of me. Trevor won't stop unless he's dead. So I'm going to make him dead."

A smile curved her mouth. "I believe you."

"Good." At the moment, she probably had more confidence in me than I did. I wasn't wired for killing. The idea of taking someone's life was physically repulsive. Thinking about it brought cold sweat and the urge to reach down my throat and rip my own guts out. I understood part of the reason. My first time out, I'd watched my then-partner drop a bystander with a single bullet just because the man had seen his face. I'd seen the light leave the dying man's eyes. Had nightmares about that moment for a month. And sworn I'd never be the one to pull the trigger.

I thought I could get away with it this time, because I didn't see Trevor as human. I was pretty sure I'd have no qualms over crushing a snake bent on murdering me and everyone I cared about.

"Donatti, I'm having second thoughts."

I looked at her. "About what?"

"The mirror thing. Cutting out. Everything." Her features struggled with emotion. Most of it was rage. "Not that I don't trust you . . . well, maybe I don't completely, but that's not it. That bastard killed my sister. Now he's trying for my son." Her whole body clenched, a five-foot fist. "I don't want to run. I want to tear him apart and burn what's left."

My gaze traveled to the sleeping figure on the bed. I didn't have to say a word.

"I know," she said. "Cy comes first. There's no question about that, and I'll do what I have to for him. Even if it means leaving Trevor to you."

She emphasized *you* as if she suspected the average fourth-grader had a better shot at taking Trevor out than I did. So much for confidence.

"You know, that's a little insulting," I said without looking at her. "Is your opinion of me really that low?"

She didn't reply.

"I'll take that as a yes."

She let out a sigh. "I'm sorry. Really. It's not what I think about you that matters."

"Thanks a lot."

"No. I mean . . ." She laid a hand on my arm. "I need to make sure he doesn't hurt my son. Ever. When I saw Trevor holding that gun on him—damn it, I would've killed him right there if I could. Almost did. But that would have killed Cy, too." She closed her eyes and shuddered. "I have to know he'll never get the chance to finish what he tried to start."

"Jazz." I waited until she looked at me. "I won't let him get the chance."

She searched my face, and finally said, "Okay."

Not exactly the gushing gratitude I'd hoped for, but I'd take it. I slid an arm around her and, when she didn't slug me for it, pulled her close. "So what do you think about me? Since it doesn't matter, you can tell me, right?"

She groaned. "Donatti, this isn't the best time to talk about you and me."

"Why not? We've got a semiprivate room, already paid for."

"You're unbelievable."

"Thank you."

"That wasn't a compliment."

The bitterness in her voice reminded me how badly I'd screwed things up with her. I beat back a tsunami of regret. I knew damned well that trying to joke about this would only make things worse, but I couldn't stop myself. I didn't want to face the reality that my apologies had come three years too late. Of everyone I'd hurt in my life, she topped the list of mistakes for which I'd forever kick my own ass.

"I don't hate you, you know," she said gently.

For an instant, I thought Ian must have taught her some mojo I didn't know he had, because she'd read my mind. I hitched a smile. "I don't hate you, too—er, either. Wait. What I mean is . . ."

She smirked. "Shut up, Donatti."

A breath later, I had no choice but to obey the command. Her mouth stopped mine.

Three years dropped away, just like that. I knew her mouth so well—the feel of her lips, the taste of her tongue. Heat seeped from her, infiltrated my head, and traveled down, detonating tiny shocks through my body. Everything I'd missed came back. She felt so right. Like home.

Jesus. How could I have left this?

The bathroom door opened mid-kiss, and something in me wept at the impending loss. Probably my roaring libido. "Akila is ready for you." Ian didn't sound even a little contrite over the interruption. "Bring the child. You do not have to wake him, if you would prefer not to."

Jazz pulled away. "Don't just try to stay alive this time," she said. "Do it. If you die, I'll never forgive you."

"I promise," I lied with a smile. Not that I didn't appreciate her concern, but it wouldn't do much good. Sorry, Trevor, but you can't kill me because Jazz will hold it against me forever. Oh, yeah. That would give him pause—for about ten seconds, while he finished laughing.

"Well . . . here we go." She scooped Cyrus off the bed and headed for the bathroom. I followed and heard her sharp intake of breath just before I stepped in. She'd seen Akila.

I moved in closer, caught sight of the image in the mirror, and wondered again how in the hell Ian had scored a woman like her. With her dark hair and smooth bronze skin, she could've almost passed as Egyptian despite those strange whiteless eyes—but even Cleopatra had nothing on Akila.

Ian had drawn the same symbol as before, in blood on the upper left corner of the mirror. With no bullet wounds handy, he'd sliced his left index finger open to do it. I'd have to thank him later for not demanding my blood. That tingle of familiarity hit me again. Where had I seen the symbol before?

"Greetings, Jazz and Cyrus." The djinn woman's ethereal voice sounded stronger and clearer than last time. She looked more there, too. Must have been because Ian hadn't broken this mirror—though he probably still blamed me for that. "I am delighted that you will join me for a time. Please, come forward. There is nothing to fear."

Jazz glanced back at me and inched toward the mirror. "Hey," she said to the ghostly reflection. "It's, uh, nice to meet you."

"What beautiful eyes." Akila's smile would have made Miss America feel like a toad. "Are you a sorceress?"

"Am I what?"

"A sorceress. A mage." She inclined her head to one side. "Your eye coloring is a trait of a magic user, is it not?"

Jazz's brow furrowed. "Don't think so," she said. "I'm only magic behind the wheel, and that's pure skill."

Akila laughed. "Gahiji-an, luck has indeed favored your Donatti, to pair him with such a girl."

"I don't know how favored he is." Jazz flushed, but a smile lifted her lips. "Thank you. So, how do we do this?"

"You must pass through one at a time. It may be better for you to enter first." Ian rubbed a thumb over his cut finger and traced the symbol with fresh blood. "I want to ensure that the connection is as strong as I can make it. Let the thief hold the child while you cross over."

"Me, hold him?" I blurted.

Jazz smirked. "I don't see another thief in here, besides me."

"Um . . ."

"Relax. You won't drop him." Jazz half-turned, edged closer to me, and deposited Cyrus in my arms.

My son. I didn't worry about dropping him. I worried about letting him go. Holding him made everything real, and despite Jazz's injunction to live, I couldn't help feeling this first time would be the last. He still slept, with his lips curved apart and his eyes closed and fluttering. I stared at him and tried to memorize his face. It wasn't hard. His resemblance to Jazz was so strong he might have been a clone.

I wished I knew more about him. What he enjoyed playing with, his favorite foods, whether he liked to sing in the shower—well, probably the bathtub, in his case. Did he dress himself? Fall asleep watching cartoons? When did he take his first step, and what was his first word? I'd missed everything, and now I might never know anything.

"Hey, Jazz?"

A small frown surfaced on her face. "What's wrong?"

"Nothing. I just . . . what's his favorite color?"

"You mean Cy?"

"Yeah."

She paused and stopped frowning. "Brown," she said.

I smiled down at him. "Me, too."

Ian made a hesitant sound, then beckoned for Jazz. "Go

through," he said gently. "Akila will assist you on the other side."

Jazz swallowed and faced the mirror. "Through the looking glass," she whispered. "I hope I don't shrink. Can't afford to get any shorter." With a weak smile, she stretched an arm over the sink and touched fingertips to the mirror's surface. Ripples distorted Akila's image, and Jazz's fingers plunged through the glass like it was smoke.

"It's freezing!" Jazz yanked her hand back and stared at it. She gave me a nervous glance. "If anything happens . . . keep him safe."

"You'll keep him safe. Nothing will happen." I forced assurance into my voice and nodded at the mirror. "Go. You'll have him back in a minute."

Cyrus stirred and opened his eyes, as if he knew we were talking about him. He stared up at me and sighed. "Ga," he said, sounding almost reproachful. Either he'd decided that was my name, or it was baby language for *Geez, not you again.*

"Hey there. Your mom's gonna do a neat trick." I shifted him so he could see her. "Watch and learn, little man."

Jazz shook her head. "Here goes." With a final worried frown, she climbed up onto the sink, took a breath, and plunged through the mirror. The surface rippled and settled. And became a mirror again.

"Jesus. Where is she? Did she make it?" Holding Cyrus one-armed, I moved in front of the mirror and pushed a hand against the glass. Cold and unforgiving. Only my reflection stared back. "Ian. Please tell me it's supposed to do that."

"It is. Stand back." Ian squeezed new blood from his finger and retraced the symbol. Placing his palm in the center of the mirror, he closed his eyes and began chanting rapidly in his tongue. The surface darkened and appeared to fill with smoke. Akila's face emerged. Worry stitched her elegant features.

"You must hurry, Gahiji-an."

Ian slumped against the sink. I suspected he would have collapsed if it wasn't there. "The child, Donatti. Bring him here."

Nodding, I approached and turned Cyrus around. Ian finished and waved once toward the mirror. He steadied himself with both hands on the counter, and his head dropped forward as if it weighed a hundred pounds.

I lifted Cyrus onto the back of the sink. "You can go inside there now, just like Mommy did. She's waiting for you."

Cyrus looked back at me for a moment. Once again, I imagined his thoughts exceeded his spoken vocabulary: *You're crazy, Mister. Mirrors are made out of glass.* He put one hand on the surface, over one of Akila's eyes, and giggled when it went through. The other followed quickly. Laughing outright, he ducked and thrust his head into the rippling surface. The rest of him slid smoothly after, as though Akila had pulled him in from the other side.

I stared at my reflection in the mirror, returned to normal now that Cyrus was gone. "So that's it?" I said. "They're both okay, aren't they?" I glanced at Ian and did a double take. "Ian, what's wrong?"

Ian's complexion had gone ashen—in fact, it was almost gray. He looked out of place, like an old black-and-white actor superimposed on a Technicolor world. Sweat matted his hair and beaded at his temples. He drew a single, gasping breath, and a coughing fit overcame him. His knees buckled. He dropped to the floor, bouncing off the edge of the sink on the way down with a sharp crack that sounded extremely painful.

I moved to help him and froze when a shift in my peripheral vision commanded attention. The mirror. Smoke swirled behind the glass and slowly took the form of a face.

It wasn't Akila.

"Uh, Ian . . ."

Ian shook his head and struggled to his feet, his back to the sink. In the mirror, a stern male visage pulled itself together. This new djinn looked sixty or so in human years. I figured that made him around ten thousand. And his current level of pissed-off made Ian at his worst seem like a slightly grumpy guinea pig.

"Crud. Ian, I really think you should—"

"Gahiji-an." The reflection cut me off with a voice like a hammer on steel. "I might have known you were responsible for this disruption."

Ian flinched and jerked upright. Stiffening, he whirled to glare at the image. "Kemosiri. I see you are still in denial."

"Insolent whelp. How dare you show such disrespect?"

The djinn's ringing voice pierced the air. Heaviness clogged my throat. "Ian," I whispered. "What the hell happened?"

Ian ignored me along with Kemosiri's reprimand. "Where are the girl and the child?"

"Humans are not permitted in our realm, Gahiji-an. You know the law."

"God damn it, where are they?" I yelled at the mirror. "They'd better be all right, or I'll come through there and kick the—"

"Silence the human."

Ian gestured at me. My empty threat continued unvoiced: *living shit out of your magical ass, djinn or not.* It took a few seconds for my brain to realize that my mouth had stopped moving. I glowered at Ian and lobbed a handful of wordless barbs his way.

"Hold your tongue, thief. You will only make things worse," he said under his breath. Another gesture, and control of my lips returned.

I kept them shut.

Ian faced the mirror. "I'll have a word with you, Kemosiri. Your selective blindness has gone on long enough."

"You'll not have a word. I will accept nothing less than absolute proof of your foolish imaginings." The image flashed a cruel smile and added a long statement in djinn.

Ian blanched. "You cannot . . ."

"Those are the conditions. And regarding these humans, the Council will decide their fate. Any others you send will be executed immediately."

"Don't you fucking touch them." The word *executed* banged around in my head, obliterating any restraint I might have still possessed. I launched myself at the mirror and realized the older djinn had disappeared seconds before imminent impact with solid glass.

Ian snagged the back of my shirt and arrested my momentum, saving me from multiple lacerations and a hell of a room bill. His reflexes weren't enough to stem my murderous rage. I diverted it to him.

"You son of a bitch. Call this a good idea? Get them back, now! Who the hell was that bastard, and why didn't you say something about him before?"

He flinched like I'd slapped him. "That bastard," he said slowly, "is the leader of the Bahari clan. And Akila's father."

CHAPTER 16

Before I could interrogate Ian, he passed out.

Nothing gradual about it. One minute, he stood in front of me, alert but still looking like reconstituted death. The next, he was facedown on the bathroom floor.

"Ian." I knelt and gripped his shoulder, shook him. No response. Christ, was he even breathing? I had no idea whether djinn had pulses. Reasoning that if he could bleed there had to be a heart to keep things flowing, I held two fingers to his neck and found a slow, steady beat.

At least I wouldn't have to attempt mouth-to-mouth.

I straightened and stared at the mirror, as if it might tell me what to do next. Only my reflection greeted me—an ordinary, unremarkable face made distinctive by the smudges and scrapes that marked my recent encounter with Trevor and an expression that would have consigned me to a few lifetimes behind bars if cops were allowed to make arrests for suspicious appearances. Bloodlust and helpless frustration didn't combine attractively.

Despite knowing what I'd find, I reached out and rested a

hand on the mirror. Cold, smooth glass met my touch. No high and mighty human-hating djinn materialized to taunt me with my complete inability to do a damn thing for Jazz and Cyrus.

No Akila appeared to assure me that they would be all right. Or to tell me how to revive her unconscious husband. I'd just have to wing it.

I crouched beside Ian and arranged him on his back, with his limbs as straight as I could make them. At the least, I'd try to get him onto a bed. Hooking my arms under his, I stood and dragged him—or tried to, anyway. He weighed about as much as a pickup truck full of rocks, and moving him felt like hauling said truck by the front bumper. With the emergency brake on.

Then I made it across the tiled bathroom floor, onto the carpet, and it got worse.

By the time I reached the closest bed and heaved Ian onto the mattress in a tangle of loose limbs, he'd begun to come around. Sort of. A low growl idled in his throat, as if he'd started the change to his wolf form but stopped at the vocal cords. He stirred, straightened a leg. A long, slender object fell from a coat pocket and hit the floor with a solid thud.

The sound seemed to galvanize him. His eyes flew open and found me. "Kemosiri. Is he gone?"

"Yeah."

A blast of harsh sounds issued from his lips. I assumed they were curses. "We must go. Find his proof. Akila . . ."

"Whoa. Hold it." Not only did I have no clue what he meant, but my brain could barely process words, much less respond with them. Exhaustion and draining adrenalin conspired to push me toward gibbering-idiot territory. I was sick of being in the dark about everything Ian concerned himself with. And I had to know what was going on beyond the mirror. Whether they would be safe. *One thing at a time.* "First of all, you dropped something."

Quick as a tripped alarm, Ian snagged my wrist and prevented me from bending to retrieve it. "I will get it myself," he said.

I sensed reluctance beneath the steel in his tone, of the I-don't-want-you-seeing-that variety. Naturally, this meant I had to. "No, it's okay. I'm right here," I said. "I'll pick it up."

"Don't." He came close to moaning. His fingers gripped harder.

"No more secrets, Ian. You're going to level with me from now on."

I pulled away from him. The object had slid on the low-pile nylon carpet and into the shadows under the bed. Kneeling, I felt along the floor until my fingers brushed something solid. I brought it into the light, and my breath left in a rush as if I'd taken a blow to the gut.

A full minute passed before I could speak.

"You son of a bitch. This is your fault. All of it." I stood slowly. My head throbbed, and my hand shook as it clutched an old dagger, the item I'd stolen for Trevor . . . which Ian had apparently stolen from me.

The bastard really had been following me for a while, at least since the day after I lifted it. Maybe longer. Shock prevented me from taking any sudden actions, which probably would have included kicking the shit out of him, if I thought it'd do any good.

Ian pushed himself into a seated position. He didn't say anything. A smart move on his part.

"What the hell is wrong with you? You must have known

this is what Trevor's after. None of this would have happened if you'd just left me alone. Now Jazz is who knows where, and maybe they'll kill her and my son. And I'm stuck here with you."

Ian didn't interrupt or try to defend himself. I barely knew what I was saying. Pacing away, stalking the length of the room, I inspected the knife again: a standard utility piece, plain and unremarkable, housed in a tarnished iron sheath. Heavy and practically useless. The blade probably wasn't even sharp. I drew it out and proved myself wrong. It was definitely unusual—I'd never seen a copper knife before. Like the pendant Trevor wore, it seemed ancient, but the blade gleamed as if time had never touched its surface.

"Why did you take it?" I demanded. "I don't even know why Trevor wanted this worthless piece of . . ." I stopped. Stared at him. I may not have read the classics, but I'd seen the Disney version of Aladdin. "This is your tether."

"Yes."

"Trevor wants me, so he can get to you."

"Yes."

I sat down. Didn't care where I landed. It happened to be the floor. "Shit."

"Agreed." Ian eased his legs over the side of the bed and leaned forward, arms propped on his thighs. "Though I do not expect you will believe it, I am truly sorry for the deception. I saw no other way to slow them down."

"But what are they doing? And who's they? I don't understand any of this." I managed to stand and make my way to the other bed. "Tell you what. You level with me, right now, and I'll believe your apology. Hell, I'll even forgive you. I'm feeling magnanimous."

"Are you, now?" Ian sighed. "Very well. *They* are the Morai. They wish to rule my realm. And yours."

"What? Wait a minute. They're trying to take over the world?"

"More or less."

"Jesus Christ. I need a cigarette." I patted my pockets to make sure I still had some and scanned the room for something that'd work for an ashtray.

Ian gave me a dry look. "I believe this is a nonsmoking room."

"Criminal. Don't care." I did care, under normal circumstances, but my nerves were already shot from sending Jazz and Cyrus over to Wonderland. Hearing that a bunch of evil djinn wanted to rule the world definitely did not help. I grabbed the ice bucket off the desk, sat back down, and lit up. "Okay. If these assholes want to take over the world, why haven't they just done it? I mean, we're human. They're not. They're magic, and we can't kill them."

"They dare not risk the wrath of the Council. They must control the djinn realm first."

"Kemosiri said something about the Council. I take it they're your government."

"Yes. The ruling body of the djinn." The disgust in Ian's voice could've curdled milk. "Only the noble clans are permitted to seat the Council. The Morai are not among them. Nor are the Dehbei. And Kemosiri occupies the highest seat."

"That bastard's in charge of all the djinn?"

Ian nodded slowly. "The Council is rife with corruption. They can be bought, or silenced, with favors and wealth. It has been so for thousands of years. Kemosiri is the worst of them."

"And he's your father-in-law." I flicked ash and took a new drag. "Lucky you."

"Indeed. He has never been pleased that his daughter is bonded with a barbarian."

"Ouch." I had a feeling that *not pleased* was an understatement. *Barbarian* didn't sound like a friendly insult. "So, your Council makes sure none of the djinn tries to conquer the humans."

"It is among their concerns, yes." He crossed his arms and stared at his feet. "That is why the Morai seek to gain control. They would once again be able to do as they please—there and here."

I picked up on the important word in that statement. "What do you mean, again?"

"They have tasted power in your realm before." He looked up, his features grim. "The Morai were once gods among humans. Your Greeks and Romans worshipped them. Feared them. And with good cause."

"Are you saying Zeus and Apollo and those guys were *Morai*?"

"I am."

"Christ." A cigarette wasn't going to cut it. "Got a beer on you?"

"Not this time, thief."

I scowled and dragged on my smoke. This was crazy. All that fate-of-the-world crap belonged in stories about prophecies and ancient evil, not out here cutting takeover deals with nutjob fences like Trevor.

Then again, so did the djinn.

"All right," I said. "How'd they stop them last time?"

Ian shook his head as if he didn't want to tell me. "With the

Morai playing at gods and other clans inciting . . . certain incidents of massive destruction among humans, the Council sent the combined forces of several clans here to bring every djinn back. They then forbade the use of tethers to travel between realms. Except, of course, for certain members of the noble clans who were permitted under the guise of research." The contempt he infused the last word with suggested that they meant research in the same way Victor Frankenstein meant to cure death.

I frowned. "But they're here now. Did they just decide to ignore the whole forbidden thing, or what?"

"No. Without the backing of the Council, it is nearly impossible to move between realms. The creation of a tether involves air magic, a strength of the Bahari. The Morai use fire magic. They can perform the binding spell for a tether, but it is temporary, and should the spell break down while a djinn is still in this realm, that djinn dies."

Now things really didn't make sense. "So how'd they do it?"

Ian's jaw clenched. "The Council banished them here."

"What the hell? Why would they do that, after they pulled them out for fucking everything up?"

"Because of the clan wars."

"Clan wars," I repeated. "Do I even want to know?"

Something that looked a lot like pain flashed in his eyes. "The Morai felt they had been humiliated by the Council when they were forcibly removed from this realm. At the time, they could not retaliate, but they spent centuries preparing for revenge. They practiced inbreeding to produce more offspring. They trained every member of their clan, male and female, from birth as soldiers. They developed and perfected powerful spells intended to cripple and to kill. And they planned a massive assault on the noble clans."

Patient bastards. But with the djinn's ridiculously long life spans, maybe centuries wasn't such a long time. "I take it they lost."

"In a manner of speaking." Ian lowered his arms, and his hands clenched hard enough to whiten his knuckles. "They were defeated but not without great losses to . . . other clans."

I hated to ask, but I had to. "What other clans?"

For a moment, Ian didn't answer. He closed his eyes and drew a deep breath. "Geographically, my clan, the Dehbei, was nearest to the Morai. We did not trust them and frequently sent spies to ensure that they would not attempt to conquer our village, as they had others. We learned of their plans to attack the nobles mere days before they intended to mobilize." A muscle jumped along his jaw. "The Dehbei leader, Omari-el, insisted that we warn the Council. Twenty of us set out immediately for the palace."

"When you say us, did that include you?"

"Yes. I was among them, as was Omari-el." He looked at me, and his eyes blazed with anguish. "The Morai also had spies. When they discovered we had gone to warn the nobles, they . . ." His breath hitched. "They diverted to our village on their way to the central lands. They slaughtered everyone there. Male, female, child. And then burned what remained to the ground."

"Jesus, Ian. I . . ." No wonder he hated them so much. "I'm sorry."

He made a weak, dismissive gesture. "Our party did reach the palace first. Some of the Council, Kemosiri in particular, refused to believe us. The word of barbarians meant little to those bloated and pampered louts. Only when another noble clan, the Kelimei, reported seeing the army of Morai did they decide to prepare. It was nearly not enough. Both sides suffered heavy casualties." He shifted on the bed, and his shoulders slumped. "But they were defeated, and those Morai who survived were sealed inside tethers and sent here."

"Well, that was fucking brilliant of them." My forgotten cigarette had burned out. I dropped it into the ice bucket and fired up a fresh one. "They didn't want the dangerous clan over there, so they dropped them on a world full of defenseless humans. Remind me to thank Kemosiri. Preferably by breaking something important, like his skull."

"It was a terrible decision. However, the tethers were supposed to have remained sealed. I will not excuse the actions of the Council, but if it were not for the greed of humans, the insatiable lust for power, the Morai would not have been unleashed."

"Come on, Ian. You really expect me to believe humans somehow let a bunch of djinn out of their tethers? We don't do magic. Well, I guess I do, sort of, but . . . hold on." I couldn't believe I hadn't thought of this before. "How many descendants are running around here?"

Ian gave a bitter laugh. "Descendants did not release the Morai. It is a complicated process that requires a great deal of power. Not so simple as rubbing a lamp." He smirked. "There was magic here, long ago. Earth magic. And there were human sorcerers who had learned to wield it. They released the first of the Morai and attempted to enslave them, to use them as familiars. They failed."

"Uh-huh. Like Merlin and shit."

"Merlin, though that was not his true name. Nicolas Flamel. Rasputin, the last great sorcerer. A few others. But once a handful of Morai had been loosed, they no longer needed the human mages. They developed ways to free their kin them-selves, mostly through blood spells. They formed human cults and demanded mass sacrifices. Eventually, your world forgot its own magic, but it no longer mattered. The Morai had already gained a hold. And they have been growing in strength since."

I shook my head. I'd always known the world was a messed-up place, but this was beyond bizarre. *Twilight Zone* stuff. I couldn't exactly refuse to accept it, because I'd seen plenty of evidence—but that didn't mean I had to like it. "So basically," I said, "you came here to save the world. Right?"

All of the exhaustion vanished from him and left pure rage. "I am here because of Kemosiri," he said through gritted teeth. "When the worm finally realized we spoke the truth about the Morai coming to attack the Council, coward that he is, he pan-icked. The Bahari fancy themselves scholars, while the Dehbei are warriors. Omari-el would have given our assistance anyway. But Kemosiri deemed it necessary to force us into his service." He paused and shuddered with fury. "He cast a powerful en-chantment on Omari-el. A curse, called the *ham'tari*. It is a truth spell that binds the bearer to a promise, on pain of death. And the promise he extracted was the complete destruction of the Morai at the hands of the Dehbei."

"My God," I said. "What an utter dick."

Ian nodded in terse agreement. "Omari-el was killed dur-ing the battle. The Morai general, Lenka, murdered him when Omari-el attempted to negotiate for Kemosiri's life. How-ever, the great Council leader still held us to the terms of the *ham'tari*. Only twelve Dehbei survived the clan wars, and when the djinn learned that the Morai had escaped their tethers in this realm, Kemosiri had us banished here to finish the task he could not. He did deign to send a small contingent of Bahari to assist us. All of them young and inexperienced. Shamil and Taregan were among them."

I remembered Shamil. The battered shell Trevor kept chained in his basement. "Who's Taregan?"

"He was a friend, once. He and I had a . . . parting of ways."

I opened my mouth to ask what happened and got interrupted by a Gestapo-style pounding on the door of the hotel room.

My gut told me that whoever was out there wasn't the smoking police.

CHAPTER 17

I needed a weapon. I grabbed Ian's tether first, but a gut feeling told me that was a bad idea. So I did something even worse—I handed it back to him.

He accepted it with a doubtful expression, as if he suspected treachery. No time to explain that I did, too. "You should disappear," I whispered.

Ian nodded and vanished.

The knocking repeated. I crept toward the door with one hand in my pocket, closing around the knife formerly known as Pope's. A look through the peephole revealed a blue-clad motel employee bearing a clipboard. Early thirties, brown hair and blue eyes. The name stitched on his shirt was George.

I didn't trust him. He lacked that certain minimum-wage-isn't-enough-to-put-up-with-this-shit vibe most third-rate-motel staff put out.

He knocked again. "Mr. Davis?" He used the name I'd given at the front desk to check in. "I'm sorry to disturb you, sir. We need your signature for the deposit agreement."

That almost sounded credible. I hadn't signed anything

when we got here. Maybe he was just an employee—they probably weren't used to people paying in cash.

But I still wasn't going to open the door.

I kept my grip on the knife and moved back, hoping he'd go away. There was a longer pause, then more knocking. "Mr. Davis?"

Just when I'd decided to say something brilliant, like I'd go to the office and sign the damn thing later, the door emitted the distinctive electronic bleat that said it'd just been unlocked. It opened fast, and the guy strode in brandishing his clipboard at me.

I almost laughed—until I saw the muzzle of a gun under the board.

Crud. Another smart thug. He stood less than five feet from me, and he'd already closed the door behind him. No way I could pull the knife before I got shot. I settled for glaring at him and hoping Ian could come up with a brilliant idea. Preferably one that didn't involve me bleeding.

"Hands out, please," he said.

I complied with a frown and tried to figure out what kind of thug said *please*.

He tossed the clipboard in my direction. Like an idiot, I grabbed it out of the air. Maybe I could use it as a shield if he fired on me. It might slow a bullet down by half a second.

"I take it your name isn't George," I said, deliberately not looking in the direction Ian should be. *Do something, damn it.*

"No. It's Quaid. And you're a hard man to find, Mr. Donatti." He reached behind his back and produced a set of handcuffs. "You do know why I'm here, don't you?"

"Yeah. Trevor's too good to come after me himself. You know, I thought he'd be running out of thugs by now."

His confusion lasted only an instant. "Maybe you should be grateful I found you before these thugs," he said calmly. "I'm collecting you for theft. You'll probably be safer in jail."

Shit. If he was a cop, he would've flashed a badge by now. And he'd said collect, not arrest. That left exactly one possibility. "You're a bounty hunter."

"Actually, I prefer the term 'bail enforcement agent,' though technically you're not a skip. There's a fairly large personal reward being offered for you by the rightful owner of a copper dagger, which is currently in your possession." Quaid flicked open a cuff one-handed. "I don't suppose you're going to come quietly."

I decided to skip the small talk and smashed the clipboard down on his gun hand.

The gun thumped to the floor. I shoved Quaid hard and kicked the weapon away. By the time I realized the bounty hunter hadn't moved much, he'd found a new weapon—handcuffs that doubled as brass knuckles. His metal-enhanced fist felt like a wrecking ball when it rammed my gut. I dropped, gasping, and tried to scuttle back.

That was when the pepper spray hit my chest.

I didn't scream. Couldn't breathe enough to get sound out. I had time to wonder why he hadn't gone for my eyes before I realized it didn't matter. My face was on fire, and the tears streaming from my eyes weren't putting it out. Burning mucus streamed from my nose. I would've been disgusted if it hadn't hurt so much.

Something—probably a foot—pushed me flat on the floor. A hand grabbed my wrist and forced my arm back.

"Release him." The voice wasn't Quaid's.

To his credit, the bounty hunter didn't react strongly to

what must have been the startling sight of Ian materializing out of nothing. He did, however, release me.

"Took you long enough," I panted. Righting myself proved difficult, but I managed to gain my feet. Fuzzy shapes swam before my eyes. I swiped a palm under my nose and cringed. "Can you cuff him to something?" My voice wheezed from my swollen throat. I hoped I'd articulated enough for him to understand. I heard footsteps, then clanks and clicks.

"You're only delaying the inevitable," Quaid said, still as calm as a hot bath. "I'll find you again. It would be much simpler for you to just give up now. I'll go easier on you than your thugs or the police."

I shook my head and blinked a few times. My eyes refused to stop tearing, but my vision cleared a little. Now the smudges had different colors. Ian had chained the bounty hunter to the headboard of the first bed in the room. He sat on the floor, watching both of us with an expression that suggested he actually expected me to take him seriously. It creeped me out.

"Sorry, Quaid," I said. "I'm really busy right now. You'll just have to bust me later, okay?"

He nodded once. "I'll take you up on that, Mr. Donatti."

I turned toward a blurred, Ian-shaped smudge and wished for a tissue. "Let's get out of here. Where's the door?"

Ian grabbed my arm and pulled me outside. The door closed. "Why did you not tell me about this man?" he said.

"I thought he'd make a fun surprise," I snapped. "Christ, Ian, I've never seen him before in my life. Why'd you wait so long to stop him?"

"You seemed to have things under control."

"Right. Before or after he pulled the gun?" I took a few

steps and walked straight into a light pole that jumped in front of me. "Crud." I rubbed my forehead. "Who put that thing there?"

Something resembling a laugh escaped Ian. "You look terrible."

"Thanks." I sidestepped the pole and headed for a big dark blur I assumed was the parking lot. A click sounded behind me. I spun around and fell against Ian. He grabbed me but didn't let go.

Quaid stood on the sidewalk just outside the room, frowning at us. He'd retrieved the gun. Crud. Why hadn't I thought to tell Ian to get his keys? I almost said something before I realized we were probably invisible. Assuming this was the same deal as the wolf, I figured we'd be all right if I kept my big mouth shut.

Still, the bounty hunter seemed to be looking right at us. Quaid stood motionless in front of the door. His nostrils flared a few times, almost as though he was smelling for us, like a dog. He glanced to both sides, moved forward, and raised his gun.

I couldn't tell whether he had a bead on us. And I didn't want to find out.

Ian tensed and jumped, hauling me into the air like an arcade crane machine extracting a stuffed prize. Oh, good. And me without my barf bag. I indulged in a few seconds of hating him for flying off like this, but the bullet that passed just under my feet changed my mind.

This time, we didn't make it far. Ian wobbled through the air, no more than twenty feet above the ground. He brought us down in a patch of woods within sight of the hotel and let go considerably sooner than I expected.

Falling five feet wouldn't have hurt so much if I'd known

it was coming. My face wasn't designed for shock absorption. Ian saved himself from a stern lecture by crashing down next to me in what looked like a more uncomfortable position, mostly because of the broken stump he bounced off before coming to rest in a crooked heap.

I moaned. Ian didn't.

I scrambled up, moved to him, and tried to check for visible damage. Not that I had much in the way of visibility. No blood was apparent, but he'd taken on that Charlie Chaplin pallor again. I crouched and said, "Hey. Do you need, uh, contact or something?"

He opened his eyes. "I cannot amplify . . . what is not there." He sounded as if he'd run the Boston Marathon.

"What?" I rocked back and stared at him. "You mean you don't have any mojo? Why?"

Ian shifted an arm and pushed himself into a seated sprawl. "Sustaining a portal between realms requires a massive amount of power. I have just done it twice."

"How do you get it back?"

"Time."

Perfect. The one thing we definitely didn't have. "Okay. Did that guy see us back there? I mean, we were invisible, right?"

"Yes. And I do not think he could actually see us. He seemed to be tracking with other senses. Or perhaps he is simply lucky."

"Great." At once, Quaid had moved out of fringe worry territory and approached full-blown threat. I shifted until I could almost see the motel. The blurring had more or less eased, and now everything resembled a double-exposed photo taken with too much flash. A figure that had to be Quaid approached our spit of trees. He moved slowly. Ambled, really. As if he didn't have a care in the world.

"We need to get out of here," I said. "Can you walk?"

"Probably."

"Well, that's encouraging." I offered a hand, but he ignored it and stood on his own.

The last thing I wanted was to move around, but hiding out here would be like trying to get lost in a post office lobby. "We need wheels," I announced.

Ian gave me a doubtful look. "Your woman's van will be recognized. We cannot risk it."

"I know. We're gonna have to boost a car."

"You want to steal one?"

"Yeah. Like, now."

"Fine." Ian sighed. "Does it not bother you to steal from other people?"

"Look, we don't have time for an ethics lecture." I shoved him in the opposite direction from the hotel. "I'm a thief. It's what I do. Besides, I'd never steal from somebody who couldn't afford it."

"How admirable of you."

"That's me. A modern-day Robin Hood. Come on."

We set off south, toward the smell of money and away from Quaid, sticking to the fringe of woods. The usual little prickle from my conscience had become a full-blown chafing, thanks to Ian's reprimand. Stealing had never bothered me before.

I decided to hate him for a while. It made me feel better.

A good fifteen minutes passed bounty-hunter-free. Ian looked a few shades better, and I could almost see the edges of the world again. I glanced behind us, didn't spot any movement. Then again, my vision wasn't exactly a hundred percent.

"Ian," I said softly. "Is he still close?"

Ian blinked and tossed a look over his shoulder. "I do not see anyone."

"Good. Maybe he gave up." Doubtful. Still, I managed to drop my guard a bit. "Soon as we hit civilization, we'll grab a ride."

"Wonderful. While we are stealing cars, perhaps we should rob a bank as well."

"Shut up. You can't fly, you don't have enough juice to disguise the van, and we can't walk clear of the danger zone."

Our path had drifted closer to the narrow access road leading out of the travel center. In the distance ahead, a series of squarish blobs suggested a commercial district. Perfect.

Something hummed nearby. Tires on pavement. I twisted around, squinted back, and saw a vehicle I couldn't identify bearing down on us. Instinct suggested this was Quaid.

The shot fired from the front window confirmed my hunch.

"Move!" I grabbed Ian and pulled him along, full speed away from the road. The scruff of trees thinned and stopped altogether, and soon we were pounding over the soggy ground of a pseudo-swamp. Dead bushes bleached to skeletal sticks thrust from the ground at irregular intervals. I didn't bother avoiding them. Cold muck splashed my jeans, and the occasional hard step sprayed droplets in my face, adding to the already delightful blend of dried tears and snot. The stench threatened to close my throat permanently.

I kept half an ear out for the sound of Quaid crashing through behind us. Didn't hear him, but my own heart pounded loud enough to drown a rock concert.

Eventually, I lost forward momentum when Ian came to a

dead halt. I jerked the arm I still held and damned near went facedown in the mud.

"Stop, thief," Ian whispered. "Be silent. Even if he catches up to us, he cannot see us."

I stared at my hand, his arm. The invisibility sheen surrounded us, as it had back at Trevor's. "Thought you didn't have any power left," I whispered back.

"I do not. You are doing this."

"Holy—" I clamped my mouth shut, afraid I'd break whatever I was doing if I kept yapping. Slowly, I turned my head back in the direction of the road. A figure I assumed to be Quaid was moving away. He'd almost reached the trees and his car beyond them.

I watched until the car disappeared from sight and let go of Ian. "Damn. Wish I knew how that worked. It'd be a hell of a lot handier if I could control it."

"No doubt it would assist you with your work," Ian said. This time, he didn't sound quite so pissed.

I smirked and took in the drying filth that coated me from the waist down. "I don't suppose you could conjure up a shower?"

"No."

"Didn't think so. Let's get out of here."

Despite my hatred of flying, I probably wouldn't have minded levitating a little. Walking back through the swamp sucked worse than running.

SMALL TOWNS NEVER CEASED TO AMAZE ME. OUT OF THE FOUR cars parked behind a little diner down the road from the hotel, three were unlocked. I decided on the newer Acura sedan, because it looked just expensive enough to carry theft insurance, and lured Ian into the passenger seat with a promise to make sure the owner got it back after we'd escaped with our lives.

How I'd keep that promise, I had no idea. I only hoped we'd survive long enough to figure it out.

I opened the driver's door and shoved the seat all the way back. "Do me a favor," I said, rummaging through pockets for the butterfly. "Tell me if anybody comes out of there. This shouldn't take long."

Ian stared down at me. "What are you doing?"

"Baking a cake." I found the blade and pried the cover off the steering column. "What's it look like? I'm getting the damned car started."

"Must you break it to get it started?"

"Will you just shut up and play lookout? We're not gonna get very far if we get arrested."

"Fine."

Under the weight of Ian's we-do-not-approve vibe, I stripped and twisted the red wires together, then exposed the ignition wire and sparked it. The engine revved and stopped twice before it finally caught. I climbed in and pumped the gas a few times, glanced at Ian. "Seatbelt," I said.

He fastened it with slow deliberation. "It seems superfluous to follow traffic laws when you are stealing a vehicle."

"Yeah, well, safety first." I adjusted the seat and buckled my own. "Let's roll."

We made it onto the road without incident. I headed for the Thruway but changed my mind halfway there. Easier for cops to spot a stolen vehicle on an open highway—and my luck dictated that if we got pulled over, the jake would be on Trevor's payroll. Instead, I hit Route 31 and swung east, hoping for a bright idea about where the hell to end up.

Wherever it was, it couldn't be far. With zero sleep in forty-eight hours and my stint in Trevor's basement, not to mention pepper spray, stimulating romps through woods and swamps, and a handful of Ian-induced adrenalin spikes, I'd passed empty six crises ago.

I glanced at Ian. His color had more or less returned, and he looked as normal as I supposed a djinn in a human suit could. "Hey. You know how to drive?"

Ian frowned. "Why?"

"Because I can't see too well, and I'm beat. Any minute, I'm going to start weaving all over the road, and we'll attract unwanted attention, if I don't ram us into something first."

"Oh. Perhaps we should find a place to rest, then."

"So you can't drive?"

"No."

"Great." I leaned over and switched the AC on full blast. Frigid air poured from the vents as if it was being piped straight from Alaska. "I need coffee or something. Tell me if you see a Dunkin' Donuts."

"A what?"

"Never mind." I slowed and stopped for a red light, using the opportunity to scope the vehicles around us. Had to watch for tails. A green car and a white truck idled on the opposite side. Behind us, a rust-scarred Escort rolled to a stop ten feet back with a prolonged squeal. Bad brakes. I sympathized with the condition—must've replaced my pads three times in less than a year. Older Escorts ate brakes like candy.

The light turned. I went straight, and the Escort waited to hang a looey. We weren't being followed. Yet.

Ian crossed his arms and rubbed them. "This is freezing. How can you tolerate being so cold?"

"I have to stay awake somehow." I took another glance around. No tails. I didn't dare relax, though. "Once we've put some miles behind us, we're going to have to stop somewhere."

"We must keep moving."

"I need sleep."

Ian sighed. "Fine. Perhaps another motel?"

"No. Too risky. I'll find a place to pull off the road for a while and crash in here." A few more miles, and we'd hit El-bridge. I'd been through there once after a job in Syracuse and hidden in a huge public park for a while to let the heat die down. I could make it that far. Probably. After that, we'd have to make some decisions. Couldn't keep running forever.

"So. How long do we have until the Morai conquer the world and enslave humanity?"

Ian stared at me like he was trying to decide if I was serious. "At the moment, that is not possible," he said. "I have ensured that they cannot return to the djinn realm."

"Yeah, you said that before. How does it become possible? I'm guessing there's a chance somewhere."

He looked away. "It will be possible when there is no Deh-bei blood remaining in this realm."

"Why?" I stifled a yawn. "Is your clan the only one who can do that thing with mirrors?"

"No. Blood magic is a shared strength among all the djinn, because it is direct in nature." His features went blank. "When we were first banished here, we sought a way to contain the Morai. Under Kemosiri's terms, we could not return until every Morai had been destroyed. The twelve of us created a barrier between the realms through which no Morai could pass."

"That sounds . . . complicated."

He nodded. "The theory resembles that of your human

DNA. The spell refuses Morai blood and is kept functioning with Dehbei blood. It took all of us together to generate the enchantment, but the existence of any living Dehbei ensures that the barrier will not fall."

I thought I understood. I'd seen enough forensic cop shows to grasp the basics. "So they can't get back unless all of you die," I said. "Where's the rest of your clan?"

He flinched. And didn't answer me.

"Ian?"

His eyes closed. "Dead."

He whispered the word, but it felt as if he'd backhanded me with it. "All of them?" I croaked.

"Yes." His lips barely moved. "In our realm, killing one another is no simple task. Here it requires only possession of the correct tether. None of my clan had ventured to your realm, even before the Council banned travel between them, so we failed to lend this condition sufficient importance. The Morai did not." He swallowed hard. "In addition, they had learned to use humans to amplify blood magic. They had been here longer and were far more powerful. One by one, they destroyed us. And now, I am the last of the Dehbei."

All of the breath left me at once, and I almost crashed the damned car. I couldn't come up with a thing to say. Sympathy had never been my strong suit, and I didn't think *Sorry about your clan's impending extinction* would be appropriate. Jesus. If I was him, I'd have probably committed suicide three or four centuries ago.

Finally, I decided I had to say something. "How did you survive?"

He gave a bitter laugh. "I learned to use blood magic as well, though I did not stoop to the level of the Morai and force humans to drink my blood. Instead, I produced offspring with humans. Descendants who would carry my blood and allow me to amplify my power without the need to harm or enslave them."

I would've been pissed that he'd fathered a bunch of kids just to use them for magic, but he obviously hadn't had a choice there. "Why didn't the Morai do that? Make descendants, I mean."

"They cannot. The spell that binds us to our tethers also renders our fertility dormant. Only the stronger Bahari can undo this dormancy. Akila has done this for me." He looked down. "I had intended only to survive, but I soon realized there was another benefit to having descendants. They contain Dehbei blood. And should I be destroyed, the barrier will stand as long as my descendants remain."

A shiver crawled up my spine. Reluctantly, I said, "How many do you have?"

"Initially, I went too far," he said softly. "I had lost my entire clan, and my bloodlust for revenge drove me to crave power. As much as possible. I impregnated dozens of human women, as I mentioned before. For a time, it seemed I would succeed. No Morai could stand against me, and I alone reduced their numbers by half. They learned to hide from me rather than seek to destroy me directly. Eventually, they discovered what I had done and began to hunt down and kill my descendants."

"Hold on," I said. "I thought the djinn couldn't kill humans."

"It is possible under certain extreme conditions and then only when in animal form. But the Morai had no need to create these conditions. They simply used humans, who have no difficulty killing one another. Just as Trevor is being used in their attempt to destroy you."

As chilling as his explanation was, he still hadn't answered my question. "How many are left, Ian? How close are these bastards to overthrowing both of our worlds?"

I guessed the answer before he gave it. "You and your son are the last."

"Of course we are." My hands squeezed the wheel hard. Damn it, I never wanted this. I was just a two-bit thief. Saving the world wasn't on my to-do list. But I'd have to go through with it if I didn't want to die or get the son I'd just found out I had killed in the process.

My fantastic luck never let up.

After several moments of silence, Ian spoke without prompting. "They will be safe."

"Huh?" I knew he'd spoken English, but I must have missed something. Maybe I'd fallen asleep for a few seconds. Not a good sign. "What'll be safe?"

"Your woman, your son. Akila will protect them from the Council."

I nodded, my throat tight. Somehow I got the feeling that there was no one to protect Akila. "Thank you. That means a lot to me."

"I know." He clasped one hand over the other and rubbed his right thumb against the base of his left index finger, the motion absent and reflexive. A glowing band of golden light appeared. It shone brightly for a moment, then faded away. I wasn't sure how, but I knew right away what the band meant.

At least the djinn didn't have to worry about losing their wedding rings.

"When two djinn are bonded, it is for life," Ian said. "I am not certain whether human bonds embrace the same vows, but it is obvious you love this woman. Hold to the knowledge that you will be reunited." He turned to the window. "Distance can be overcome. Death cannot."

For the first time, I considered how hard this must be on Ian. They'd banished him for trying to save them, and he'd been separated from his wife for centuries. She'd obviously waited for him all this time. It had to be torture, never to touch each other, communicating with blood through cold mirrors or whatever else passed for a reflective surface . . .

The symbol. I knew I'd seen it before, and I suspected figuring out where would help. The recollection lurked somewhere in the fog just outside my sleep-deprived brain: crescent, dot, squiggle. Not drawn in blood but . . . carved? Maybe I'd seen it in a museum somewhere, though that didn't seem likely. I'd never been culturally inclined.

But I knew someone who was.

At once I remembered exactly where and how I'd seen the thing: Fremont. Lark, the mythology-obsessed hookup I'd damn near killed. His place was practically a museum anyway, so I hadn't given a second thought to the stone tablet he'd covered up fast when he noticed me looking. Twelve squares, bearing what looked to me like *Hieroglyphs for Dummies*. One had been Ian's symbol.

Twelve squares, for twelve Dehbei. Lark knew about the djinn.

He also hated my guts. I hoped being able to introduce him to a real live djinn would soften him up a little . . . at least enough to prevent him from killing me on the spot.

I grinned despite my exhaustion. When Ian gave me a look that suggested I'd lost my last few marbles, I said, "Ever been to Fremont?"

CHAPTER 18

Sycamore Point boasted acres of trails and paths—plenty of room to ensure a little privacy. I drove to a deserted spot near the back of the place, pulled the Acura offroad, and parked behind a massive evergreen. When I announced my intention to pass out, Ian didn't protest. In fact, he offered to keep watch while I slept in the backseat.

Somehow I wasn't surprised to wake two hours later and find him gone.

I hauled myself out and panned the area. Saw nothing but nature. Fantastic. I resolved to have a little talk with Ian about wandering off and leaving me asleep and defenseless against thugs, cops, and bounty hunters. Soon as I found him.

Sudden thirst drove me in the direction of water sounds. Maybe a little rehydration would clear my muzzy head. Still, two hours of sleep had done wonders for my attention span.

Now I could really concentrate on what deep shit we were in.

I spotted the source of the rushing sound through a clump of trees. A small brook ran through the grounds, complete with wooden footbridge and a few benches along the opposite bank. As I neared the bridge, another sound came in under the water's whisper. Foreign words, spoken low and fast. I stayed out of sight and looked for the source, though I suspected I knew.

The brook curved away from a reflecting pond several yards to my left. Ian lay on his stomach at the edge of the pond, staring into the surface like a cat mesmerized by fish. One hand trailed in the water. He said something, paused, shook his head.

I crept closer, until I could see the pond's surface and Akila's face just beneath it. She looked like someone had just shot her puppy.

Alarms shrilled through my head. I dropped caution and closed the distance in microseconds. "What happened?"

Ian stiffened as if my voice was a knife in his gut. "Must you creep up on me like that?"

"I'm a thief, remember? Stealth, surprise, all that shit." I sat next to him with a frown. "You know, you're a lousy lookout. I think you and I have different definitions of standing watch. To me, it means sticking around to make sure the bad guys don't kill me in my sleep."

"You were in no danger."

"Yeah. Sure." I glanced at Akila's reflection again. She'd tried to smile, but it was an empty funeral expression. A sorry-your-life-is-over kind of curve. *Jazz*, I thought immediately. "Tell me what's going on. Please."

"Nothing."

"Gahiji-an . . ." Akila whispered.

"Nothing," Ian repeated firmly. "I wanted to ensure that your woman and son were safe. They are. Now give me a few moments' privacy."

"Gahiji-an, you should tell him."

"It is not his concern." Ian closed his eyes. "Leave us, thief. I will join you in a moment."

I didn't budge. "Not until you spill. I thought we talked about this. We're in this together, remember?"

"How could I forget?" he said under his breath.

When he didn't elaborate further, Akila spoke in tight tones. "The Council has agreed to shelter them temporarily. However, they are—"

"Akila!"

"He must know." A flush colored her skin. "They have realized that the child carries Gahiji-an's blood. They seek the one who broke his dormancy and allowed him to create descendants in the human realm, as it is forbidden. Further, my father has entered a motion to extend Gahiji-an's banishment permanently. The Council debates this now."

Her desolate words kicked me in the teeth. "Ian, I can't . . . damn. I'm so sorry. I shouldn't have agreed to let you send them. Can't you cancel this, have them come back? I'll find a way to keep them safe."

Ian shook his head. "It is done, thief. And they will not be safe here. You know that."

"But . . ." I dropped to a whisper. "You can't stay here forever. I mean, what about your wife? You'll never see her again. Because of me."

"You are not at fault, Gavyn Donatti." Akila's voice shivered as a slight breeze rippled the water's surface. "This is my father's doing."

"Kemosiri would have found a way to accomplish this, even if I had not sent them," Ian said. "He hopes the Morai will destroy me here, but if I should survive, he wishes to ensure that I do not return. So my barbarian blood does not taint his lineage." He turned his attention back to Akila. "Perhaps you are better off without me, love," he whispered. "He would not make things so difficult for you then."

"Do not say such things." This time, there was no breeze to blame for the catch in her voice. "My discomfort is nothing compared with what he's put you through."

Ian lifted his head and gave me a cool stare. "You are still here."

"Um, yeah."

He sighed. "A moment, Donatti. Please."

"Oh. Right." I scrambled up and strode back toward the car. It wasn't easy, but I'd actually started to sympathize with King Grumpy—at least when it came to the women in our lives.

I LOCATED THE CAR AGAIN WITHOUT TROUBLE. BUT WHEN I opened the driver's-side door, something sharp stung the back of my neck. I slapped at it, expecting a bee or a wasp. Instead, I dislodged a slender object tipped with a metal point and capped with a crushed ball of white cotton. A dart.

I bent to pick it up—and my body kept going down. Muscles that had turned to water no longer responded to my mental demands to move. I was melting like the Wicked Witch.

"Whaargh . . ." I managed to garble before my mouth succumbed to the spreading lethargy. Curled on my side, unable to move, I watched a pair of sneakered feet enter my field of vision and stop. They seemed familiar.

The feet stepped over me. "Don't worry, Mr. Donatti. The effect is temporary."

Quaid. I tried to curse him, but the words in my head emerged as a stream of loose vowels. How in the hell had he found me so fast?

The bounty hunter flopped me onto my back and knelt. "I don't suppose you have it on you? Don't bother answering. I'll find out." He frisked me with thorough professionalism, extracting the few tokens I had left. After he removed my shoes and shook them, he rolled me facedown and started over from the top.

My eyes watered in defense against the blades of grass thrusting into them. I warbled a protest. In response, Quaid cuffed me and flipped me over again. He sighed down at me, shook his head, and hauled me up to prop my sagging torso against the side of the truck.

"That's an interesting trick your friend has, disappearing like that. But it doesn't look like you can do it without him." Quaid crouched in front of me and glanced up at the Acura. "Grand theft auto is a felony, you know. I'll search this vehicle for the dagger in a minute. However, while I have your attention, I think I'll attempt to reason with you."

I tried to laugh. All I produced was a wheeze.

"This is not a complicated situation, Mr. Donatti. I'm not out to get you. All I want is my employer's property returned. Just hand it over, and all of this will go away."

Another wheeze from me brought him up short. Dudley Do-Right here actually thought Trevor would find out he'd brought Ian's tether back to where I'd stolen it from, chalk it up as a loss, and forget about it. What kind of criminals did he usually chase—people who ripped tags off mattresses?

"I'm going to assume you disagree." Frowning, Quaid stood and peered into a side window of the sedan. "I will find it, and I will return it. That dagger doesn't belong to you. It belongs to my employer."

"Actually, it belongs to me."

Quaid whirled at the sound of Ian's voice. A meaty thud sounded, and the bounty hunter dropped unconscious on the grass.

"What a troublesome human."

I slurred indistinct agreement.

Ian made an exasperated sound. "Why are you still sitting there, thief? We must go before he returns to consciousness."

Glaring lost its effect with the inability to raise my head. *Can't move, jackass. A little help here, please.*

"Oh, for the love of the gods . . ." Ian reached down and pulled me to my feet. I sagged against him. "What is wrong with you, Donatti?"

"Aagh. Ee ohg ee." Didn't sound anything like *He shot me.* Drool filled my mouth and spilled over my lip, as it had when Trevor Tasered me. I gave a long sigh and tried to think louder. *I'm drugged. Can't move.*

"You are restrained."

Nice going, Einstein. How about the paralyzed part?

Ian held me back with one hand and gestured with the other. The cuffs opened and fell off. My arms flopped at my sides like wet spaghetti.

"Have you been poisoned?"

"Eh!"

Muttering, Ian moved his fingers again. Sensation flooded me within seconds. I stiffened and gasped. Ian removed his supporting hand, and I toppled over like a headshot victim.

"Thanks," I murmured into the ground. Pushing myself up required more effort than it should have. I gathered my scattered gear, stuffed my feet into my shoes, and snatched Quaid's cuffs. "Help me with him."

We dragged the inert bounty hunter to the nearest tree.

Quaid twitched a bit, and his eyes fluttered under his lids. After we'd secured him with his arms around the trunk behind him, I went through his pockets and located his keys. Not that he could unlock himself this time, but I wasn't taking any chances.

He came around while I worked the handcuff key off a ring with a plain brass tab that held several interesting items, including a few safe-deposit keys, a slim penknife, and a mechanical lock-pick set. Quaid took stock of the situation and offered a disappointed sigh. "All right. We'll do this the hard way."

"You think this is easy?" I pocketed the cuff key and dropped the ring into his lap. "Nice toys you have there, Quaid. How did you find me this time?"

He tried to shrug. "I suppose I'm just lucky."

"Uh-huh." I glanced around and spotted another vehicle far back along the park road. Had to be his. I'd search it on the way out. "Look. You've got to drop this gig, or you're going to get yourself killed. You're not the only one after this dagger—and like my friend said, it belongs to him." I couldn't believe the word *friend* had just left my lips in association with Ian. Whatever'd been on that dart must've snapped a few circuits somewhere.

Quaid smiled. "Oh, I know all about Mr. Maddock. He originally tried to purchase the dagger from my employer, and when his offer was refused, he hired you to steal it."

I cringed at the idea of anyone referring to Trevor as Mr. Maddock. "All right. If you know about Trevor, then you have to know why I can't take you up on arresting me. Don't get me wrong. It's tempting. I'm not enjoying this, and I hear they make a great pot roast in prison. But whether or not you get the dagger, Trevor's still going to kill me. And I really don't want to die." I decided not to go into the whole djinn thing. The less he knew, the better.

"Don't you think you're being a bit dramatic, Mr. Donatti? I'm sure Mr. Maddock wouldn't actually murder anyone."

"Oh, man. You . . ." I struggled to hold back laughter. "Yeah. He's a fine, upstanding citizen. Someday you might realize it's a good thing I got to you before him. Honestly, though, I hope you don't. Come on, Ian." I started for the car.

"Are you just going to leave me here?"

I turned. "The park rangers will find you before dark. Don't worry, Quaid. It's only temporary."

Quaid's assured gaze didn't leave me while I climbed in and drove away. I had no doubt he'd find me again. My life would've been so much easier if I just killed him, but I couldn't bring myself to do it. Only Trevor inhabited my list of people I wouldn't hesitate to murder.

I'd just have to hope I lived long enough to escape Quaid next time.

CHAPTER 19

When we'd put a few miles behind us, I broke the bad news to Ian. "He's got a GPS locator in his car."

"And this means what to us, exactly?"

"He's tracking us. That has to be how he found us so fast." I refused to believe Mr. Grand Theft Auto Is a Felony had some kind of psychic ability that led him straight to me. Maybe he was lucky, but luck didn't explain his performance so far. He knew exactly what he was doing. "He couldn't have bugged the vehicle, because he wouldn't have known I'd steal this one. Has to be on one of us. Ian, did he touch you at all back at the hotel?"

"No. Wait . . . yes. He grabbed my coat while I was securing him to the bed."

"Okay. Look for something you don't recognize. It'll be small, probably plastic."

After a minute, he held up a slim black square about the size of a driver's license.

I flashed a grim smile. "Jackpot."

"Should we destroy it?"

"No." I glanced out the window. Ahead, a sign announced five miles to Cortlandville. "I've got a better idea."

When we entered the town, I pulled around to the back of the first convenience store I saw. I left the engine running and turned to Ian. "Gimme that thing."

He handed it over with a wary expression. "What are you doing?"

"Throwing the dog off our scent." I ducked out and headed for the front entrance.

Inside the store, the young cashier didn't look up from the newspaper she was reading. There were two security cameras—one near the front of the store, the other above the beer coolers. Four customers occupied the place. A middle-aged man browsed the magazine stand, his gaze flicking up to the blacked-out skin rags encased in plastic on the top row as if he was trying to screw up the guts to touch one. In front of the soda display, a teenage couple huddled over a cell phone, laughing. An elderly woman shuffled down the center aisle and stopped occasionally to pick something up from a shelf, sneer at it, and put it back.

She'd be perfect.

I palmed the transmitter and started through the aisle next to the old lady. Keeping my head down, I stayed just ahead of her and waited. She grabbed something that rattled gently. A bottle of pills, I guessed. "Eight dollars," she grumbled aloud. "How is anyone supposed to afford anything these days? Eight dollars, and for twenty-five pills. It's a crime, that's what it is."

She placed the box firmly back on the shelf. It clattered a bit, and she went on her way.

I strode to the end of the aisle and waited, feigning interest in rows of peanuts and diet bars. When she stopped again, I rounded the corner, walked straight into her, and slipped the bug into an outside pocket of her oversized maroon leather purse.

"Oh!" The old woman glowered at me.

"Excuse me. I'm sorry, ma'am," I said.

She wasn't impressed. When I stepped aside, she harrumphed and moved on.

I left the store fast, hoping we'd have a few days before Quaid caught up with us. Competent bounty hunters were worse than thugs—at least men without morals were predictable.

We made Fremont around two in the afternoon. I parked the Acura behind a gas station half a mile from Lark's place, shoved the panel back on the steering column, and wiped everything down for prints. No reason to lengthen my record.

"Are you sure the owner will get it back?" Ian asked as we headed away.

"Yeah. The gas station'll have it towed eventually. They'll run the plates and track the owner down." I smirked. At least, whoever drove that thing would never leave the doors unlocked again. Hell, I'd just done a public service. "Come on, we'd better move."

I set a fast pace. I wanted to get in, find out what Lark knew, and get out before then. No sense dragging anyone else into this. Of course, getting Lark to open up to me could prove problematic. The last time I'd asked him to trust me, he'd ended up in traction.

"Who is this Lark person again?" Ian asked.

"He's a hookup. The guy who can get stuff." I left off the part about him despising me. Ian didn't need to know that yet.

I veered off the road and cut through an abandoned lot. From here, it was a straight shot up a hill to his place. "Weapons, equipment, connections—pretty much anything. He's a one-man Walmart for criminals."

"I see. And he knows of the djinn?"

"Unless you copied that symbol you use on the mirrors from something else, I'd say he does. It looked like he was collecting them."

Ian nodded. "He must know something. Though I cannot imagine how."

"Yeah. Let's just hope it's not because he's cozy with Trevor." I doubted that—Trevor put guys like Lark to the curb with devastating regularity—but I'd been wrong before. "There it is. We'll go around to the front."

The place looked deceptively small from the outside. A ranch-style cabin with a wraparound porch and a massive stone chimney suggested a summer vacation spot. However, the house extended belowground, and the lower level was easily four times the area of the surface floor. Lark practically had his own catacombs.

I stopped at the side of the building and glanced back at Ian. "How are you doing, powerwise?"

Ian's eyes narrowed. "What are you up to, thief?"

"Nothing. I just thought it might be better if he didn't see you right away."

"Why?"

I cleared my throat. "I might need some leverage."

"You want to use me as a bargaining tool?"

"Uh. See, Lark doesn't exactly like me. I kinda dropped him off a building once. Accidentally."

"You seek help from a man who hates you?"

"I didn't hear you offering any brilliant ideas."

Ian huffed. "Do not expect me to jump in front of any more guns for you." At once, he winked out of sight.

I headed for the front yard with a sigh. Behind me, Ian grumbled under his breath in his language. The disembodied-voice bit creeped me out, but at least I knew he hadn't taken off. Up a wooden ramp that hadn't been here before, across the deck. I tried to keep myself angled away from a straight shot with the security camera mounted above the door while I hit the buzzer.

Maybe he wouldn't recognize me right off. If I'd been thinking, I would have grabbed a few random brochures from the gas station and pretended to be a Jehovah's Witness. At least then he'd be furious for different reasons.

Two minutes passed before the door finally opened. The guy on the other side wasn't Lark, unless he'd grown two feet and dyed his hair. And gone tanning. And started wearing eyeliner.

Speaking of eyes, his were just like Akila's—gray-green irises filling where the whites should have been and a slim black ring around the edges. Crud. This raven-haired, coffee-skinned, tall drink of angry looked suspiciously like a djinn. So much for leverage. Was there a convention around here or something?

My mouth twisted down. "I don't suppose Lark is around."

"Who are you?"

"An old . . . friend." I realized Ian couldn't see inside from his position and stepped back, hoping to give him a glimpse and a chance for recognition. For all I knew, this guy could be one of the Morai. "I wanted to do business with him, if he's available."

"He's not. Leave your name and go."

Come on, Ian, do something. "Can I ask who I'm leaving my name with?"

"I'm Tory." He moved forward and let the door swing open. "Now, who—"

"That is not what I have called you, Taregan."

The sound of Ian's voice would've been a relief, if I hadn't remembered what he'd said about this guy back at the hotel. I hoped their parting of ways hadn't been as abrupt and violent as mine and Lark's—otherwise, we might've had better luck knocking on Trevor's door and just asking him to drop the whole assassination attempt.

CHAPTER 20

If Tory had a gun, he probably would've shot me. "How do you know that?" he snarled. "Answer me!"

"Hey, whoa." I held my hands up and backed away. "Not me. Him." I jerked a thumb in Ian's direction. At least he'd made himself visible again.

Tory stepped through the doorway and froze. "Gods, it's you. Go crawl back under whatever rock you came out from."

My jaw fell to China. So much for peaceful separation.

"Taregan, please . . ."

"I told you, it's Tory. And I have no use for traitors, Gahijian. Leave. Take your pathetic human with you."

"Traitor! Are you suggesting that I betrayed your clan?"

"No, I'm not. I'm suggesting that you got us booted to this wasteland and then deserted us. For three hundred years."

Ian flushed sickly pale. "I did not desert—"

"Don't feed me any more bullshit." Tory's hands clenched into fists, and his lip curled in disgust. "Our fearless leader. Where were you when they slaughtered our kin and drove us into hiding? They've marked us all. We're just waiting to die now."

"I am aware of that." Pure misery reflected in Ian's eyes. He flashed me an apologetic look. "If you will just let me explain . . ."

Tory folded his arms. "Oh, this should be good. Go ahead. Explain away three centuries. Tell me why you left us for those bastards and never came back."

Ian looked at me again. I got the feeling he didn't want me to hear this, but I wasn't going anywhere. I wanted the truth. How much more had he conveniently omitted from his history?

"I thought it best," Ian said at last. "I did not know they would become so powerful in adulthood, and I thought to contain them. They would have caused massive destruction—"

"They *did* cause massive destruction, Gahiji-an. Let's start with the St. Bartholomew's Day massacre."

"Hold on." I had no idea why I felt the urge to intervene, but I rarely disobeyed my instincts. Probably not the best strategy when my mouth tended to run five minutes faster than my brain. "I thought you guys were on the same side."

"Taregan is not referring to the Morai," Ian said. "He speaks of my descendants. A number of them banded together and attempted to exploit their power, and mine." He returned his attention to the other djinn. "I gave in to their demands to leave my kin, and my friends, to serve them and their frivolous wishes. I had intended to neutralize them."

"Well, you didn't," Tory replied. "Obviously."

"No. I could not. Since they were directly descended, they possessed enough power to prevent me from harming them while they remained together. I could only contain them and limit the damage."

"Right. And was there some reason you couldn't have left them and come back to us, once you found this out? We would've helped you *neutralize* them."

Somehow, I got the impression they had different definitions of the word.

Ian made a helpless gesture. "Yes. There was a reason."

"Something Akila would have been all right with, I'm guessing."

"Leave my wife out of this, Taregan." Ian's voice tightened around the statement. "She had nothing to do with my decisions."

"Funny. Because I thought she had everything to do with it—or should have. How many humans did you sleep with? How many times did you betray her, Gahiji-an?"

Ian's expression flickered through a landslide of emotions. His fury melted to stunned surprise, then pain. Sorrow. Apathy. Back to rage. And then he vanished.

"Ian!" I swiped a hand at the place he'd been standing. Nothing. I thought I heard a rush of air, as if he'd taken off in flight. Tory stayed where he was, stone-faced. "That was dirty," I said. "You should've let him finish talking."

"What he's done is worse than any insult I could throw at him. Besides, he knows where to find me now. He'll be back."

"He'd better be."

"Or what?" Tory sneered. "You're human. Obviously, you know what I am. I don't think I'll worry about cowering in the face of your vengeful wrath anytime soon."

As much as Ian annoyed me, this guy beat his asshole quotient by a landslide.

"Look," I said. "I need to see Lark. Is he here or not?"

A troubled look eclipsed Tory's face. "I don't know. He's

not really interested in company anymore. But if you're an old friend . . . who are you? You still haven't told me."

"Yeah, about that. Maybe we could skip the introductions?"

"No. We can't."

"Didn't think so." I gestured vaguely and hoped whatever was between Tory and Lark wasn't too personal. Maybe he hadn't said anything about me. "The name's Donatti."

Tory's disgusted expression suggested he'd heard of me. "You're in luck. I think he might have something to say to you. Wait here."

He backed into the house. The door closed, and I stifled a groan. I doubted whatever Lark had to say would be lucky for me.

I WAITED ON THE PORCH FOR A GOOD TEN MINUTES BEFORE TORY deigned to return. He opened the door and grunted.

"You'd better come in, before Lark changes his mind."

"I take it he still hates me."

"Yes."

I sighed and followed Tory inside. The place was darker than I remembered, and not just because of an overall change in furnishings—though the velvet-draped walls and stone fixtures certainly didn't cheer things up. Ultra-low-wattage lights and a general absence of anything that wasn't brown, gray, or black created an atmosphere better suited to a cave than a house. The only things missing were bats and dripping water.

"So," I said, convinced that I'd start hearing horror-movie violins any minute if I didn't talk. "You're with the hawk clan, right? The Bahari?"

Tory turned and glanced at me with raised eyebrows. "I'm

surprised you know about the clans. Gahiji-an doesn't believe in explaining our world to humans."

"Yeah. I got that impression." I could see the animal resemblance. Where Ian was shaggy and lean, Tory was sleek and quick, with an aquiline nose and bright black eyes that seemed to miss nothing. Feathers would look right at home strung in his hair.

We crossed the main room and entered a short hallway. Tory gestured to an open door on the right and said, "He's in there. I'll let you two catch up."

"Thanks a lot."

Moving past the djinn, I walked into a room made of bookshelves and shadows. A single lamp on an end table revealed a small, unoccupied sitting area. My eyes adjusted slowly to the gloom, but I didn't see any Lark-shaped lumps.

"Gavyn Donatti. You've got balls showing up here."

He sounded as if he'd eaten a grill full of used charcoal. I squinted in the general direction of his voice, just beyond the sitting area, and finally made out an extra chair with what looked like someone sitting in it. "Uh . . . hey, Lark," I said. "Look, I'm really sorry about that accident we had. I swear to God, I didn't know they were building up there."

The chair moved smoothly to the left and passed behind the lamp. I caught a glimpse of chrome and rubber and realized it was a wheelchair. *Damn.* No wonder he still hated me.

"Oh, I'm over that." His words were grit and gravel. Why did he sound so awful? "You started an avalanche, asshole, and you didn't stick around long enough to get caught in the slide." The chair pulled even with the end table. A strangely stiff hand reached for the lampshade and lifted it off.

At the sight of him, I came close to losing every meal I'd

eaten in a month. Maybe it was my fault he was stuck in a wheelchair, but I sure as hell hadn't ever set him on fire.

A gruesome patchwork of alternating rough wrinkles and shiny, stretched pink skin covered Lark's face and hands. A milk-white cataract overlay his right eye, and the outside corner was a mass of red pulp. His right ear no longer existed.

"What happened?" I managed to say.

"Trevor happened." Lark lifted something from his lap—a white half-mask Phantom of the Opera style. He fixed it in place, leaving only his mouth and lower jaw visible. Must have decided I'd gaped at him enough. "Apparently he wanted that item you were supposed to help me lift. He didn't get it, so he decided to take it out on me. He rigged my car. Never bothered to find out whether I'd survived."

"Goddamn psycho," I said. "He really . . . wait. You're not blaming me for that, are you?"

Lark sighed and reached for something in a side pocket of the chair. "I know he's got a contract out on you. If I thought it'd make me feel better, I'd turn your ass over to him. But I'd rather he didn't know I made it out. So I'll just do this instead."

He'd found what he was after—a 9mm Beretta. Was there anybody besides me who didn't pack heat? "Christ, Lark. Do you really think shooting me will make you feel better?" I backed away, prepared to dive behind something.

"It might. Tell you what. You give me one good reason why I shouldn't, and I won't."

"Uh, you'll go to jail?"

"Not good enough."

He raised the gun, but it wasn't exactly pointed at me. In fact, he'd miss me by a few feet if he fired where he aimed. Fresh sorrow assailed me as I realized why. "You're blind."

"As a fucking bat, thanks to you. But I can still hear. I'll hit you eventually."

He sounded serious. I moved in the general direction of not in his line of fire and tried not to make too much noise. "Wait. I only came here to find out what you know about the djinn."

"More than you. What the hell's that got to do with me dropping you?"

I held up my hands before I realized the surrender gesture was pointless. "I know a few things. I ran into one . . . well, actually, he ran into me. And I think we can save Tory from the bad guys. Bad djinn, I mean."

Probably the stupidest thing I'd ever said in my life. I had no idea how to breach Trevor's defenses, let alone get the Morai's tether—if Trevor even had it. And maybe Ian wouldn't come back, in which case I was completely screwed. It was a bluff of Trojan-horse proportions.

A shot fired before I realized Lark hadn't bought it.

I lunged aside as a small vase next to me exploded. The floor seemed like a good spot, so I stayed down.

"Not good enough," Lark called on the tail of the report's echo. "I made you a promise, Donatti. I said I'd kill you the next time you turned up, and here you are. So you're dead." Another shot whined past my ear and thunked into the carpet somewhere. My heart rattled like a loose screen door.

"Lark, I'm serious," I said, backing away to scramble around a chair. "Trevor's mixed up with the Morai, and I know they're trying to wipe out the other clans."

Silence. I held my breath in case he was trying to aim at the sound of air feeding my lungs. At last, he said, "How do you know about the Morai?"

"I told you, I met one of the djinn. He came here with me."

I tried to move without sound and managed to knock over a small stand of books. Thumps and flutters exploded behind me. So much for stealth. "I remembered seeing this symbol he uses here at your place, and I thought you might be able to help. I think we can stop them."

I peered around the chair. Lark lowered the piece and held it in his lap, as if he'd change his mind any second. "How, exactly, are you going to do that?"

Crud. So much for buying my bluff. "Well, er, that's why I need your help."

"You don't have a plan, do you?"

"Not really."

Something resembling a grin formed on his scarred lips. "You always did work better without one, anyway."

"Does that mean I can come out now?"

"I won't shoot you. Yet." Lark returned the gun and rested his arms on the chair. "Now, I think we need to have a chat first, so we're on the same page. Where's this other djinn you brought along?"

I stood and brushed a few porcelain fragments from my sleeve. "He . . . uh, stepped out."

"What'd you do to him?"

"Nothing." I took a long breath to stave off a rant. Why did everybody assume when things went wrong, it had to be my fault? "He had a disagreement with your buddy Tory. He'll come back. In the meantime, do you have a spare room I could crash in? We've been moving all night, and I'm so beat I can't even remember my own name."

Lark nodded slowly. He punched a button in a console built into one of the wheelchair's arms. "Got a minute, Tory?"

"For you, I got two of 'em."

Tory's voice seemed to come from the chair. Lark must've had speakers built in somewhere. I imagined there were more than a few surprises packed into that contraption. Lark and gadgets went together like Mickey and Mouse.

"Our guest needs to rest for a while," Lark said. "Can you show him to the back room?"

"Sure. Want me to turn the sheets down for him?"

"That won't be necessary."

I knew code-speak when I heard it. If I wasn't completely drained, I would've been a little offended that Tory'd just offered to kill me.

Lark waved a hand in dismissal. "He'll be right outside the room. We can talk tonight, provided your djinn shows."

"Thank you." I headed for the door, uncomfortably aware of the meaning hidden in Lark's words. If Ian didn't come back, I was useless—and therefore expendable.

Despite the knowledge that Lark's back room possessed only one quick escape—a picture window with a balcony seat that faced the backyard and the woods beyond—I hit unconscious harder than a featherweight on the wrong end of Tyson. A close-range explosion couldn't have woken me.

But someone lurking in the room could, and did.

I kept my breathing even and opened my eyes to near dark. I'd slept for hours. Night had crept in, leaving only a silver-white moon to cast contours over my unfamiliar surroundings. I heard again the indistinct rustle that pulled me from sleep and strained to find its source without moving. My fingers curled around the knife I'd appointed a just-in-case position under the pillow. After a minute, whispered words penetrated the stillness.

"It is my fault."

It was damned hard to recognize Ian in that shell of a voice. I winced, sat up, and spotted the tall silhouette to the right of the window. He stared outside, holding himself so rigid it looked as if he might shatter with a touch.

"No, man. It's not." I loosed a sigh. "That was a shitty thing he did, walking all over you like that. And dragging your wife into it."

"You do not understand." Ian faced me. The moonlight caught his eyes and revealed the devastation in them. "Taregan called me a traitor. I am. This has been my fault from the beginning. I am responsible for my clan's demise."

"You're not making any sense. Did you stop speaking English again?"

My wisecrack failed to lighten the mood. If anything, he looked even more miserable.

Ian paced a few steps and sank onto the window seat. A single breath shuddered from him, and he closed his eyes. "You wished for the truth. I am giving it to you. I am weak and impulsive. A fool. Were it not for me, my clan would have survived."

I frowned. "Come on. How could it be your fault?"

He leaned back against the glass. "I allowed the Morai to destroy our village."

"What are you talking about?"

"I never wanted the Dehbei to become involved. It was not our war, and the Bahari had not been our allies. They had always looked down on us, believed themselves superior. And when we learned the Morai plotted against them . . . for a time, I hoped they would be victorious." He crossed his arms and rubbed them. "I told him not to send our scouts or warn the

Bahari. I pleaded with him. I did not feel it was our place to help those arrogant windbags, to risk our lives doing so—and I knew Kemosiri would not listen. But he insisted it was the right thing to do."

I straightened and stared at him, wondering if he'd been hit in the head recently. That definitely didn't make sense. "Who's he?"

"Omari-el. The Dehbei leader." He let out a shaking breath. "My father."

My brain insisted on filtering this little piece of information through the story he'd told me, and my stomach rebelled. No wonder he was so pissed. "Ian, I still don't see how any of this was your fault."

"You do not? I suppose I can understand why." He returned his gaze to the window. "When our spies brought news of the Morai's plans, my father did not hesitate in deciding to warn the nobles." He paused for a beat. "We fought. He insisted that I stay behind to watch over the village while he carried the news to the palace. I did not want the responsibility or the tedium. And since he insisted on warning them, I wanted to confront Kemosiri myself." His jaw firmed, and he brought a fist down hard on the window seat. "If I had stayed behind, I could have prevented the Morai from slaughtering our women and children."

Guilt dripped from his words, thicker than roofing tar. A twinge of empathy shot through my chest. "You're serious, aren't you?" I said. "Come on. Wasn't there a whole army of those fuckers? I doubt you'd have been able to stop them. You'd be dead right now, too."

"It does not matter. I should not have left. I should have taken my responsibilities seriously. I should have sent more spies among them and monitored our village more carefully. I should have been there when they invaded our homes and murdered the children . . ." His voice fell flat, and I recognized the tone as a litany of wrongs he must have tormented himself with over and over through the years. The centuries.

I had a long list of self-accusations, too.

"I could not even save my father," he whispered. "Lenka was too powerful. He is both son and grandson to the Morai clan leader. His twisted blood and his madness feed his strength." He bent his head, pinched the bridge of his nose. "He murdered my father in my presence. I watched, and I could do nothing." Fury crimped his features, but it didn't last long. "The worst of it is that Omari-el died attempting to save Kemosiri. And you have seen how that bastard repaid his sacrifice."

"Ian . . ." I stood and approached him but couldn't manage anything more than an awkward pat on the shoulder. Words seemed rude to offer. Finally, I said, "Does Tory know about this?"

"He does now."

I whirled at the brittle sound of Tory's voice, just in time to see him pop into view beside the closed door of the room. "Jesus Christ. Can't a guy get a little sleep without invisible djinn sneaking around all night? How long have *you* been here?"

Ian jumped to his feet as if he'd been doused with ice water. "Taregan."

Tory stalked across the room. I moved forward in an unconscious attempt to shield Ian, but he held an arm out and gently pushed me away. "Let it be, thief," he said quietly. This time, his calling me thief seemed more endearment than insult.

"Why?" Tory stopped in front of him and gripped his upper arm hard. "Why didn't you tell us about this before?"

Ian regarded him with a cool stare. "My shame is mine to bear, Taregan. Why should I wish to humiliate myself further by allowing you to know of my failures?"

"Gahiji-an, have you really blamed yourself for the attack on your village all this time?"

"Of course. I was responsible."

Tory shook his head. "You couldn't have known what they'd do. Look, Gahiji-an, you're a brilliant strategist. A great general. If you hadn't come to the palace, we would have lost the city, and the Morai would be in control right now. I'm sure of it."

"General?" I blurted. "I thought you were just tagging along."

"The clan leader is also responsible for the command of the clan's armies. As son of the *ra*, this duty fell to me upon my father's death, though there were but a handful left to lead." Ian's face fell. "It makes no difference now."

"It does," Tory insisted. "You've got to stop blaming yourself." He backed away, and a frown surfaced. "I'm sorry I didn't hear you out earlier. You do understand, though—it's Akila I'm worried about. She doesn't deserve to be treated like an afterthought."

Ian blanched. "I have done nothing to Akila, and I will thank you to leave her out of this discussion. She is not your concern."

"The hell she isn't! How can you say you've done nothing, when you screwed as many human women as you could get your hands on behind her back?"

"You do not understand—"

"I don't have to. You never wanted the marriage, but she loved you anyway. And this is how you repay her. Screwing around like a college frat boy."

"A *what?*"

"It's a human thing. You wouldn't get it." Tory flashed a poisoned glare. "I don't blame you for the war, but I won't let you hurt her. If I ever see you so much as touch another woman, I'll kill you myself." He whirled and stalked from the room.

I glanced at the pillow where I'd hidden my knife. "Guess I should've stabbed the bastard after all."

"No." Ian sat down hard on the window bench. "Allow him his anger. I've no desire to discuss personal matters with him."

"But why is it so damned personal? I mean, she's your wife."

"Yes. She is." Ian closed his eyes. "For many centuries, Taregan's family has served as bodyguards, and more, to the royal Bahari. They call themselves the Guardians. When he came of age, Taregan was assigned personally to Akila." A smile tugged at his lips. "He takes his duties quite seriously. Even when I attempt to relieve him of them."

"So he thinks he's her godmother—er, father?"

Ian almost laughed. "Something like that."

I choked back a snort at the idea of Tory doing a Marlon Brando impersonation. "Well, don't you think it'd help if he knew why you made all those descendants?"

"Perhaps. But he does not seem inclined to stop berating me long enough for an explanation."

"True. He's got a mouth on him." I slipped the blade back into a pocket and finger-combed my hair, a useless attempt to look presentable. No way I'd get back to sleep now. "Well, at least you've got me on your side."

Ian smirked. "How fortunate for me."

"Just a guess, but I'd say you're better off with me than your other descendants. I haven't started any massacres lately."

"Take care, thief. Your arrogance is showing." A small smile belied any bad intentions. "My apologies for not trusting you sooner. I had to be certain that you were not like your predecessors."

"Yeah, I can see that."

He shifted sideways and drew his knees up to his chest. "I did attempt to return. To Taregan and the others. By the time it was safe, they had moved on."

"Safe. You mean from your descendants?" A shiver stole through me. "I didn't know they were trying to kill you."

"Not me," he said. "Taregan and Shamil. You see, the one who called himself their leader had located their tethers. He threatened to destroy them both if I did not remain with them and continue to indulge their desires. I had to wait until the humans died on their own. Killed themselves with their excesses and foolish behavior. It took nearly a century for those who had turned on me to pass away, and at last I was able to take the tethers. But I could not locate the Bahari. Dehbei do not possess strong scrying abilities." He leaned back against the sill. "With the Morai hunting us down, it was not safe to keep the tethers with me. I hid them among ancient human remains, deep underground, on separate continents. However, it seems not even the dead are sacred to humans. They were found before I could return to retrieve them."

"Yeah. Looks like Trevor's been collecting them."

"He has Shamil's, and he nearly had mine." Ian closed his eyes briefly. "I can only hope Taregan has located his own.

Though I suppose it would do no good to ask him, as he will simply blame me for that as well."

By the time Ian finished talking, I wanted to hurt someone. Several someones. Since a bunch of them were already dead, and one of them was in his fortress by the lake, that left Tory.

"I'm sorry, Ian. That really sucks." I would've offered something a little more sympathetic, but eloquence had never been one of my strengths. "Look, I . . . have to take a piss."

He looked confused.

"You know, urinate."

"Oh. That."

"Yeah, so I'll be back in a few, okay? Gotta find a bathroom."

He nodded vaguely and stared out the window.

I left the room, relieved that he hadn't prodded me any. If he'd known what I really intended to do, he probably would've refused to allow it. Or tried to, anyway.

Tory wouldn't listen to Ian. Fine. He'd damned well listen to me.

CHAPTER 21

Four in the morning wasn't my idea of a good time for an argument.

It wasn't hard to find Tory. I just had to follow the trail of angst leading to Lark's living room, where a plasma TV blared old Bugs Bunny cartoons at a volume suitable for old folks with broken hearing aids. The djinn sprawled on a couch, shirtless, beer in hand. He'd obviously adjusted to life as a typical American. In the blue-white glow of the screen, I made out armband tattoos that matched Shamil's. For some reason, the sight of them pissed me off.

Probably because I knew where Shamil was right now. Didn't seem right that this asshole should sit here drinking and damning Ian while his clan member took Trevor's abuse.

I moved between Tory and the television. He lifted bleary eyes and let out a grunt. "Fuck off, monkey."

"You sound like Lark. Besides, I thought you liked humans."

"I don't like humans who choose to associate with Gahiji-an. Especially the female ones." His gaze narrowed. "Or humans who go around crippling people and then screwing them over."

I winced. Couldn't defend what I'd done to Lark, but I wasn't about to let his idiotic tirade against Ian continue. "Let's get a few things straight here," I said. I reached down and hit the TV's power button.

"Hey! I was watching that." Tory grabbed for a remote lying on a side table.

I got there first and threw it across the room. "No, you don't. You're going to listen to me, damn it."

"Why should I?"

"What are you, five years old?" I folded my arms, took a breath. "Okay. First, I can't tell you how sorry I am about what happened to Lark. I would've stuck around and tried to help, but he asked me to leave. Actually, he told me if I stayed, he'd kill me."

Tory glowered. "He should have."

"Maybe. But he didn't, and that's for him to decide. Now, about Ian."

"I don't want to hear it."

"You're going to if I have to tape your mouth shut."

"Not if I turn you into a frog."

"Oh, come on. A frog? I do know a little about djinn, and I'm pretty sure you can't do that. But maybe I'm wrong. If I am, go ahead and prove it."

Tory sank lower into the seat cushions and knocked back a swallow from his can.

"Thought so." I relaxed. A little. "Ian didn't desert you."

"Right. I just imagined him going off with those half-breed morons."

"Shut up and listen." I had to drop my arms and clasp my hands behind my back to keep from strangling him. "Those morons had your tether, and Shamil's. They were going to kill you both unless Ian did what they wanted. He had to wait until they died to get the tethers back, and then he couldn't find you."

Tory sprang to his feet. "You're lying."

"No—"

"Gahiji-an cares for no one but himself. He rejected me, the same way he rejected . . ." The color drained from his face, and he slid back down on the couch. His features slackened.

"Uh, Tory?" I said when he didn't continue. "You're gonna have to give me a little more to go on. I'm not following you."

"Is that really what happened?" His lips barely moved.

"Well, I wasn't there, so we've only got Ian's word on it. But I believe him."

"Gods." Tory hung his head. "I'm such an idiot."

"I would not go so far as to say that."

Ian's voice jangled my unsuspecting nerves. "Would you stop doing that?" I snapped as he popped into view across the room. "I thought you trusted me now."

"I do. However, I knew it should not have taken quite this long to relieve yourself."

Tory stood and faced Ian. "I . . ."

"It is all right, young one. I cannot fault you for believing as you did."

"Whoa." I glanced from Tory to Ian. "Isn't he like a thousand years old, too?"

"Not quite," Ian said. "He was a mere century old when Kemosiri sent us here. A child, by our standards." A tiny smile graced his lips. "And already insisting on shouldering more responsibility than was required of him."

"I wasn't a child. I'd been trained by the Guardians."

"Training is no substitute for experience."

I sensed another imminent explosion. "Breathe, guys," I said. "Whatever it is, can't it wait? We've got more important things to worry about than our respective maturity."

"Your pathetic human is right, Gahiji-an." Tory smiled. "He's got balls, too. Where'd you find him?"

"Under a rock." His eyes flashed with amusement. "The pathetic human calls me Ian. Perhaps you should as well, to avoid confusing him."

"Watch it, genie boy. I can name-call right along with you." I had to grin myself, from pure relief. At least they wouldn't try to kill each other now.

Unless the subject of Akila came up again.

I leveled a look at Ian. "Isn't there something else you want to explain, now that he's listening?"

"I do not recall anything else."

I sighed. "Subtlety isn't one of your strengths, is it? Descendants, wife . . . any of this sound familiar?"

"Good point, Donneghy." Tory raised an eyebrow. "Go ahead. I'm listening."

"It's Donatti," I said.

"Whatever."

Ian made a dismissive gesture. "Listen all you like. I have nothing to say."

"Why am I not surprised?" Tory snorted. "Like I said, you've never wanted her."

The expression on Ian's face made me regret bringing it up. I hoped Tory's tether wasn't anywhere close. He might end up disintegrating—or whatever happened to a djinn when his tether was destroyed. "He must have," I said, trying to put myself between them in case of sudden murder attempts. "I mean, he wouldn't have married her in the first place if he didn't. Right?"

"Ah. He hasn't told you."

"Apparently not." Now what had Ian conveniently forgotten to mention?

"It wasn't his choice. Their marriage was arranged to unite our clans. And he protested it—loudly and publicly."

"That is enough, Taregan."

"What's wrong? Don't like being in the hot seat? Well, now it's your turn." Tory moved closer. "You deserve it, after you humiliated Akila."

"I did not mean to hurt her—"

"Whether or not you meant it, you did. Everyone else sure as hell saw it that way." He turned to me and said, "Your friend Ian here showed up late for his own marriage ceremony. Then, as soon as it was over, he announced that he was leaving, and he'd see his new bride in ten years when her mating cycle arrived."

"Her wh-what?" I stammered.

"Female djinn can only reproduce for a three-day period, once every three hundred years," Tory said. "Only when her time came, he was here, impregnating his human harem."

"Enough! I have my reasons, Taregan, and they are not your concern. Regardless of what you and the rest of your clan believe, Akila is my wife, and we have every right not to share the details of our personal life with you."

Tory reeled as if he'd been slapped. "Please," he said softly. "I'm not asking for details. This has nothing to do with clans or politics. I just . . . gods, Ian. She loves you so much. It breaks my heart to think you don't return the feeling."

Something in Ian's rigid stance relented. "I have always

loved her. More than you can know." He looked away. "Akila is aware of my descendants. In fact, she made it possible by breaking the dormancy component of the tether spell. Without access to blood magic, I could not defend myself against the Morai—and I wished to do so without human sacrifice. I also needed blood descendants to ensure that the barrier would not collapse."

"I thought all the Dehbei created the barrier together," Tory said. "You're telling me their blood won't keep it from collapsing?"

All the color drained from Ian's face. "They are all dead, Taregan. Only I remain."

It took Tory a full minute to pull himself together. "Ian, I . . ."

A short electronic tone cut through the room and amputated the conversation. Lark's voice followed. "Tory. Where are you?"

Tory shook himself. He unclipped a small, slim black rectangle from his waistband and held it near his head. "Upstairs. Our guests are up and about."

"Good. We have a problem. Bring them down."

"Be right there." Tory replaced the device and frowned. "Come on. If Lark says we have a problem—"

"Then we're five minutes away from gruesome death," I finished for him. "Right?"

"Exactly."

Crud. I'd wanted to be wrong this time.

CHAPTER 22

Tory lurched us down to the basement in an old-fashioned birdcage elevator that creaked and complained and had me praying we'd survive long enough to find out what the problem was. I considered introducing Lark to the technological wonder of WD-40 but decided he'd probably take it the wrong way. We stepped out, and the décor changed from ancient cave to Bat Cave.

The central room of Lark's subfloor hadn't changed much since my last visit. Banks of equipment lined the perimeter, projecting a kaleidoscope of indicator lights and screen glow. A row of digital clocks still displayed the current times in every major metropolitan area on earth, and the industrial gray linoleum and cool, dry air still reminded me of a morgue.

But the sarcophagus in the glass case hadn't been there before.

I took a closer look and recognized the unusual piece. It was about three feet tall, as if it'd been made for some obscure midget pharaoh. King Tiny the Terrible. Its angular, blank-eyed, inhuman face sported a traditional Egyptian headdress trimmed in onyx and gold, and long folded wings crossed its chest in place of arms.

When Lark first showed me a photo of the thing, before we failed to steal it and I crippled him, he'd said it was a falcon and that it contained mummified remains of said bird. Aside from the wings, I couldn't see the artistic vision. It just looked damned freaky.

"Lark, how in the hell did you get this?"

Too late, I realized he couldn't possibly know what *this* was, but he wheeled around from the screen he'd been facing to cast me a twisted smirk. "Wouldn't you like to know."

"Matter of fact, I would."

"Well, tough shit. You're a master thief. I'm sure you know every trade secret there is to know, so I'm not going to bother explaining." He turned back, and I could've sworn his chair harrumphed at me.

"Fine." I squinted through the glass. The sarcophagus leered back. "This thing's even uglier in person. Why's it still here? I thought you had a buyer lined up."

"I did," Lark said without turning. "And I delivered."

"So this is a figment of my imagination, then, right?"

"No. I commissioned a dupe."

"Impressive dupe." I was no collector, but I'd stolen plenty of art, and it looked exactly like the original to me. "Who'd you get it from?"

He laughed. "No. The one I delivered was a dupe. That one's real."

"You're shitting me."

"Afraid not. That's the genuine article, and some sucker in Italy paid half a mil for a fake." Lark gave a thin shrug. "We needed it."

"We?"

"Thank the gods." Ian had come up behind me to stare into the case. "You did find it."

"Whoa, hold on," I said. "You've seen this thing?"

Ian nodded. "It is where I attempted to conceal Taregan's tether."

"Oh, you did more than attempt to hide it," Tory said from the doorway. "Took me forever to find the damned thing, and when I finally did—"

Lark interrupted with a snort of laughter. "He tried to steal it. And he got busted."

"I wasn't trying to steal it." Tory flushed and crossed his arms. "I was just going to get my tether out. They could've kept the damned coffin."

"Yeah. That's like saying you didn't want the *Mona Lisa*, you were just going to take the frame." Lark smiled, shook his head. "He's lucky I was already working on the guard who grabbed him. That's how we met. I had a buyer lead for a different piece at the OCM in Albany, and when I went up to feed the bribe, there was Tory trying to talk his way out of a trip downtown. He'd told the guard he dropped his watch into the exhibit, and it somehow mysteriously landed in the sealed sarcophagus, and he had to get it back."

Tory rolled his eyes. "You just love this story, don't you?"

"You know it." Lark shifted his chair around and almost relaxed. "I ended up having to use the bribe money to get him out. Lost the lead, gained a partner. Fair trade."

"Something like that." Tory looked away, but a faint smile lingered on his lips.

I felt like an ass all over again. "So that's why you were so hot to lift this thing," I said. "And I . . ."

"Yeah, you fucked us. But we managed." Lark stiffened and swiveled back to the screen, which displayed a topographical map. "Tory, I need your eyes."

Tory crossed the floor to stand beside him. "What's up?"

"I listened to the audio feed twice, but you know how garbled the scanner is. Check the police band for the county sheriff."

Nodding, Tory leaned in front of the wheelchair and punched some buttons. A ticker-tape banner scrolled across the bottom of the screen. I couldn't read the text from where I stood, but I got the general gist of it when Tory said, "Shit. How could they know?"

"I've been trying to figure that out myself. Funny, but I can only think of one possible answer. Why don't you ask him?"

Tory straightened and glared at me. "You sold us out."

"What? No, I didn't."

I managed two steps toward him before Ian pulled me back. "Let us clarify things before anyone does something regrettable," he said. "Taregan, I can assure you he's done no such thing."

"Really. So it was you, then?"

"Will you let me talk?" I shrugged Ian off and restrained myself from lecturing him. He might have been a few thousand years old, but he had no idea how to deal with criminal protocol. I did—and I had a feeling Tory knew a thing or two, if he'd hung around Lark for long. "All right. What, exactly, is the code?"

"A ten one-oh-seven and a four eighty-seven. Two squads and a Frank dispatched. ETA thirty minutes."

"Jesus. What did you steal, the mayor?"

Tory hesitated. "Sure you don't know anything about this?"

"I'm clueless. Like I said, came by to ask for help." I stifled a laugh at Ian's baffled expression. "Suspicious person, grand theft, four officers, and a detective en route," I explained. "They expect Lark to resist arrest. But I swear to God, I didn't tip them. I'm not looking for amnesty. Do you think . . . wait." Certainty struck me like a pile driver. "It was Trevor."

Lark swiveled and faced my general direction. "How? He doesn't know where I live, or he'd have tried to finish me off by now."

Ian uttered something garbled and explosive. It sounded like the same curse he'd spat in Trevor's yard. "He used Shamil to pinpoint our location."

"*What?*" Tory looked at Ian like he'd just forecast a snowstorm in hell. "Shamil would never work for them. And only the tethers can be traced, remember?"

"I know," Ian said. "That disgusting son of a jackal has Shamil bound and sealed. Trevor uses his blood to whore himself to one of the Morai. And . . . I carry my tether."

Tory stood silent for a moment. "So that's why you're not dead. Well, Ian, this is a bit of a mixed blessing, isn't it? They can't break the barrier as long as you live, but you're leading them straight to us."

"Shamil can only trace to a fixed point, and he won't be able to repeat the spell for several hours. No matter what they do to him." Ian shuddered. "We will have to move."

"Hey. Excuse me. The blind cripple objects." Lark slapped a palm on the arm of his chair. "I can't run. And besides, this is my fucking house. That bastard'll destroy it if no one's around when his rent-a-cops show up."

Ian glanced at me. I didn't like his expression. Before I could throw in some objections of my own, he said something stupid.

"We cannot protect your house. But we can remove your other objections."

Tory stepped in front of Lark. "He's not expendable, Ian. Don't even think about it."

"Come now. Do you really believe I intend to kill him?" Ian forced a grim smile. "The thief and I will heal him."

I had to assume Ian meant me. Which obviously wasn't going to work. "You're crazy. Seriously. I can't do that mojo stuff."

"You've enough to contribute, and you will have to learn to control it quickly. I cannot do this alone."

I shook my head. "What about Tory? I mean, he's gotta have more juice than me."

"Ian," Tory said. "What is he babbling about?"

Ian looked uncomfortable. "Donatti is my descendant. And there is one other who lives still."

"Holy shit. How did he dodge them?" Tory sent me an approving smile. "You must be the luckiest human alive. No others have managed to escape the Morai once they've been marked."

"Uh, right. Lucky. That's me." Except that when it came to my fellow humans, I was a disaster waiting to happen. Everything that kept me alive ended up hurting someone else. How fortunate. "Like I said, why can't you and Tory do this? You're both full of djinn."

"Because Taregan and I combined are merely two. You and I are bound, thief, like it or not. And together we are exponential. Now, concentrate."

"On what? Damn it, Ian, I have no idea what I'm doing. This is stupid. I don't have magic powers."

"Hold on. Donatti has a point." Lark wheeled forward with a frown. "Are you sure you have the right guy? I don't think he's really your descendant. I mean, he doesn't have a competent bone in his body."

"Jesus Christ. I'm not that bad—"

"Besides," Lark interrupted, "Tory already tried to heal me. Obviously, it didn't work."

"Taregan is young and . . . alone." Ian averted his gaze. "And I am certain Donatti is descended from me. I would not have found him otherwise."

"Have you actually seen this clown do anything magical?"

"All right. Enough bullshit," I said. "Lark, if you don't want us to try, that's fine with me. I don't want to make a fool of myself, because I don't think it'll work, either. But you'd better come up with another idea fast. The cops aren't going to wait for us to formulate an escape plan."

Tory crouched next to Lark's chair. "Ian is right, *adjo*," he said. "This guy really is descended from the djinn. I can sense it, too."

Lark turned his head in Tory's direction. "Do you think they can do it?"

"They've got a better shot than I did."

"I don't know. He's still an idiot."

"Okay, that's it. I'm not doing this." I backed away and looked around the room, trying to think of another option. No way I'd be able to work any magic, and Lark would hate me even more when I failed to help. "Cops aren't here yet. Maybe one of us could carry you or something. You do have a vehicle stashed around here somewhere, right?"

"Donatti." Lark's ash-coated voice shook. "I'm sorry. If there's any chance at all that this crazy scheme might work . . . for God's sake, please try. Trevor can have the fucking house, if it means I get my eyes and legs back."

"Way to lay a guilt trip on a guy," I mumbled. At least he'd apologized. "What if I screw this up? I mean, I've managed to fuck everything else over so far."

"You couldn't possibly make me any worse."

"Right. Let's see you say that when I turn you into a frog." I sighed and looked at Ian. "What am I supposed to do here, chief?"

"Well, you . . ." He blinked. "I do not know. Concentrate. Focus."

"You're not helping. D'you think you'd have been able to get us here if I plopped you behind the wheel and said, 'Just drive'?"

Ian gave an exasperated snort. "You have already experienced invisibility. Do what you did to achieve it, but direct it at Lark."

"I don't know what I did to achieve it! It was an accident, remember?"

Tory held up a hand. "Maybe I can help. I'm going to guess you've only been accidentally invisible when you really needed to not be found, right?"

"Yeah. So?"

"The key here is need. In order to affect something, you have to need it to happen."

So that was why Ian would only give me what he thought I needed. At least something made sense. "Okay. I'll try." I stared at Lark and tried willing him better. Nothing happened—at least, not that I could tell. "Should I wave or something?"

"You can, but it might not help you," Ian said. "I use gestures to focus. Perhaps you should try closing your eyes. You may have more success if you rid yourself of distraction."

I did, and attempted to tune out the small sounds in the room: the muted hum of computer fans, faint breathing from the others, a distant steady ticking from the synchronized clocks. I really, really wanted to heal Lark. Unfortunately, it wasn't the same as need. Easing the burden of guilt over getting him busted in the first place would have been great, but I'd still feel responsible, and I had plenty of other shit to feel guilty about.

Like Jazz and Cyrus. I hadn't let myself think about them. I needed to stay alive. I'd promised Jazz. And if we didn't get the hell out of here, I couldn't keep that promise.

Something raw and hot balled in the center of my chest. I focused on the sensation, felt it sprout tendrils and spread through me, seeking a target. The stuff felt alive, electric.

It fucking hurt. A lot.

Lark. Heal Lark.

A sound pierced my concentration. A gasp. My eyes flew open just in time to see Lark jolt to his feet. He stood in place for a few seconds, mouth agape under the mask, still and silent as an after-hours bank vault.

Then he pitched forward and fell flat on his face.

"Lark!"

Tory's shout competed with the sickening crunch of face meeting floor. I would've worried whether I'd killed him if I wasn't busy being in pain. Dropping to hands and knees, I watched Tory help Lark up and discovered what had made the awful breaking sound. The mask lay shattered on the gray linoleum. My smudged vision wouldn't reveal whether his face looked much better.

"Well done, thief." Ian sounded as bad as I felt. He slung an arm around my waist and hefted me to my feet, then supported my weight while my body attempted to let gravity take over. "You will feel better in a few moments."

"Don't think so." My words slurred together, and my brain insisted that I'd been Tasered again. "He okay?"

"Yes."

"Good. I'm not." The room spun a few times. I felt like the ball on a roulette wheel. "Shit. Does it hurt like that for you?"

It took him a few seconds to answer. "Only in your realm."

"Oh." No wonder he wanted to go home. I shook my head and squeezed my eyes shut. When I opened them again, the world had more definition. I made out Lark, standing unassisted, staring at me. Only a few faded patches of scar tissue remained on his face. His cheeks glistened in the low light, but it wasn't blood.

I squinted. "Lark. You crying?"

"Can't help it. First thing I see in six months is your ugly mug. It's depressing." He turned away and walked unsteadily toward the terminal he'd used to access the police scanner. Tory followed, trying too hard not to look as if he was hovering. His overt attentions had me wondering again just what kind of relationship existed between them. Obviously, they weren't blood-related, or the healing bit would've worked when Tory tried it.

"You're welcome," I mumbled in the general direction of Lark's back while I eased away from Ian and found I could stand, at least. I'd been physically exhausted plenty of times, but this felt different. If I was the poetic sort, I'd be tempted to believe my soul had been drained. Ian was right—this magic was no trifle, no parlor trick. I hoped I'd never have to use it again.

A coughing fit seized Ian and doubled him over. I moved to help him, but he held a hand out and eventually straightened on his own. Then he stared at me as if I'd just sprouted horns and cloven feet.

"What? Is there something stuck in my teeth?"

"I do not enjoy being wrong." He shook his head and smiled. "Your abilities are far stronger than I suspected, thief."

"Yeah, well, if you're planning to see what else I can do, don't hold your breath. No way I'm going through that again." I could feel my legs now. They protested supporting the rest of me. I had to overrule them, since my arms weren't up to the challenge. "That's some powerful mojo. He's already walking around, after being in that chair for years?"

"Yes. Because your own magic is strong, he has been almost completely healed. The atrophied muscles have regenerated."

"Oh." I wondered if Lark heard that—and kind of hoped he didn't. Something might still go wrong, and he'd blame me for it. "So why are we all standing around? Shouldn't we haul ass out of here? I hear Hong Kong's nice this time of year."

Lark hit a button. A crackling burst of static filled the room. Even with Lark's advanced technology, police scanners still had crappy reception. Maybe it was against the law for them to communicate effectively.

"*Code one, unit four-alpha-six. We are in sight of target, repeat, we are in sight. ETA two minutes. Ten-oh, all units copy.*"

"Oh, Christ. We're dead."

Ian looked at me. "You understood that gibberish?"

"Unfortunately." I glanced at Lark, whose grim features reflected the dread sinking hooks in my gut. "They can see the house. They're already here."

CHAPTER 23

S hit," Lark said. "I wanted to pack a few things first.
We'd better get moving."

He didn't sound nearly as terrified as he should,
considering that by the time we made it upstairs, we'd be facing
down at least six armed cops. I wondered if Ian and I had done
something to his brain when we healed him—like deleted his
common sense and self-preservation instincts. "I vote for staying right here," I said. "Maybe they won't find us."

Lark gently pushed Tory out of the way, jerked out a
keyboard, and ran his fingers rapid-fire over the keys without
looking. "Are you nuts? Of course they will. And even if they
don't, they'll wreck the place, maybe set it on fire. Trevor loves
a good torching."

"Right." The skeletal, smoldering remains of Molly's place
shimmered in my head. "So what's the plan? We gonna talk
them out of shooting us?"

Lark gave a long sigh, as if he couldn't fathom the depths of
my stupidity. "You're not playing with a full deck, are you? We
aren't going up there."

"Did I miss a memo or something?" Lark had to be the

crazy one here. Our choices were stay down or go up, weren't they? Ian seemed more confused than I did, but Tory looked amused. "Okay, spill it," I said. "What's going on?"

Lark ignored me. He moved to his abandoned chair, reached under the seat, and pulled. The distinct sound of snaps unfastening preceded the appearance of a battered leather portfolio. He slung the bag onto a shoulder, then yanked the Beretta he'd almost shot me with from the side pocket of the chair and handed it to Tory. With no further explanation, Lark made a follow-me gesture and headed out of the room.

"You know why I bought this place?" he asked when we'd stopped at the elevator.

"Because you're a paranoid son of a bitch."

He grinned. "Exactly. But I'm paranoid about all the right things—just like you. Think I'd stay anywhere I couldn't get out of in a pinch?"

"Holy shit. You've got a way out from down here."

Lark nodded. "Remember your history lessons?"

"Uh, kinda." Most of my memories of school consisted of flint-eyed Catholic matrons at the orphanage with sharp tongues and sharper rulers who found me a more pleasing target than anyone else. They'd probably had a party when I didn't come back after ninth grade.

"We're in Underground Railroad territory here. There's a tunnel. Leads to one of my properties outside town. We'll take that."

For a moment, I wanted to hug the paranoid son of a bitch. Thankfully, the feeling passed.

Lark opened the grate, reached inside, and hit a button. The elevator started up empty, groaning and complaining all the way. He fished in his bag and came out with some kind of remote. After he fiddled with it, a smooth grinding noise resonated from the elevator shaft and ended in a metallic bang. "Firewall," he explained. "Even if they figure out there's another floor, they won't be able to get down here without a big-ass blowtorch and a couple of days to spare."

I had to laugh. Even running for his life, Lark looked out for his gear first and his ass second.

The computer equipment wasn't the only thing down here worth saving. Lark led the way through a corridor and into a cavernous room stuffed with old things. Ancient things. Brittle rolls of parchment, statues and figurines, vases, jewelry—a few museums' worth of artifacts, no doubt worth a fortune or three. Most of it was legally his. The rest he'd had stolen, but the former owners had been dead for a thousand years, so they wouldn't file any complaints.

When we reached the opposite end of the room, Lark opened a rough wooden plank door and flipped a light switch inside, revealing a spacious closet with floor-to-ceiling shelves lining the left and right sides. He located two flashlights and handed one to Tory. "Sorry. I hadn't planned on more than two using this route. Tory, you want to go first? I'll cover the back."

"Oh, could I?" Smirking, Tory slid a panel of the back wall aside. "This is gonna be fun."

I saw immediately why Lark had insisted he couldn't run. The packed earth tunnel wasn't more than four feet high and maybe two and a half wide. We'd have to crawl through. No way his chair would've fit in there. Cool air and the distinct smell of damp dirt wafted from the blackness. But it didn't seem so bad—I could deal with a chill and a couple of cramps in exchange for my life.

When Tory switched his light on and played the beam into

the space, I almost changed my mind. Squeaks and squeals, skittering paws, and the flash of tiny eyes in the distance announced the presence of mice. And all those cobwebs meant we'd have to tangle with spiders, too. I hated them almost as much as mice.

Good thing I wasn't claustrophobic.

"Wait." Ian stepped up to the mouth of the tunnel and peered through. "Where did you say this ends?"

"A little shack on my property. No one lives there."

"And have you been through this passage recently?"

"No. Why?"

Ian frowned. "Taregan, give the light to the thief. You can create your own."

"Oh. Right." Tory handed me the plastic tube. He held a hand out, and a shower of sparks burst above his palm in midair. In seconds, a fireball blossomed and hovered in front of him.

Lark stared at him, enrapt. "I didn't know you could do that."

"I'm limited but not completely powerless. Oh—we'll need better ventilation." Tory pushed his free hand at the tunnel. The cool air leaking out became a slight breeze.

"I will lead. We do not know what to expect." Before anyone could protest, Ian glowed and morphed into the wolf. He sniffed the air a few times, pawed the floor, and leaped through the hole.

Tory glanced at Lark and shrugged. "His form is better suited to this. I'd just fly into the walls. Come on." He moved the hand with the fireball to the opening, held it in place, and slowly pulled his palm back. The flame stayed put and then hovered at a consistent foot in front of him as he wedged himself into the tunnel.

"Go," Lark told me.

I eased through after the djinn. The instant I'd crawled clear, Lark scooted in behind me. He executed an awkward half-turn and moved the panel back into place, leaving only the two flashlights and Tory's floating campfire to cut through the gloom. As we started forward in single-file crawl, I was half tempted to break out whistling. "Anyone know any good mining songs?" I said.

Tory groaned. Lark didn't exercise similar restraint. "Shut up, Donatti. Every time you try to lighten things up, somebody falls off a roof."

"Not every time," I said. "Occasionally, they get arrested. Or ditched."

He grunted. "Yeah, I heard about Jazz. How's she doing these days? Still pissed at you?"

"Probably." At least, I hoped she was—because right now, she'd only be calm if she was dead. I crushed that idea and concentrated on more pressing matters, like the scratching, skittering sounds from the darkness ahead. Some of them were Ian. Too many weren't.

"Too bad," Lark said. "Thought you two had a thing going a while back. She's gorgeous, that girl. A living work of art."

"Don't even think about it."

The venom behind my words surprised me, but Lark's answering laughter replaced it with confusion. "What's so funny?" I demanded. "Think I won't kick your ass just because you're a recovered cripple?"

"You really don't know, do you?"

"Apparently not."

Lark chortled under his breath. Tory and Ian had gotten

several feet ahead and didn't seem to be paying attention to our conversation. "I'm not a ladies' man," he said.

"So?"

"Fuck's sake, Donatti. I'm gay."

"Oh." My brain processed the knowledge that he wouldn't compete with me for Jazz and moved on. Then it stopped. And backtracked. "*Oh*. You and—"

"Yes." He cut me off forcefully. "Let's leave it at that, all right?"

"Okay." I almost added *sorry*, but I didn't want him to think I felt bad about his sexual preferences. Or his choice of lover. In fact, if I were gay, I'd be jealous. Not everyone got to bang a djinn.

Silence settled between us, marked by the soft sounds of our progress in the cramped passage. After a few minutes, Lark said, "By the way . . . thank you."

"Huh?"

"How much bone you got in that head? Thank you for what you did. You know. Healing me and all."

I grinned. "I heard you the first time. Already said you're welcome."

"Yeah, I know. Sorry about that. It's just . . . well, I'd resigned myself to never seeing or walking again. Having it all rush back like that, I couldn't think straight. Didn't even believe it at first."

"Ha. Me, neither." My body still tingled with the aftereffects of power. I'd accepted that it came from me, but I refused to consider how it would affect my future. I didn't want this. On top of everything else that had been piled on me in the last forty-eight hours or so, suddenly possessing magical ability tipped the weirdness scale toward insane territory.

Lark made a strange sound—half sigh, half cough, as if he'd tried to swallow a big dose of pride. "I can't believe you're descended from the djinn. You're damned lucky."

"I really wish people would stop saying that," I muttered. "I'm so far from lucky, I'm kissing its ass from the other side."

"Come on. It's not that bad. Like Tory said, you're still alive."

"Yeah." For now. But with Trevor actively trying to revoke my living-and-breathing status, this particular streak might not last long.

The ground seemed colder now, and the tunnel somehow smaller, though I knew its dimensions hadn't changed. I still had a foot or so above my head and a few inches on either side. We'd only been moving for about ten minutes, but it already felt like hours. My knees ached, and my hands approached numb.

Unfortunately, they weren't far enough along to spare me from feeling the thing with way too many feet trundling across the back of the left one.

"Gah!" I stopped and shook my hand in front of me. In the faint light from Lark's beam, I watched a four-inch-long critter made of legs and attitude cling to my pinkie like an organic grappling hook. I cringed and smacked the thing against the wall. It plopped onto the ground, and I could've sworn I heard it stomping away. "Oh, ugh. What kind of mutant caterpillars you got around here?"

Lark chuffed softly. "The centipede kind. Try not to let those things bite you. They hurt."

"Terrific." I tried not to moan and started forward again. If I got out of this alive, I was moving as far from nature as possible. "How long is this tunnel of yours?"

"Half a mile or so."

"Is that all?" At the rate we were going, we'd be down here for an hour. "Don't suppose you have a shower in your storage building."

"No, but there's a nice freezing pond nearby."

"I'll pass."

Conversation ceased by unspoken consent in an attempt to conserve energy. As my strength drained steadily, I wondered how babies managed to crawl around all day without collapsing. Twenty minutes in, every one of my muscles throbbed and screamed for mercy. The worst were the heels of my hands, right along my thumbs. The flesh there felt packed with burning coals. I gritted my teeth, fisted my hands and knuckled along, noting that the gap between humans and djinn had widened considerably. Ian, at least, had it easy moving on all fours.

"Gotta stop a minute." Lark gasped behind me.

I froze and craned my head around. "What's wrong?"

"Tired. Been sitting on my ass for too long." He rolled to one side and scrunched until he managed to sit with his back against a wall. "Tell 'em to hold up . . ."

I hadn't heard him over my own labored breathing. Now I caught the rattle and wheeze, the almost desperate gasps in his struggle for air. His skin looked like wax paper. He should've stopped before now.

Feeling like a world-class wuss, I inched ahead and held my flashlight out as far as possible, without leaving the circle of light from Lark's. "Ian. Tory. Would you mind joining us back here for a minute?" I called.

No reply. Maybe they were too far ahead. I saw the faint, flickering cast of Tory's fireball ahead and shadows that had to be them. I moved forward and tried again.

"Anybody up there? We need a break. Lark's beat."

"We heard you the first time. We're coming."

Tory's voice bounced hollow along the tunnel back to me. Aware that it would take them a minute to get turned around, I backpedaled slowly, spacing my hands wider to keep from losing my balance.

My right palm landed on loose earth and sank a few inches. The ground came alive beneath it. Within seconds, hundreds of tiny legs swarmed up my arm and into my shirt. Pinpricks of burning pain lanced me, a dozen at once. And kept coming.

"*ARRR*goddamnsonofa*get'emoffme*!"

Lark's flashlight swung on me in response to my garbled litany. I brushed frantically at the ten or so centipedes milling around on my arm. A few refused to let go. So I bashed them into the wall, gagging when they popped and smeared on my skin.

What felt like hundreds of the bastards still crawled around inside my shirt, occasionally stopping for a nibble of Donatti Delight. With a choked howl, I threw myself flat on the ground and rolled hard from side to side in the narrow space, slamming my torso against the walls until nothing moved but my own convulsing body. I stopped, flipped onto my back, and peeled my shirt off. Smears of yellow-green paste bristling with hairy black legs decorated my torso. The bug guts contrasted nicely with the angry red and purple bites dotting my flesh.

I clenched my throat against rising bile and closed my eyes. As I lay there panting, something trundled up my side and across my stomach. I groaned, lifted a hand, and smashed it into oblivion without looking.

A throat-clearing cough demanded my attention. I cracked an eye open to see Tory kneeling over me. "Excuse me," he said. Without waiting for a response, he clambered across me and plunked down next to Lark. His ball of flame settled near the opposite wall. "You all right?"

I scowled at the ceiling. *Yeah, I'm fine, thanks for asking.* At least I knew Tory returned Lark's feelings for him.

Lark nodded once. He closed his eyes and leaned his head back. "Just catching my breath. Haven't had much exercise lately." The corners of his mouth turned down. "They're burning my place," he whispered.

"What?" I sat up and stared down the tunnel toward the house. I saw nothing but blackness. "How can you tell?"

"The smoke. Can't you smell it?"

I drew a deep breath and tasted dirt, sweat, and the acrid tang of destruction by fire. "Oh, Christ. I'm sorry, man. Bastards didn't have to do that."

Lark turned his face away. I suspected he was crying. "Yeah. Well, they probably think we're still in there somewhere. Trying to flush us out like rabbits. We'd better keep moving."

I twisted around to grab my shirt and flinched. The space that had been empty a second ago was now full of wolf. "Shit. Ian, don't sneak up on me like that. We have to—"

He gave a low, menacing growl.

"What's wrong?" Before I realized he couldn't possibly answer me, I figured it out for myself. The ground beneath us trembled. A heartbeat later, a muffled explosion rattled the far end of the corridor. The shaking grew more intense, and tiny showers of dirt erupted from the tunnel ceiling at irregular intervals.

Tory's fireball flickered and sputtered from existence.

"It's coming down!" Tory shouted.

A distant rumble rolled toward us like thunder, growing

louder by the second. "We can't just sit here and die," I said. "Isn't there something *yeeARGH!* What the—"

The agony in my arm stemmed from Ian's teeth clamping into it.

Instinctively, I tried to yank free. The wolf held fast and stared at me. My blood streamed from the punctures at his fangs. It dripped on the ground and ran into his mouth.

The blood is the bond.

"Fuck." I snagged Tory's wrist with my free hand and indicated Lark with a curt nod. "Hold on to him. Now."

Tory didn't question me. I reminded myself to thank him later for that.

This time, I knew exactly what I needed: to get the hell out of there. The knowledge didn't ease the pain, but at least the energy built faster. Burning tendrils shot through my limbs almost instantly—and at once we moved up, through the dirt ceiling like soda in a straw.

Shifting cold earth smothered my senses. Just when my lungs hovered on the verge of oxygen starvation, daylight replaced dirt. For a moment, we were air-bound. Then gravity asserted itself and brought us down in a heap on cool green grass.

Ian pulled his fangs free. I scrambled clear of the pile, coughing and panting. After a brief glimpse of our surroundings, I decided we might have been better off buried alive.

A black-and-white squad car perched on the edge of the sinkhole we'd created in emerging from the ground. It was the only thing blocking us from the view of the cops, who stood at a safe distance from Lark's burning house, their backs to us, waiting for the rabbits to run.

CHAPTER 24

I dragged myself farther behind the car while the others sorted themselves out. "Maybe they won't see us," I whispered.

A loud groan split the air. The squad car rocked a few times and slowly slipped into the edge of the loose dirt pit, where it started to sink. Puzzled shouts erupted from the direction of the cops. Running feet approached.

"Crud. Anyone else have a brilliant idea?"

Ian whined. He belly-crawled closer to me and nuzzled my hand. I took it as an apology. "It's okay. I understand," I said. Since we were ten seconds from being busted, I figured he wanted to make amends before we died.

His lean features reflected exasperation. If wolves could roll their eyes, he would have.

"Look, I'm tapped. I can't even—"

"Stay on the ground. All of you." One of the uniforms had reached the sinking car. He drew his piece and trained it on me. "This is a police—*hey!* I've got Donatti over here!" he roared over his shoulder. The smug grin on his face faltered when he scanned us. "Who the hell are the rest of you assholes?"

Tory pushed me aside and struggled to his feet. He muttered something in djinn. "Donatti's over there," he said, pointing toward the conflagration on the hill.

Confusion flooded the cop's eyes. "Wha . . . ?" He half turned and shouted, "I see them! Coming out the back!"

A second cop joined the first. "You bring the dog? I thought you said he was over here, Mathers. What gives?"

Tory whispered and gestured. The new arrival drew a sharp breath. "Shit. Move out. They're headed for the woods."

"Come on," Lark hissed in my ear. He dragged me back and helped me stand. "Whatever he's doing, it isn't going to last long. Just walk. And act natural."

"Natural. Right." Nothing at all bizarre about three guys— one shirtless, all of them filthy and staggering—out taking their giant wolf for a stroll. On some base level, I understood Tory had somehow temporarily confused the cops. But my mind occupied itself with the more urgent matter of moving fast. Difficult, considering that my legs felt like stones and the rest of me seemed to be on fire.

I managed five or six steps and dropped to my knees. "Can't do it," I mumbled. "Jus' let 'em shoot me. Got plenty of blood left."

Something big and furry slid in front of me and stopped. I slumped across Ian's back, struggling to swing one leg over. At last, I achieved a clumsy grip around his neck and lay draped over him like a worn saddle blanket. "We walk, we die." I gasped. "See any cars we can steal?"

Ian's muscles bunched beneath me. I damn near slid off when he started down the incline at a slow lope. Dimly aware of Tory and Lark following, I watched the world jounce past. A dark blue blur ahead resolved into a sedan, an unmarked cop car. Ian circled the vehicle and stopped next to the driver's-side door.

"Great. Anything more obvious around? Ice-cream truck, hot-air balloon, Howitzer . . ." I let go and oozed to the ground, then hauled myself to my knees and fumbled with the door handle. Locked. No surprise there. "Ian, would you mind changing into something with opposable thumbs, so you can give me a hand?"

A brief snarl escaped him, but he lit up and turned biped again. "I do not typically transform in sight of humans," he said in a harsh whisper. "What do you want?"

"Shut up and unlock the damned door."

To my shock, he actually did both.

I pushed up to a crouch, and the whole world dipped and spun around me. No way I'd be conscious long enough to get us out of here. "Lark," I said, "you here somewhere?"

A voice sounded at my shoulder. "Yeah."

"You're driving." I eased my knife out of my pocket and clambered onto the seat. At least this was an older model. Didn't have to worry about breaking the steering column. I popped the cover off the ignition stem, jammed the blade in, and jiggled it around until the engine caught. "Right. Let's go."

I meant to step out and climb into the backseat. Instead, I found myself flat on my back with my legs still inside the car. "Ow. Pavement."

Someone—I couldn't tell if it was Ian or Lark—hooked me under the arms, hauled me up, and folded me onto the back-seat. A door slammed shut, then another. Everything headed sideways in a slow, smooth motion.

Just before I passed out, I felt phantom centipedes crawling on my skin from head to toe. I didn't bother brushing them off.

For a moment, I failed to grasp the significance of the sand coating my mouth or the rash of hot, itchy bubbles stippling my back and chest. I wrenched an eye open. Things didn't improve. Darkness splashed across my vision like spilled oil. Was I captured? Dead?

I groaned and tried moving. One hand twitched. I was pretty sure it was mine. Flexing my fingers, I dragged the hand inward and felt a rough, cool surface. I hoped it wasn't Trevor's basement floor.

"Welcome back, thief."

"Mmph." At least Ian sounded halfway normal. Maybe he wasn't as drained as I felt. A slight breeze indicated that wherever we were, it was outside. I forced both eyes open and focused on the closest object, which happened to be a twisted wreck of a car. "Damn, Lark. Where'd you learn to drive, Jersey?"

"What are you . . . oh. We ditched the plain wrapper a while back."

I blinked a few times and realized the wreck used to be a green convertible. It had company, too. Rusted hulks stretched in a row under a blazing near-full moon and terminated in a mountain of scrap metal. A junkyard. And I was sprawled on Abraham Lincoln's refrigerator.

How much worse could our refuge options get? At this rate, we'd end up hiding from Trevor in a sewage pipe.

Sensation returned to me reluctantly. I pushed up and sat on the edge of the ancient icebox, pointedly not looking at the multitude of bites—centipede and wolf—that scored my flesh. Ian huddled on the ground next to me. Tory and Lark slumped on oversized wooden spools to my right. I'd seen more cheerful expressions on prisoners headed for their executions.

I decided to discuss less urgent concerns first. "Anybody got a spare shirt?"

Ian stood slowly. "I will heal you, if you wish."

"No. Really, I'm fine. Just a little chilly." Knowing exactly how much it hurt him to use power made me reluctant to ask for anything. "I'll survive."

"Very well." He slipped his jacket off and held it out to me, leaving him in only a vest.

"I can't take that."

Ian frowned. "You are cold. I am not."

"Fine." Instinct told me there was no sense arguing. "Thank you."

I had to stand to put it on. The material, some kind of leather, felt warm and pliable and not nearly as heavy as I expected. It seemed to mold to my shape. After a moment, I realized the jacket really had changed. With the difference in height between us, the lower edge should have dragged on the ground. It didn't—it was a perfect fit. "What's this made from?"

"Human skin."

"Ergh." I had one arm halfway out before I noticed the smirk on Ian's face. "You know, you could've just said 'none of your business' if you didn't want to talk about it. Is this another one of those things my pathetic brain can't understand?"

"No. It is leather. Which comes from cows. You did know that, did you not?" The smirk grew. "I simply thought you might enjoy a more colorful explanation."

"Since when does cow leather adjust itself to whoever's wearing it?"

Ian shrugged. "I may have made a few modifications."

"Great. I'm wearing an enchanted coat. Do I get glass slippers, too?"

"If you wish."

I laughed. "Thought you said I didn't get any wishes."

"Donatti."

Lark's strained interruption let reality leach all the calm out of me. "What?"

"If you two are done fucking around, maybe you could give us a hand figuring out how we're going to survive until dawn."

"Right." I sat back down. "Who's got a plan?"

No one replied. I figured that meant we were screwed.

"I must contact Akila," Ian said. "Stay here. I will return in a few moments."

As if we had the choice to go out and catch a movie while he was gone.

I watched Ian head down between rows of smashed cars and then slumped in place. Three days of fragmented sleep, combined with expending energy I didn't even know I possessed, had managed to turn everything inside me to mush. "Okay. What happened while I was out?" I said. "You all look half dead."

Tory shrugged. "That car was too hot. We had to leave it, so Ian and I flew part of the way."

"You're kidding. We were airborne, and I didn't wake up?"

Lark shuddered. "Yeah. Lucky bastard."

I let my head drop and indulged in closing my eyes for a moment. "Well," I said without looking up. "First thing we have to do is figure a ride out of here. How close are we to civilization? Maybe I can boost another car somewhere."

Silence. I lifted my gaze to find Lark glaring daggers.

"What'd I do now?"

Lark spat on the ground. "You and your pal Ian are on your own from here, Donatti. There is no *we*."

"Lark, wait," Tory said. "I think we should talk about—"

"No, we shouldn't!" Lark stalked a few paces away from the djinn and turned his inferno gaze back to me. "Breaking my spine wasn't enough for you? Thanks for showing up and ruining my life again."

"You're welcome." I didn't bother reminding him that I'd healed him, too.

"God damn it." He closed the distance between us and stopped half a foot from my face. "I should beat you into the ground, right now."

I shrugged. "Go ahead."

"What?"

"If it'd make you feel better, go for it. I won't stop you." I managed to stay calm on the outside. To have half a chance at making this clusterfuck work, we needed everyone focused. Including Lark. Even if he had to take a few swings at me to get there.

Couldn't blame him, really. I'd do the same.

His eye twitched. "You smug bastard. How can you do this? You sic Trevor on me, get my place burned down, force me underground, and now you think you're gonna take the only thing that matters to me anymore."

"All right, Lark. You lost me. What am I taking?"

He sent a helpless glance at Tory, who seemed to have decided that Lark and I needed some one-to-one time and kept his distance. "This isn't his war. Can't you leave him out of it?"

"Whoa." I stood and tried to think calm thoughts. "Nobody's making him do anything."

"You haven't left him much of a choice. You brought the djinn who ditched him four hundred years ago back into his life and dumped his problems in our laps. What's he supposed to do now?"

"Come on. I came to ask you for information." My calm was disappearing fast. Contrary to Quaid the bounty hunter's belief, there were some people you just couldn't reason with. "I didn't know you'd hooked up with him, and I sure as hell didn't mean to bring the cops down on you. Or Trevor."

"Well, you did. And now he'll end up—"

"*Adjo.* What's going on?"

Lark flinched when Tory came up behind him and put a hand on his shoulder. "Nothing," he muttered. "Just championing a hopeless cause."

Tory smiled. "You're good at that. But I think we should talk about what we're going to do now."

"Can't we just leave?" The slight tremor in Lark's voice didn't stem from anger. "I don't owe Donatti anything, and you don't owe Ian. They can sort this out themselves."

"Lark, you know why I have to help him."

I got the impression I'd been left out of something and the distinct feeling I wouldn't be brought in.

"Yeah, I do. I've heard plenty about the great Gahiji-an, haven't I?" Lark jerked away from his touch and turned his back. "You're going to get killed because of *his* war. And if you do survive, you'll go back with him."

Tory's face fell. He stepped toward Lark, hesitated. "I may be killed," he said quietly. "But if I'm not, I won't leave you."

"That's a big fucking if!" Lark whirled. His gaze skated past Tory and landed on me. "You don't need us. You're a descendant, so you and Mr. Amazing can handle this alone. I can't—"

He drew a sharp breath and finally met Tory's eyes. "I can't lose you."

"Gods," Tory whispered. "Why would you do this to me? We've talked about this. I don't like it, but I have to help. Do you really think I want to die for the realm?"

"What about what you're doing to me?"

"Lark, cut the crap." I moved toward him, intent on shutting him up for a minute. I still didn't know exactly what they'd discussed, but I understood enough to figure out which one was the jackass. "Don't you think you're being a little selfish here?"

Something solid slammed my jaw. After the stars cleared, I realized it was Lark's fist.

I shook my head and decided to give him a free pass for the blow. Had that one coming for years. "Happy now?" I said.

"Fuck you." He drew back with a snarl. "This is all just fine with you, isn't it? You have nothing to lose."

Screw calm. I couldn't let that one slide.

"Lark. I'm going to tell you something, and I want you to think real hard before you shoot your mouth off again. You listening?"

"If I have to."

"You do." I came close to slugging him anyway. Instead, I clenched my fists hard enough to feel my nails dig in. "Remember when Ian said he has another descendant besides me, who's still alive?"

"Yeah. Got a point?"

"The other one's two years old. Cute kid, lots of curls, big blue eyes. And right now, he's with his mother. I think you've met her. She's about four-eleven and a breath. Likes wearing shades and kicking people's asses."

Lark appeared to deflate. "You mean . . . you and Jazz?"

I chose not to dignify that with a response. "Yesterday, they walked through a mirror in a hotel room, into the djinn realm. And according to Ian's father-in-law—big pissed-off guy, leader of the djinn, doesn't like humans—they aren't coming back unless we stop these Morai bastards, who by the way are planning to take over the world after they overthrow the djinn realm. Oh, and Trevor wants the kid, too. So he can kill him while I watch." I forced my jaw to relax a bit, before I seriously damaged my teeth. "But I've got nothing to lose. Right? So go ahead and beat me into the ground. Just keep in mind that when you're finished, it's my turn."

It took him a minute to respond. "Well. Shit."

"That's the short version."

Lark shook his head and backed down. "Donatti, you have lousy—"

"Don't say it. I know." I was getting pretty tired of hearing the L-word. "So can we call a truce, or do I have to let you kick my ass?"

"All right. Truce." He looked over my shoulder with a frown. "What the hell is he doing?"

Tory and I followed his gaze. Down the corridor, beneath a security light, Ian knelt on the hood of a rusted pickup with one hand against the edge of the roof and the other through the intact windshield. He drew his arm back with someone else's attached. A slender golden-brown arm that was familiar enough by itself, before the rest of Jazz followed.

CHAPTER 25

I bolted toward them, not caring whether Tory and Lark came along. The fact that she appeared unharmed didn't make me feel much better. She wouldn't have been here if something hadn't gone wrong. Right now, she was probably furious.

When I got there, she seemed less than concerned. In fact, she was hugging Ian.

I couldn't stop the scowl that formed on my face. "Do you two want a room?"

Jazz drew back and leaned on the pickup. "Donatti, this is no time to turn green."

"Relax, thief," Ian said. "I was simply assisting her down."

I ignored him and rushed to Jazz. "Why are you here? Where's Cyrus?"

"Nice to see you, too." She tucked a strand of hair behind an ear and shivered. "Damn, that's cold."

"You're not answering me."

She glared. "Do you really think I'd leave him if I didn't know he was safe? He's with Akila. And I'm fine, thanks."

"Jesus Christ, Jazz. It's not like I'm running into you at the grocery store here." I forced myself to step back, breathe, think. Had to be an explanation for this. "Okay. It's good to see you, but why are you here?"

Something dark flashed in her eyes. With an obvious effort to keep from screaming, she said, "I got kicked out."

"What?"

"Kemo Sabe, or whatever the fuck his name is—"

"Kemosiri."

"That's it. He said Cy could stay because he has djinn blood, but I couldn't."

"Son of a bitch." I whirled on Ian. "I thought you said this would work. Can't you do something? Make him change his mind!"

Ian's jaw hardened. "Kemosiri's mind cannot be changed."

"It's all right." Jazz offered a heavy sigh. "I'll just—"

"No, it's not. You can't be here," I blurted. For the first time since I'd met her, some other emotion overruled the concern that she might kick my ass for contradicting her, and my mouth took off on a kamikaze mission. "You were *safe* there. Ian, send her back. Please."

"Don't you dare patronize me." Jazz straightened with ice in her gaze. "Let's get something settled, Donatti. I didn't need you when Cy was born, and I don't need you now. I'm going to handle this. Understand?"

She couldn't have hurt me more if she'd sandblasted my skin and rolled me around in salt. I tried to nod, but my head refused to cooperate. At last, I managed to speak. "Fine. What are you going to do, then?"

"Kill Trevor." She smirked. "Can't let you have all the fun."

A chill stole through me. "Didn't you hear the part about the evil djinn he's working with? You can't . . . you've got to hide out somewhere. A motel, maybe. Bed and breakfast. Fucking KOA, even. Another country would be great. I'll buy you a plane ticket." Jesus. I was gibbering like a moron, and I couldn't stop. "Just get as far away from Trevor as you can."

"No. Damn it, I'm not going to hide."

Her tone said she was two seconds from slugging me. I swallowed my immediate protest. "Can you at least tell me why you won't go somewhere safe?"

"Because Trevor is trying to murder my son." The raw edge in her voice was painful to hear. "And if he succeeds because I *didn't* do anything, I'm as good as dead anyway. I would've stayed with Cy, but since I can't—and I know he's safe—I'm going after the bastard."

Damn it. How could I tell her that everything she felt for Cyrus I felt for her? It'd be a hell of a lot easier to keep her alive if she wasn't here to get shot. Or tortured. Still, I knew there was no changing her mind once she'd made it up. I'd just have to make damned sure she survived. "Okay," I said. "But you're not handling Trevor alone, so don't try. We stick together."

She smiled. "I was counting on that."

Ian cleared his throat. "If you are finished, perhaps we should attempt to determine a mode of transportation." He nodded back down the corridor, where Tory and Lark waited with almost identical frowns. "We cannot remain in one place for long. They will find us."

"Wait a minute," Jazz said. "How's he going to find us here? We're a county away, in the middle of nowhere. Aren't we?"

I gave her a puzzled look before I remembered that she'd missed the whole tether-tracing thing. "Long story," I said. "Ian's right. We need to move. Any ideas?"

By unspoken consent, the three of us walked toward Tory

and Lark. Jazz scrutinized wrecked cars as we passed them. "Guess we're probably a long walk from civilization," she said. "But we'll have to hoof it, anyway. I doubt there's a salvageable ride anywhere in here—and even if there was, I don't have my tools."

My brief hope of hotwiring a wreck guttered. If anyone could make that statement, it was Jazz. She'd forgotten more about cars than I'd ever figured out.

But she didn't know much about djinn magic.

I grinned. "Maybe you won't need them."

"Are you nuts? I can't hand-tool an engine. I'm not Superwoman."

"No." I jerked a thumb in Ian's direction. "But he is."

"Did you just call me a woman, thief?"

"Relax. It's a metaphor." I shook my head and reset my train of thought. "Jazz, remember what he did to your van?"

Her expression brightened a bit. "Yes . . ."

"With your skills and his mojo, I think we can rig something."

She nodded. "I'll find a likely candidate." With that, she turned and headed back toward the pickup.

"Yeah," I muttered after her retreating form. "Why don't you do that?" Sighing, I pivoted to find Lark right in front of me.

"Well?" he said. "What's going on? Isn't that Jazz?"

"Brilliant observation," I said. "Yes, that's her. She . . . didn't want to be left out of the vengeance party."

Lark nodded, but sympathy was reflected in his face. "Guess we're both stuck in this."

"You could say that." I turned to Ian. "Any idea how long we have until they find your tether again?"

"Not long. Perhaps two days and then the time it takes for

his closest minions to reach us." He grimaced. "They will not wait for Shamil to regain full strength."

Not as long as I'd hoped. "All right, so what are our options? We keep moving, or . . ." I hesitated. The thought forming in my head had the hallmarks of a made-for-television B-movie sequel. *Stupid Donatti Strikes Again.* Still, it was just nuts enough to work. Maybe. If I could manage to stave off my lousy luck for what would come down to the most important gig of my life.

"Okay. What if we break into Trevor's place and steal his surveillance system?"

Lark snorted. "You can't steal a system, Donatti. And even if you could, you'd have to presteal it so you wouldn't get busted."

"I meant Shamil."

Three pairs of eyes tried to burn holes through me.

"Let me explain," I said. "We're never going to get anywhere if we stay on the defensive. If he's using Shamil to track us, we can take that away from him—and a few other little things. I mean, he asked you to free him, didn't he?" I looked at Ian, hoping for a little support.

Ian winced. "That is not what he meant. He wanted me to . . . destroy his tether."

"No." Tory stood fast, almost knocking Lark over. "Ian, you can't. We've got to get him out of there."

"Taregan, you've not seen what they have done to him."

A shiver shot through me with Ian's strained words. I had.

"Well, you two can heal him. Can't you? I mean, you did it for Lark."

"I do not know if that is possible. It may take more power than we are able to produce."

"We can try! You can't just kill him."

"It is what he wants."

Tory glared daggers. "Always the general, Gahiji-an. Sacrifice the one for the good of the many, right? Let me ask you something. If it was you in there, would you rather we murdered you than try to save you?"

"If it would mean sparing the realm, saving the others, then yes. I would."

Though Ian returned a cool stare, I knew Tory had hit him where it hurt. Right in his pride.

"All right, this isn't helping," I said. "Look, if Shamil still wants to die after we bust him out, he can tell us himself. And I think we can do it. If we pull this off, we might be able to save your friend and get rid of Trevor and his Morai pal at the same time."

Ian was already shaking his head. "I am not convinced we will be able to destroy this Morai," he said.

I blinked at him. "You know which one it is? Does it even matter?"

"In this case, it might. I believe Trevor has allied himself with Lenka."

"Of course he has." Just my luck to have my mortal enemy hook up with the strongest possible bad guy. What had Ian said about him? Powerful, inbred, and crazy. Terrific.

Tory's jaw looked as if it might fall off. "Lenka? Shit, Ian. You could've mentioned that before." He crossed his arms. "Maybe we should come up with a different plan."

"Come on," I said. "You said it yourself, Ian. All we have to do is get his tether."

Ian gave a deep frown. "You do not know Lenka. Destroying him will not be an easy task."

"Just hear me out, okay? And I need Jazz to listen in. She's important to the plan." Besides, she'd kill me if I made monumental decisions about Trevor without her. I spotted her leaning over the engine bay of a solid-looking Cadillac, prodding wires and yanking out dipsticks. Damn. If all mechanics were that sexy, I'd have gone in for a lot more repairs. I cupped my hands and shouted her way.

She strode back, wiping grease-smudged hands on her thighs. "That one might do it," she said. "Why do you all look like somebody spit in your drinks?"

"Your friend De Rossi here thinks he has a plan," Tory said.

I sighed. "It's Donatti."

"Whatever. Just spit it out."

I drew a breath and explained what I was thinking. They came around. Eventually.

Ian smiled. "It is a good plan."

"Thanks. I'm a brilliant strategist when it comes to saving my own ass."

"If this works, you will save more asses than your own." Ian glanced at Tory, who looked away just long enough to seem apologetic. "Are we in agreement, then?"

No one objected. I guessed that was as close to agreement as a bunch of humans and djinn who were probably planning their deaths could get.

WHILE JAZZ BANGED AROUND UNDER THE HOOD OF THE CADDY and instructed Ian on the finer points of vehicles that didn't sport pull-me-over signs, I ran reconnaissance on an important mission: finding needles in a haystack. Or, more technically, finding knives or knife-shaped metal objects in a thousand tons of jumbled scrap metal.

Inspired by Lark's bird mummy, I'd persuaded Ian to make dupes of his tether—one for each of us to carry. He'd stash the real one here among the junk, so none of us would have it when we broke into Trevor's place. It wasn't a permanent solution. If we got caught, it would only buy us time. I hoped that would be enough.

Ian had explained that transformation worked best when the thing being changed resembled the original. Jazz and Lark didn't do blades, so that left us with one between us, the butterfly I'd lifted from Pope. I was glad to donate it to the cause. Using another man's blade was like wearing someone else's underwear. Now I only had to locate four more knives.

Might as well look for Atlantis in here. I'd probably find it sooner.

I left the long rows of junked cars and headed for the giant piles of scrap. There weren't quite so many lights on this end of the lot, and the jagged mounds of metal cast deep shadows over the narrow pathways. The place smelled like fresh earth and old blood. At the base of one mountain, an idle yellow Cat stood with scoop upraised, as though its driver had given up hope of ever moving that formidable mass and run screaming from the yard at mid-push.

The flashlight Lark lent me, a mini Mag with a halogen bulb, should have cut through the gloom like butter. Instead, it created a murky brown puddle near my feet. I slapped it against my thigh. Blue light flashed forward, throwing the junk ahead into strobe relief. For an instant, I thought my chest tightened and my arms tingled, but whether magical need or old-fashioned brute force had brought the light around, I welcomed it.

I recognized a few of the twisted, bent, and generally broken objects stacked to the sky. Bed frames, filing cabinets, pipe fittings, and ladders studded the less recognizable mash of splinters and chunks. Eventually, I unearthed a jumbled pile of tableware, fished out four reasonably solid table knives, and wandered back toward the others with my rust-spotted bounty.

Apparently, Jazz and Ian hadn't resolved their technical differences yet, because I arrived to find them in the middle of a small war. Jazz had the Caddy jacked up and was halfway through stripping the lugs on a bad flat. A fresh tire stood propped beside her, and a frustrated Ian stood scowling over her.

"This is not necessary," Ian said. "I can repair the tire in far less time."

Jazz didn't even look at him. "With magic? No, thanks. I've got it."

"Why not?"

"Because I don't want this bitch to blow while I'm driving."

"It will not 'blow.'"

"How do you know? This thing's a human contraption. And maybe everything that works in your world doesn't work in ours. Besides, when it comes to cars, nothing beats mechanical soundness. The less jerry-rigging we have to do, the better."

Ian grunted. "At least allow me to loosen those fastenings."

"Will you shut up and let me work? I said, I've got it."

"I found your knives," I said loudly.

Ian's head swiveled in my direction. "Would you inform your woman that djinn magic is not like your charlatan stage performers and will not cease to function if one should sneeze while driving a vehicle?"

"And would you inform your *genie*," Jazz said, emphasizing the word with a hard twist on the lug wrench, "that I'm perfectly capable of changing a goddamned tire?"

"Hey, look. I'm not translating English into English." I shoved a fistful of knives against Ian's chest. "Take these. First of all, where's Lark and Tory?"

Ian snatched the bundle and waved a hand off to his right. "They seek a suitable location to conceal my tether."

"Okay." I crouched next to Jazz. "I'm not saying you're wrong, but he's right."

The look she gave me said she would've punched me if her hands weren't full of tire iron. I reminded myself not to argue with her when she possessed a lethal weapon. "I'm busy," she said. "Back off."

"Come on, Jazz. It'd be faster if you let him do it."

"I've. Got. It." She freed the last lug with a crack and yanked the tire off as if she was plucking a leaf from a branch. "Look, Donatti. I've got to contribute something, okay? I don't have any magic."

If she were anyone else, I would've thought she was jealous. But I knew what she meant. Watching someone else get even for you wasn't satisfying enough. "All right," I said. "Just try to remember that you don't have to do everything alone. We're on the same side here."

"Yeah. Thanks." She scooped the scattered lugs into a hand and frowned at them. "Shit. These are stripped to hell. I'll never get them back on." With a sigh, she held them toward Ian. "Can you . . ."

"Of course." Ian set the knives aside. "Though I am not quite certain what you need me to do. What is stripped to hell?"

Jazz smirked. "I'll show you."

After fifteen minutes of explanations punctuated by subtle and not-so-subtle jabs, Jazz pronounced the thing drivable.

She'd helped Ian create a set of plates that would pass a cursory glance from a cop, though we had no idea what'd happen if anyone ran the tags. We hoped we wouldn't get the opportunity to find out.

"Now," Ian said when we stepped back, "we must create the duplicates. I will need your assistance, thief."

"Whoa. What, with making them?" I held up a hand. "Come on, man. I already had enough doing Lark. I'm not real interested in frying myself again."

"Doing Lark?" Jazz cocked her head. "What'd you do to him?"

I sighed. "He was in a wheelchair when we found him. And . . . otherwise fucked up. Ian healed him. I guess I helped."

"You unparalyzed him?"

"He did." Ian thrust one of the table knives in my direction. "And he is going to assist me further, because I do not have the strength at the moment."

"Oh, I gotta see this." Jazz boosted herself onto the hood of the Caddy and sat cross-legged, watching me with something like awe. Or serious doubt. Maybe utter disbelief.

I snatched the knife. "Fine. Just for the record, though, I'm not looking forward to this."

"Why?"

"Because it hurts. Remember?"

"Only too well."

The catch in Ian's voice reminded me how much longer he'd been doing this. I decided to lay off. "Sorry, Ian. What am I supposed to do?"

"I will show you, if you would hand me my tether."

"Oh. Right." I'd forgotten I was wearing his coat. I patted the pockets, discovered a lump, and gave him the dagger.

He took it and held one of the replacements in his opposite hand. "As Taregan explained, it is a matter of need—or, in this case, will. You must will one object to resemble another." He offered a small smile. "Do not worry, thief. Transformation is a strength of the Dehbei. This will not hurt as much."

"Great. That's very reassuring."

"Pay attention." Ian held the table knife on an open palm. He passed his tether slowly over the length of it, and a copy of the dagger emerged inch by inch. When he held them both up, I knew he could've put them behind his back and shuffled them, and I wouldn't have been able to spot the original. He handed me one with a nod. "It is your turn."

I swallowed and took the dagger. His instructions sounded like a knockoff Nike commercial. *Just will it.* There had to be more to this stuff than feelings, didn't there? Just because I shared a few genes with Ian, that didn't mean I should be able to make unnatural things happen when I wanted them to. It almost seemed wrong. Like cheating.

Then again, I supposed stealing wasn't much better.

I arranged the knife in my hand the way he had and stared at the dagger for a long moment. Maybe if I memorized the shape of it, my will would have an easier time imposing itself. I felt far from ready when I copied Ian's motion and passed the dagger over the knife.

No pain. And no change.

"Brilliant," I said. "Maybe I should stick with accidental invisibility."

I tried to give the dagger back. Ian didn't take it. "Try again, thief. You have made progress."

"No, I haven't. This thing is still just a rusted . . . er, wait." I held up the table knife and blinked. Along the flat blade, copper had replaced silver beneath the corroded surface streaks. The handle seemed thicker, too. "I'll be damned," I murmured.

Without waiting for a prompt, I lowered the knife and tried to concentrate. To tune out everything but the dagger and my need to make this work. After a minute, my chest tightened. Warmth spread through my torso, down my arms. Only a mild ache instead of the intense pain Lark's healing had caused. I moved the dagger over the base of the knife, and it rippled and expanded against my palm.

For the first time since I'd met Ian, wonder struck me and demanded acknowledgment.

Magic. I possessed magic. It was in my blood. I could *feel* it, a tingling sensation through skin and bone, raw and comforting at once. Like toweling off in a cold room after a hot shower. The realness of it lodged in my throat.

When I looked down, I realized I hadn't quite gotten the hang of it. The handle looked almost right, but the blade was still dull and rounded. The world's first table dagger.

A hesitant laugh escaped Jazz. "You missed a spot."

I glowered at her and tried again. The same feeling moved through me. I forced my mind to think dagger thoughts. Finally, I finished the pass and fought a whisper of vertigo. A glance at the dupe revealed I'd gotten it right this time—or at least close enough. "No problem," I said with a slight slur. "Let's make a hundred of 'em."

"You really did it?" Jazz slid down from the hood and plucked the copy from my hand. "Holy hell. Ian, you sure you didn't help him with this?"

I made a face. "Your confidence is underwhelming."

"Sorry." Jazz smiled and squeezed my hand. "Guess I picked the right nickname for you after all, Houdini. I'm impressed."

I grinned. *Impressed* in Jazz-speak was one step shy of worship. Maybe she really didn't completely hate me.

"I will be impressed if you manage to transform the remaining three." Ian handed the knives to Jazz, then absently tucked the dupe he held into his waistband. "You must use the true tether as a guide for each transformation. Be as quick as you can. The sooner we depart, the more time we will have before we are discovered."

"Wait a second. Why do I have to do it? I mean, if you want fast, you should probably do this yourself. I suck at magic."

"I have explained this. I have no power left. After two transformations, flight, bridging to the djinn realm, and repairing that vehicle, I am drained." Ian hitched a half-smile. "And you need the practice, thief."

"Terrific. Well, don't blame me if they end up looking like shit."

I managed to get through the rest in a few minutes. They didn't look half bad.

"Well done." Ian put a hand on my shoulder. "Now, we must conceal the true tether. I cannot allow Lenka to control me."

I glanced around at the mountains of junk. "Well, if we had to pick a place to hide it, I'd say this one's pretty good."

"Yes. Taregan has prepared a spot where it will be difficult to recognize." A strange look flickered across his face. "Come. I wish you to know where my tether will be."

My brow furrowed. "Why?"

"You may need this information eventually."

"Yeah. If you say so." I followed him anyway, thinking that whatever was on his mind, I probably didn't want to know.

TORY HAD CREATED A NEST OF METAL SCRAPS AND PIECES OF daggers, all the same color and style as Ian's tether. Once we buried it in the pile, he levitated a couple of cars and piled them on the spot. The feat used up the rest of his mojo, too. I'd seen corpses that looked more animated than Ian and Tory by the time we dragged ourselves back and loaded in the car.

Jazz insisted on driving. No one objected. She eased the Caddy onto the main road and pointed us in the general direction of Trevor's place. She'd suggested that Tory ride shotgun, since he was the least wanted. The rest of us crammed into the backseat and tried to shrink, to avoid touching each other. I wished we'd rigged a van instead. Close quarters made me itchy.

"This is a bad idea," Lark said for the hundredth time.

I let my head fall back against the seat. "Like I said, you got a better one? Jazz knows what she's doing. We'll be fine."

Lark muttered something that sounded suspiciously like *Go fuck yourself*. Up front, a station giving the news and weather droned. Tory perched rigid and alert in the passenger seat, scanning the night for dangerous creatures like cops or stray deer or maybe innocent-looking hitchhikers who were actually evil snake djinn in disguise.

I slumped between Lark and Ian and tried not to think that things couldn't get any worse. If I let myself believe that, fate would be eager to prove me wrong.

"It will not work." Beside me, Ian toyed with the dupe he carried, regarding it with an expression normally reserved for offensive things like shit on a shoe and Canadian bacon.

"Sure it will." I sounded about as convincing as a politician's promise. "It's a classic con. The old shell game. They'll never see it coming. I mean, there's no way to tell these things are fake, right?"

"There is one, outside of my obvious failure to die when one is destroyed."

"And that'd be . . ."

"Blood tells."

I frowned. "That doesn't sound good."

Ian unsheathed the dagger and ran a finger along the flat of the blade. "A tether reacts to the blood of the one tied to it. If my blood were spilled on the real tether, my symbol would be revealed. These false ones will not mimic that response."

"Great. Does Trevor know this?"

"I am not certain. But Lenka does."

"So we'll just have to stay away from Lenka. Wherever he is. It'll work out."

Ian sighed and stowed the dagger in his vest. "Perhaps. But we should plan for the possibility that something might go wrong."

"What could happen?"

The instant I said it, I wished he wouldn't answer. I could imagine plenty of things going wrong. Sudden death. Drawn-out, painful death. Or worse, as Trevor had promised on my last visit with him.

"I am their primary target." Ian spoke soft and low, as if he didn't want the others to hear him over the radio babble. He looked at his hands and touched the index finger that carried his bond with Akila. The golden glow shone briefly. "They will attempt to take me first. If they succeed, they will use me to find you and the boy before they destroy me. And I've no wish to exist as Lenka's plaything."

"Ian. Don't even think about it."

"We *must* think about it." His gaze held mine, and I couldn't look away. "If I am captured—"

"No. I won't—"

"—you must destroy my tether."

The words hung between us, impossible to take back. "I can't do that," I whispered.

"You can. Your abilities are more than sufficient. If you destroy me, it will be far more difficult for them to hunt you down. You and your son will survive. The barrier must remain."

"I can't kill you. I won't."

A small smile tugged his mouth. "Then do not. Free me."

"Calling it something else doesn't change what it is."

"Perhaps not. Still, it must be done." He gripped my shoulder. "Promise me, thief. Promise me you will do what is necessary to save my realm and your family. Your world. Every human will suffer if the Morai are permitted to regain control."

Was anyone listening to this insanity? Lark faced the window as if his life depended on looking anywhere but at me. Jazz concentrated on the road. I glanced at Tory's profile. In the gloom, it was hard to tell whether he'd heard our discussion, but I thought his eyes seemed too bright, his jaw too firm. "How am I supposed to get to it?" I said. "I can't lift cars."

"You will find a way," Ian whispered. "You must."

I didn't say anything for a moment. When I couldn't come up with another excuse, I snapped, "Fine. Damn you, I promise. But it's not going to be necessary. This will work."

"Thank you. I do hope you are right." Ian sank back into the seat and closed his eyes, as if asking me to kill him had taken more power than creating a dimensional portal.

I kept my mouth shut and fought the urge to protest further. Ian was wrong. Killing him wouldn't save my family, because he was part of it. Like it or not.

After five minutes of unsuccessfully trying not to remind

myself that I'd just promised to murder someone—and worse, someone I cared about—I decided to attempt distraction. I leaned between the front seats and touched Jazz on the arm. "So," I said, "what's it like over there?"

She blinked. "Give me some context here, Donatti. Over where?"

"The djinn realm."

"Oh." She gave a one-shouldered shrug. "It's okay, I guess."

"That's it? Just okay?" I scooted forward as far as I could without falling off my seat. "C'mon, Jazz, it's not like you were visiting Boston or anything. It's a magic realm. There must've been something interesting, right?"

"Well, I—" She glanced in the mirror, and I realized with a start that she'd looked at Ian. Did she need his permission? Finally, she cleared her throat and said, "It's beautiful. Like a dream. Ian . . . I won't talk about it if you don't want to hear it."

A sad smile arranged itself on his face. "No, lady. It is all right. I would not mind hearing of home."

Jazz nodded. "It's hard to describe, but everything is alive. The furniture, the clothes they wear, even the walls. Everything moves like it's breathing, and the air—you know how people say there's music in the air? It's real there, the music. You can just hear it, all the time, bells and voices and whispers. But it's not singing. It's the wind and the water. It's life music."

I grinned. "You're downright poetic, Jazz."

"Hey, you wanted to hear about it." She smiled back. "They have this statue in the palace courtyard. It's a tree. A Joshua tree, I think. It's made out of flowing water, and the leaves are flames. It just hangs in the air and rotates. You can touch it and get wet, but it doesn't lose its shape. Cy . . ." She drew a quick breath and laughed softly. "The first time we saw it, Cy splashed around in the trunk for half an hour. Then he asked if he could have a wet tree in his bedroom."

"The elemental fountain," Tory said. "I'd almost forgotten. A tree of fire, rendered in water, suspended in air. At sunset..."

"It catches the light and burns red." Ian trailed fingers down the window glass. "It is supposed to represent unity, though the hypocrisy of the Council makes a mockery of its own symbol."

"Anyway," Jazz said after an awkward pause, "they have this amazing hot drink. I don't know what they put in it, but it tastes like silk sugar coffee with berries and nuts and cream, and it makes our fancy gourmet stuff seem like muddy water."

"*Asir'an de labaan*," Ian said. "The nectar of the gods."

"Yeah. That." Jazz tightened her grip on the wheel for an instant. "I didn't really see anything outside the palace, though. We were more or less under house arrest."

Ian sighed. "I am not surprised. Kemosiri would not wish the entire realm to know he had allowed humans into the palace." He gestured in the air, a quick blur of motion that left soft, glowing fingers hanging before him. They faded so fast I was sure I'd imagined them. "It is a shame you were not able to visit the outlying realm—the misted mountains of the Bahari proper, the lush forests of the Lycheni clan, the glittering lakes of Amahnri. And the eastern lands, the painted desert. The country of my clan held such beauty before the wars. Fine colored sands and cascading rock, blooming *lo'ani* and the sweet barbed flesh of the *kaktao*. And music! Our nights were filled with it. We danced and sang beneath the spangled sky until dawn burned the dunes. We were..." He closed his eyes, and pain twisted his mouth in a grimace. "Free," he whispered.

Ian's impassioned speech wove a spell of silence through the car. After a moment, Jazz shattered it with a throat-clearing cough. "What was all that about?"

"Didn't you hear him?" I said. "He was talking about forests and lakes and colored sand and music. Dancing, Ian? I never would've pegged you for a dancer."

Tory sent me an odd look. I frowned, glanced at Lark, and discovered him staring at me as if I'd just lost the last marble rolling around in my skull.

"What?"

Lark ignored me. "Is he right?" he asked Tory.

Tory nodded.

"I'll be damned." This from Jazz, who smirked and offered a disbelieving headshake.

"What's going on?" I caught Ian's gaze, but he looked just as confused as I was.

"I don't think he knows." Tory broke out in a grin. "Seems Ian temporarily forgot about the mixed company here. He was speaking djinn."

"He was?" I slumped back against the seat. It hadn't sounded like djinn to me, but I hadn't really been listening for words. I'd just let his speech wash over me and found an almost painful comfort in the rhythm of his descriptions and the emotion behind his recollections. I understood it so completely that I'd practically been there with him.

The connection unnerved me. If I felt this way just hearing about everything he'd lost from his home, how could I possibly deal with being forced to kill him?

Somehow, I'd have to make sure it didn't come to that.

CHAPTER 26

I wasn't sure how long we'd been driving, but we were within sight of a town called Shamrock when we heard the siren. And I thought shamrocks were supposed to be lucky.

I guessed my bad karma negated even the luck of the Irish.

Jazz swore under her breath. "Ian, are you sure you put three letters and four numbers on those plates?"

"Of course I did."

"And Trevor couldn't have found us with magic yet?"

"Correct."

Jazz glanced in the rearview and tapped the brake. "Left taillight's out. Shit!"

Biggest understatement I'd heard all night. No word existed in English to describe how deep we were in. Even if this cop wasn't Trevor's dog, we were busted the second he ran the fake plates.

Red and blue lights flashed across the interior of the car, painting stricken faces. The cry of the siren blasted through Tory's open window. My brain shuffled through a dozen different scenarios. None of them ended fortunately for us.

And none of them started with Jazz pulling over. Which she did.

"What are you doing?" I hissed. "Keep moving! You can outrun him."

"No, I can't." She pointed at the windshield.

I leaned forward. We'd stopped just before a bright orange detour sign that pointed to a crooked dirt path with no right to call itself a road. A few hundred feet ahead, concrete barriers with yellow-and-black striped lines spanned the pavement. Black letters on white above them announced: ROAD CLOSED.

"We've got to do something," I said. "He checks us out, he'll have us under the gun while he calls for backup."

"I know." Jazz drummed fingers on the steering wheel and stared straight ahead. "I'm thinking."

"What about confusing him?" I looked at Tory. "You know, that thing you did with the cops at Lark's place. The whole these-aren't-the-droids-you're-looking-for trick."

Tory shook his head. "I'm tapped. Used everything I had for sealing spells."

"Ian?"

"I have nothing."

Crud. "Lark, you still have that Beretta? Maybe you could shoot him."

"Have you lost your fucking mind?"

"Yes!" I glanced out the rear window. The cop idled behind us. A million-watt side floodlight trained on the Caddy kept me from seeing anything beyond the cruiser's hood. Any minute now, he'd come strolling up with his gun and his badge and his serious belief that people who drove around with burnt-out taillights were threats to the public. Why couldn't cops chase real criminals?

I conveniently ignored the fact that's what most of us were.

"Donatti," Jazz said, "I have an idea."

"Call it."

She smiled. "Remember Virginia?"

"Oh. That." I reached automatically for my seatbelt. Hell, yes, I remembered Virginia. "If anyone's not buckled in, you better get that way. And find something to hold on to."

Shuffles and clicks sounded in rapid progression. I skimmed the belt over my waist and went for the buckle end, only to find it missing. Not good. I shoved a hand into the crack between the seats. Dust and grit but no buckle. Definitely not good.

I sighed and eased the belt out to full length. "Sorry about this, Ian," I said.

The question on his lips died when I threaded my loose belt through his secure one and tied the stiff canvas as tight as I could. I wedged my feet under the front seats, gripped the edges of the seat beneath me, and waited.

A shadow passed through the flood of white light behind us. The cop getting out. Jazz waited until a figure appeared beside her window and tapped on the glass.

Then she wrenched the wheel to the right, slammed the gearshift into drive, and sped off.

I watched the cop. He tried to dive out of the way, but the rear bumper caught him on the hip and sent him sprawling. With Jazz rocketing down the dirt road, he disappeared fast. The last I saw was him gaining his feet, headed for his cruiser at a crooked sprint. Determined son of a bitch. A minute later, the wail of his siren filled the world again.

Jazz screamed around a corner, kicking dust clouds over the red wash of the taillights. She straightened and gathered speed. The car rattled across uneven surfaces like the downhill stretch of a roller coaster. If the road stayed unpaved much longer, it'd shake my teeth right out of my mouth.

Pulsating lights behind us gained slowly. The cop had a few skills of his own—and probably better shocks.

Another detour sign flashed past. I hoped that meant blacktop. Ahead, a stop sign loomed.

Jazz gave no indication of slowing, much less stopping.

Ten feet from the sign, she executed a textbook bootlegger turn, with a hard twist of the wheel and a generous application of emergency brake. The rear end of the car jackknifed left with a rubber scream, mashing me against Ian and Lark against me. Full stop lasted half a breath before she peeled off down a marginally less jarring street. The force of the acceleration pushed us back against the seat in an awkward tangle.

I made a mental note never to play Twister with these guys.

We'd gotten onto a country route, one of those seemingly endless single-lane roads with no streetlights, few turnoffs, and plenty of curves and dips. I suspected Jazz had never been here before, but she navigated the twists and turns at top speed as if she'd driven it daily for years. Little by little, the siren diminished, and the whirlies fell back.

My short-lived relief ended when we topped a rise and smashed over a bone-jarring pothole. Almost immediately, the car dipped left and rattled hard with the double *whump* of a flat tire.

Jazz gripped the wheel. The Caddy's speed fell to a fast wobble. "Got any bright ideas?" she said through her teeth.

Ian nudged me in the ribs. "You must repair the tire, thief."

"How? I can't see it."

"You need not see it! Do you not know what a tire looks like?"

"Jesus. This is crazy." No sense protesting that I couldn't do it, since our other choice was to get busted. I closed my eyes and pictured a tire that wasn't flat humming along the pavement. Concentration didn't come easy, and the mechanical earthquake that used to be a Caddy didn't help. For a long time, nothing happened. The siren provided fierce competition for the metal thunder of the wheel. An acrid stench, like burning plastic, invaded the interior as shredded rubber let the rim scrape asphalt.

I need to fix the tire. I need to stay out of jail. I need to make sure Jazz doesn't turn us all into a crunchy pile of flesh and metal when she loses control of this thing.

Finally, pain gathered in my chest and sliced through my limbs. An audible pop sounded outside, like a suction cup unsticking from tile. The ride smoothed instantly.

Jazz let out a war whoop and tromped down on the gas. "Fuckin' beautiful! Donatti, you keep pulling off saves like that, and I might consider partnering with you again."

"Yeah. Piece of . . . something easy." I gasped. Everything ached, from my toenails to the tips of my hair. I wasn't saving anything anytime soon. I leaned back and hoped we'd be spared from needing any more miracles.

Several minutes passed, with nothing but the hum of tires and the fading siren as Jazz put distance behind us. I almost wished I could've seen the cop's reaction when a fugitive vehicle with a crippling flat managed to pop back up and speed away. Hadn't even had the chance to find out whether he was a sheriff or a trooper. Or whether he was on Trevor's dime.

When I could feel my fingers again, I straightened and looked through the windshield. A landscape steeped in country dark spread in front of us. It had to be around two in the morning. Few lights shone in the sparse houses dotting field-sized yards. Every place seemed to have a garage or a barn that was bigger than the actual house. "You find a good place to lose him yet?" I asked.

Jazz shook her head. "Too much open territory out here. See that hill?"

"Yeah." It was hard to miss. A mile or so of flat road ahead, then a sharp uphill slope that climbed halfway to the moon.

"If there's a turnoff on the down side, I should be able to grab it before he clears the rise."

"Great." I hoped the down side wasn't as steep as this cliff. With Jazz's brand of turning, we'd end up in a roll that no seatbelt could protect us from, and I doubted that djinn magic could heal the dead.

When we hit the base of the hill and started up, a pale glow appeared at the top. It swelled fast to white light. Seconds later, red and blue pulses joined the show. Hello, backup.

Tory breathed out hard. "I think we're in trouble."

"Shut it." Jazz clenched her jaw and drove faster. A new cruiser sailed over the hill, with another on its tail.

She didn't slow down.

I grabbed handfuls of seat. "Jazz, what the hell—"

"I know what I'm doing."

"Is killing us what you're doing?"

"Come on, Donatti. Haven't you ever played chicken?"

"Not with cops!"

"They'll move."

"I don't think so."

"Trust me. They'll move."

Horns blared and bleated. Sirens whickered and whined. A thousand feet lay between us and imminent death. The cruisers looked as if they were slowing, but I couldn't tell—might have been Jazz gaining more speed. I wanted to close my eyes, but I couldn't look away from the oncoming half-ton of cop car. "Jazz," I said with a crackle in my voice, "they're not moving."

She ignored me. Six hundred feet. Four hundred. A final barrage of blasting horns assaulted the night, and both cruisers jerked left. Jazz flicked the wheel a hair to the right. The Caddy responded with a lurch that put us on two tires for a terrifying millisecond before we dropped back to level and shot over the hill.

Somewhere behind us, squealing brakes and a dull thud suggested that one or more cruisers had just dropped out of the race.

Halfway down the other side, a blue road sign pointed to County Route 38A. Jazz made a neat swing turn and rocketed down a lane that was less residential, unless trees counted as denizens of the land. When we didn't encounter helicopters or Army tanks, I finally remembered to breathe.

"I was wrong," Lark said. "He's not crazy. You are."

"You're alive, aren't you?" Grinning, I leaned toward the front and said, "You never did that in Virginia."

Jazz shrugged. "I never did that anywhere."

"So you didn't know they'd move?"

"Not really."

I had to laugh, as much from relief as anything. I might have been unlucky, but being around Jazz made up for it.

NEARLY AN HOUR PASSED WITH NO MAJOR DISASTERS. JAZZ stuck to the back roads until she estimated the fuel tank would reach critically empty unless we rediscovered civilization soon. She hooked up with the county route, and endless trees gave way to the occasional house. Road signs promised gas stations, shopping centers, and other convenient delights a few miles ahead.

That was when the Caddy decided to surrender.

The engine sputtered and belched a cloud of black smoke. A rattling purr drew itself out, slowing its pulse in time with the decreasing speed of the car. Jazz uttered a string of expletives that would've gotten her kicked out of a biker bar. She eased over to the side of the road and cut the engine. "Anybody got a flashlight? I'll take a look, but it doesn't sound good."

While Lark patted his jacket pockets, Tory pointed to the bottom of the windshield. "I don't think it's supposed to do that," he said.

I followed his gesture. Thin orange flames licked from the defroster vent and sent heat ripples through the darkness pressed against the glass.

"Everybody out!" Jazz popped her door and dove from the car.

Tory and Ian followed suit fast, but Lark sat in place, his gaze riveted to the fire. I nudged him hard. "Move! Open the door and get out."

He blinked once. And still didn't move.

"God damn it." Aware that I wouldn't be able to drag him out, I reached over him and opened his door, then pushed him through. He tumbled onto the grassy shoulder. I jumped over him, prepared to try to manhandle him away from what was probably going to be a tower of flame in a few minutes. I could already smell the gasoline.

By the time I turned, Lark had gained his feet. "Maybe we should run," he said.

"Good idea."

We made ten yards before the ground trembled with the force of exploding Cadillac. I turned just in time to watch the hood burst open and release a fiery blossom, an oversized, glowing rose spitting sparks like pollen. One hinge tore free when the hood smacked the windshield, and the metal tongue tipped to the ground with ripples of flame cascading down its underside.

We were gonna need a new ride.

Lark and I walked to join the others, who'd made it farther down the road. "What happened to you back there?" I said.

He looked confused. "What happened when?"

"In the car, man. You blanked out or something."

"Oh, that. Isn't it obvious?" He shook his head and continued in strained tones. "I've already had the experience of being trapped in a flaming car. Once was enough."

"Jesus. I'm sorry." I'd almost forgotten about Trevor trying to blow him up.

"Don't worry about it. It's over." Beads of sweat rolled from his temples, and I could practically feel him trembling. "We'd better keep moving."

"Yeah," I muttered. "Let me just pull some roller skates out of my ass."

"What?"

"Nothing. Let's make sure they're all right." I waved toward Jazz, Tory, and Ian, who stood ten feet ahead of us, staring back at the burning wreck.

"Why'd you wait?" Jazz demanded when we reached them. "That wasn't exactly a good time to break out a round of 'Kumbayah,' you know."

"The door stuck," I said smoothly. "Took both of us to bang it open."

Lark flashed me a brief, grateful look. I half-nodded and faced Jazz. "Any idea how we blew up the damned car? I have to admit, I've never seen one go off like a firecracker before."

"Must've ruptured something on the rough spots," she said. "Lines, seals, maybe both. Probably ended up mixing gas and oil. The engine was overheating anyway."

"So I'm guessing you can't fix it, right?"

Jazz shot me a narrow-eyed glance. "You're not serious."

"Doubt it."

"I hate it when you do that."

"What did I do?"

"Can't you pretend, just for a minute, that you know how to pay attention?"

"Stop." Lark looked ready to punch one of us. Probably me. "We can't stand around arguing all night."

"He is correct. It will not be long before we are discovered, particularly if we remain in this area." Ian stood rigid with his back to the flaming car and looked to the sky as if the moon held the answer. "I do not yet have the strength to fly."

I had to offer a silent prayer of thanks for that. I'd rather ride double-back and helmet-free on a moped with a suicidal stunt biker than fly with Ian again.

"I do, but I can't carry all of you." Tory walked over to Lark and put an arm around him. His eyes widened. "*Adjo*, you're shaking. What" wrong?"

"Nerves, I guess," he murmured. "I'll be fine."

A porch light flashed on just up the road, illuminating a small blue house. The front door opened. A figure in a bathrobe poked out, looked around, and withdrew quickly. "Shit," I said. "Somebody's about to call nine-one-one. We'd better shake out before some good Samaritan tries to help us."

"So what are we going to do, walk to Trevor's?" Jazz frowned and wiped her hands on her jeans. "We might get there sometime next week."

She wasn't off by much. It'd probably take the better part of a day to walk. "We should at least get off the road," I said. "And I guess we could boost another car somewhere."

"An excellent plan, thief. After all, it has worked so well before."

I glared at Ian. "You got a better idea, genius? It's not like we can call a cab here—"

"Lark!" The alarm in Tory's voice drew everyone's attention. "What is it?"

"I can't . . ." Lark hitched a breath and let it out in a moan. With a thick sound that might've contained a choice word or two, he pushed away from Tory, stumbled a few steps, and went down—and promptly emptied his stomach into the grass.

Tory went to him and pulled him back from the mess, then knelt and cradled his head on his lap. Lark's eyes were sunken and glazed, conscious but unaware. His breathing came fast and ragged. Tory smoothed his hair back with a gentle hand. "Lark," he whispered. "Can you talk? Tell me what happened."

"Somebody get me a light." Jazz nudged me aside and crouched beside Lark. She looked from him to Tory. "Is he sweating?"

"No. But he's hot—way too hot. Feels like he's burning." Tory extended a hand, and a ball of blue flame burst into existence above his palm. He held it next to Lark. "Is this enough light?"

"That'll work." Jazz barely blinked at the impromptu magic show.

But Lark did more than blink. He flinched away, and a thin,

desperate sound wrenched from his throat between shallow pants.

"Oh, Lark. I'm sorry," Tory whispered. "It's all right. You're safe." He gave Jazz a stricken look. "Please hurry."

"Right." She pressed fingers to Lark's neck. Her lips moved without sound. After a beat, she held one of his eyes open gently and frowned. "He's dehydrated. Needs fluid, and lots of it. How long's it been since he's had anything to eat or drink?"

"Maybe a day," Tory said, extinguishing the fireball with a flick of his hand. Lark relaxed a fraction, and some of the strain left Tory's features. "But how could this happen in such a short time?"

"Hasn't he been in a wheelchair for a while?" Jazz pulled back. "He's probably exhausted, too. No one thought to bring food or water, did they?"

"Not exactly. We were kind of distracted with all the guns and the burning house." I turned to Ian. "Can't you just magic some water? You know, transform some dirt or something?"

"No."

"Why not?"

"Transformative magic does not change what something is, merely how it is shaped and perceived. If I did this, it would look, feel, and taste like water, but it would still be dirt."

"Oh." I wouldn't mind a swig of perceived water right about now, but it would do nothing for Lark's condition. "In that case, we need to go shopping. Gotta be somewhere around here with sports drinks. And we need supplies anyway."

Jazz stood and looked down the road. "The last sign said three miles, but that's driving, so there's probably a turn or two somewhere. It'd be faster to cut across ground. And safer. I just don't know which way to go."

"I'll find out," Tory said. "Can somebody sit with him a minute?"

"Yeah." Jazz moved closer. "I got him. Do your thing."

Between them, they managed to prop Lark up and get him halfway sitting against Jazz. He blinked and gave a weak cough, and his eyes focused a little. "Tory," he slurred. "I could really use a drink. Screwdriver'd be great."

Tory smiled. "Time for that later. Hang on, *adjo*. I'll take care of you." He glanced at me and Ian. "Be right back," he said, and vanished.

"Damn," Jazz said. "Don't think I'll ever get used to that."

Lark shifted slightly. "Jazz?" He looked sideways at her. "Never told you . . . nice to see you again, beautiful."

"Same here, slick." She smiled. "Now, stop talking. You're a wreck, and you need to relax."

He coughed again, and a smirk surfaced. "Might need mouth-to-mouth."

I only saw red for a second. "If you do, we'll get Ian to give it to you," I said.

Behind me, Ian cleared his throat. "Do not bring me into your personal affairs, thief."

"Why? Do you think Tory'll get jealous?"

"All right, you two," Jazz said. "Stop provoking the sick guy."

"He started it."

She laughed. "Donatti, you're too much."

"Thank you."

Before she could inform me that it wasn't a compliment, Tory materialized in front of Lark. Jazz let out a gasp. "Jesus. Warn people before you come out of nowhere, will you?"

"Sorry. We need to head that way." He pointed away from

the road, ahead to the right. "About a mile and a half. And there's no way you're walking, *adjo*. I'll carry you."

Lark flashed a tired smile. "Not gonna argue this time, hon."

Their brief exchange held a teasing familiarity, as if they'd had the same conversation a dozen times before. My throat clenched a little when I realized they must have. They'd met before I screwed Lark up, and Tory had stuck with him through being first crippled, then blinded and disfigured. He'd probably done a lot of carrying, and knowing Lark's stubborn streak, he'd likely done it over protests and some nasty verbal abuse.

That was love.

A distant and unsettling sound pulled me back to cold reality. Sirens. Lots of them. "Crud. We're gonna have company. Let's move."

Part of me wondered how many of those approaching fine boys in blue reported to Trevor before their superiors. The rest of me didn't want to stick around and find out.

CHAPTER 27

If there was one thing nearly every American could count on, it was that there'd be a twenty-four-hour Walmart situated near any population of fifty or more. The sprawling cement-constructed store we approached was open and fairly deserted. I guessed not many people felt the urge to shop for quasi-fashionable clothes and cheap toiletries at four in the morning. This one happened to be a super Walmart, with its own garage, fast-food place, eye doctor, nail salon, and a bunch of other crap. Probably only a matter of time before they put in a merry-go-round and a few roller coasters for the kiddies.

On the way, I'd gotten Ian to magic me a shirt and given him his coat back. Couldn't go out in public looking like a drunk bum. Just going into this place was risky enough.

Tory had finally consented to let Lark walk when we reached the parking lot, but he obviously wasn't going to make it much farther. If he wasn't leaning on Tory, he'd be on the ground. At least he'd stopped trying to talk.

"Okay," I said when we'd gotten halfway across the lot. "We need to make this quick. Anybody have any cash on them?"

Jazz pulled a wad of bills from a back pocket. "How much do you need?"

"Not that much." I grinned. "Give Tory a twenty, so he can take care of Lark. You do know what Gatorade is, don't you?"

Tory rolled his eyes.

"That's a yes. Buy a bunch of them, and get him drinking. Then make your way to the back of the store, and wait for us by the tires. We're leaving from there." I'd been in enough of these places to know there were exits at the garage, and the area wouldn't be open yet. There'd be alarms, but if things went well, we'd be out of sight before anyone caught up with us.

"The back?" Tory shot me an uneasy look. "If we're buying shit, why do we have to break out of the place? There's already cops in the area, and they're going to be looking for us. Can't we just go through the checkout and walk out the front door, like normal humans?"

I shook my head. "We're not paying for everything."

"You are planning to steal from this place?" Ian's lip curled. "You cannot be serious. You are—"

"I know what I'm doing," I said before he could tell me what a lousy thief I was. "Look, I may not believe in killing, but I believe in the right tools for the right job. We can't go up against Trevor's firepower with a couple of tricked-out blades and some harsh language. So unless any of you has an arms dealer in your pocket, we're going with this."

Nobody protested. It almost shocked me enough to make me forget the rest of the plan.

"Jazz, you're with me," I finally said. "You're driving."

"I thought we nixed the car-boost thing."

"I meant a shopping cart." I had to turn away to keep from laughing at her fuck-you expression. "For a while, we'll be a couple of regular people, out picking up random things at four in the morning. We save the tricky bit for last."

She smirked. "You're not exactly regular."

"Same to you, babe."

"Did you just call me babe?"

"Nope. I said 'eh.' Practicing my Canadian accent." I coughed and turned to Ian. "You're the distraction."

"I am what?"

"You get to run interference. You keep as many employees and customers as you can busy while we load up."

He leveled a black look at me. "And how do I accomplish this?"

"Should be easy. You're a natural asshole, so just be yourself."

"Thank you. But I still do not understand what I am supposed to do."

I sighed and pointed in the general direction of the store. "Go in there and start yelling. Complain about everything— the parking lot, the shopping carts, the lousy layout, whatever. Demand to speak to a manager. And then a different manager. Tell them you want phone numbers. Try to give us twenty minutes or so, and then say you're going to buy more shit and meet us in the back."

"This is ridiculous," Ian muttered. "I know nothing of your commerce system."

"Good. Then you'll sound like every other average no-brain jerk bitching about the customer service they deserve." We'd reached the crip spaces at the front of the lot. I slowed my pace. "We'll stagger entry. Tory and Lark first, then Ian, then Jazz and me. Pretend we don't know each other."

Tory's brow furrowed. "This'd better work, Dermotti."

"Christ, man. It's Donatti. Not that hard to say, honest."

"Uh-huh. Come on, Lark."

Lark murmured something that made Tory laugh, and they moved toward the automatic glass doors without looking back. So far, so good. Now we just needed a little good luck—or a lot of dumb luck. I figured we had a better shot at the latter.

WE GAVE IAN ABOUT THREE MINUTES BEFORE WE WENT IN. I heard him shouting the minute the doors whooshed open. Couldn't make out the words yet, but he sounded pissed.

I gave myself a mental pat on the back. Knew he'd be good at this.

Jazz pried a cart from one of the massive lines and pointed it toward the security arches. She was struggling not to laugh. "Shall we?"

"Let's." We moved into the store at a brisk clip—casual fast. Shoppers on a mission for the essentials. Food, water, and guns. Because plenty of people impulsively bought rifles along with their cereal bars and bottled water.

Ian's voice clarified itself as we passed the mostly deserted checkout lanes. ". . . parking lot is disgusting! There is trash everywhere. I stepped on gum."

The poor cashier he'd cornered squeaked a reply. In my peripheral vision, I made out two other employees—one with a handheld CB and a set of keys—moving toward the confrontation.

"This excuse for cleanliness is unconscionable," Ian roared on. "I wish to speak with someone in charge, this instant. And I have not even mentioned the bathrooms . . ."

"Oh, he's good," Jazz said in low tones. "Way better than

the last distraction you brought in. What was his name, Sheik, some bullshit like that?"

I grimaced. "Shake. Yeah, he was a mistake." Shake's specialty had been faking fits. He had two acts: epilepsy and Tourette's. He could make himself foam at the mouth on demand. Unfortunately, he had a tendency to pull a gun on anyone who touched him during a fit, including EMTs and cops. He'd lasted a gig and a half.

"Okay," Jazz said. "Where to first?"

"Housewares, I think. We need a mirror."

"Right." We moved down a main aisle toward the lamps and bath towels, and Jazz let out a soft breath. "This is so . . . bizzare."

"What?"

"These guys. The djinn." The corners of her mouth twitched. "Magic."

"Tell me about it." I still couldn't get over the idea that I had these weird abilities. That I wasn't entirely human. I couldn't deny the truth of it, but acceptance didn't come as easy as the evidence. There'd never been anything special about me.

She turned down an aisle stocked with mirrors, framed prints, and curtain rods and waited for me. When I caught up, she said, "How does it feel?"

"The magic?" I studied the selection and tried not to look directly at my own face. "Well, like Ian said, it hurts. But it's warm, too. Down deep and primal. It's physical and mental— you have to think about it to make it work right." I gave a half-hearted laugh. "Mostly it's just fucking unreal."

"Yeah, I'll bet."

Jazz fell silent while I investigated a likely choice. About four and a half by two and a half, lightweight, cheap plastic frame with cardboard backing. Easier to transport than the decorative wooden models. I lifted one out of the slot and stood it in the cart.

"Cy's going to be doing this stuff someday," Jazz said. "Isn't he?"

"Stealing from Walmart? Christ, I hope not."

My attempt at levity didn't have the intended effect. She looked like she wanted to eviscerate me with a dull spoon.

"Sorry," I said. "Unfortunately, I'd bet his odds are good for developing magical tendencies. But I can't say for sure. I barely understand any of this." I shrugged and looked away. "You should probably ask Ian."

"I'll do that."

The modulated hostility in her voice gave me the shivers. At least it was directed at Ian this time and not me.

We made fast work of the remaining incidentals. Grabbed a big hiking pack and a smaller canvas bag, an assortment of sustenance that wouldn't spoil or squash, some bungee cords and duct tape, and a decent set of screwdrivers. I surveyed the contents of the cart and summoned a grim sliver of determination. "All right. Next stop, sporting goods."

"I hope the rest of these clowns are ready for this," Jazz murmured.

"Everything's under control," I said, hoping to convince myself, too. "We're a go."

"Sure we are."

I declined the bait and kept walking. "See what you can do about packing up," I said. My gaze automatically panned the area while we moved. I took in shelf angles and potential blind spots, department phones and staffing checkpoints, the numerous black-bubble security cameras dotting the ceiling and the occasional thin white cameras mounted on columns. The system probably wasn't live-monitored, but I intended to act as if it was.

With casual, almost unconscious movements, Jazz opened the backpack and slipped a few items into the main compartment while she pretended to check out a rack of DVDs. We lingered a few seconds, moved on, walked past sporting goods. We approached and deliberately ignored Tory and Lark, who were feigning a debate over which brand of motor oil to buy and whether it was worth an extra two bucks for the synthetic.

I drifted to the other side of the cart so I'd be next to them when we bypassed. "Back door in five," I said under my breath. "Do a walk-by on Ian."

Tory offered a barely perceptible nod. "Whatever you want," he said to Lark. "Just get the damned synthetic. I need some of that tire-wash stuff, too."

"Fine." Lark grabbed a bottle off the shelf. He still looked like hell, his complexion pale and pasty beneath a sheen of sweat, but at least he was on his feet. "Let's go."

Jazz and I circled back toward the sporting goods. She'd already gotten most of the supplies in the pack, and I hadn't even noticed. Damn, she was good.

I skimmed a glance over the glass-fronted gun case. Standard cylinder locks on the doors. The selection wasn't terrific, but I'd take what I could get. The lower portion of the case held ammo. A few dozen boxes, and most of them were BB and air-rifle pellets. I'd have to clean them out of the heavy stuff.

"You're lookout," I said. "Be ready to move, and try not to freak out," I added with a grin. "I'm going to disappear."

"Great." Jazz positioned herself at the perimeter of the department, in front of a display of fishing lures. "See you on the other side, I guess."

I winked, grabbed the smaller canvas bag from the cart, and walked down one of the narrow aisles. Once I hit a spot that wouldn't be picked up by the cameras, I took a second to collect myself and did the invisible thing. The brief pain was manageable enough. I unzipped the bag, then headed for the guns.

I still had my lock picks, but it'd take me precious minutes to open the cylinders that way. And I'd have to crack at least three locks, maybe four. I figured if Ian could unlock a car door, I might be able to magic them loose somehow. All I had to do was need it to happen.

Since the ammo shelves were lower and less noticeable from the camera angle, I knelt to go for that first. The boxes I wanted, .22 cartridges and shotgun shells, were in the same compartment. I debated half a second before resting my fingertips on the glass around the lock and thinking, *I need this fucking thing to open.*

A jolt to my chest blurred my vision for an instant. I expected the lock tongue to turn or the cabinet door to slide. Instead, the cool glass against my fingertips warmed and softened, and my fingers went right through it. My palm hit the metal of the lock and pushed it out of the glass. The whole locking mechanism thumped onto the top shelf of the display.

That'd work. I could get used to this magic stuff.

I slid the panel open and tossed boxes into the bag, listening for a signal from Jazz. Nothing yet. I shouldered the bag, stood, and reached for the upper lock on the .22s. My internal clock insisted on keeping track of my time. A minute and a half. A minute forty-five. The lock collapsed. I swiped four rifles and started on the next case.

In less than three, I had all I could handle. I glanced back at Jazz and gave a low whistle. She sent an uneasy look in my direction, but she slipped the backpack on and grabbed the mirror. She started at a fast clip for the darkened tire center, where three figures stood around trying to look as if they had every reason to stare at a locked door.

I caught up to her, still invisible. "Looks like everybody made it," I said.

"That is so fucking creepy," she whispered.

"Sorry. I don't want anyone to see me walking around with an armful of guns, if I can help it."

"Yeah. It's a pretty handy trick."

"Something like that."

Ian's furious expression grew darker when we reached him. "Where is the thief?"

"Right there somewhere." Jazz waved the hand that wasn't holding the mirror. "We've got everything."

"Then we had best leave quickly. There are police in the front of the store."

"Damn." I must have lost my happy thoughts or something, because the minute I spoke, Jazz flinched back, and I knew I was visible again. "Ian, can you get that door open?" I nodded at the exit leading to the store garage.

"As you wish." The snarling sarcasm suggested he'd prefer breaking the glass with my head, but he moved to the door and held a hand out.

Tory stared at me. "Good gods. There's only five of us. How many guns do we need?"

"Trevor has a lot more than this. Besides, we—"

"Hey! You can't be back there." An unfamiliar female voice called out from further in the store. Keys jingled with the approaching footsteps. "The tire center opens at eight. We can check you out at the front . . . oh . . . *shit* . . ."

I half-turned and saw the woman, apparently a manager, staring slack-jawed at me. And my guns. She pivoted and darted down an aisle, already grabbing for her handheld.

"Jesus Christ." I shoved half the rifles at Tory. "Take these. We need to disappear. Ian, hurry the fuck up."

"It is done."

"Good. Jazz, don't flip out." I made myself vanish and grabbed her free hand.

She jerked a little, stared at me. "You're flickering."

"So are you. Don't let go, okay?"

"I won't."

Ian popped out of sight, followed fast by Tory and Lark. The exit door swung itself open. As we filed through, a cacophony of sounds filled the building—shouts, pounding feet, beeps, and static bursts from CB sets. It sounded like the entire NYPD converging in a parking garage.

Not that I'd know what that sounded like.

I led Jazz down the corridor running along the side of the garage. The door at the end opened before we reached it. Ian was still in front of us, then. Through the door was a back parking lot and then a grassy hill leading to a stretch of woods. Thank God for rural shopping centers.

"Head for the trees," I said as loudly as I dared, hoping Tory and Lark were still right behind us.

Jazz squeezed my hand hard when we hit the outside. "They can't see us," she whispered. "Right?"

"Right." *I think.* I really didn't want a bullet in the back to prove me wrong.

Just in case, I shifted position so I was behind Jazz. They could shoot me first.

It seemed to take an hour to reach the edge of the lot. The cops poured out just as we mounted the hill. I heard them, but I didn't look back. There was no gunfire. We hauled for the trees and kept going straight for a good fifty feet. Finally, I tugged Jazz back and let go of the invisible shield.

"Everybody here?" I said cautiously.

Ian shimmered into sight ten feet ahead. "I do hope Taregan has kept up."

"Way ahead of you." Tory stepped from behind a huge pine tree in front of Ian. He had Lark on his back, and Lark held the rifles across Tory's chest as if he was reining a horse. "That was fun," Tory said. "Let's not do it again. Ever."

"Agreed." Ian stared at me. "Well, thief?"

"I don't know." I knew he expected me to give the next step. But the adrenalin rush was already crashing, and I could've lain down and given up right there. "They'll search through here. Probably sooner than later. I have no idea how far these woods go, so we might run out of cover in two hours or five minutes. I'm open to suggestions here."

Ian looked at Tory as if he was trying to gauge his condition. At last he said, "We have no choice. We fly."

I groaned. "I was afraid you'd say that."

CHAPTER 28

It wasn't any easier the third time.

A feeble band of gray-white ran along the horizon to the right, the first whisper of dawn. The world spread below, little more than a patchwork of shadows and pitch speckled with lights. Some people might have found this a breathtaking sight.

It took my breath, all right. But only because I recognized it for what it was: a great big rock that would reduce me to roadkill if—*when*—I fell.

Tory, who'd agreed to fly with a cheerfulness that made me want to break his teeth, carried Lark and Jazz with him. Jazz had the mirror harnessed to her back with bungees, and Lark held a few of the guns. I expected Tory to stay lower and wobble along under the weight of two people plus supplies, but he'd taken off like a greased bullet. I guessed it had something to do with him being part bird. It probably helped that Jazz and Lark together almost made a full-sized adult.

The arrangement left me a solo passenger on Air Ian, which was definitely an economy flight, judging from the turbulence. I'd taken the backpack and the rest of the guns, tied over the pack in a makeshift sling. The extra weight didn't help my sense of balance. Neither did the whole being airborne thing.

I tightened my locked hands and closed my eyes. "I think we lost them!" I shouted. "Can we get down?"

"Not yet." Ian tensed beneath me. "But we must land soon. I do not have much strength left."

"Soon is too long. How about now?"

"No."

I waited a few seconds. "Now?"

He twisted sideways. I would've screamed, if I could remember how to work my vocal cords. But for an instant, a vision of my own broken body commandeered my brain and drove everything else out.

"If you wish to land sooner, thief, you can do so without me."

"You're a bastard."

"Yes. And?"

"That's all I got." I almost laughed. He didn't like being airborne any more than I did, so I let the attempted murder slide. "Where are we headed?"

"I do not know."

"Great. So you're just flying until you get tired, then setting us down in the middle of wherever?"

"No. You must inform me when we are close to Trevor."

"Right." I glanced at the unreadable blur sliding past a million miles beneath us. Should've stolen Quaid's GPS. "How the hell am I going to do that? I can't even tell if that's Earth or Mars down there."

"You will be able to in a moment."

I finally realized that either the trees were getting bigger or the ground was getting closer. Quickly. "What the hell are you doing?" I gasped.

"Gaining a better vantage point. Do you recognize this area?"

I swallowed hard and leaned over a few inches. A ribbon of water below cut a near-black chasm through vegetation that appeared bleached in the creeping light. I made out a narrow, unpopulated access road leading left from the river. Far ahead lay the southern tip of Owasco Lake. "Yeah," I said, drawing back so I wasn't looking down anymore. "You made good time. The lake's just there, and there's a little town over that way. Waterfall Haven, Cape Cascade, something like that."

"And can you find a safe place nearby? We must regain our strength."

I thought for a minute. We couldn't check into a motel or anything. The bastard would find us. There were a few people I used to know in the area, but they must have either moved or gone pro-Trevor, if they were still alive. Finding forests between here and his place wouldn't be hard, but I didn't exactly welcome the idea of sleeping on leaves and branches and God knew what else. The only nearby park sat on state land, a difficult place for a criminal to take an illegal nap. Our least disagreeable alternative lay half a mile from Trevor's. I could see it from here. Unfortunately.

We wouldn't even have to worry about the neighbors calling the cops. They were all dead.

"Okay," I finally said. "Dead ahead. There's a big old cemetery right near Trevor's place. Plenty of crypts to hide in, no surveillance. We should be all right there for a few hours."

"Well, then. That is where we are going."

At least it was close. I squeezed my eyes shut and kept them that way until we stopped moving. When I opened them again, we hovered above a cluster of pines across the road from the boneyard gates. A dark shape approached through the air. Tory and his two passengers resembled a deformed camel tossed from a catapult. The djinn looked exhilarated, the humans as if they'd just swallowed bugs.

I smirked. I wasn't the only one who knew people were strictly ground animals.

We descended through close-set branches. I let go the instant Ian's feet hit dirt and staggered away to lean against the nearest trunk. My legs shook like flagpoles in a hurricane. I was a cocktail fresh from the blender. Pulverized, not stirred.

Tory touched down a few feet away. Jazz disentangled herself fast and sat hard, barely avoiding breaking the mirror. "That sucked," she said. "But thanks for not dropping me."

Lark slid off with a prolonged moan to land in a heap. Tory turned and leaned down to him, and Lark muttered, "Don't touch me. I like it here."

Tory sighed and sat next to him with an exasperated expression.

I would've laughed if I wasn't busy fighting the urge to puke. "Crud," I said weakly. "Why does flying screw us up like this?"

Ian dropped to his haunches and hung his head, apparently in no great shape himself. "It is not your element."

"Really. I hadn't noticed." At once, sitting seemed like the best idea since TV dinners. I obeyed the impulse and introduced my ass to the ground. "It's not yours, either, is it?"

"More so than you but not by much. Tory's clan is far more

skilled with air abilities." He gave a soft laugh. "The wolf does not often fly."

"So, what's your clan skilled at? Biting?"

Ian shook his head. "It is not that simple. We are elemental beings, you and I. All of us. Fire and air, earth and water. Djinn and human. Like two halves of a whole that is more than the sum of its parts."

"Okay. You lost me."

"That is not difficult to accomplish."

Jazz struggled to her feet and approached slowly. "All right, color me confused. What are we doing here—did somebody die?"

"We're holing up," I said.

"This is practically Trevor's backyard."

"Yeah. So if you were Trevor, would you look for us here?"

Jazz arched an eyebrow. "No," she said. "Good thinking, Houdini."

I grinned. "Watch it. If you keep complimenting me, I might think you care."

"Couldn't have that." She gave me a smile that melted my bones.

"If you two are finished, let's move," Tory called. "We're too exposed here."

Ian nodded agreement. "Lead the way, thief."

I really wished he hadn't said that. Leading wasn't my style. But at the moment, I didn't have a choice.

At least it wasn't a sewage pipe.

The Black Oaks Cemetery held the remains of enough people to populate Allegheny County twice. Situated on acres of flat land, it was divided into two sections. The front part was laid out in a fairly open grid pattern, with paved drives dividing groups of graves. A wrought-iron fence spanned the length of the property near the road, and empty fields stretched back thirty feet to the first of the headstones. Plenty of room for more dead people.

About half a football field back from the road stood a ruler-straight line of tall, thick trees. Black oaks, I presumed. A break in the line marked a wide, worn stone path leading straight back. More trees grew at uniform attention along both sides of the path, and wooden benches had been placed every twenty feet or so, accompanied by old-fashioned gas-light-style lamp posts. For anyone who felt like hanging out in a graveyard after dark. The lamps hadn't come on yet. We'd set a good pace, and it was still daylight when we limped collectively down the path. Almost dinnertime, my stomach reminded me. Sadly, the cemetery didn't have a wide selection of restaurants. At least we had the prepackaged crap to tide us over.

The path led to the old section, with plenty of enclosed mausoleums and no mourners—unless the surrounding area was occupied by melancholy vampires. The tomb of the Trumbull family provided chambers hidden from casual view and a lovely selection of crypts to sleep on. Not exactly a Motel Six, but we'd be better off on graves than in them.

I entered first. I perched on a stone box that held the remains of *Joseph Trumbull, Who Departed This Lyfe on 2 Jan. 1909, He Sleeps in Jesus* and shrugged the hiking pack off, to the delight of my shoulders. I hoped Jesus made a comfortable resting place, because Joseph sure as hell didn't.

Jazz plodded in and propped the mirror next to the entrance. She settled beside me, closed her eyes, and leaned back without a word. Dark, deep hollows under her eyes betrayed her exhaustion. I wondered if she'd slept at all since she'd crossed over to the djinn realm.

Tory slumped against a wall and slid down to the floor. Lark all but collapsed next to him.

Ian entered last. He didn't even try to sit down. "You must learn a few things before you rest, thief. Come here."

"Are you sure this is a good idea?" Tory said. "What if he can't do this? No offense, Delini, but you're no djinn. And you're ten or eleven generations removed from his line."

I didn't bother correcting him this time. "I'll be fine." *I hope.*

"Maybe you will. All the same, Ian, I think we should get some help."

Ian went still. "And who do you suggest we call on? Shamil? Perhaps you can locate other Bahari here in the next six hours. In case you have forgotten, Taregan, I am the only surviving Dehbei."

Tory blanched. "I haven't forgotten," he whispered. "But we can still contact the Council. They'll send reinforcements."

"No, they will not. Your clan leader has persuaded the Council not to interfere. No one will come to assist me, whether or not you are involved."

"What about Akila?"

Ian's eyes narrowed. "I will not risk her life. And you should know better than to ask such a thing, for your *rayani* to betray her father's directives. No, we do this alone."

"Then we die!"

"It is possible. However, the most likely outcome is that I will die. The rest of you will survive, and my death should be incentive enough for your leader, in his infinite wisdom, to act against the Morai. At the least, it will please him." Ian made a rough grab for the mirror. "Donatti, if you do not mind, I would prefer that we practice outside."

He stalked out without waiting for an answer.

Although the last thing I wanted right now was to torture myself trying to use magic, I decided it'd be less painful than what would happen if Ian didn't get some distance between himself and Tory. "Jazz," I said gently.

She opened her eyes. "They still catting?"

"No." I glanced at Tory, but he'd turned his attention to making Lark comfortable. "I'd better go with Ian. Do you want to come out with me?" I had the feeling things might get a little tense in here.

Jazz seemed to understand my unvoiced concern. "I'll be fine. Wanted to check on Lark anyway, make sure he's had enough fluid." She eased forward, stood, and stretched. "Go. Do what you have to."

"Right." I let out a breath. "Sorry about all this. Soon as we're clear of Trevor, I'll try to explain everything to you. It's a long story."

"I know." She smiled. "Akila gave me a crash course in djinn politics."

"Oh." I should've guessed that. Jazz didn't enjoy not being as informed as possible. She probably had better stories than I did. I hoped I'd get the opportunity to hear them someday.

"You should get out there. Ian's waiting for you."

"Yeah, I guess I should."

She brushed my arm and moved toward Lark and Tory. I grabbed a bottle of water and an energy bar from the pack, hoping to ply my protesting body with food and drink, and headed out after Ian. Outside, I found him leaning against the outer wall of the mausoleum. "Hey. You all right?"

"Yes. Fine," he said, sounding anything but. "My apologies, thief. I did not realize Taregan was so opposed to your assistance."

"Yeah, me, neither." Unfortunately, I could see Tory's point. It would be safer if we had another djinn or two. Or a hundred. Taking on Trevor was risky, even as just a regular brutal, underhanded bastard. Now he was a bastard with power. Damn near untouchable.

But there was no one else. Just a couple of djinn, two humans, and a whatever I was.

Ian straightened and propped the mirror upright. "There are three components to forming a bridge. Symbol, words, intention. The intention is the most difficult to master, because it is imprecise."

"Well, let's just jump right in," I muttered. "It's not like I just robbed a store and burned up my reserves or anything."

"We have no time to waste. Power takes time to rebuild, and you must be as close to full strength as possible when we attempt this for real."

I sighed and shuffled over to him. "Okay. Let's do the easy part first."

"You'll use my symbol. You are my descendant, so it should work."

"Should?"

"It will work." Ian frowned, pointed to the mirror. "Pay attention."

"Sorry."

"Do you know how to form the symbol?"

"Yeah. In blood. There's a wavy line and a dot . . ."

"Show me."

Crud. I was hoping this would be more of a theory lesson.

I used the knife to slice my left index finger and smeared what looked like a reasonable facsimile of Ian's squiggles onto the top corner of the mirror. "Right?"

"Good enough." Ian stepped back and motioned for me to stand before the glass. "With the words, you must have the intention. Concentrate on your destination, and call on the desire to bring it to you."

"Hold on. I'm supposed to bring some other place to me?"

Ian made an exasperated sound. "You simply have to desire being there."

"Why didn't you say so?"

"The words," he said sharply. "*Insha no imil, kubri ana bi-sur'u wasta.*"

I blinked. "That's a lot of words."

"Say them."

I tried. And failed spectacularly.

Frustration flooded Ian's face. He drew a quick breath, held it, and exhaled slowly. "All right. Move away for a moment." A half-smile tugged his mouth. "I have never found occasion to teach this to anyone, you know."

"Yeah. I guess it's pretty natural for a djinn." I stepped aside and tried to recall the words in my head, but all I could come up with was *eenie meenie miney moe.* That probably wouldn't cut it. "Can you say the middle part again?"

Instead of replying, he moved behind me and gripped my shoulders. "Try to relax. Close your eyes."

I did, hoping he wasn't going to give me a massage. "I don't know how relaxed I'm going to get here."

"Silence, thief. Listen." He paused, then repeated the incantation. It still sounded like gibberish to me. "Do not attempt to memorize the sounds and spit them back out. Feel the words, understand their shape. You have this knowledge already—find it." He said them again.

This time, a glimmer of understanding penetrated. My mind automatically translated part of the chant: *Go quickly and connect.* I stood trying to tune out everything but the words and plant them in my brain.

At last, I opened my eyes. "I think I got it."

"Try again." Ian released me. "Remember to focus on your intention, your destination."

"Wait. What's my destination?"

"Oh." Ian cleared his throat. "Yes. You should not attempt to arrive in Trevor's basement yet." He scanned the area, and his gaze fell on the water bottle I'd left by the entrance. He grabbed it, twisted the top off, and poured the water carefully into a small stone basin next to the doorway. "This will do for the moment."

"Uh . . . Ian, I don't think I'm going to fit in there." The basin was about two feet in diameter, and the puddle he'd created was considerably smaller.

"You do not have to pass completely through to test the bridge. Just put your hand inside."

"Right. No problem," I lied. I stared at the basin, trying to establish it as where I wanted to be. It wasn't easy—I wanted to be in some tropical foreign country, with Jazz and Cyrus, where no goon or evil djinn would ever find us. But that wouldn't happen until I figured out how to work this bridge trick.

Finally, I faced the mirror and projected my intentions.

"Insha no imil, kubri ana bi-sur'u wasta." The sound of my own voice surprised me. My lips moved almost automatically, and the words came out low and rhythmic, the same under-breath chant Ian used. I felt my chest tighten, my limbs thread

with painful tingling. The surface of the mirror rippled and shivered. My reflection vanished. Distorted, cloud-spotted blue sky took its place. I glanced at Ian. He nodded.

I held out a hand, hesitated, and eased fingertips against the mirror. Through the mirror. A freezing sensation penetrated my flesh and bit clear to bone. It was like reaching into a snow bank. When it disappeared to the wrist, I risked a look at the basin.

My hand jutted from the water, solid and undamaged.

I wiggled my fingers and watched them wave at me from way over there. I yanked my arm back with a strangled yelp. "Christ. That's just . . . ugh. Glad I don't have to see that again." I shook my hand viciously to make sure it was still attached. It didn't fall off, but imaginary pins and needles crawled around my wrist and up my palm.

"Well done, thief." Ian sat cross-legged on the ground and motioned me to join him. "Just one further task before you rest."

"Is that all?" I sank down on the grass, already feeling the drain. "What now, flying? Honestly, if that's it, don't trouble yourself. I'd rather swim in a cesspool."

Ian withdrew his false tether from a pocket. "You must learn to destroy these."

"Come on, Ian. We won't have to—"

"Nevertheless," he said firmly, "you will learn. Perhaps you will have the opportunity to destroy Lenka's tether first."

I grimaced. "You didn't sound very convincing. Wanna try and tell me that again?"

"No." Ian averted his eyes and drew the dagger from its sheath. The copper blade glinted in the sunlight. He laid it on the ground between us, pressed his lips together, and explained.

The process was simpler. Blood, a decent amount, no symbol required. Focused power, lots of it. And words. *Ana lo 'ahmar nar, fik lo imshi, aakhir kalaam.* Through blood and fire, shatter and be gone, for eternity.

I got the words right the first time. And prayed I'd never have to utter them again.

CHAPTER 29

leep came easy. Staying that way didn't.

I woke hard on the tail end of a muddled nightmare, cold and disoriented. After I figured out I wasn't restrained in Trevor's basement again, things started to clear up. The warmth next to me was Jazz. A paler shade of dark indicated the entrance to the tomb. Nightfall but not yet late. Probably eight o'clock or so. One of these days, I'd get myself a watch. Soft, rhythmic breathing marked the others as still unconscious. At least now I knew djinn did sleep sometimes.

For a few minutes, I tried to ease back into slumber. My bladder had other ideas. At last, I gave up and wrenched my stiff muscles into motion. Swinging my legs over the side of Joseph Trumbull's crypt, I stood and bent forward, attempting to sneak some feeling back into my flesh. Sleeping on stone hadn't done any wonders for my back, but waking up beside Jazz sure didn't hurt. I probably would've slept on nails and broken glass if she asked me to, though I would've preferred a bed. And considerably less company.

I headed out in search of a tree to water. Outside the crypt, a medley of sounds made a mockery of the phrase *silent as the grave*. A brisk wind rattled bushes and whistled around corners, carrying the chirps of crickets and peepers and the occasional hoot of a nearby owl. My footsteps rustled the grass, making small thunder.

When I stopped walking, I still heard footsteps. Behind me.

I turned, reaching instinctively for something to throw. My pocket yielded the wire spool. Useless. Several bulky shapes lay between my position and the crypt. One of them was moving.

The breath I'd been holding exploded in relief when Jazz stepped out from behind a headstone. "I knew it," I said. "You're trying to kill me."

"If I was, you'd already be dead." She came toward me with a smirk, but her expression eased into genuine concern. "You all right? You look awful."

"I've had better days." Pressure stabbed my groin. I grimaced and squeezed my legs together hard. "Uh, I'm just going to step around this a second," I said, waving at the nearest grave marker. "Otherwise, it's gonna get a little wet down south."

Jazz shrugged. "Suit yourself. But it's not like I haven't seen your equipment before."

"You are evil, woman."

"Sometimes."

I moved out of her line of sight and relieved myself fast. When I came back, she'd taken a seat on a stone bench in front of one of the bigger monuments. She patted the empty space beside her. "Saved you a spot."

"Thanks." I sat down. "So, what about you . . . are you all right?"

She shook her head. "Oh, yeah. My son's in some magical realm that I can't get to, and I'm hiding from Trevor in a cemetery. I'm great."

I wanted to dig up a coffin, crawl inside, and bury myself alive. Sorry wasn't going to cut it, so I didn't say anything.

"That was a joke," she said. "Guess it wasn't funny."

"I'm laughing on the inside." I sighed and stared at the ground. "Jazz, I—"

A muted ring tone drifted from her pocket. She frowned and pulled out her phone. "No data," she said. "It could be Trevor again. He's blocked his number before."

Crud. If it was, I doubted he was calling with a discount subscription to *Time* magazine. "You wanna answer it?"

"No. But I should. I'll put it on speaker." She hit a button. "Yeah."

"Miss Crowe?"

It wasn't Trevor, but I'd heard the voice before. Recently. I just couldn't place it.

Jazz gave a deep frown. Nobody called her Miss Crowe. "Who is this?"

"I'm looking for a friend of yours. One Mr. Donatti." The identity of the voice hit me in the brief pause before he added, "My name is Quaid."

"Son of a bitch," I blurted.

Jazz shot me a look. I groaned and hung my head. Damned speaker phone—should've kept my mouth shut.

"Ah. So you are there, Mr. Donatti."

"You don't give up, do you?" I said. "You'd better forget this number, asshole, however you got it. She isn't involved in this."

Jazz cleared her throat. "What the fuck is this about? Who's this Quaid guy?"

"He's a bounty hunter," I muttered.

Her eyes widened. "You've got bounty hunters after your ass, too?"

"Just this one."

"Mr. Donatti." Quaid sounded downright indignant. "I think you'd better listen to me."

"I don't have it, Quaid."

"Have what?" Jazz said. "You know, Donatti, we really don't need this right now."

"I'm aware of that," I said through my teeth. "Look, can I explain everything after I deal with him? This is getting really confusing."

"Fine," she said. "But you'd better—"

Quaid cut in. "I've contacted the police."

I stared at the phone. "So? They're already looking for me."

"I can make them stop looking for you. If you return my employer's property."

Even Jazz laughed at that. "No, you can't," I said. "You can't do shit for me."

"I have contacts in every sheriff's department across the state."

"Are you trying to cut me a deal, Quaid?"

"I'm offering you an opportunity to stay out of prison."

I snorted. "You're not very good at this part."

"Which part is that?"

"The deal." I rolled my eyes. "See, when you're dealing with criminals, you've got to have something concrete to bargain with. Police contacts don't mean jack when half the force is working for our side anyway. Criminals don't trust anyone. Ever."

"So, you admit it."

"What?"

"You're a criminal."

"Uh . . . yeah. I am."

"Which means you're no different from Mr. Maddock."

Ouch. "Wrong. I'm nothing like Trevor."

"But you are." Quaid sounded smug, as if he'd just scored a hit on some mental Bingo card for insults. "Unless you return the property you stole, you're exactly the same. People make mistakes. If they make them intentionally and illegally, with no thought of correcting them, they are criminals."

"It's not that simple." I didn't have time for a philosophy discussion with a bounty hunter looking to extract a payday from me. "Trevor isn't just a criminal. He's an animal. A cold-blooded killer. He'll shoot you for being you and smile when he does it."

"All you have to do is return the dagger. Then you won't be a criminal like Mr. Maddock." Quaid spoke in a tone that suggested it'd be stupid to disagree with his logic. "To be honest, if you fail to produce it this time, I'm afraid I'll have to take the matter up with him instead."

"You're insane." I didn't like this guy, but that didn't mean I wished him dead. "Look, Quaid, you've got to stay away from him. I'm not kidding. He'll kill you."

"Oh, I don't know about that. Have you ever tried reasoning with him?"

"Reasoning? With *Trevor*?"

"You have until midnight tonight." Quaid gave an address in the small town we'd flown over on the way here. "If you don't return the item to me by then, I'll bring the situation to Mr. Maddock." He paused. "I assume, at the least, that you fear him more than the police."

"You idiot! You can't—"

The phone clicked and went silent.

Jazz put it away with a frown. "How long's he been after you?"

"He showed up right after you went over to the djinn realm. Bastard keeps finding me. This is the third time." I dropped my head in my hands. "Jesus Christ. He's going to get his righteous ass murdered."

"What's he want?"

I looked at her. "Ian's tether."

"Shit. Guess we can't give him that." She put a hand on my leg, and a delicious shiver zipped through me. Bad timing, as usual. "Well, he doesn't seem like much of a threat."

"He's not. He's really more annoying than dangerous." The bounty hunter was about as threatening as a nun's tongue, compared with Trevor. I held out some hope that he'd take my warning seriously and set his path in a direction that didn't lead to certain death.

Not much, though.

BY TEN OR SO, EVERYONE WAS MORE OR LESS AWAKE AND HANG-ing around outside the crypt, looking about as lively as the bodies in the ground. Ian and Tory still weren't speaking, and I was too wired to care. Still had a few details I wanted to work out. It was nice to have weapons, but shotguns and rifles weren't exactly designed for ideal portability or close-range work. And I was a lousy shot with them.

Not that I was much better with handguns. But put a rifle in my hands, and I'd miss the broad side of a blue whale.

I brought the guns out of the crypt and laid them on the ground. "Don't suppose anyone has a tubing cutter or a hack-saw handy," I said.

Jazz smirked. "Sorry. I packed light."

"You're not going to saw those off," Tory said. "You'll ruin them."

I shrugged. "Can't anyway. But if I had the tools, I'd do it. Carrying these things around is gonna be a pain in the ass—and so's firing them."

"Give 'em to me." Tory stalked over and scooped up the pile. "Lark, come on. I need some technical advice."

Without a word, Lark followed him around to the back of the crypt.

"Touchy," I said. "I guess we all are, though."

"It is best to let him be." Ian sat cross-legged on the ground, eyes closed. "Taregan can be quite stubborn."

"Yeah. Not unlike some other djinn I know."

Ian ignored that. "I assume at this point we are as prepared as possible."

"I can't think of anything else." I turned to Jazz. "You?"

"Not really." She folded her arms and shivered. "Except . . . I'd like to talk to Cy before we do this. If I can."

Ian looked at her. He started to frown, but the expression slid away into understanding. "Of course, lady," he said. "It will have to be brief. I must conserve my power, so I will not be able to keep the bridge open long."

"Understood." She gave him a hesitant smile. "Thank you."

Ian nodded. He stood and went to the mirror still leaning against the outside wall of the crypt. After a pause, he drew out the fake tether and nicked a finger, then did the spell. I couldn't be sure, but I thought there were a few different words from the one he'd taught me. A faint flash traveled over the surface of the mirror, and the reflection became a bedroom illuminated with glowing balls of light on the walls. Akila sat on the floor, Cyrus in her lap. She was reading to him in the djinn tongue from a massive book lying open in front of them.

"Hello, love," Ian said softly.

Akila caught a breath and looked toward the mirror. "*L'rohi*," she whispered. She stood and carried Cyrus closer, until the two of them filled the frame. "You are worried. What has happened?"

"I am simply tired, my heart. And the lady wishes to see her son."

"Of course." Akila smiled. "Cyrus, your *muut* is just there. Do you see her?"

Cyrus grinned. "Hi, Mommy!"

Ian moved aside and gestured to the mirror. Jazz blinked fiercely a few times and stepped forward. "Hey, baby," she said, a slight tremor in her voice. "Having a good time?"

"Me and 'Kila's readin'," he announced.

"I see that. Is it a good story?"

"Yep. No monsters." He leaned his head back and yawned. "Come read, Mommy."

"Oh, Cy." She managed to smile. "Mommy has . . . something to do, but we'll read double stories tomorrow night. Okay?"

"'Kay. C'n I get my drink?"

"Sure, baby. I love you. So much."

"Love you, Mommy." He slid down and out of sight.

Akila turned to watch him and faced back. "He is a beautiful child," she said. "A true delight. He will be strong."

"Thank you," Jazz whispered. "For taking care of him." She pivoted and walked away from the mirror fast, as if she couldn't stand to look at it anymore.

While Ian moved to talk to Akila, I went after Jazz. I

touched her arm, and she stopped with her back to me. "Not now," she said thickly. "I need a minute."

"Jazz . . ."

"I said not now."

I almost let her go. But I had to try. "You don't have to be alone," I said.

She hesitated. Just when I thought she'd take off anyway, she turned back. She said nothing, but I could feel the conflict in her—she was hurting, vulnerable, and she hated it. She didn't want to want comfort. Especially from me.

At the risk of bodily harm, I put my arms around her. She shuddered and held back for a fraction of a second, then leaned in to me and buried her face in my shirt.

I held her as close as I dared. She finally stopped shaking, but I didn't let go. I never wanted to let go. If a few hours were all I had left in the world, I wanted to spend as much of them as I could with her. It wasn't enough for an apology. But maybe she'd remember that I cared and that I'd never meant to hurt her.

In a flash of spectacularly shitty timing, Tory came back around the opposite side of the crypt with Lark in tow. He deposited an armload of guns that weren't long-barreled anymore on the ground. "Problem solved," he said. "Now, can we—what the hell's he doing?"

I assumed he meant Ian. I glanced over and saw him kneeling in front of the mirror, his forehead resting on the glass, one hand pressed flat to the surface above his head. The band around his finger pulsed faintly. His shoulders twitched once, the barely perceptible motion a testament to his struggle not to give in completely, not to burden Akila with his pain.

From where Tory stood, the image in the mirror wasn't

visible. I glared at him. "Maybe you should ask him that," I said.

"Fine." Tory stalked toward Ian. He made five or six steps and stopped dead. "*Rayani?*"

The hand on the mirror convulsed, clenched in a fist. Ian didn't look up. "This is not your concern, Taregan."

"Taregan?" Akila's voice was faint but audible. "You have found him. Thank the gods."

"I would not thank anyone yet." Ian straightened and sent a fierce glower in Tory's direction. "He still has not learned to be responsible, and he makes foolish choices."

"Nevertheless, I am pleased he is with you," she replied with gentle reproach.

"I am not certain I agree." Ian turned back to the mirror, his anger supplanted with regret. "I must go, love."

"I know," she whispered. She said something in djinn, and Ian replied in kind.

I couldn't quite grasp a translation, but the meaning of the words reached for my soul and plucked a few strings. I almost felt guilty for being able to hold Jazz.

Ian stayed on the ground for a moment. When he stood, he stared at Tory. "I hope you are finished with this childish game of ignoring me. We have work to do."

Tory blinked. His defensiveness evaporated. "Of course, *rayan*," he said. "My apologies." There wasn't even a hint of sarcasm in his formal delivery. He was practically bowing and scraping.

Nodding, Ian gestured to the pile of guns. "Show me what you have done here."

Tory started to explain. In calm, deferential tones.

Jazz stirred and looked up at me. "What's a *rayan?*"

I'd understood that one. "Prince."

"What happened to Tory?" she murmured. "Somebody whack him with a chill-out stick?"

I shook my head. "Guess he forgot about that whole royalty thing for a while. Maybe seeing Akila reminded him." Or maybe he'd finally realized what was painfully obvious to me, after knowing Ian for all of three days—that he loved Akila more than should've been possible.

"Oh." She leaned back and peered around me at Ian and Tory. A tiny smile surfaced. "Let's go check out the new toys."

"Sounds fun." I dropped my arms reluctantly and reached for her hand.

She didn't pull it away.

CHAPTER 30

A full moon in a clear sky turned the world into a scene from an old movie. The five of us huddled under gray trees with brown leaves and looked over silver-white grass fields at a mansion straight from the set of *Frankenstein*. Unfortunately, there were far scarier things than Boris Karloff in green makeup waiting inside.

I leaned against a tree and watched Tory impersonate a zombie. He'd been motionless, with eyes wide open, for at least five minutes trying to locate Lenka's tether. Apparently, the hawk clan specialized in scrying—which I'd finally gathered meant "finding stuff"—illusions, and generally being pompous jerks. The last must have been a male trait.

At last, Tory blinked and sagged back. Lark rushed to him, ducked under his arm, and helped him ease to the ground. "It's in there." Tory gasped. "Something small and round—a ring or a coin. In Trevor's pocket. Front left."

Great. It'd be easier to rob the White House than pick Trevor's pocket.

"So before we go in, let's run through this real quick. You break Shamil out, and I find Trevor and somehow relieve him of a pendant around his neck and a ring or a coin in his pocket. Not that it's a problem," I said when Ian opened his mouth, probably to remind me about the Walmart thing. "I can get them. And then . . . what? Do I destroy Lenka's on the spot?"

"That would be preferable," Ian said.

"Okay. Fine. But isn't somebody going to notice the whole destruction thing? I mean, I've never seen a djinn die, but I'd guess it doesn't happen quietly. Where is Lenka, anyway?"

Ian shook his head. "I have been unable to locate him. The traces of his energy are muffled. However, I believe he is near."

"Any more good news? If there is, don't tell me." At least everyone had a gun. Except Ian—he'd insisted he wouldn't be able to use it anyway. Apparently, he'd never fired one in his life. I clenched my jaw and turned to Jazz. "You're set with your end of things, right?"

"I'm good. I've done a dry run on his garage before."

"You have?"

"Yeah. After he horned in on a gig I was doing and kept the score, I considered boosting his blue roadster to even things out. I've always liked that car."

"You are crazy."

"No. But Trevor is, and that's why I didn't take it. At least, not the whole thing."

"What did you take?"

She smiled. "The gearbox."

"You're terrible." I grinned back, but my good humor faded fast. "All right. You pull your sabotage act and then come back here. Give us two hours. If we're not back, get the hell out and find some backup."

"See, that's the part I don't like," she said.

"Which one?"

"The leaving-you-for-dead part."

I closed my eyes and tried to stay calm enough not to blow it. "Jazz. You can't go after Trevor yourself. Not that I don't think you could take him," I said quickly. "But it's not just Trevor we're dealing with here. He's got serious protection— and I don't mean Leonard the Land Mass."

She scowled and looked over in Lark and Tory's direction. "What about him? He's a djinn."

"Tory? He's kinda young. And not really too strong." I spoke low to make sure he didn't hear me. "Please don't do anything . . . rash. You can't get killed. Cyrus needs you."

Jazz looked away. "I hate it when you do that."

"What'd I do now?"

"You made sense." She leaned in to me for a moment. "Don't you die on me, Houdini."

"Yes, ma'am." Reluctantly, I straightened and walked to the mirror, where Ian stood in silence. I glanced back at Tory. "You'll take care of them and guard our escape route here, right?"

"Yeah." Tory didn't look too thrilled with his assignment. "I'll stay."

"All right," I said. "Let's get this over with."

Ian nodded. "Taregan, you will help him retrieve my tether if it becomes necessary."

"Gods, Ian." Tory's voice shook, not entirely from exhaustion. "I still say we should contact the realm. Akila will—"

"No. She is safe there. I will not endanger her."

"She won't be in danger. Lenka only wants you."

A stricken look crossed Tory's face the instant the words left his mouth. He obviously hadn't meant to say that out loud. I almost felt sorry for him.

Ian didn't. "Understand this, Taregan." His hands tightened to white-knuckled fists. "Sometime before the attack, Lenka requested a marriage bond with Akila. He was denied, but only because the Council overruled Kemosiri's consent. I do not know whether this decision contributed to the Morai's revolt, and I will not take the chance that Lenka no longer desires her. Do not contact my wife."

It took Tory a moment to recover. "Fine. But will you just listen to me for a second?" Tory struggled to his feet, wavered. Lark supported him and glared at Ian, as if it was his fault Tory was acting like an idiot. "Haven't you ever wondered why I agreed to help you hunt down the Morai in the first place? I'm Bahari. We were sent to watch, not to fight."

Ian's eyes narrowed. "I assumed you wanted to protect the realm, and your *rayani*."

"Screw the realm." Tory spat on the ground. "There's nothing for me there—politics and bullshit and courting and war. I've found what I want here." His hand rubbed Lark's arm, and he flashed a smile. It died fast. "I'm helping you because I made a promise. To Akila."

"You did *what?* What promise?"

"I came to watch you, not the others. I promised to keep you alive long enough to return to her. I spent three centuries thinking I'd failed her, and then you came waltzing back. So I'm not going to stand here and watch you march to your death."

Ian closed his eyes, opened them. "Very well. Then I release you from your vow."

"You can't do that."

"I can. I have." Ian raised his hand. The band around his index finger glowed. "We are bound, and I can speak for her in matters that concern me. You are absolved of responsibility."

"You son of a bitch. What do you think will happen to her if you die—do you think that won't hurt her?"

"Yes. But far less than it will hurt to see the Morai conquer the realm and enslave her kin. *Your* kin, Taregan." Ian turned his back and punctured a finger with his teeth. He scrawled his symbol on the mirror with crude strokes. "If I must die to open Kemosiri's eyes and force him to deal with those snakes, so be it. Your clan would never have accepted me anyway." He snarled the words to open the bridge and plunged through without hesitation.

Tory stared after him with a crumpled expression. "I would have accepted you," he whispered.

I couldn't look at him, so I concentrated on Jazz. "Remember what you said about not dying on you?"

She nodded slowly.

"That goes for both of us." The smile I tried to summon wouldn't come. I turned away and did the bridge spell as fast as I could, then forced myself in before I could change my mind.

MY TEETH WANTED TO CHATTER, AND MY HANDS WANTED TO rub away the frost clinging to my skin. I knew I hadn't really turned into a human-sicle, but it sure as hell felt like it. Trevor's basement was a blur of flickering light and shadow, but my vision had already started to clear. The rack of pliers resolved itself first, and I wanted to kill Trevor right then. Preferably by yanking his heart out with one of his own damned tools.

"Cloak yourself, thief," Ian whispered from somewhere close.

Turning on invisibility barely registered this time. Ian shimmered into sight at the foot of the stairs, head cocked.

"I've heard no one," he said. "They may not have detected our entry."

"If they had, they'd be down here already." I pointed at the dark alcove. "Is he still in there?"

"He is . . . unconscious."

The catch in his voice suggested that the blackout state was probably the best one for Shamil right now. "Can you get him out?"

"I believe so. But it will take time, and all my power. The seal is strong." Ian held out an arm. A fireball blossomed over his cupped palm. He approached the alcove with stiff steps, and the light revealed evidence of his unspoken suggestion.

A thick gash scored Shamil's torso from shoulder to hip. The edges looked burnt, the inside raw and red. Fresh cuts marched down both arms. And a familiar symbol had been seared into the top of his bowed and shaven head. Ian's symbol.

I shuddered and looked away. After watching Tory locate a tether, I knew mutilation wasn't a necessary component of the process. This was a message. *Don't fuck with Trevor.*

"Go." Ian knelt in front of the alcove. "Try to be quick. I cannot leave this place without you, once I've freed him."

"I'm gone."

Climbing the stairs was the easy part. I paused at the top and listened through the door. No sound from the other side. I opened it slowly, slipped through, and entered a room empty of life. No thugs, no Trevor.

One room down, twenty or thirty to go. Trevor could be anywhere.

I headed for the short hallway, toward the sitting room where I'd been taken on my last visit. Three days ago. It seemed so much longer. The Gavyn Donatti who'd watched

Trevor kill a cop in cold blood and order his son kidnapped and tortured, who'd stood helplessly witnessing everything important to him fall like dominoes, no longer existed. I had power and purpose. Something—and someone—to live for. To die for.

In the hallway, I stopped again. Listened. Only silence reached my ears. I passed through the entry arch that led to the sitting room and couldn't help remembering how I never expected to leave this house alive the last time I'd been in here. Dimmed lights shone from fake sconces set in the walls at regular intervals. Without thugs and mortal terror to distract me, I noted more detail. The floor-to-ceiling columns flanking either side of the arch seemed overkill, as if they'd been included in the design just to point out how much money Trevor had. Chairs and tables weren't so much placed around the room as abandoned. He obviously hadn't seen fit to hire a decorator. And someone had gotten the cop's blood out of the pale carpet without a trace.

I moved across the floor to the closed door and paused. If I opened it and anyone noticed, I'd draw some attention even if they couldn't see me. After a listen against my cupped hands yielded no sound from the other side, I twisted the knob slowly and opened the door to a dark and empty vestibule.

The next room toward the front of the house wasn't lit, but a glow from the opposite side provided enough to get me through. Once I crossed to a longer hallway, I heard something clink from the direction of the light. Ice in a glass. A cabinet door opened and closed. Liquid poured. Someone was enjoying a late drink.

I crept down the hall and hesitated just outside a lit doorway. Drawing a shallow breath, praying I was as invisible as I thought, I leaned far enough to see into a kitchen. And found Trevor.

He'd clearly been roused from sleep. His clothes were wrinkled, his eyes bagged and bloodshot. The thin jacket he wore didn't match his button-down linen shirt—not at all like Trevor to commit crimes against fashion. Stubble flocked his jaw line and accentuated drawn cheeks. He still wore Shamil's pendant. Even without the marks of exhaustion, he looked mad enough to bite through bricks. He leaned against a counter and clutched a short glass full of amber liquid. A quarter-full bottle of Scotch stood on the surface behind him.

He seemed to be arguing with himself. And losing.

"Too soon," he murmured. "It's only been five hours. We can't force him." His brow furrowed, and he drained half the glass at once. "We'll find him. First thing in the morning."

His eyes widened. The glass shook in his hand, slipped out, and shattered on the stone tile floor. Trevor followed it down, dropping to one knee with a choked gasp. He fisted a hand and banged it on the top of the counter.

What the hell was in his drink? The bizarre performance almost made me think he'd poisoned himself, but I had to discount that idea. It'd be a stroke of luck for me.

Trevor coughed a few times and struggled to his feet again. "Don't do that," he said, his tone hollow and forceless.

I'd known he was insane, but this transcended normal lunacy.

A muffled ringing hailed from Trevor's pocket. He fished out a cell phone and keyed it. "Whatever it is, deal with it."

The pause that followed sent Trevor from annoyance to his typical ice-calm demeanor, which meant someone was about to die. "A bounty hunter. He's looking for what?"

I filled in the gap myself. Quaid had followed through on his promise. Dudley Do-Right strikes again—and now Trevor would take him out.

"Send him through. We'll meet him at the door." Trevor hung up and called for his thugs.

I pulled back just before Trevor swept out of the kitchen and followed him through the house. Now I'd have to save Quaid's ass, too. I reminded myself to thank him later for ruining a perfectly good impossible plan.

CHAPTER 31

I stood behind a potted tree in the entrance hall and prepared to watch Trevor play Quaid like a royal flush.

The two thugs behind Trevor remained poker-faced while he opened the door. On the porch, Quaid appeared alone and ridiculously unprepared, though he didn't seem nearly as vulnerable as he should have. Still, I knew he failed to understand that his reasonable attitude wouldn't score any points with Trevor.

"Mr. Maddock, I'm sorry to disturb you at such an inconvenient time." Quaid produced a small cream-white card with a magician's flourish.

Trevor accepted the card and looked from its surface to Quaid. "My associate tells me you're looking for a thief."

"I am. His name is Gavyn Donatti, and I have reason to believe you've had dealings with this man. I'd like to discuss a few things with you on behalf of my employer." Quaid nodded at the card.

"I see." Trevor motioned, and one of the thugs stepped forward. "I don't believe I caught your name, Mr. . . . ?"

"Quaid will do."

"Will it, now."

I wondered if Quaid could see the shark swimming behind Trevor's smile—because I could sense it through the back of his close-shaven head.

"All right, Quaid. Before we proceed, I'll have to insist that you remove any weapons you may be carrying."

The bounty hunter's easygoing expression faltered. "I don't see why—"

Trevor stepped aside. The nearest thug slipped past, grabbed Quaid in mid-sentence, and shoved him face-first against the wall. "Policy, my good man," Trevor said while the thug began his treasure hunt. "You wouldn't believe how many visitors I've had who were intent on harming me. One can never be too careful."

Quaid offered no reaction as Trevor's goon relieved him of enough hardware to subdue and capture the population of a small country. A thick leather roll, tied in the center, contained at least a dozen of his paralyzing darts and a segmented blow-tube. Not one or two but four sets of cuffs were turned out, along with a length of rope and some plastic zip ties. He had mace, chloroform, a handheld GPS tracking unit, night-vision goggles, a genuine stun gun, and a small velvet pouch full of crushed leaves that resembled pot but probably wasn't.

By the time the search ended, Quaid had lost his coat, his boots, and any trace of good humor.

Trevor gestured the other thug into action. They flanked the bounty hunter, one to an arm, and awaited further orders. "It's interesting that you have questions for me," Trevor said. "I have a few for you myself. They concern Mr. Donatti and his tall friend—I'm sure you must have met him. Correct me if I'm wrong."

"The police will be here soon, Mr. Maddock," Quaid said. "There's still time for you to be reasonable."

Trevor laughed. "Well, if they bother to show up, I'll just have to reduce their bonuses. They know better than to disturb me at this time of night with wild accusations." He picked up the stun gun from the pile and examined it. "I've been meaning to get one of these. You don't mind if I try it out, do you?"

The thugs released Quaid seconds before Trevor pulled the trigger. Two projectiles shot from the barrel and latched onto the bounty hunter's shirt. A loud zap, a few sparks, and Quaid fell to the floor convulsing.

Trevor calmly detached the wires. "Bring him downstairs and make him . . . comfortable. I'll be along to talk with him soon."

Downstairs was bad. Very bad. I wished djinn could read minds, so Ian could hear me screaming at him to hurry the hell up.

Trevor left first and disappeared into the house somewhere. A small comfort, but it gave me a few extra seconds. The thugs hefted Quaid's limp form and dragged him past me. "Heavy son of a bitch, ain't he?" one of them said. The other just grunted.

I waited as long as I dared. The scuffing sound of Quaid's legs sliding across the floor would have to suffice for cover. I grabbed the roll of darts, freed two of them, and followed the thugs through darkness and into the sitting room.

There, I closed the door after us.

One of the thugs turned with a wary expression. "The hell was that?"

"You really want to ask?" the other one said.

"Fuck, no. C'mon, let's get this over with. I'm trying to watch *Exit Wounds*."

"Ain't you already seen that fifty times?"

"Yeah, but it's always—ouch! What the—"

He slapped at the dart I'd planted in his neck. I skirted around and went for the other one, no longer caring about any sound I might make. While the unaffected thug watched his buddy fold to the floor with a baffled expression, I thrust the second dart in near his collarbone.

Without support, Quaid toppled over and groaned. Both thugs made loud, garbled sounds. I sprinted to the dry bar, grabbed a solid metal mixer cup, and delivered knockout blows to their temples. It took longer than I wanted.

"Who's there?" Quaid spoke with difficulty.

"Shut up," I whispered. After a few seconds passed and no one burst into the room ready to shoot me, I stopped trying to be invisible and hauled Quaid away from the unconscious thugs. "Can you walk?"

He stared at me. "How did you—"

"We can play twenty questions later. Can you walk or not?"

Quaid tensed and relaxed with a gasp. "Not."

"Okay. Hang on." No way could I drag him down the basement stairs alone. I closed my eyes and concentrated. *Heal Quaid.* The pain of using magic didn't last long. I hoped that meant he wasn't too damaged, and I still had some mojo left. "How about now?"

Frowning, Quaid pushed off the floor and stood. "What did you do to me?"

"Never mind. Come on." I headed for the opposite side of the room, stopped, and turned. Quaid wasn't following. "Can you move a little faster? I doubt we have much time."

"I don't understand."

I almost felt bad for him. He'd finally realized that he wasn't in control anymore. Still, I couldn't spend the next hour or so explaining everything to him. "Look, it's simple," I told him. "If you don't want Trevor to torture you to death—or just put a bullet through your skull—come with me. I'll get you out of here. And if you still want to bring me in after this is over, feel free."

Quaid blinked. Just when I thought I'd have to try dragging him after all, he took a step. And another. Soon, he was practically running.

TAKING THE STAIRS THREE AT A TIME MIGHT HAVE HELPED MORE if Ian had been conscious when I reached the basement.

I rushed over to the heap on the floor at Shamil's feet. Ian had lost his shimmer, so I assumed he was visible. "Ian," I whispered, dropping next to him and shaking his shoulder. "We gotta move. Come on."

His eyes opened. "I broke the seal," he murmured. "Cut him down. I've not the strength to heal him."

"Okay. I will," I lied. We'd have to come back later for Shamil—if there was a later. I grabbed Ian and started hauling him toward the mirror. He struggled to move with me and managed to stand.

Quaid stood by the table of flickering candles, his gaze riveted to the alcove. The light didn't reveal the full extent of Shamil's injuries, but it was enough to catch glimpses of his eyeless face. "My God," the bounty hunter whispered. "I've never seen anything like this."

Ian stiffened. He glanced at Quaid and back to me. "Troublesome human," he rasped. "What business has he this time?"

"Suicide, apparently." I helped Ian prop himself against the wall. "I'm going to have to send him through first. Far as Trevor's concerned, he's expendable."

"Be quick, thief."

Although Ian didn't protest, his expression clearly insisted that Quaid was expendable to us, too. But I couldn't leave him here. It'd be the same as killing him myself.

"Quaid, come here," I said.

He approached slowly and regarded Ian with vague unease. "Generally, calling someone human would indicate you're not. Human, that is."

"Yes. The mind boggles," I snapped before Ian could reply with something less than helpful. "Like I said, we can worry about all this later, okay? Just be quiet and cooperate for a few minutes. No more questions."

To my amazement, there weren't.

I fumbled the knife from my pocket and sliced a finger before my brain caught on to what my hands were doing. Concentration wouldn't be easy to come by, though I remembered the rest. Symbol, words, intention. I scrawled blood in the corner, drew a breath, and tried to envision Jazz and Lark and Tory. Trees and grass. And most important, not Trevor's basement.

"Insha no imil, kubri ana bi-sur'u wasta."

Relief accompanied the image of moonlit woods that filled the mirror. Within seconds, Tory's concerned features swam into view. "Has he freed Shamil?"

Quaid stumbled back, his complexion the color of chalk.

I grimaced. "Er, mostly. There's been a slight complication . . . no time to explain. I've got a bounty hunter here, too. I'm sending him through first. Uh—don't hurt him, all right? That's not code. He's okay."

"Fine. But hurry." Tory offered a deep frown and moved away.

I motioned to Quaid. When he didn't move, I grabbed him and pulled. "Hurry means fast, Quaid. Come on. Do you want to live for the rest of the night?"

He shook himself and came forward. A grim determination had replaced his alarm. "Sorry. What should I be doing?"

"This is a gate." I pointed at the mirror. "You go through it. Now."

"Through the mirror."

"Yes. Look." I gripped his wrist and shoved his hand into the image of forest. He shivered. "It's a little cold, but it won't last long. Now go."

He stared at me. "Thank you."

Before I could reiterate that we were kind of in a hurry, he caught a quick breath and plunged through. The surface darkened to black, then faded into a mirror again.

The first wave of exhaustion hit me hard. I managed to keep from collapsing in front of Ian. Clear certainty that three bridges were at least one too many for me to make lurked in the back of my mind. I ignored it. "Okay. Your turn," I told him, already going for the knife.

Ian touched my wrist. "Take a moment," he said gently. "Rest."

"I don't think we have a moment." Still, I dropped to one knee and closed my eyes in a futile attempt to regain a little stamina. "Trevor's really lost it," I said in the general direction of the floor. "He was up there fighting with himself. Wasn't going well for him, either."

Ian shifted instantly to full alert. "Explain."

I repeated the one-sided conversation I'd heard and described Trevor's choking act. The more I talked, the angrier Ian became. Finally, he said, "Lenka."

"What, the snake dude?"

"He is controlling the human. Trevor is nothing more than Lenka's puppet." Ian's jaw clenched. "Of course. Why did I not see this before?"

My brain entered a sickening spin. "Does that mean Lenka is here somewhere?"

"It is not necessary, but it is possible. Likely, in fact. Proximity gives us greater control—but we do not practice such magic." Disgust twisted his features. "To take over another's soul is the basest form of evil. He must be destroyed."

"Right. But I think we'll have to survive in order to do that. We really should—"

A soft click sounded from the vicinity of the stairs. The door? No footsteps followed. Surging adrenalin brought me to my feet, and I faced the mirror again.

Ian sent a grim look at the stairs. "Leave me," he whispered.

I clapped a hand over his mouth. Shook my head. And went back to business. *Symbol, words, intention.* With one ear tuned for movement, I reopened the cut and squeezed fresh blood. Scrawled the symbol—squiggle, dot, crescent. And tried to concentrate.

The first footfall sounded as loud as thunder. More followed—measured, unhurried.

I glanced at Ian. His lips formed *Go.*

My mind shuffled through options at warp speed. I could open a bridge only once before we were discovered. So I had two choices. Push Ian through, stay here, and die. Or go through myself and kill him.

I chose option three, with a big heap of I'm-gonna-regret-this.

Turning from the mirror, already going for the see-through look, I grabbed Ian and hustled him back. Away from the stairs. His expression went from shock to fury in zero seconds, but he didn't speak. He must have understood at least part of my plan, the not-being-seen part. Unfortunately, that was as far as I'd gotten. With an arm around Ian as if we were entering a three-legged race, I flattened us against the wall and waited.

Trevor reached the bottom and headed straight for Shamil. Halfway across the room, he stopped. Turned. A cold smile registered on his face.

"Gahiji-an. Could you really be that stupid?"

Ian stiffened. I urged him toward the stairs, but he didn't move.

"You have broken the seal, yet Shamil remains bound. Did you lack the strength to cut him down? I know you are here, Gahiji-an."

I silently willed Ian not to move. Maybe we could still skin out.

Trevor approached the mirror. He stared at it, reached up, and swiped a finger through the blood symbol. "You will not slip past me this time. Fool. And I thought you had learned to leave your wounded behind."

At once, I understood these were Lenka's words, delivered in Trevor's voice. A grotesque puppet show featuring a living, breathing marionette. I'd heard it once before, when Ian had rescued me from this place. When Trevor had said *I feel you . . . Gahiji-an.* And it hadn't even occurred to me to wonder how he knew Ian's real name.

Trevor-Lenka moved back to the stairs and blocked them.

"Visible or not, this is the only way out. I know you're still here, and I will find you." He pulled out a gun. "You may as well show yourself," he called out. "You've lost, General. You are an army of one. Prince of nothing."

Ian practically vibrated. I squeezed his arm hard, attempting to stop him from doing whatever stupid thing he had in mind. And I reached for my own gun. Maybe I'd have to shoot the bastard after all.

"Show yourself, and I will let Akila live."

A sinking feeling lodged in my gut just before Ian lunged from my grasp. I clamped my mouth shut against a protesting shout. One of us had to leave this place alive. Ian knew that—and he'd decided it would be me.

Damn him.

He walked out in clear view. "Lenka, you are the worst of cowards. Hiding behind a human. I've shown myself. Why do you not face me on your own?"

I read his intentions instantly: distract Lenka's control, and I might be able to take out Trevor, or at least get the tether from him. Unfortunately, Lenka read them, too.

"In good time, Gahiji-an," he said. "You will see me before you die. But after four centuries of the chase, I intend to savor this capture."

"That will be your mistake." Ian kept his gaze on the figure blocking the stairs. "Why delay victory any longer? Destroy me, and claim your prize."

"No, Gahiji-an. You will suffer first. And you know full well I require your tether. Of course, you would not have brought it here—or would you?" The cold smile widened. "We shall find out."

The gun came up. Trevor took aim and fired.

CHAPTER 32

The bullet ripped through Ian's thigh. He dropped to his knees. Trevor fired twice more, putting one in his shoulder, another straight to the gut. Ian collapsed with a groan.

I finally got a grip on the modified rifle. My hands shook so hard I half expected bullets to start rattling in the chamber and give my position away. Despite my conviction that I could make an exception for Trevor, I still wasn't sure I'd be able to go through with killing a human being—even if he only fit that term loosely. Guess I'd find out. I tried to aim for his torso. Bigger target, better chance at actually hitting the bastard. My finger rested on the trigger.

Then Trevor reached down and hauled Ian up with one arm. Might as well've been a brick wall between us. Even if I was a good shot, I couldn't have hit him.

"You have nothing left. Do you? No power at all." Trevor shook him. "You can't be as foolish as you seem. Why did you come here? What are you hiding?"

When Ian didn't answer, Trevor drove a fist into the gut wound. Ian's body went slack, but Trevor held him up.

I took a few careful steps to one side, looking for an opening to plug him. *Come on, damn it. Move.* But Trevor didn't seem inclined to go anywhere. I half suspected he knew I was here.

"You broke the seal. You must have known it would drain you. How did you plan to leave, with a weak cripple and no power of your own?"

Ian slowly raised his head. And spit at him. I damn near cheered aloud.

Trevor ignored the blood-flecked saliva sprinkling his face. "You will answer me. As I said, I have waited four centuries for this. I can be patient longer. Hours, perhaps even days."

Nothing. Ian didn't even blink.

I managed another few cautious steps. Couldn't afford to miss with the first shot, because I wouldn't get a second chance. I almost had a clear line when Trevor snarled and dragged Ian toward his collection of restraints. Away from me. Once again ruining my shot.

"We can do this the long way. In fact, I look forward to it." Still clutching Ian by the vest, he tucked the gun in his waistband and grabbed a set of iron manacles. He jacked Ian's arms behind him and cuffed them tight. "How do you prefer your pain?"

In a blink, Trevor slammed him face-first against a wall. Ian let out a breathless gasp. I drew a bead, but he jerked Ian back almost as fast as he'd bashed him. "What shall we use?" He scanned the room, and his gaze settled on the mirror. A grim smile stretched his lips. "How interesting. Your finger barely bleeds. Yet you have not healed your other wounds, and the blood on the mirror is fresh."

My breath stopped.

"You would never have planned to leave yourself defenseless. The blood is not yours. You have taught your pet some new tricks. He is here as well." He paused. "*Donatti.*"

I felt the personality switch when my name left his lips. Lenka must have been pushed back by the force of Trevor's rage. "Disgusting thief! I should've killed you when I had the chance."

Despite my horror, I couldn't help feeling a quick swell of pride. The bastard had just paid me the ultimate criminal compliment. I wouldn't add him to my Christmas card list, though.

"Come out! I'm going to rip out your tongue and feed it to my dogs, you slippery little shit!" He shoved Ian to the floor and whipped the gun back out.

Finally.

I took an extra second to attempt a steady aim and pulled the trigger before I could talk myself out of it. The boom and kick of the weapon were rifle-strength, earsplitting, slamming back down my arms and damn near knocking me over. I held my ground.

Trevor didn't. The shot took him in the side and spun him around almost completely. He hung unbalanced on one leg for a heartbeat and toppled over like a bowling pin.

Bile clogged my throat, and I had to resist a compulsion to throw the gun across the room. I'd just shot a man. No idea if I'd killed him, but he was down, and he wasn't moving. Heart thumping my ribs, breath whistling like a kettle, I kept the piece on him and crept forward.

Ian coughed and stirred. He rolled onto his side with a harsh groan. "Thief . . ."

"I've got this. Just hold on."

He tried to say something else, but a convulsive coughing fit overcame him. I had to get him out of here fast.

I reached Trevor and found him still alive. His half-open eyes were twitching, rolled back to whites. He breathed in shallow hitches. The blast hole torn through his shirt revealed a bloodied eruption of glistening pink flesh. Blood soaked the material and pooled on the floor. Glimpses of the snake tattoos on him almost appeared to be writhing, as if they were trying to crawl away from the wound.

After kicking his gun away from his outstretched hand, I grabbed the pendant, jerked it over his head, and stuffed it into a pocket. The other tether . . . what the hell did Tory say? Something small and round in his pocket. A ring or a coin. I knelt and thrust a hand into the pocket that wasn't soaked with blood and came up empty. Of course. I reached into the wet pocket. Felt something solid and pulled it out. It was a coin, about the size of a half-dollar, gleaming silver under crimson streaks, embossed with worn markings that were probably djinn writing.

Trevor hissed a rattling breath. His entire body jerked. Maybe he was dying. I folded the coin in my hand and started to stand, and Trevor's hand flew up and made a grab for me.

"Jesus!" I stumbled back. His eyes were still trying to stare at his brain. He didn't move again. Might've been some kind of bizarre nerve reaction, since he couldn't see me. I was still invisible.

Ian let out a moan. At least he'd stopped coughing. He tried to get up.

"Don't," I told him. "We're leaving in a minute."

He made a garbled sound. If there were any words in it, I didn't catch them.

I crouched near Ian. If I could manage to destroy Lenka's tether, everything stopped. Still holding the gun, I reopened the cut on my finger with my teeth and smeared blood on the face of the coin. Easier than opening a bridge, I reminded myself. Just the blood and the words. And every bit of strength I had left.

Trevor screamed and jolted up to a seated position, as if someone had tied a rope around his neck and pulled. Pink-tinged foam bubbled from his lips. His arms jerked and flapped like a kid playing airplane, and his head lolled forward bonelessly.

He was half-dead, and Lenka was still moving him around. I had to finish this now.

Focus. The familiar electric sensation balled in my chest and built to a rapid crescendo of pain. I tuned out the horror show that was Trevor and Ian's now-breathless attempts to speak. Nothing but me and the coin. Seconds away from ending this nightmare.

Another chilling scream left Trevor's mouth. He fell over and flopped a few times. Then he raised an arm and slapped his own face. His eyes flew open, and one hand jerked and twitched toward the inside of his jacket.

The grotesque display robbed most of my focus, and gathering the threads again took precious seconds. Ian gasped something that I failed to understand. Some distant part of my mind realized it was probably important, but I couldn't stop now. Words. I had to say them.

I opened my mouth to speak—and realized I wasn't invisible any more.

At once, Trevor bolted to his knees and lunged at me with impossible speed. I brought the gun up and fired twice. At least one shot hit him. But he still collided with me and knocked me flat.

A new pain exploded in my throat. Electric but manmade. Taser.

My muscles went on strike. I crumpled to the floor, vaguely aware of the coin clattering from my fingers outside a cocoon of agony. Something that felt like a wrecking ball rammed my stomach. The blow cleared some of my mental fog, but then the Taser went off in my side. The world blurred again.

Dimly, I heard Trevor shrieking while he juiced me over and over. I fought to stay conscious. And lost.

EITHER THERE WAS AN EARTHQUAKE IN PROGRESS, OR SOME-one had surgically implanted a giant joy buzzer in my stom-ach.

I opened my eyes and realized that was about all I could move. It didn't look as if I'd been out too long, though. Trevor knelt on the floor six or seven feet from me. The second shot had taken him in the thigh. His head hung limp, a broken thing. He gasped every intake of breath and cried out every exhale. The bloodied coin lay on his palm.

"Thief." Ian's voice behind me, raw with shock.

I wasn't sure I could answer him. It took three tries to re-member where my tongue was. "Wha'?" I slurred through a mouthful of drool.

"You are visible."

"Noticed." I squeezed my eyes shut, opened them, and tried to move. Anything. One finger might've twitched. The vibrating buzzer in my core sent out needles.

"*Sssilence.*" The awful, grating word came from Trevor.

His head winched up with a series of popping jolts. Tendons bulged in his neck. Agony and rage blazed from his eyes. His fingers spasmed around the coin, and his arm lifted with the same jerking fits.

"... *no* ..."

Despite his strengthless protest, Trevor's hand stayed on course and shoved the coin into his mouth. He gagged immediately and tried to spit it out. His eyes widened so much that I was convinced they'd burst in their sockets. Finally, he swallowed hard and gasped for breath. Tears streamed down his cheeks. "Kill you," he spat. "Swear ..."

He went completely still. More spasms and twitches moved through him, puppeting his arms, stripping away his tattered shirt. The tattoos looked sunken into his flesh, as though they were squeezing him.

Immediately, one of the snakes glowed fire-red. Not just a trick of the light this time. And from Trevor's agonized expression, whatever lit those lines didn't tickle. His arms rose, his head fell back. Slender wisps of smoke formed along the edges of the coal-bright snake. The smell of burning flesh wafted through the room, and I suppressed a gag.

This explained the unusual qualities of Trevor's tattoo work. No ink involved. Just fire.

I couldn't look away from him. The glow spread to encompass the entire area between the outlines of the snake. His skin blistered and bulged until a thick, bright red tube looped around his torso, over one shoulder, under the other. Red faded to black and became glistening, close-set scales. A snake. Sliding in lazy motion across limbs and body as if Trevor was its favorite tree.

Lenka, I presumed.

The snake's head lifted from behind Trevor's shoulder, bobbing and weaving like an Indian cobra in a charmer's thrall. It gave a threatening hiss and streaked down Trevor's body to coil on the floor. White light enveloped the snake, and its shape shifted. The transformation yielded a tall figure clad in deep blue velvet robes. Pale white skin, as cold and smooth as marble save for the tattooed scale pattern on his hairless head. Eyes the color of fresh blood, with narrow slits for pupils. And serrated ivory teeth nearly as sharp as the fangs of the snake he'd been seconds before.

The instant Lenka completed his transformation, Trevor collapsed.

Ian snarled something in djinn. It was definitely not a friendly greeting. Smirking, Lenka kicked Trevor's inert form aside and crouched in front of me. He tipped his head and stared at me as if I was an exhibit in a freak show.

"My hair on fire?" I croaked.

"You intended to destroy me. Didn't you, thief?" Lenka flashed a ghoulish grin. "Clever. I admit, I never would have guessed that Gahiji-an would teach you this. Or that you would be able to learn. Such a smart dog. But as clever as you are, I doubt you can pick a stomach."

"Release him, Lenka." Ian's voice wavered like an old man's. "You have me."

Vicious laughter answered him. "The dog is more intelligent than his master. No. He will stay and witness your death. Then experience his own. My pet wants this one for himself."

I made a sound that would've been a laugh if my lungs worked. "Think your pet's dead."

"I am afraid he is not. How unlucky for you." Lenka rose

and hovered over Trevor. He held a hand out and chanted in djinn. The gaping hole in Trevor's side started knitting itself back together.

Great. Now that I'd shot him, he was really going to be my best friend.

He finished in less than a minute. Trevor shot to his feet, teeth bared, and grabbed my gun off the floor. He knelt and pressed the muzzle to my forehead. "I'd blow your skull apart right now, Donatti, if it wasn't too good for you. You aren't worth wasting one of your own bullets."

"Patience, my hot-blooded pet," Lenka said. "It will be time to hurt them soon."

I pulled a grimace. "Can we reschedule? I have a hot date."

Trevor grabbed a handful of shirt, hauled me up, and back-handed me with the gun. Lightning flashed through my head and sizzled across my vision.

"Enough," Lenka commanded. "Bind him, and summon your men."

"Fine."

Trevor dropped me. I landed hard and coughed out a spray of blood. He stalked over to the restraint collection, grabbed a length of rope, and returned to kick me facedown, then knelt on my back and started tying.

"Get the pendant from him," Lenka said when he finished.

Trevor got the right pocket on the first try. He tossed Shamil's tether to Lenka and pulled a phone from his back pocket. He dialed and almost immediately barked, "Get your asses down here, right now."

"Now, then." Lenka moved toward the alcove, where Shamil remained bound and unconscious. "I have little use for the *sharmoot* now, save for one last infusion. And so I will allow him to keep this." He snapped the cord, reached in, and tied it tight around Shamil's neck.

Ian loosed a wordless roar. He almost managed to stand. But almost wasn't enough.

"You are displeased?" Lenka sneered. "I have returned his tether to him. I cannot be blamed that he does not take advantage of the opportunity."

"You've not changed, Lenka. You and your kin have always excelled at crushing the weak and defenseless." Ian paused for a wheezing breath. "Face me fairly. Prove you can best me, as you failed to do before."

Lenka's smile didn't waver. "I swear it will be done, and soon. Perhaps sooner than you may wish, Gahiji-an." He pulled something from his robes with a showman's gesture. A short, curved knife. Turning back toward the still form in the alcove, he reached up into the shadows and came back with a gold-plated goblet. He pushed the cup against Shamil's stomach and sliced his flesh just above the rim.

Shamil's head flew up, tilted back. The cord prevented him from making a sound as his blood pulsed into the goblet. Shock kept me from screaming obscenities, and Ian groaned in sympathy.

"Come and drink, my pet." Lenka gestured at Trevor.

As Trevor made his way across the room with faint disgust stamped on his features, the sound of an opening door drifted down the stairs. Heavy footsteps followed. Four thugs filed into the basement, Leonard among them.

Trevor took the cup. He finished fast and dashed it aside. "Happy?"

"Nearly." Lenka's expression lost its amusement. He pointed at the thugs. "Bring them to the sitting room, and search them both. We will join you shortly. I want full power to deal with them."

The goons split two and two. Of course, I got the pair with Leonard. They each grabbed an arm and dragged me toward the stairs. I couldn't have walked if I'd wanted to, but some of the feeling was starting to flood back into my limbs. It wasn't a warm, soothing feeling.

But I didn't exactly expect a massage and a foot rub in my immediate future.

CHAPTER 33

eing tied to a chair wasn't a new experience for me. Last time, though, I hadn't been naked. Well, I was almost naked. They let me keep my drawers on, but it didn't make the wooden seat any softer or less cold. My ass had fallen asleep by the time Trevor and Lenka entered the room.

"Found this on him." Leonard approached Lenka with the fake tether—for all the good it'd do. Having a dupe now defeated the purpose. They'd figure it out pretty quickly when Ian didn't die.

Lenka took it with raised eyebrows. He stared at Ian, who'd been tied on his feet to one of the pillars across the room. "What a shame. I had thought you a better strategist, Gahijian. Unless this is another of your tricks?"

"You are too quick for me, Lenka." Ian's words sank under the weight of his sarcasm. "I question how I have managed to evade you for so long."

Lenka fell silent. His gaze traveled the room slowly, as if he was searching for the perfect tool to teach Ian some manners. Finally, he waved a hand at the two remaining thugs. "Leave us.

I want everyone up and on guard. Search the grounds—these two may have brought reinforcements."

My last spark of hope was snuffed out with his orders. We were all dead.

The thugs filed out and closed the door behind them. Lenka looked from Ian to me and back. "I do not trust you not to lie, Dehbei scum. Perhaps this is your tether, perhaps not. We shall find out soon." He moved toward Ian. "If this is not your tether, I will enjoy persuading you to locate it for me."

Ian pulled a smile. "You have gotten uglier since I saw you last."

"I take pride in my clan, Dehbei," Lenka snarled. "Your appearance is disgusting. You degrade yourself, aping these pitiful humans." He pointed a finger and murmured.

Ian screamed and writhed against the ropes holding him.

"Ah. It has been long since I cast a flame curse. How satisfying." After a long minute, Lenka gestured. Ian slumped immediately. "Do not trouble yourself thinking you will die in the same manner as your father, *rayan*." The djinn word fell heavy with mockery. "No. I have something special in mind for you. Something that will take far longer."

"Gods curse you." Ian gasped. "Or better yet, allow me."

His lips moved. One hand shifted in the ropes. Lenka's mouth opened, and thick black fluid poured out to splash down his robes.

Garbled sounds rose from the Morai's throat. He dropped to one knee and clapped a hand over his mouth. The black stuff leaked from his nostrils and seeped between his fingers. It dribbled from his eyes like black tears. I had no idea what that gunk was, but it looked as if it hurt. And I didn't think Ian knew any destructive spells. Too bad he never got to show me that one.

Now I knew why he hadn't done anything in the basement. He must've been conserving what he could for this.

Lenka raised his free hand and gestured with a cutting motion. The black flow ceased. He coughed once, rose to his feet, and murmured in djinn. The streaks and splashes of liquid decorating his face and clothing seemed to be absorbed back into him. His lips peeled back in a sharp-toothed smile. "Well done, *rayan*. A flawlessly executed soul drain. Quite futile, as you see, but you showed excellent form. However, I would suggest that you conserve your power for what is yet to come."

Despite looking like overworked bread dough, Ian sneered. "I am surprised that you still have a soul to drain, snake."

"There is no need to flatter me," Lenka said. "Now, then. A test."

He drew the fake dagger and plunged it into Ian's chest.

I bit back a scream of my own. Whether it was some aspect of our relation or just plain empathy, I felt echoes of every blow Ian took. But he didn't voice this one. Blood bubbled from his mouth in place of sound. Bastard must've punctured a lung.

And Ian would live. Lucky him.

Lenka wrenched the dagger free. He wiped the blood from it on Ian's pants and inspected the gleaming blade with the care of a suspicious dealer sniffing for counterfeits. "This does not carry your mark." He flashed a cruel smile. "We will have to do this the hard way."

Trevor glanced at Lenka. "The thief might know something."

"All right, pet. I will leave it to you to find out."

From the look on Trevor's face, he'd just won the lottery. And once again, I held the losing ticket.

———

TIME DOESN'T FLY WHEN YOU'RE BEING TORTURED.

The grandfather clock near the mantle claimed only thirty minutes had passed—at least, it had the last time I could see clearly. Which might have been a few hours ago. In that time, I'd gained at least two broken bones, along with other assorted injuries, and lost two fingernails.

Ian was ahead of me. I wasn't sure how many bones he'd broken, but Lenka seemed to enjoy the fingernail-ripping game. He'd taken seven of Ian's so far.

"Maybe I'm going too fast. Should we slow down, Mr. Donatti?"

"Why? You getting tired?" I didn't bother turning my head to look at him. It hurt too much. "Take your time," I muttered. "Don't have plans for tonight."

"Once again, then. Where is that tether?"

"On the moon. Third crater to the right."

Trevor gave a disappointed sigh. "This one's going to be difficult. They're always hardest to rip free. You see, they tend to stick at the cuticle."

He grabbed my thumb and clamped it to the arm of the chair. The pliers settled at the tip of the nail. "Are you sure you don't want to modify your response?"

"No, thanks, Regis. That's my final answer."

Part of my mind begged me to spill, or at least force my mouth to stop making it worse. But my gears were stuck in auto-kiss-my-ass.

"Well, then. If you insist."

For an instant, I thought Trevor grinned at me. Then the pain came. No other senses existed. He did this one slowly, and I felt every centimeter of torn skin. Hot blood gushed over my thumb like the world's smallest volcano. Finally, as Trevor had promised, it stuck at the cuticle. He yanked it free and dropped the bloodied bit into my lap with the other two.

Would've bit my tongue, but I needed all my strength to scream.

I couldn't understand why I was still conscious. Why I bothered expending the effort to stay alive. It was over. We'd been reduced to euphemisms. Entered the eleventh hour. The fat lady had sung. Time had run out.

If only that were true. But time insisted on continuing, and pain rode the minutes like a desperate whore.

Eventually, I realized why I hadn't confessed the location of Ian's tether yet. Trevor hadn't promised to kill me if I told him. He didn't even try to lie and say he would. As Skids had me back when the world was normal, he just wanted to hurt me. Extensively.

He'd gotten his wish.

Trevor's face loomed into my blotchy vision. His lips moved. That probably meant he was saying something. I laughed at my own joke, a rusted wheeze that showered splinters through my chest.

My amusement cost me another fingernail. On the plus side, I couldn't scream anymore.

For an instant, gray haze obscured my vision. Then something harsh stabbed my nostrils. It felt like a urine-coated fork. My breath quickened, and my eyes flew open. I hadn't realized they'd closed in the first place.

Trevor held a small glass bottle under my nose. Industrial-strength smelling salts, with extra ammonia.

"Wake up, Mr. Donatti."

I blinked at him. "What's up? Time for breakfast?"

He slapped me. Constellations exploded behind my eyes. "Your attitude isn't doing you any favors."

"Very osser . . . obber . . . smart of you." I shook my head. Some of the stars went out. "This is pretty stupid, Trevor. I'm not telling you. Don't you have better things to do? Terrorize businesses, scare little kids . . ."

Renewed screams drifted across the room from Ian's side. I managed not to vomit, but it was close.

Trevor pushed the bloodied point of the pliers into the hollow of my throat. He didn't break skin, but air refused to pass in or out. "If I don't get anywhere with you, I'll just have to keep you alive until I can find your son."

He pulled back. A coughing fit scalded my lungs and prevented my reply. I almost went for the taunt, almost said he'd never find Cyrus. Instead, I decided to bluff. "Tell you where he is," I said. "Won't matter. He's already dead. Jazz, too," I added as an afterthought. Might as well bluff big.

"You lie." He slammed the pliers down on the table he'd dragged over to hold his toys and my body parts and picked up the Taser. Juiced me forever and a few extra seconds.

"Dead," I gasped when my teeth stopped chattering. "We tried to hide 'em. The digie . . . genies, they don' like human visitors. They k-killed both. Of them. Second they crossed." I didn't have to manufacture the misery in my voice. No matter what happened, Jazz and Cyrus were dead to me. I'd never see them again.

Incredibly, Trevor bought it. Or seemed to.

"Well, Mr. Donatti." He replaced the Taser and crouched to eye level with me. "I suppose you're right. There's no point in continuing when you have nothing to lose."

I didn't dare agree out loud.

"So it comes to this. Tell me where his tether is, and I'll kill you right now."

My lips stretched without my permission. "Liar."

Trevor laughed. "Right again. But you might as well tell me anyway."

"Why?" I croaked. "Why do you hate me so much? It's not like I kicked your dogs, raped your wife. If you had one. I only lost a lousy knife."

His eyes glittered. "And I paid for it. You have no idea." Trevor darted a glance across the room, as if he expected Lenka was listening. "He's in my head," he hissed. "Constantly. Inside me. It's agonizing. He won't leave until he gets this lousy knife."

A nauseating stench invaded my nostrils. At first, I thought he'd shoved the smelling salts up my nose, but the thick, bittersweet odor didn't slice like ammonia. It reminded me of an outdoor barbecue. I finally realized it came from Trevor. Everywhere the snake markings had been, his flesh had warped, cracked, or outright melted. His torso glimmered with a mixture of fluids. Some of it was blood. I couldn't tell what the greenish-yellow gunk was, but it probably shouldn't have been seeping from his wounds like that.

I'd lay odds he didn't sign on for that when he took up with Lenka.

Trevor grabbed me by the throat. "I want my payment, and I want him gone. You're the key. You will tell me where it is!"

It was hard to feel sorry for a guy who was treating my windpipe like a tube of toothpaste. I almost did. But not enough to confess.

Someone pounded on the door of the sitting room. Trevor released me abruptly. I dropped forward so hard I damn near toppled the chair. My head refused to rise again, and my eyes forgot the meaning of focus, but my hearing still worked.

"What?" Trevor snarled through the door.

Leonard replied from the other side. "Found somebody tryin' to crash the party, boss."

I felt as if I'd been stuffed in a freezer. *Please don't be Jazz.*

The door opened. And Trevor loosed the most chilling laugh I'd ever heard. "Welcome back, dear lady. How was the afterlife?"

I was beginning to hate being right all the time.

Scuffling sounds. The door slammed. Silence. My name carried on a broken whisper, in the last voice I wanted to hear right now. She should've been with Tory and Lark. Should've been safe and long gone from here. Fate could *not* be this cruel.

Raising my head seemed harder than cutting concrete with a spoon. I had to inch my eyeballs in the direction of the door. Absolute terror kept me from focusing clearly on her face, but I didn't need visual confirmation.

The sight of Jazz—handcuffed, under Trevor's gun, and pissed enough to chew iron and spit out nails—hurt a hundred times more than everything he'd done to me. And it was about to get worse.

CHAPTER 34

Trevor shoved hard against her cuffed hands. Jazz stumbled a few steps and righted herself. "You look like shit," she said. "And you're torturing him? Idiot. You know that never works."

Although she spoke steadily enough, she avoided looking directly at me. It was enough to tell me she cared more than she'd let Trevor find out.

Trevor ignored her admonishment and held up one of the dupes. I assumed it was the one she'd carried. "Are they giving these away at the grocery store?" He tossed it to Lenka. "Considering what happened with the other one, I doubt this is real. But you might as well find out anyway."

"With pleasure."

Lenka's voice came from far away. I knew what came next, so I fixed my blurred gaze in the general direction of Jazz. She stared open-mouthed across the room. Through my pounding head, I realized this was her first eyeful of Lenka. A nasty sight. Almost as bad as Trevor.

Ian's harsh cry when Lenka tested the dagger made her look away fast.

"You are correct, pet. This one is false as well. Such clever humans."

"The hell they are." Trevor moved toward me, dragging a chair with one hand, Jazz with the other. He forced her into it, facing me. "Move, and he dies. Understand?"

Jazz gave a bitter laugh. "I don't know, Trevor. I might not be clever enough to get it. But I'm smart enough to finish the job I started on your roadster. The rest of your pretty collection, too." She stared up at him. "Nice wheels you used to have. Oh, and you're running out of goons, too. I took out three."

Trevor flushed maroon. He raised a hand but stopped just short of striking her. "Just so you know, bitch, I'll be taking payment for my cars out of Donatti's hide."

Jazz's lips thinned. She didn't respond, but I caught the apology in her eyes. And I couldn't help noticing that Trevor didn't give a shit about his thugs. Nobody would ever nominate him for a humanitarian award.

"Who is this?" Lenka appeared next to Trevor.

"A good friend of Mr. Donatti's." Trevor smiled. "A very good friend."

It hurt to look at her. I turned away—and spotted something even more painful. *Ian.*

How could there be that much blood? It looked as if he'd bathed in the stuff. Blood soaked the carpet under his feet and splattered the wall beside him. Something white stood out in all the red on his left shoulder. Took me a while to realize it was his collarbone.

I closed my eyes and swallowed bile. No wonder he'd wanted me to kill him.

". . . stimulate his memory." Lenka's voice faded in as if someone had just turned up his volume knob. He and Trevor must have been talking strategy, but I had no idea what they'd said. Jazz's horrified expression suggested she did.

Trevor picked up the pliers.

"Don't tell them anything." Jazz glared at Trevor. "I was going to trim my nails anyway."

"In that case, maybe we should start with your teeth." Trevor motioned to Lenka. "Could you hold her down for me, please? Molars tend to be stubborn."

"*No.*" My mouth finally caught up with my brain. "Keep your hands off her."

Lenka pointed at me. Words flew from his mouth and set me on fire.

Someone screamed. Must have been me, because no one else moved. I saw flames engulf my legs and lick at my torso. Saw my flesh blister and blacken. Smelled smoke and cooked meat. Trevor's Place, now serving well-done Donatti with a side of death.

The back of my head smacked against something solid. The flames vanished, and I found myself staring at the ceiling. Unburned legs stuck out from the chair I'd managed to knock over. An illusion. Only the pain had been real.

"The only thing we want to hear from you, thief, is how to find Gahiji-an's tether." Lenka sounded fairly pissed. At least he'd stopped slicing Ian for a few minutes.

Trevor loomed over me. He grabbed my hair and pulled me back up, chair and all. "Don't bother protesting, Mr. Donatti. You know this game. And you decide when it ends."

He moved away. I tried to focus on Jazz. She sat as still as a stone, every trace of resolve vanished. Tears slipped from her eyes, one by one, like mourners paying last respects.

"Don't cry," I mumbled. "Won't let him. You need teeth."

"I'll get dentures." Her voice shook hard enough to rattle windows. "You just keep your mouth shut. Please."

"No. Gonna tell him. Kill me, not you. That's the deal."

Jazz opened her mouth, but Trevor's voice cut in. "I'll agree to those terms."

"Please don't," Jazz whispered. "You don't understand—"

"Shut up!" Trevor screamed, lunging between us. Somehow, he'd acquired more rope. "One more word from you, and I will gag you. He's going to tell me." He looped a length around her waist and the chair.

"Let her go first," I said. "She goes, I talk. Way it works."

Trevor ignored me and finished tying her down. "She goes when I have that tether in my hands and not a minute sooner. I don't trust you."

"And I'm supposed to trust you? You'll just kill us all when you get it."

"Ah, Mr. Donatti." Trevor shook his head. "This is a difficult impasse. She won't be any use to me now, and I have no need to kill her. But you'll never believe that . . . will you?"

I wanted to. Desperately. "No," I said weakly. "I can't believe you."

He held something in front of my face. Pliers. "Then I suppose we'll have to revert to the original plan."

Jazz made a horrible, desolate sound. Everything inside me withered and drained away. I forced myself to look at her—and caught a tiny smile on her lips.

"Cavalry's here," she whispered.

A hoarse sob reached my ears. Female. Not Jazz. She hadn't made the first sound, either. I moved my pounding head in the direction of the cry, the open entrance from the basement hallway. And promptly forgot to breathe.

Akila in person was a thousand times more stunning than her reflection. A goddess. Tory stood beside her and kept her from collapsing at the sight of her brutalized husband. A hawk, bedraggled but alert, perched on Tory's shoulder. They must have helped Shamil transform. And Jazz had taken on the distraction role for them.

I wanted to cry myself—but not for joy. We were deader than ever.

"Gahiji-an . . ."

Half cry, half moan. Pure pain. Akila's voice could have melted all of the ice at the North Pole. But I doubted it would sway Trevor or Lenka.

The sound must've pierced whatever shell Ian had wrapped himself in. His body heaved against his bonds, and a grating breath exploded from him. "No. Gods . . . *why* . . ."

Trevor grabbed the Luger and thrust it against Jazz's temple. "She's first. Then him." He jerked his head at me. "Don't do anything stupid."

"Stop." Akila wavered, then seemed to pull herself together. "Lay down your weapon, human. We are here to bargain."

"Bullshit," Trevor snapped.

"Do as she says, pet." Lenka sounded as smug as a gambler holding four aces. "They are powerless. Bahari are weak to begin with, and they have expended themselves healing the *sharmoot*. Let her speak."

Trevor lowered the gun. With extreme reluctance.

"Akila, no. He will not—"

Ian's breathless protest ended in a scream when Lenka flung another curse at him.

"Enough!" Akila cried. "If you hurt him again, there will be no bargain."

Lenka gestured. Ian slumped. "Very well, *rayani*. Let us hear your proposal."

"Yes. My proposal." Akila closed her eyes briefly. "Spare Gahiji-an's life, and I will join with you. My father will have no choice but to allow your clan back into the realm."

"I am nearly tempted. However, there is the small matter of your bond for life."

"There is a way to break it," Akila whispered.

Lenka laughed. "You would mutilate yourself for him?"

"I would."

A broken string of djinn fell from Ian's lips. The translation lurked just beyond my grasp, but I understood the general sentiment. He was begging her to stop, to leave this place before it was too late.

My gut told me it was half past too late already.

Lenka ignored Ian. "Interesting. Give me a moment to consider." He turned, and a look passed between him and Trevor.

Before I could shout a warning, Trevor fired two shots. One dropped the hawk to the floor in a small explosion of feathers. The other blasted through Tory's shoulder and drove him to his knees.

Again, Lenka seemed to move instantly. He appeared behind Akila, wrapped both arms around her upper body, and dragged her away from Tory. "I do not agree to your terms," he said with a nasty grin. "Kemosiri would sooner allow you to remain banished forever than lift the barrier for us. But take heart, *rayani*. I have a proposal for you."

Akila squirmed in his grasp, ranting away in djinn. Lenka held fast. "Since I have declined your bargain, do you think I will hesitate to hurt your precious Gahiji-an if you make things difficult?"

She went limp.

While Lenka secured Akila in place, Trevor produced his cell phone and called for reinforcements. Within minutes, three armed thugs joined us—four and a half, if you took into account Leonard and the theory of relativity.

"Now, then. Here is my offer." Lenka pointed to Ian. "Produce his tether, and I will destroy him quickly. And I will also refrain from slaughtering your entire clan when I return to the realm." A smile snaked across his mouth. "I guarantee this is your best option, and I suggest you take it. You will not like the alternative."

"She agrees." Ian's voice still cracked, but it sounded stronger. Almost commanding. "Swear to return her unharmed, and you will have my tether."

Lenka smirked. "I swear it."

"No." Akila struggled to free herself. "Please. I will bring you to the realm. Somehow. Let him live . . ." She trailed off into sobs. Even she'd realized the futility of reasoning with Lenka.

"Taregan," Ian gasped. "You must retrieve my tether and bring it here. The thief cannot break the seal."

Tory groaned and lurched to his feet. "I can't . . ."

"She must live. Protect your *rayani*. I do not matter."

Lenka drifted closer to Ian. "Those may be the most intelligent words you have uttered in your entire life. How far is it? I do not want to wait long."

"Miles. Buried in a garbage dump. If you are in such a hurry . . ." He choked and let out an anguished groan. "Have one of your rats drive him," he finally breathed.

Lenka turned his vicious gaze on Tory. "No. I have a better idea."

CHAPTER 35

Trevor had one of his thugs bring a full-length mirror into the sitting room.

"Go." Lenka shoved Tory toward it. "You have ten minutes. If you are not back, I will start killing them. And hurting the ones who cannot die yet."

Tory glared at him. "It's not enough time. I need to lift a couple of cars, and I'm spent."

"Fine. Fifteen, then."

For a moment, Tory didn't move. "You won't defeat Kemosiri. Our clan outnumbers yours. You'll be wiped out, just like his." He motioned to Ian but didn't look in his direction.

Lenka gave him an ugly smile. "That is why we plan to send the humans first. Did you think us idle for the last four centuries? Our army is poised to invade, once the barrier is broken. We will not fail again."

I recognized the look on Tory's face. He and I'd just arrived at the same conclusion. Lenka told us his plans—and that meant none of us would leave this room alive, no matter what promises they made.

"You are down to fourteen minutes, Bahari. I suggest you move faster."

"Son of a—" Jaw set, Tory positioned himself in front of the mirror. He used blood from the wound in his shoulder to paint a symbol on the glass.

Ian croaked something in djinn. Tory paused, winced. He pulled the dupe he carried from a pocket and dropped it on the floor. "That's not real," he said weakly. "Don't bother testing it." It took him another minute to gather his resolve, cast the bridge, and step through.

"Lenka," Akila whispered. "Let me say good-bye. Please."

"Very well."

He released her, and she crossed the room slowly. Ian managed to lift his head enough to look at her. She raised a hand, and her fingertips hovered just short of his battered face. "*Ana uhibbuk*," she said.

One corner of his mouth lifted. "*Ana bahibbik*."

I didn't need a translation for love.

Privacy was a moot point, but I still looked away from them. All the better to concentrate on my own impending demise. And Jazz—what I wouldn't give to make the same deal with Trevor that Ian had with Lenka. Anything to let her live. Everything I had. Unfortunately, one hundred percent of nothing was still nothing.

At least Cyrus wasn't here. I assumed he'd been left with Lark, since I knew Akila wouldn't have deserted him in the djinn realm. Maybe Lark would make a better father than me.

"Donatti."

Jazz pulled me back to reality. I met her eyes with a questioning expression. God, she was beautiful.

"Know what you're thinking," she said.

Smiling hurt, but I did it anyway. "No, you don't."

"He's safe."

"I know." So that was it. She thought I blamed her for putting Cyrus in danger. But it was her I worried about. Much as I'd really rather not die, she had more to lose. More to regret. She wouldn't get to see Cyrus grow up. He would spend his life in hiding with Lark or, more likely, in a string of orphanages and foster homes and stretches of hard-scrabble solitude. Like father, like son.

The thought wrenched my gut. Growing up alone never did me any favors. It wasn't the life I wanted for him. But at least he would be around to live it.

Jazz hung her head. "I'm sorry."

"Don't." I waited until she looked at me. "Don't be," I insisted. "None of this is your fault, Jazz. *I'm* sorry . . ." *For leaving when you needed me. For dragging you into this. For getting you killed.* ". . . For everything."

Her lips twitched. "I love you. Just so you know."

"Love doesn't cover it for me," I said. "I . . . worship you. Always have."

"Now you tell me."

"Better late than never."

Jazz glanced at the nearest gun-toting thug. "This is pretty fucking late."

"Still have ten minutes."

"Enough," Trevor said from somewhere behind me. "You've had your moment. Now, stay quiet, unless you want to start screaming again."

Jazz clamped her lips together. Her eyes glittered with restrained emotion, but I couldn't tell whether she was about to cry or laugh.

I knew which one I'd choose.

Despite my intense desire to spend the rest of my shrinking life in my head, away from reality, my brain insisted on assessment. A good thief always had a backup plan. I didn't at the moment, but years of necessary resourcefulness insisted there had to be a way out of this. An alternative escape route, a window I'd missed. An outcome that was less final than death.

Nothing came to mind. But I did feel different. The agony racing through my body had throttled back to mere excruciating pain. I could speak without sounding as if my mouth was full of marbles. My mutilated fingertips zinged with pins and needles.

I glanced at the hand tied to the arm of the chair. One of my nails had grown back.

Ian. It had to be him—but how? He barely had enough power to stay conscious. I looked over his way. Akila still stood in front of him, and it seemed they'd lapsed into the part of good-bye that didn't need words. But I thought I saw his fingers move. Just a little.

I had to conclude that he thought there was still a chance. Damned if I knew what that chance was, though.

TORY DIDN'T WALK BACK THROUGH THE MIRROR. HE FELL through and landed facedown on the floor with one arm outstretched. His fingers curled loosely around Ian's tether.

Lenka snatched it from him before the mirror's surface had returned to normal.

We'd all been returned to our designated death stations. For some reason, Trevor had dismissed the thugs. Maybe he thought they were too stupid to witness death by magic, but

I didn't think it would faze them. Murder was murder. And they'd already seen Lenka's ugly mug.

I'd gained another nail. Compared with thirty minutes or so ago, I felt downright perky. For all the good it'd do me.

Lenka prodded Tory's limp form with a toe and nodded in Trevor's direction. "Make sure he does not interfere."

"Gladly." Trevor stepped up and emptied the rest of the gun into Tory's back.

Both women screamed. Jazz's cry was peppered with choice names for Trevor—half of them too dirty to scrawl on a bathroom wall. I wished I could join them, but I was too pissed off to open my mouth.

Silence settled like dust over the wake of the violent outburst. I made a mental sketch of our conditions, still trying to thwart the inevitable. Had to scratch Tory from the list of possibilities. Shamil—or what was left of him—hadn't stirred since Trevor shot him. Ian remained somewhat alert, but he was bleeding like a wet newspaper. Grief had paralyzed Akila; fury did the same for Jazz.

That left me. So we were out of luck.

Lenka drew the dagger and lodged the sheath on the back end of the handle. "I almost desire to find this another trick," he said. "It would extend my enjoyment. However, I suspect you have run out of surprises." He approached Ian, wiped the flat of the blade across his bloodied chest, and repeated the gesture with the other side. Streaks of golden light shone through the crimson coating near the base of the blade. Ian's symbol.

Akila gave a desperate sob. Lenka grinned.

"Do not trouble yourself, *rayani*." He gazed almost fondly at the dagger and watched until the glowing symbol faded.

"Once we have taken the realm, I will allow you to remain in my court. You will become my favored *hag'gar*."

Something in my head spit a loose translation—*sex toy*—an instant before Ian's guttural curse confirmed the Morai's intent.

"I would sooner take my own life," Akila said. "You will not have me."

Lenka's twisted smile vanished. "The choice is not yours. If you do not give yourself of your will, I shall take it from you."

"You will not have the opportunity, Lenka." Ian trailed off to harsh, wracking coughs. When the spell abated, he rasped, "You cannot take the realm."

"Two score strong we are, and a hundred times that in human fodder." Lenka sneered. "Kemosiri and his bloated, simpering Council will fall within a fortnight. The moment your life ends, our rule begins. Over both realms."

I shuddered. Given free rein, even a handful of djinn could take over the world—and we pathetic humans couldn't do a damn thing to stop them.

"Well, then," Ian said evenly. "Why do you still wait? You hold the key to your kingdom in your hand."

Lenka glanced at the bloodied dagger. "I did swear to destroy you quickly, Gahiji-an," he said, wiping the blade clean again on his own robe. "So be it."

Ian straightened as much as possible within the ropes. "Thank you."

"What?"

"It is about time." A constant tremor threaded Ian's voice, as if it took everything he had to push the words out. "I thought you would never destroy me. I welcome death at your hands."

"What trickery is this?" Lenka roared. "You cannot be grateful, you pathetic wretch."

Ian returned his glare without blinking. "You murdered my father. You have wiped out my entire clan. What better way for me to join them? And you have already sworn to destroy me, so you cannot stop now. Send me home, Lenka."

"No." Lenka sputtered. "I will not allow . . . wait." He stared at the dagger and turned in a slow half-circle. His blood-red eyes settled on me. "*You* will finish him."

Ian snarled the protest that refused to leave my clenched throat.

"Yes. It is beautiful. What is it you humans say? Ironic." Lenka spoke in a soft, deadly cadence. "Ah, Gahiji-an. You have trained your pet to destroy me, and now it will be used against you."

My voice returned. I started to refuse, but a look from Ian stopped me. He wanted me to do it. Was it the principle of the thing or something else?

Lenka advanced, holding the gleaming copper blade in front of him like a shield. The dagger captured my reflection in miniature, throwing my pitiful condition back in my face. My mind seized the image. And a single, absolutely insane idea stole my breath.

"I see this troubles you." Lenka flashed his fangs. "I would suggest you consider this an honorable gesture, but thieves do not hold honor in regard." He touched my ropes. They loosened and slithered away. "On your feet."

With shaking legs and a heart that threatened to hammer my ribcage apart, I complied. I might have found a window, but even Houdini would have trouble squeezing through this one.

CHAPTER 36

It wasn't hard to feign complete weakness. I dropped to one knee and let the dagger fall from my hand. Groaned, picked it up. "Think I'll stay here." I gasped.

"Get on with it," Lenka snapped. "And do not attempt to play the hero, or your woman will die slowly."

I gritted my teeth. His implication was clear. Slowly, as opposed to quickly after I killed Ian. "Don't worry about me," I said. "Couldn't stab a marshmallow now."

I drew the blade across my palm, wincing at the fresh pain. Utter silence mocked my ridiculous attempt at a plan. I couldn't let Lenka hear me. Ian's distraction act would've been useful right about now. Hell, I'd even take a fan or a ticking clock. Or an argument. Maybe I could start one.

"Hey, Jazz," I said softly. "Remember Philly?"

A puzzled expression flitted across her face. Anger chased it away.

"Actually, I do," she snapped. "You owe me half a million dollars, Trevor."

I struggled to keep my pride from showing. We'd done the bullshit-argument bit to slip away from the heat on a gig in

Philadelphia, and she'd taken the bluff crown without breaking a sweat. Whatever she was leading up to, she'd pulled it out of her ass.

"What the hell are you talking about?" Trevor said.

"You know damned well what I mean. The Benz deal."

"*What?*"

"I delivered a carrier full of Benz to your back-ass chop shop, and he wrote me a rubber check. You owe me."

She'd picked the right fakeout. Trevor rarely bothered running checks on his chops.

"Idiot! What does that matter now?" Trevor shouted. He moved toward me, probably intending to kick me or zap me with the Taser again.

Lenka scowled at him. "Do not interfere. The thief has a task to perform."

"He's right, you slimy son of a bitch." Jazz bared her teeth. "Maybe it doesn't matter, but if you're going to kill everybody and their grandmother, you could at least pay up first."

The shouting continued. I tried to tune it out. Keeping the dagger as close to me as possible, I used a torn finger to smear Ian's symbol near the bottom of the blade. I concentrated on the memory of the shining coin Trevor had swallowed and whispered, "*Insha no imil, kubri ana bi-sur'u wasta.*" When no one shot me or set me on fire, I figured they hadn't noticed.

The surface of the dagger facing me rippled. Copper darkened and showed vague suggestions of shadowed, glistening flesh. Hello, Trevor's intestines.

"Silence!" Lenka's roar threatened to shatter my concentration. I clung to my intentions hard enough to manifest them physically. Sweat drenched my forehead and rolled into my eyes. "It should not take you this long, thief," Lenka said. "You have sixty seconds before she loses the first finger."

No time for a smart-ass remark. Nodding as if I'd just lost my last nerve, I wrapped my sliced hand around the tapered end of the blade and slipped my cut and still bleeding index finger through the base end. So cold. I glanced at Trevor. A slight frown surfaced on his face, and he rubbed once at his stomach. But he didn't seem overly concerned.

I curled my finger around carefully until I felt the edge of the coin. Focused everything I had on it. And forced myself to meet Ian's eyes.

"*Ana lo 'ahmar nar, fik lo imshi, aakhir kalaam.*"

A band of pain clamped around my finger where it still stuck through the surface of the knife. I wasn't sure if I'd done the spell right. Either the bridge was closing, or I'd destroyed Ian's tether instead of Lenka's. I tried to pull my hand back, and the copper blade solidified—taking my finger off clean at the first knuckle, newly grown nail and all.

I wasn't the only one in pain, though.

Trevor's eyes opened so wide I didn't think they'd stay in his skull much longer. He crossed both hands over his stomach and opened his mouth. Blood poured out and drenched his chest, his arms. He fell hard on his knees. A few wisps of smoke drifted from between his fingers. He toppled to one side like a warped domino.

Horror replaced the triumphant smirk on Lenka's face. He managed a single step, a single word, before his hands and feet burst into flames. Real ones, not illusions. The fire raced along his limbs, transforming his flesh into showers of ash as it went. Although his legs burned and crumbled, the rest of him stayed in place. Finally, nothing but a core remained. A floating fireball. It grew bigger, surged bright and hot. And exploded.

Sparks filled the room, covering everything. It was like standing inside the grand finale at a fireworks display, without the ear-shattering booms and third-degree burns. The bright flecks faded into shimmering air and then calm.

This time, I welcomed the silence. It let me hear my ragged breathing and galloping heart. Good indicators that I wasn't dead.

"Like to see you magic *that* away, you twisted fuck," I muttered.

The floor beckoned to me. I accepted the invitation.

"GAVYN."

What? I tried to say. Wasn't sure if I actually managed to speak. I tried again. My lips didn't seem to move.

"*Gavyn.*"

"Jazz," I whispered—or thought I did. My throat vibrated. Had any sound come out? I needed a drink. And a transfusion. Maybe some nice drugs . . .

Someone made a choked sound. Probably not me. An arm slid under me and guided me up. Two went around me. Something warm and wet dripped on my shoulder.

I pried my eyes open. "Ow."

"Oh, God." Jazz pulled back. Tears bathed her face. Why was she crying? My muzzy brain seemed to think we'd won. Or something. "I'm sorry," she said. "Didn't mean to hurt you. I just thought . . . well, you looked dead."

"Not yet. Dead doesn't hurt this much." I tried to pull myself together and managed to sit in crooked Indian style. "*Mmph.* Think I need more practice."

"I'd say you have come quite far, thief."

"Ian?" I squinted at the tall, thin blur standing behind Jazz.

"Oh, good. You're alive, too. Wait . . . maybe we're all dead."

My vision doubled and resolved. I made out Ian, unbound, minus the blood. The smile on his face contrasted with the tears in his eyes. Crying was contagious today.

"I had intended for you to destroy me." His voice hovered on the edge of cracking. "But I think your plan was better."

"Brilliant strategist. That's me," I muttered. "How'd you get healed so fast?"

"The destruction of a tether releases a great amount of power. Any djinn within range can absorb it and use it for a short time."

"So, Tory and Shamil . . ." I tried for a better view of the room. Akila stood beside Ian. Wasn't a shock to see her crying, too. Tory sat a few feet away, and a considerably less bedraggled hawk kept him company.

Besides me, only Trevor hadn't experienced a miraculous recovery. There was a smoldering crater where his stomach used to be. The sight relieved me enough to tolerate the stench. For an instant, my conscience stabbed me, but the discomfort didn't last long.

Technically, I hadn't killed him. Lenka's tether did.

"Okay," I said. "Anybody spare some healing mojo for me? Mine's out of order."

"Of course." Ian started for me.

Akila touched his arm. "Gahiji-an. Let me help him." Before Ian responded, Akila came to my side and knelt. "Gavyn Donatti," she whispered. "I sensed your strength, but even I underestimated your cunning. I cannot thank you enough. His life—*my* life—is yours."

I smirked. "Don't want your life," I said. "Got one of my own, thanks. But I'll take that healing, if you don't mind."

She smiled and nodded. "You have sustained great damage. It will take a bit of time, but I will heal you."

I felt better already.

Akila chanted in djinn. For a full minute, I welcomed the tingling sensation that spread through my aching body. Just when I'd started to feel halfway human again, an enormous crack echoed from somewhere inside the house. Now what? Were Trevor's thugs breaking the door down?

Across the room, a chunk of plaster dropped from the ceiling and shattered on the floor.

Ian swore loudly. He rushed over and helped me stand. "We will have to finish this outside. This house is going to collapse."

"Wha . . . why?"

"Lenka must have made some modifications. Probably to entice Trevor to his side. Now that he is gone, the spells are breaking down." A bigger slab of ceiling crashed down in the corridor by the basement. "We must move quickly. I will carry you, thief."

I couldn't object much. Right now, my top speed wouldn't beat a slug in a crawling race. Still, I did have one request.

"Hey, Ian?" I said when he settled me on his back.

"Yes?"

"Let's stay on the ground this time."

He laughed. "Your wish is my command."

CHAPTER 37

Trevor's remaining thugs were no match for four djinn at full strength.

I stopped noticing them after the first one went down. In fact, I didn't notice much of anything. Exhaustion beat at me, and it took everything I had not to fall from Ian's back. At one point, I thought something exploded. Maybe my brain had finally popped from overload.

A gray fog settled over me. Eventually, everything went black. And then green.

Leaves. Lots of them. A blanket of rippling green floated high above me, dotted with chinks of blue sky. Somehow, I'd acquired clothes again. Not mine, but I hadn't wanted them back anyway. Bloodstains never came out. I breathed in sweet, clean air and let my lungs release the remembered stench of crisped Trevor. Nature wasn't so bad after all.

"Ga."

I blinked and turned my head to the side. Cyrus squatted next to me, regarding me with serious blue eyes. He held a stick in one small hand.

"Hey, little man. Hope you're not planning to prospect me for treasure."

Cyrus looked over me. "Mommy, he's waked!"

"Huh?"

I followed his gaze and saw Jazz striding toward us. "Gavyn?" She sounded almost like herself again, except for calling me by my first name. I kinda liked that. "You're conscious," she said.

"No, I'm not." I closed my eyes and sighed. "If I was awake, something bad would be happening."

"Hungry," Cyrus announced.

Jazz smiled at him. "Didn't you already eat all the Pop-Tarts?"

"Not yet."

"Okay. Go ask Lark to get you another one."

While Cyrus ambled away, I pushed myself off the ground. Jazz appeared next to me and held me steady. "How long have I been out?" I said.

"Hours. It's almost noon."

"How far'd we get? We make Canada yet?"

Jazz laughed. "Don't turn around. You can still see Trevor's place from here . . . well, what's left of it, at least."

"Great." I decided I could live without seeing the wreckage for now. Getting on my feet dizzied me for a few seconds, but the pain had vanished almost completely. A slight ache lingered in the new, shorter tip of my index finger. It had been healed but not restored.

I figured an inch of skin and bone wasn't much to pay for six lives.

"Where's everybody else?"

Jazz pointed. "There."

I followed her gesture. Four djinn, Lark, and, to my surprise, Quaid occupied the clearing we'd set up the mirror in. No one seemed inclined to chat or move more than necessary. We all needed to sleep for a week or two.

"Come on," Jazz said. "They'll want to know you're up and around."

She stepped toward them. I grabbed her. "Wait."

"What's wrong?" She searched my face.

I smiled. "I feel lucky."

"Do you?" She moved closer and pressed against me. Her arms wrapped around my waist. "What a coincidence. So do I."

"Mmm." I couldn't come up with any words. The feel of her drove me to distraction. I leaned down and brushed her lips with mine.

"Call that a kiss?" Her eyes sparked. "You do need practice."

She laced her hands behind my head and showed me the right way. I could've died happy right then.

I moaned when she pulled away. "Can we get a private forest?"

"Animal." She gave me a playful shove. "They're waiting."

"Let them."

"Gavyn!"

"Fine." I settled an arm around her shoulders. "Tell me something. How did Akila and Cyrus get here?"

"It's a long story. Basically, Tory brought them through."

"Any idea why? I mean, if she could have come over before, why'd she wait?"

Jazz shrugged. "I guess she finally decided not to listen to her father anymore. Especially when Tory told her Ian was about to get his ass killed."

"That's what I thought." I shook my head. "Ian's gonna be pissed."

"Probably. But I'm glad he did that, instead of letting you and Ian die." She shuddered against me.

"Yeah," I whispered. "Me, too."

She smiled. "Your friend Quaid has a way with kids. Cyrus took right to him."

"Whoa. Since when is Quaid my friend?"

"He seems to think so, since you saved his life."

"Oh, great. Any more friends like him, and I'll be in jail or dead before I'm forty." I rubbed her arm—and started when she pulled back. "Hold on. Where are you going?"

"Breathe." Jazz put a hand on my chest. "Just thought we should join everyone else, before they send out search parties. I'm not going anywhere."

"No, you're not. I'm never letting you out of my sight again."

She leaned in to me. "No more disappearing acts, Houdini?"

"Never."

"Good." She gave me a squeeze and stepped back. And laughed. "You've gotta see this."

I turned and followed her line of sight. Cyrus stood in front of the mirror, a half-eaten pastry in one hand and a thoughtful look on his face. He stuck a finger into the filling and smeared a little on the surface. After a pause, he spoke a bunch of nonsense words that actually sounded damned close to the bridge spell. Nothing happened, but he still smiled as if he'd pulled a rabbit out of a hat. It was the cutest damned thing I'd ever seen.

"He gets that from me," I said.

"Great. Can't wait to find out what else he gets from you."

"Bet he'll kick the other kids' butts at hide-and-seek."

Jazz shook her head. "That's what I'm afraid of."

———

"Welcome back, thief."

Ian strode across the clearing and hugged me. This time, I didn't mind. But I still hoped he wouldn't make it a habit.

"Ian. Thank you for not flying." I grinned and stepped back. "Hey . . . everybody."

"If it isn't the hero." Lark sent me a grateful smile. "Donatti, I'm officially not pissed at you anymore."

"Thanks. I think." I glanced at Tory, who stood behind Lark with an arm clasped possessively across his chest. "Interesting strategy you had there. I wouldn't have crossed Ian. You've got balls."

"You were taking too long. I had to do something." He smirked in Ian's direction. "He'll forgive me. Eventually."

"This was not the help I had in mind." Ian drifted over to Akila. "You should not have listened to him, my heart. But I am grateful that you did."

"I could not lose you again." She buried her face in his chest.

I left them to their moment and turned to Quaid. "Still waiting around to arrest me?"

"Well. About that." He hesitated for the first time I'd ever seen. "It seems you saved my life, Mr. Donatti."

"Sure does seem that way. But you never can tell. Maybe Trevor would've been reasonable with you."

"I have my doubts." Quaid looked over at Cyrus, who'd wandered off again with Jazz watching over him. "You have a wonderful son. He's something special."

"Thank you."

"It would be a shame for him to be deprived of a father. If, for example, you were in prison."

My eyes narrowed. "Yes. It would."

Quaid's serene smile resurfaced. "In that case, I believe I'll be on my way. I doubt our paths will cross again, so I wish you well on yours."

"Wait." If I'd calculated right, we could still help Quaid cash his bounty in. "I think my friend Lark here has something for you."

Lark glanced up at the sound of his name. "Whatever you're telling him, Donatti, don't drag me into it."

"He won't bother you. If you'll just give him the dagger you're holding, he can get going."

"Are you ... oh. That dagger." Lark pulled his dupe from an inside pocket and tossed it to me. "Knock yourself out."

I grinned and presented it to Quaid. "Now we're square."

"You're sure you want to part with this?"

"We've done what we had to. It's all yours." When he accepted it uncertainly, I said, "So, this means I'm not a criminal anymore. Right?"

Quaid laughed. "I suppose it does. Good-bye, Mr. Donatti."

I watched him walk away. When Quaid was out of sight, silence of the uncomfortable variety descended. I had the feeling I'd missed an important discussion. I looked around, and my gaze fell on the mirror still propped against a tree. Understanding hammered me in the face.

They were going home.

"Well," I said, trying to sound normal, though I felt as if my insides had been scooped out. "Guess you'd better get moving."

Ian frowned. "Do you have a destination in mind?"

"Don't you? I mean, you wanted to go home. Now you can, right?"

"Oh, yes. Home. A fine idea." He stroked Akila's hair and

smiled. "Love, are you certain you did not neglect to heal his head?"

"Okay. You lost me."

Ian sighed. "Did you not hear Lenka? Apparently, there is an army of humans and Morai waiting to invade the realm. My work is not through here, and therefore I am still banished."

"So . . . you're staying?"

"Yes. I am afraid you are stuck with me, thief."

My grin felt wider than the Grand Canyon. "Lucky me."

"We shall see how lucky you are." He turned and gestured. "Shamil, if you are ready, I will open the bridge for you."

A shaded silhouette I'd taken for a tree moved, and Shamil approached. Someone must have magicked him some clothes. He looked like a traditional genie: open vest, silk sash around his waist, baggy pants, and bare feet. He'd grown some hair—it resembled Tory's, only shorter. His small smile revealed new teeth. A blindfold covered his eyes, dimpling in over the empty sockets. Apparently, transformation healing didn't extend to regeneration.

He stopped in front of me and bowed his head. "I am pleased to meet you, Gavyn Donatti. It seems I owe you my life."

"Likewise. And no, you don't." I nodded back. "Nice to see you up and around."

"Yes. I had not expected to taste freedom again." His voice wavered. "I am ready, Gahiji-an. I will report to Kemosiri immediately. He will not be able to ignore this situation any longer."

"Hold on." Tory broke away from Lark. He pulled a slim black box from a pocket and tucked it into Shamil's waistband. "Don't forget this."

I stared at it. "Is that a recorder?"

"Lark's idea," Tory said. "Absolute, irrefutable proof. I had it going the whole time we were in there. That asshole won't be able to find a loophole now."

I had to laugh. "Lark, you would be the one to introduce technology where it has no place. Next thing you know, all the djinn will start carrying cell phones."

"Do not count on it. We are slow to adapt." Smiling, Ian moved to the mirror and did his thing. Shamil came up beside him. Ian stood aside and clasped his shoulder. "I will contact you soon to hear the Council's decision. Luck be with you, brother."

"And with you, *rayan*." Shamil bent at the waist and stepped through the mirror.

Ian stared after him for a long moment. At last, he turned and held a hand out. "Akila," he said in strangled tones, "if you return now, you can accompany Shamil to the Council. Your word will be taken."

She walked up to him. Stopped. And sent him a look that could've frozen Mount Vesuvius. "Return? Perhaps it is *your* head that is in need of healing."

"But you must—"

"What? Persuade my father to step out from his ignorance and make a stand for the realm? If Taregan's recording cannot do this, nothing will." When he opened his mouth to protest again, she laid a finger on his lips. "No, Gahiji-an. I will not go back and pander to the Council. And I will no longer be bound by my father's ridiculous notions of loyalty to clan. I have made my decision. My place is with you, my husband. My home is wherever you are. If you stay, I stay."

"Akila—"

"I am staying. Do not bother telling me that I must return for my protection. I will not leave you again, and you cannot—"

He stopped her mouth with his. Apparently, he wanted a private forest, too.

"*Adjo anan,*" he murmured when he pulled back. "I am not the Council. You've no need to convince me. Stay, love, if that is your wish."

She smiled. "It is."

"Well," I said a little too loudly. "I hate to interrupt, but don't you think we should get going? I don't know about you guys, but if I don't get food and sleep soon, I think I might get a little cranky."

An unsteady toddler zipped past me. Jazz reached my side and stopped to catch a breath. "I just realized something," she said. "I'm the only one with a house."

"She's got a point," I said. "Think I might have a little cash left. We can get a room for the night."

Jazz pounded my arm. "No way, Donatti. You're coming home with me."

I grinned. "I knew you'd see it my way."

"Oh, for . . ." She rolled her eyes. "Aren't you ever serious?"

"No." I caught Ian's gaze and saw amusement. "Is that a problem?"

She coughed, but I detected a laugh in there. "Let's go home."

Those three words sounded better than a winning lottery ticket to me.

CHAPTER 38

After sleeping for twelve hours straight, I felt almost normal again. Except for the part about waking up in a bed that wasn't in a cheap hotel or the backseat of a car. I could count the number of times that had happened in my life and still have a few fingers left over.

The only thing missing was Jazz. I'd been pretty sure I left her right next to me when I passed out.

I rolled off the mattress and tried to remember how to get to the bathroom. It didn't take long. After all, I'd been here a few times before—though we hadn't stayed in the bedroom much. We usually hadn't made it that far and ended up settling for the downstairs couch. Or the floor.

Why did I ever think leaving her was a good idea?

The minute I stepped into the upstairs hall, the smell of breakfast attacked me. Bacon, eggs, coffee. Maybe even toast. The idea of Jazz cooking for me induced a kind of happy delirium. Only nameless line cooks and grudging nuns had ever made me breakfast.

I took care of business and headed for the stairs. On the way, I passed the room I'd watched Jazz tuck Cyrus into last night. The door stood open a crack, and I couldn't resist peeking in. Morning light behind curtains decorated with cartoon dogs bathed the room in a soft glow. Cyrus sprawled on a pint-sized bed with sturdy plastic rails, a sheet tangled around his legs and a thumb resting loosely in his mouth. He somehow managed to occupy the entire mattress, even though it was twice as big as him.

My son. The phrase still seemed distant and muffled, like a dream. But it was getting easier to accept the title of father. I only hoped I'd prove worthy to carry the role.

I backed out and moved down the hall. A baby gate blocked off the top of the stairs. I took one look at the latch and stepped over it. No way I'd be able to get that thing open without at least a cup of coffee in me. Of course, if it had been a locked bank vault, I could've cracked it in my sleep. The irony did not escape me.

Downstairs, the door to the spare room Jazz had given to Ian and Akila remained closed. I smiled and moved on to the kitchen. Didn't expect to see them for a while yet. They had four hundred years of catching up to do.

Jazz looked up from a newspaper spread on the table in front of her when I walked in. "Morning, Houdini. Want some breakfast? It's on the stove."

"In a minute." I hung back and took in the sight of her. Oversized white cotton shirt, form-fitting tan pants, bare feet. No jewelry or makeup—she didn't need it. She'd stopped wearing sunglasses in the house, probably for Cyrus, and her mismatched eyes were beautifully unapologetic. And despite the horrors of the past few days, she seemed relaxed and content.

I knew she wasn't recovered, but she'd never let on about it. Typical Jazz.

She gave an exasperated snort, as if she'd just read my mind. "You going to eat before it gets cold or just stand there all day?"

"Sorry. Just enjoying the scenery." I grinned and moved to the stove to help myself.

A page rustled behind me. "Did you just call me scenery?"

"Me? Never." Plate full, I carried it over and settled in a chair next to her. I nodded at the paper. "Anything interesting in there?"

"Some rich guy's house on the lake collapsed, night before last. Killed him and at least two other unidentified individuals. Tragic, really." The ghost of a smile traced her lips, and she flipped back a few pages to show me an article accompanied by a flat color shot of Trevor's half-toppled house. "Local Art Collector Dies in Unexplained Accident", the headline stated.

"Mm-hm. A shame." I forked a pile of scrambled eggs and tasted bliss. "Thank you for this," I said.

She seemed to know I meant more than just breakfast. "You're welcome."

Conversation entered an easy lapse. I ate, she read. When I finished, I cleared my dishes, procured some coffee, and sat back down. Some of my contentment evaporated. I had to discuss a few things with her, and they weren't going to be easy.

Jazz sensed my disquiet and put the paper aside. "What's up?"

"I love you."

That hadn't been where I meant to start. It did get her attention, though. She smiled and covered my hand with hers. "I feel a 'but' coming on here."

"Yeah. A big 'but.'" I swallowed hot coffee. Despite the

sugar I'd loaded it with, a bitter taste lingered in my mouth. "Being here with you, like this . . . it's amazing. I've never been happier. I mean that," I said before she could voice dissent.

She arched an eyebrow. "Get to the 'but' already."

"However," I said with the hint of a smile. It faded fast. "I can't do this full-time. You know. Settle down and stay here forever."

"Really. Have a lot of people to rob, do you?"

I probably deserved that, but it still hurt. "Actually, no. I've decided to retire."

"Then what's the problem?"

"Ian." I sighed and looked away. "There's still almost a hundred of those bastards out there. The Morai, I mean. And Ian has to hunt them all down by himself." I shook my head, backtracked. "Well, he's got Tory, but I don't know how much help he'll be."

Jazz smirked agreement. A few hours in Tory's presence was more than enough to realize that, five hundred years old or not, he still had some growing up to do. He and Lark had opted for a high-end hotel stay while the team Lark had already hired rebuilt his house. It wouldn't take long. Lark's money worked faster than djinn magic.

"Anyway, Ian would never admit to it, but I think he needs me." I couldn't begrudge him that. Didn't think I'd ever admit that I needed him, too. "I'm going to help him. The thing is, as long as these guys are trying to get back to the djinn realm, they'll be after me. And Cyrus. I just can't—"

"Gavyn."

"Wait, let me finish." If I didn't spit it out now, I'd give myself time to change my mind. "I've got to help him. It won't be easy, and I won't be around as much as I want. I'll be ditching you both. Again. I promised no more disappearing acts, and I'm already breaking that promise." My voice cracked at the end.

She looked at me. "Are you done?"

"Yeah."

"Good. Now I can tell you what an idiot you are."

"Christ, Jazz. Tell me something I don't know."

"You obviously don't know this."

"I'm aware of my own stupidity, thanks."

"Shut up, Donatti."

I did. And she kissed me. I wanted to be angry—didn't she know this was rubbing it in?—but my primal senses drowned everything except her lips on mine.

Jazz drew back. "I love you. But if you weren't doing this, I don't think I'd like you very much."

"Huh?"

"I'm saying I agree with your decision. More than agree. And I'm going to help any way I can." She touched my face and smiled. "You'll stay when you can. Go when you need to. Think of it as a home base."

"What about Cyrus?"

Her expression took on a touch of exasperation. "What about him? If you think he's going to grow up hating you for not being around all the time, you don't know little boys. He'll think you're a hero."

I grunted. "Not likely."

"You will be in his eyes. And mine."

For a moment, I forgot how to speak. What I felt was too big for words. Finally, my mouth lapsed into habitual behavior.

"What kind of fringe benefits do heroes have around here? At the least, I expect to get the babe in bed."

She kicked my shin. I yelped.

Low laughter from the doorway alerted me that my performance had been witnessed.

"You cannot help yourself, can you?" Ian said.

"With what?"

"Trouble. It clings to you like a shroud."

"Yeah, and sometimes it follows me around like a djinn." I grinned and added, "Good morning, trouble."

Ian nodded in amused acknowledgment. "Tell me. What is this delightful smell?"

"Breakfast." Jazz stood and gestured to the table. "Have a seat, Ian. I'll get you some."

"Oh, sure. Wait on him."

"He complimented my cooking." She rubbed my shoulder on her way to the stove, and I felt better. A little.

While she piled food on a plate, I refrained from glowering at Ian. "How long were you standing there this time?"

"I have only just arrived."

"No invisible eavesdropping?"

"Not this time, thief."

"Good."

Jazz set the plate down in front of Ian with an authoritative *thunk*. "Settle down, boys. It's too early for this."

"Thank you, lady." Ian sent me a smug look.

I drank my coffee and congratulated myself on my restraint.

A short electronic squawk behind me drew my attention. I turned and saw a squat plastic speaker box with a row of red lights and a short antenna sitting on the counter beside the stove. "That's a pretty low-tech scanner you got there, Jazz. Does it transmit in Morse code?"

"It's a baby monitor, you dope." She reached over and twisted a knob. A steady hiss of air drifted from the speaker. Seconds later, there was a soft thump, then another. Like two pajama-clad feet landing in succession on the floor.

Cyrus's voice came through as clearly as if he was in the kitchen with us. "Where Teddy?" Something rustled. "Ga. Teddy?" *Crash!* "Uh-oh. Boke it."

Jazz grimaced and switched off the monitor. "Oh, boy. I'll be back."

I watched her rush from the room, then held my empty mug aloft. "Want some coffee?" I asked Ian. "I'll pour, and you won't even have to compliment me."

He laughed. "Thank you, yes. That would be pleasant."

"So." I fished out another mug. "Where's your wife?"

"She is resting." Concern knitted his features. "Dealing with Lenka has exhausted her. I do not think she will recover quickly."

"You might be surprised. Women are tougher than we think."

"I do hope you are correct." He accepted the cup I handed him and wrapped both hands around it. "I must remember to thank your Jazz for allowing us to rest here. Once Akila has regained her strength, we will move on."

"Why? I'm sure Jazz won't mind if Akila stays."

He blinked. "She would rather I did not?"

"That's not what I meant. She wants everyone to stay. I'm just talking about while we're gone. I figured we could take this in stages—you know, maybe bag two or three and take a break. It'll take a while to find all those evil snake dudes."

Ian gave me a strange expression. "Did you say 'we'?"

"Yeah. Why?"

"It is my place to destroy the Morai. My responsibility. Not yours."

"Well, now it's mine, too."

"You cannot—"

I glared at him. "Are you saying I can't do it? Because I seem to remember exploding that slimeball pretty good."

Ian sighed. "I did not mean it that way."

"So you don't want my help, then?"

"No. I . . ." He paused. "You have already done more than enough. You have seen Lenka. The rest of the Morai are no better, and they will not hesitate to kill you, given the opportunity." Ian shook his head. "You have a family now, thief. I cannot ask you to continue risking your life for the realm. For me."

"That's retired thief to you," I said. "And you don't have to ask me. I've already decided, all by myself."

"I do not understand. Why would you do this?"

"Because Jazz and Cyrus aren't the only family I have."

He looked at me as if I'd started speaking Martian.

I laughed. "You've got a lot to learn about humans, my friend. Or should I call you Grandpa?"

"That will not be necessary. Ian will do." His features grew serious. "You are certain this is what you want?"

"Does a bear crap in the woods?"

"What?"

"Never mind." I clapped his arm. "Look. You told me you were going to help me achieve my life's purpose. Yeah, you were lying through your teeth at the time, but it worked anyway." I looked at the silent baby monitor and imagined Jazz and Cyrus upstairs. "This is my life. It's with her and with you."

I grinned. "Besides, why go back to stealing when I can save the world instead? Always wanted to be a hero."

Ian smirked. "Did you, now?"

"Sure. Only not Superman. He flies."

I decided not to tell Ian—or Jazz—that I planned to keep practicing. I wouldn't actually steal anything, but I wanted my skills to stay sharp. Just in case we ended up needing a window.

Being a thief did come in handy sometimes.